Agent of Rome: The Siege

NICK BROWN

Agent of Rome: The Siege

HODDER &
STOUGHTON

First published in Great Britain in 2011 by Hodder & Stoughton
An Hachette UK company

1

Copyright © Nick Brown 2011

Map © Rosie Collins 2011

A CIP catalogue record for this title is available from the British Library.

Hardback ISBN 978 1 444 71485 2
Trade Paperback ISBN 978 1 444 71494 4
eBook ISBN 978 1 444 71487 6

Typeset in Plantin Light by Palimpsest Book Production Limited,
Falkirk, Stirlingshire

Printed and bound in the UK by
CPI Mackays, Chatham ME5 8TD

Hodder & Stoughton policy is to use papers that are natural, renewable and
recyclable products and made from wood grown in sustainable forests.
The logging and manufacturing processes are expected to conform to the
environmental regulations of the country of origin.

Hodder & Stoughton Ltd
338 Euston Road
London NW1 3BH

www.hodder.co.uk

For Mum and Dad

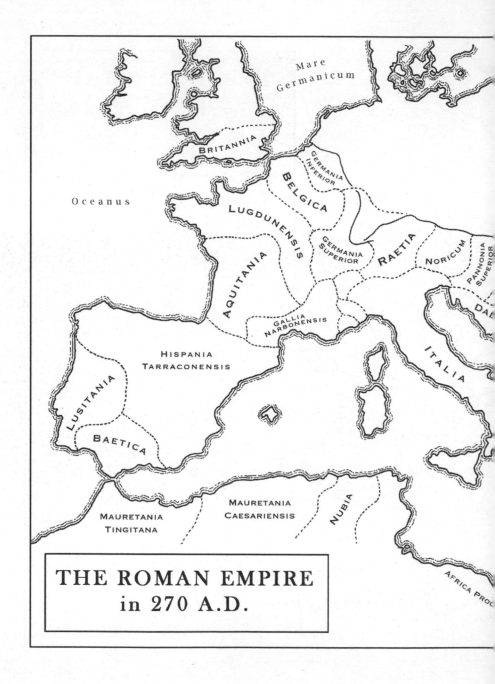

Mare
Germanicum

Oceanus

BRITANNIA

GERMANIA
INFERIOR

BELGICA

LUGDUNENSIS

GERMANIA
SUPERIOR

RAETIA

NORICUM

PANNONIA
SUPERIOR

AQUITANIA

DAL

GALLIA
NARBONENSIS

ITALIA

HISPANIA
TARRACONENSIS

LUSITANIA

BAETICA

MAURETANIA
TINGITANA

MAURETANIA
CAESARIENSIS

NUBIA

AFRICA PROC

THE ROMAN EMPIRE
in 270 A.D.

DACIA

MOESIA
SUPERIOR

MOESIA
INFERIOR

Pontus Euxinus

THRACIA

MACEDONIA

ASIA

GALATIA

CAPPADOCIA

CILICIA

MESOPOTAMIA

R. Euphrates

SYRIA
COELE

PHOENICA

ARABIA

Mare Nostrum

Desert

CYRENAICA

AEGYPTUS

ULARIS

Miles

0   200   400   600

Antioch

Seleucia

Beroea

Chalcis

Anasartha

Apamea

Androna
Seriane

Tripolis

Emesa

Palmyra

Damascus

■ – City
● – Town

High
ground

Miles

0   30   60

Alauran

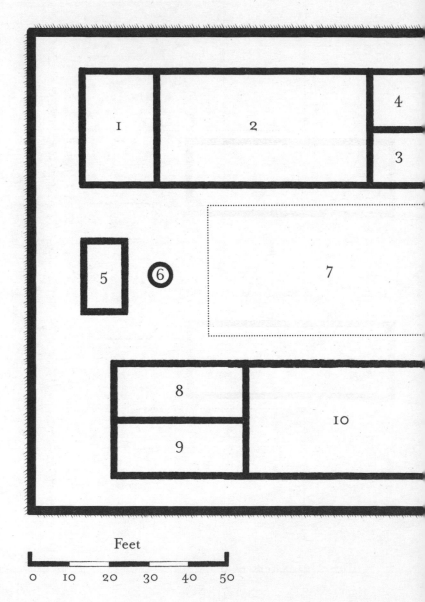

Feet

0   10   20   30   40   50

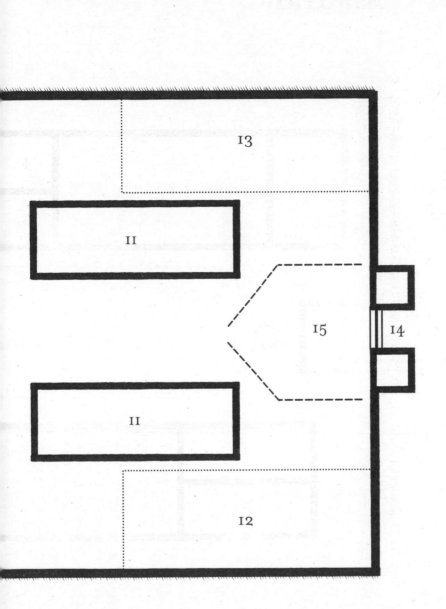

1	Officers' Quarters	6	Well	11	Dwellings
2	Barracks	7	Square	12	Syrian Camp
3	Aid Post	8	Stables	13	Marketplace
4	Inn	9	Workshop	14	Gatehouse
5	Temple	10	Granary	15	"Killing Area"

Summer, AD 270

Marcus Aurelius Valerius Claudius, Emperor of Rome, rules a divided domain threatened by invasion and revolt.

In the East, the Persians have long posed the greatest challenge to Roman dominance. Control of the eastern provinces has been ceded to Odenathus, Roman ally and emperor of the Syrian city-state, Palmyra. Having won the second of his major victories against the Persians, Odenathus has been mysteriously murdered.

His ambitious and charismatic widow, Queen Zenobia, takes command of his empire and army. Not content to remain guarantor, she unleashes a rebellion against Rome. Having already attacked Arabia, Palestine and Egypt, she now looks north to the mighty Syrian capital: Antioch.

I

Cassius Quintius Corbulo nudged his horse towards the side of the alley, taking them both out of the glare of the bright morning sun. He sighed impatiently, twisted in his saddle and stared down the line.

Some of the men were mounted, others were on foot. There were more than a hundred of them, but they were an un-impressive bunch: mainly clerks, engineers and slaves. The handful of legionaries were mostly injured and unfit for service. Supplies hadn't reached the area in months; not one soldier had a full set of equipment.

Cassius had made a note of every name and occupation. He also knew each man's age and had checked three times to confirm what he already suspected: at nineteen he was the youngest in the column.

Unfortunately, he was also in charge of it.

The alley ran alongside a walled square in the centre of Nessara, an isolated town on the edge of the Syrian desert. Until that very morning, the compound had housed a tiny garrison, now part of the column. Though long neglected and soon to be abandoned, the compound retained its most valuable feature: a working well. The Romans would not depart until every last man had filled every last barrel, canteen and gourd. They faced a long march, and if the previous week was anything to go by, it would be conducted in blistering, unrelenting heat.

'Give that back!'

A local man hurried past, in pursuit of a burly Roman heading for the end of the alley. Opposite Cassius was the Syrian's stall, a meagre selection of fruit laid out beneath a sagging awning.

3

The Roman turned round. It was Ammianus, the man in charge of the Nessara garrison. He held no rank but had assumed command on account of his age and years of service. Cassius had not enjoyed working with the vulgar Thracian over the last two days. He was by trade a stable master and seemed ill-equipped to deal with men, maintaining a particular antipathy for the locals.

In his hand was a palm leaf full of dates.

'Give it back!' repeated the stall owner, now switching from Greek to passable Latin.

'Well, well,' said Ammianus with a mocking smile, 'an educated peasant. But not educated enough to know when to bite his tongue. Back to your stall now or I'll slice it off!'

The Syrian was dark and well built. He squared up to Ammianus.

The other legionaries watched with interest, absorbed by the prospect of an impending fight.

Across the street was a group of six local men. They too looked on, heads bowed, jabbering excitedly. The departure of the column meant freedom from their Roman masters, for the time being at least. Most of their compatriots had been conscripted as Roman auxiliaries while others had elected to fight alongside the Palmyrans.

Had there been more men of fighting age, Cassius might have worried about some kind of uprising. He was still wary of having such a large group gathered together in the centre of the town. Ammianus and his like had done little to enhance relations. Tensions were running high; even the smallest incident might get out of hand.

Sighing again, Cassius patted his horse's neck, slid off his saddle and walked towards the quarrelling pair. The dull ache that had been building in his head all morning was rapidly worsening.

'What's going on here?'

'Nothing to concern you, centurion,' answered Ammianus with an oily smile.

As usual, Cassius felt a pang of unease when so addressed. Technically speaking, he was not a centurion at all.

The Syrian spat a burst of invective in his native Aramaic. Cassius held up an appeasing hand and quietened him down before speaking to Ammianus again.

'Perhaps you should return the fruit. Or at least pay for it.'

'Since when do Roman soldiers take orders from locals, sir?'

There were a few murmurs and nods from the other legionaries.

Cassius had lost count of the times his instructions had been questioned since arriving in Syria. Most of the soldiers had never encountered such a youthful officer; they were used to experienced veterans promoted after years of service. Cassius had given up explaining to them that the army was now recruiting young, educated men to bolster the hard-pressed forces in the East. If not for the stripe on his tunic, the crest on his helmet and his signed set of orders, he doubted he would have got anything done.

Cassius was naturally rangy and his long, slender limbs made it impossible for him to pass for an older man. Even the rigours of training had added only a limited amount of bulk and this added to his sense of inadequacy. In truth, he felt very much like an actor playing a role and, as he had a little experience of theatre, he had decided early on that he should at least put considerable effort into his performance.

He gestured towards the horses.

'In case you haven't noticed, Ammianus, we are leaving. Retreating, in fact. Hardly the time to antagonise our hosts.'

Cassius spoke in Greek so that all present would understand what was being said. Most Syrians knew enough of the language to get by. Only those who dealt closely with the Romans picked up any Latin.

'Hosts?'

One of the legionaries laughed.

'I've been stationed here almost a year, sir,' continued Ammianus, 'and I have always taken as I pleased.'

The Syrian suddenly stepped forward and made a grab for the fruit. Cassius blocked his way.

'Try that again. Please,' said Ammianus, one hand on the horse-whip hanging from his belt.

5

A couple of the Romans cheered. More locals had gathered at the end of the alley, including the men from across the street.

Someone brushed past Cassius' shoulder. He turned to find a tall legionary beside him, one arm bound by a bloodstained bandage, the other holding a gleaming five-foot throwing javelin.

'Why not let them fight, sir? We could do with some entertainment.'

There were more cheers. Some of the Syrians pressed into the alley. One of the mounted soldiers spat into the dust at their feet.

'Move back,' Cassius said to the tall legionary. The man smiled contemptuously and took a quarter-step backwards.

'Damn all you Romans,' said the stall owner through gritted teeth, eyes locked on Ammianus.

'That's enough out of you!' snapped Cassius.

'Let me teach him some respect,' suggested Ammianus. 'These dogs only understand a good thrashing.'

'Drop that and I'll fight you right here,' countered the Syrian, nodding at the whip.

'Any way you want it.'

The Romans roared again. The tall legionary clapped his hands and waved to another man who had dismounted close to the end of the alley.

'Cinna! Come quickly or you'll miss the action! I'm betting on the Syrian.'

The legionary laughed. Ammianus frowned.

Some of the bolder Syrians pushed their way into the alley. As Cinna passed them, comments were made. Though spoken in Aramaic, their mocking tone was unmistakable.

'Say that in Greek!' Cinna barked.

Cassius' headache was now an ever-enlarging ball of pain above his eyes. Beads of sweat had popped out across his face and back. His fingers, gripping the top of his belt, were wet against the slick leather.

He knew he had to act.

'You!' he shouted, pointing at Cinna. 'Back on your horse! That's an order!'

After a brief hesitation, the legionary removed his hand from his sword pommel and reluctantly retreated. Two others who had dismounted got back on their horses.

'And you,' Cassius said, speaking over his left shoulder, 'can do the same.'

Cassius was taller than most legionaries but this man had a good three inches on him. He was bulky too, with thickly muscled forearms criss-crossed by scars.

Cassius waited, trying to look unperturbed.

The soldier didn't move.

'Alternatively, I can take your name. And you can prepare yourself for a lengthy discussion with your commanding officer upon our return to Antioch.'

The legionary tapped the javelin lightly against his shoulder, then finally backed away.

Cassius let out a breath. After a moment's thought, he struck on a solution and turned towards Ammianus.

'What if I pay for the dates?'

Ammianus looked surprised, then his face broke into a grin. Cassius imagined he was thinking of future drinking sessions, of boasting about the time a centurion bought him his lunch.

'Fine by me, sir.'

Cassius reached into the small leather bag tied to his belt and pulled out a couple of bronze sesterces.

'That should cover it,' he said, handing the coins over. The stall owner looked satisfied; he'd been paid well over the odds. As he hurried back to his stall, a couple of the legionaries groaned with disappointment.

'Caesar himself wrote about the importance of feeding an army,' Cassius announced loudly. 'And it is my responsibility to ensure that the most important individuals in our group are well nourished.' Then, before Ammianus could react, he snatched the palm leaf from his hand, walked back to his horse and held the dates under its muzzle. The animal noisily devoured the fruit.

Cassius stared back at the dumbstruck Ammianus and smiled genially.

The tall legionary was first to react, chuckling at the sour look on the Thracian's face. Some of the other soldiers joined in, adding a few quips at Ammianus' expense. Then the Syrians began laughing too, and in moments the air of tension had been dispelled.

Cassius wouldn't have sided with the Syrian had Ammianus been more popular, but the man had brought it on himself. Still scowling, the Thracian stalked back along the alleyway. A couple of the locals shouted at his back. Cassius hurried over to them.

'That's enough,' he said, quiet but firm. 'Please move along. We shall be leaving soon.'

The crowd broke up. Cassius found himself gazing at a shapely young girl carrying a clay amphora. She had the same smooth brown skin and flashing white teeth he'd noticed all over Syria. His stare lasted a moment too long and he realised some of the locals and legionaries were watching him.

'Hurry up there!' he shouted to no one in particular, feeling his face redden. Returning to his horse, he climbed up on to the saddle, cursing quietly and reminding himself to keep control of his baser instincts. It was just such interest in the female form that had landed him in his present predicament.

'A moment of weakness' was how he'd described it to his father. Up to that point, the old man had tolerated his drinking and dalliances, happy at least that his only son's studies seemed to be progressing. Cassius had been working towards a career as an orator in his native Ravenna, hoping eventually to graduate to the forums of the capital.

However, when he had been discovered enjoying one of his aunt's handmaidens (by his aunt, at her villa, during her fiftieth birthday party), his father's patience had finally run out. Cassius' protestations that the serving girl had 'enjoyed it too' did not help and over the next week he had been dismayed to find that his persuasive powers were not as far advanced as he thought. Corbulo senior was an ex-army man and he had decided that Cassius could only be deterred from a wasteful life of excess by 'discipline, discipline and more discipline'.

Cassius cursed again and rubbed his fingers against his warm, aching brow. He still found it almost impossible to believe that such a small indiscretion had led to this. Here he was, stuck in this pit of a town; in a province facing imminent annexation; deprived of cultured company and all the finer things in life; and surrounded by barbarians, thugs and idiots.

Worse still, according to his father's terms, he had five years left in the army.

Two weeks earlier, Cassius had stood in the office of General Marcus Galenus Navio, the commander charged with the defence of Syria.

'So – a grain man, eh?' the general said, examining the sheet of papyrus as he sat behind his desk.

Cassius didn't reply. He was beginning to tire of the nickname used for agents of the Imperial Security Service. An independent wing of the military, the Service had been established during the time of the Emperor Domitian. Originally concerned with the supply and distribution of grain to the legions, its officers were spread far and wide across the Empire. Dealing so closely with the provincial populace, they were uniquely well placed to report back to Rome on all manner of issues. Over time they had become the 'eyes and ears' of the emperor and his general staff. The original name had stuck.

The Service maintained a headquarters in Rome known informally as 'The Foreigners' Camp'. Most legions were assigned several officers and, though their duties sometimes still included the procurement of supplies, Service men could find themselves acting as emissaries, tax collectors, investigators or spies.

Cassius had heard of his first posting via a missive from the Service chief, Spurius Sestius Pulcher: the same letter now in Navio's hand.

'You're a little young,' the general continued. 'Usually a man has to prove himself a lying, scheming, underhand devil before being recruited to the Camp.'

Cassius stifled a grimace. He knew that the Service suffered from what could at best be described as a mixed reputation. Several friends had advised him against accepting the post. Some suggested that the Service was riddled with corruption, others that it was an impossible job – with loyalties divided between headquarters, local governors and the military hierarchy.

'It is a rather unusual arrangement, sir, I know. My father was able to secure me a position commensurate with my level of education.'

Cassius chose not to add that only weeks of pressure from his mother had persuaded his father to call in a few favours and keep his son from front-line service.

The general grinned. Cassius noticed the thick, lined pouches of skin beneath his eyes. Though broad-shouldered and upright, Navio was quite overweight and this extra bulk sat unnaturally on the frame of what had once been an exceptionally fit man. Above his forehead was an island of grey fluff abandoned by the rest of his receding hair.

'Well, unless your education extends to the dark arts of diplomacy, espionage and assassination you may find it a post more suited to a career criminal than a scholar.'

As Navio continued reading, Cassius looked around. Considering the general was responsible for the defence of Rome's third city, his office was surprisingly modest. Well lit by a large window behind the desk, the only other items of furniture were four unused lamp stands, a neglected brazier and a holed rug. There was nothing for visitors to sit on. Cassius wondered if the general had problems with his eyes. He was taking a long time to read a short letter.

'As you can see, sir, Chief Pulcher requests that I be directed to the senior Service officer in the province.'

At last Navio put the letter to one side.

'Yes, well, unfortunately that arrogant bastard Abascantius doesn't deign to trouble me with news of his activities, let alone request my permission for them.'

The general took some almonds from a small bowl on his desk and washed them down with a mouthful of wine.

'I have no idea where he is. He disappeared into the desert two months ago without even telling me why. Not for the first time I might add. Luckily, there is no shortage of work for young, upstanding officers such as yourself.'

Despite the heat of late afternoon, Cassius felt a chill run down his spine. The prospect of five years with the Service seemed dreadful enough, but surely nothing could be more dangerous than a field posting with the legions.

'You understand the situation here?' asked the general.

'I do, sir. We face revolt.'

'I suppose you could call it that. The truth is, the Palmyrans have held the upper hand here for years. And you'll find as many folk on the streets of Antioch would as soon raise Zenobia's banner as Claudius'. But the Queen has gone too far, and seems intent on nothing less than annexation.'

'We can assume that she knows of the problems in Gaul then. Not to mention the campaign against the Goths.'

'Indeed. And that she'd be well advised to secure her position while the Emperor is preoccupied.'

Navio stood, ran a hand over his paunch and sauntered over to a large, tatty map mounted on the wall. It was marked here and there with charcoal and ink.

'Come. Show me the partition boundary.'

It took Cassius a moment to find the right line, denoting the partition between Syria Coele and Syria Phoenice.

'That's it. Phoenice went first. That's the Palmyrans' home ground. Several cohorts were lost so I withdrew the rest to key settlements further north. A few were taken but I suspect the Queen was waiting for Arabia, Palestine and Egypt to fall before committing significant forces. Now they have; so we're getting her full attention. Apamea and several smaller towns have gone in the last few weeks. All that stands between them and us is what's left of the Third Legion.'

The general made circles with his finger in an area to the south-east of the capital.

'Scattered amongst the towns here are a number of small

garrisons. Just a few engineers and clerks now. Wounded, too. I need them rounded up and brought back here. It might be only weeks before the city is besieged.'

Despite such a prospect, Cassius had felt rather reassured by his few days in Antioch. The thought of venturing beyond its walls horrified him.

The general was already back at his desk. He filled a bronze pen with ink from a pot, then began to write on a papyrus sheet.

'I'll list the towns here. Get around them as quick as you can. I'll assign a scout to help you find your way. My clerk will help you with any questions.'

'Sir, you do understand that – officially – I'm not actually a centurion. I haven't even been assigned to a legion yet.'

The general continued writing as he spoke.

'What was the name?'

'Corbulo, sir.'

'Corbulo, you have an officer's tunic and an officer's helmet and you completed full officer training, did you not?'

Cassius nodded. He could easily recall every accursed test and drill he had undergone at Ravenna's military academy. Though he had excelled in the cerebral disciplines and somehow survived the endless marches and swims, he had rated poorly with sword in hand and had been repeatedly described as 'lacking natural leadership ability'. The academy's senior centurion had seemed quite relieved when the letter from the Service arrived.

'I did, sir, but it was felt I would be more suited to intelligence work than the legions. I really would prefer—'

'And you did take an oath? To Rome, the Army and the Emperor?'

'I did sir, and of course I am happy to serve but—'

The general finished the orders. He rolled the sheet up roughly and handed it to Cassius.

'Dismissed.'

'Yes, sir. Sorry, sir. I just have one final question.'

The general was on his way back to his chair. He turned round and fixed Cassius with an impatient stare.

12

'Sir, how should I present myself to the troops? In terms of rank, I mean.'

'They will assume you are a centurion, and I can see no practical reason whatsoever to disabuse them of that view.'

Cassius could not forget that phrase, nor could he shake off a mild sense of shame every time he donned his officer's helmet, complete with its bright red horsehair crest. The helmet was made of iron, with a protruding nose guard and three hanging sections that protected the ears and neck. He was still not used to the weight, and though his headache was beginning to ease, he cursed quietly as he tightened the straps around his chin. He hated the damn thing but it seemed sensible to keep up appearances for the benefit of the locals. He could take it off once the column was clear of Nessara.

It was the last town on the general's list. Fifty miles from the capital. If they were lucky they might do it in three days. Cassius was desperate to get moving. He had gleaned enough from the soldiers and locals to know that Palmyrans approaching from the east might overrun the area at any time.

Once back in Antioch, he intended to find this Abascantius, take up the post he had been promised and hopefully avoid any more field assignments. But as he had discovered of late, looking too far into the future was a dangerous indulgence. His priority was to get the column out of the town and on the move.

It was almost midday when they left. Cassius took the lead with the mounted legionaries behind him, riding two abreast. Next came the carts bearing supplies and the wounded. Bringing up the rear were those soldiers on foot and the local auxiliaries.

Apart from the now abandoned Roman compound, Nessara was little more than a cluster of low, mud-brick houses. Despite the ravages of war and the enervating climate of high summer, life continued apace. Small groups of children darted here and there, stopping only to gaze at the column as it passed. Traders – some with stalls, others with no more than a woven basket –

offered all manner of food; from olives, dates, oranges and lemons to chicken, goat and lamb, available alive or dead. One man stood over a selection of military equipment polished to a high sheen: some Roman, some local, even a huge axe from some northern land.

Approaching the edge of town, the column passed a group of women hanging washing on lines strung between dwellings. Several stopped what they were doing and more than one pair of eyes were drawn to the unusual figure leading the way.

As if his youth and lean physique were not enough to set him apart, Cassius' other features did little to help him blend in. His family was from the far north of Italy and, like his mother and three sisters, he had light brown hair and a fair complexion. Thankfully, he had also inherited his mother's good looks and his distinctive appearance had never done him any harm in his relations with women, not to mention drawing attention from quite a few men. The effect was doubled when he found himself amongst the darker peoples of the East.

One of the younger women bent over a basket and, before he could help himself, Cassius was leering at the swell of her surprisingly large breasts. The girl caught his eye as she stood up. Hand on hip, she gave a provocative smile.

This was soon replaced by a frown as an older woman, presumably her mother, slapped the girl hard across the back of her head. Pulling her daughter's robes together to cover her cleavage, she pushed her away through the laundry before shooting Cassius a venomous glare.

The scout assigned to assist Cassius was a man named Cotta, who was waiting for the column at the edge of town by a run-down farmhouse. He stepped out of the shade provided by a wall, rounded his horse and nodded a greeting.

'Morning. Or should I say afternoon?'

Cassius was about to apologise but reminded himself that Roman officers did not offer excuses to scouts.

Cotta had a thin covering of greying hair and a heavily lined face that carried a certain air of nobility. He wore the white robes of a local, with only a traditional brooch to identify him as Roman.

'Shall we?' Cassius said, pointing towards the road ahead. It was marked by a darker shade of sand and the occasional line of stones. The lands beyond were dotted with hardy shrubs and trees. In the distance were the undulating hills that signalled a return to safer territory.

'I thought you might prefer to wait,' said Cotta.

'For what?'

'The messenger.'

'What messenger?'

Cotta pointed towards the hills. Cassius and the legionaries peered into the haze. About a mile down the road, a speeding rider had just emerged from behind a small copse of trees.

'And if my aged eyes serve,' said Cotta, 'he carries a spear with a feather attached.'

'Meaning what?'

Cotta seemed surprised by Cassius' ignorance.

'The feather instructs all who the carrier meets to clear the way or lend assistance. It means he bears urgent and important news – a military emergency.'

Cassius narrowed his eyes. Though slumped forward in his saddle, the messenger was holding a spear aloft.

Cotta was right. The feather was there.

II

Two of the legionaries helped the messenger to the ground. The man looked utterly exhausted. His skin was red, his lips cracked, his tunic soaked through with sweat. He could hardly walk and the soldiers half dragged, half carried him over to the farmhouse wall as the rest of the men crowded round.

Cassius, still on his horse, looked on as Cotta administered some water. The messenger drank greedily, coughing it up at first, then emptied half the canteen. Squinting, he pointed over Cotta's shoulder.

'Centurion Corbulo?'

'Yes,' answered Cassius evenly. He removed his helmet, dismounted and walked over.

The messenger reached into his tunic and pulled out a sodden piece of cloth. He attempted to undo it but his fingers were still too numb from gripping the reins. Cotta took over and unwrapped a roll of papyrus sealed with maroon wax.

'It carries the general's mark,' he said, offering Cassius the letter.

As Ammianus attended to the messenger's equally shattered horse, Cassius took the letter and walked round to the other side of the farmhouse. The seal was indeed the general's, the letters M, G and N quite clear. Cassius felt his stomach turn over as he scratched away the seal. Opening up the page, he recognised the same even hand that had given him his first ever set of operational orders. Now he had his second.

Corbulo,
Zenobia's advance has gathered pace. She has ordered her forces to take control of the settlements close to your position. The easternmost of these is a fort named Alauran. It should still be

*occupied by men of the Third Legion. There is a large stock of
provisions there and, more importantly, a deep, reliable well.*

*General Valens and the Sixteenth Legion are on their way
south to meet this new advance. His men will need that food
and water.*

*I do not know the size of this Palmyran force but I have
already dispatched a message to Valens, requesting that he send a
unit of cavalry immediately to Alauran. They should be there
four or five days after this letter reaches you.*

*There are no other officers in the area. Get yourself there,
Corbulo. If there's anyone of rank, give them this letter and any
assistance you can. If not, take charge of whatever forces remain.
You are, after all, employed to safeguard imperial security; this is
a perfect opportunity to do so. Prepare for an attack and hold
Alauran until reinforcements arrive.*

May the gods favour you,
General Marcus Galenus Navio

'Well?' asked Cotta, now standing close by.

Cassius wiped away the thick beads of sweat running down
his face, no longer entirely as a result of the heat. He took a deep
breath and tried to compose himself.

'A change of plan. How far to Alauran from here?'

'A day and a night perhaps.'

'And the route?'

The scout pointed to the south-east.

See the three hills there, on the other side of the plain?'

Cassius shaded his eyes once again.

'There's a pass through the first two. Get to the other side and
bear directly east into the desert. Alauran is within clear view –
there are palms by the western wall. It may have been overrun
by now. Surely we're not going there?'

'You're not.'

As Cassius walked back towards the column, he briefly considered throwing the orders away, concocting some scheme to avoid
this new mission, but the thought died, stillborn. After six months

17

of training, instructions from above carried an undeniable, irresistible weight. Orders were given, orders were obeyed. Cassius gave a grim, unnoticed half-smile. There had always been a certain inevitability about this moment; what he feared most had come to pass.

Approaching the soldiers, he was met by a line of expectant faces.

'You. Cinna, isn't it?'

'Sir.'

'You know my attendant? The fat Gaul? He's close to the back of the column. Tell him to come up with as much of my gear as we can carry on two horses. Assist him if he needs help.'

'Yes, sir.'

Cinna coaxed his mount out of the line and set off at a trot. Cassius ignored the exchange of cynical glances between the other legionaries. Young centurions were rare. Young centurions with their own manservant were almost unheard of.

Cassius hurried back towards Cotta and met him by the shaded wall.

'So, what do you know of the place?'

'I was there about four months ago. I delivered orders for their senior officer to report any sightings of the Palmyrans and prepare the defence. I assumed they had been withdrawn by now.'

'Apparently not.'

'From what I recall the fort was in a pretty poor state. There was a centurion still there but I didn't see him. He was very ill. Close to death I think.'

Cassius shook his head and cursed his father.

'And the men?'

'Unit of the Third Legion. Disorganised lot. No one else taking charge.'

'How many? A century's worth?'

'Oh no, certainly not.'

'Wonderful. Anything else?'

'They ate well. There's a granary full of grain, dried meat and fish. And plenty of wine. A little too much of which was being consumed by the men, actually. I left the orders with an old veteran. Name began with a B. He knew the place inside out. Kept going on about some man he referred to as the Praetorian.'

'A member of the Praetorian Guard? Out here?'

'That was my reaction. I never saw him but the old fellow seemed sure they would be safe as long as this Praetorian was around.'

'Sounds to me like the figment of a deranged imagination.'

'I don't know,' said Cotta, fiddling with his brooch. 'He was old certainly, but not deranged. I got more sense out of him than anyone else there. I saw a few legionaries but they could barely string a sentence together.'

Cotta mimed tipping a cup towards his mouth.

Cassius wafted away a fly. Clusters of them had begun to gather round the stationary horses.

'So. Apart from drunks, insane old men and fictitious Guardsmen, is there anyone else I should know about?'

'I believe there were a few locals left: traders, those too sick to travel, a couple of whores . . .'

As Cotta's voice trailed off, Cassius turned and saw Simo and Cinna approaching. Simo's horse was laden with gear. Cinna had two leather saddlebags perched on his lap.

'Simo, we're to be on our own for a while. You'll need to use my mount too.' Cassius nodded at his horse, pacing slowly in the shade.

Cotta held up a hand.

'A word of advice. Travelling alone you'll make for an easy target. Apart from the Palmyrans, some of the locals might be tempted now we're pulling out. Keep an eye out for bandits. You should make it across the plain before dark.'

Cotta lowered his voice.

'Are you sure you don't want to take some of the legionaries with you?'

'No. They are the only front-line troops in the column. Besides, they are still recovering from their last engagement.'

'And you are fresh and eager to face action?' asked Cotta with a wry smile.

Cassius knew there was no point trying to hide his concerns from such an experienced campaigner. He made no attempt at bravado, in fact he made no reply at all. His oratorical skills had so deserted him that he was unable even to summon a witty riposte.

'Your name's Corbulo, isn't it?' Cotta continued.

'That's right.'

'Gnaes Domitius Corbulo. The general who restored order in Armenia for Nero. Any relation?'

'Distantly I believe.'

'And he led the Third Legion. A good omen. You'll do well with these men.'

'I wish I shared your confidence. Come, there are some points of command to settle.'

The messenger had been taken to the rear of the column. Ammianus and the legionaries were back on their horses and arranged in a loose semicircle. Cotta took the reins of his own mount and followed Cassius towards them.

'I have to leave,' Cassius announced. 'Cotta here is in charge of all matters relating to the journey back to Antioch. He knows the territory well and is to be regarded as commander in this respect.'

The legionaries all nodded their assent. Cassius knew there were no soldiers of senior rank in the column but somebody had to take charge. He caught the eye of the tall legionary with the injured arm. He now had a whole bundle of the throwing javelins slung across his back.

'Your name?'

'Licinius.'

'Well, Licinius, I have a job for you. If there is an attack, you are to take over and coordinate the defence of the column. Assuming all goes well, report to the first senior officer you come across. Understood?'

Unlike many of the soldiers Cassius had encountered, Licinius seemed to respond well to being given responsibility; he sat higher in his saddle and seemed happy to take charge.

'Yes, sir.'

'And do whatever you can to keep everyone moving in the hours of daylight.'

Cassius moved towards Cotta, now also in the saddle.

'When you're ready then.'

'May Fortuna watch over you,' replied Cotta gravely as his mount moved off.

Cassius backed away from the column towards the farmhouse, looking on as the legionaries and auxiliaries followed in turn.

'Centurion!' Cotta shouted over his shoulder. 'The old man! His name was Barates.'

Cassius only just heard him over the sound of the horses.

'Barates?'

'That's it!'

They exchanged a final wave. Cassius, now back in the shade, was struck by the number of men who took the time to salute or shout a goodbye.

Simo had led the horses round to the other side of the farm-house, away from the dust kicked up by the column. He had readied his own mount and was now shifting full canteens of water on to his master's saddle. He was a big man, broad-shouldered and solid, and carrying a quarter more weight than he needed. He had an open, youthful face made older by a hefty double chin. His thick, black hair was now wet and matted to his forehead. Cassius watched him work for a moment. All things considered, Simo had adjusted to his new life rather well.

Though he had been tended to since birth, Cassius had decided against maintaining an attendant whilst in the army, mainly because he couldn't afford it. But he was not one to turn down a convenient opportunity, and during his brief stay in Antioch a rare piece of good fortune had come his way.

He had visited a friend of his father, a wealthy, aged merchant named Trimalchio. Fearing the city would fall, Trimalchio was taking his family back to Rome and clearing up his affairs in the province, not expecting to return. He and his wife remembered

Cassius as a young boy and, sympathetic to his predicament, they had treated him kindly. He had dined with them twice and those few hours had given him valued respite from the tense wait for orders.

On the day of the family's departure, Trimalchio had presented him with Simo. He was of Gaulish descent, a sixth-generation slave highly regarded by his master. No money changed hands but Cassius had been told he could make use of Simo for as long as he was required. Only then would he join the rest of the staff in Rome.

Simo looked up as he tied off the last canteen.

'A necessary measure I'm afraid, sir.'

Cassius waved the comment away.

'Go ahead. Do you think I'd rather die of thirst than pile on a bit of extra weight? You have the money, I trust.'

'Yes, sir.' Simo patted his tunic.

Corbulo senior had at least been generous enough to furnish his son with fifteen hundred denarii in silver coins: twice the annual army salary and enough to bribe one's way out of most situations.

'Is there anything else to do?' Cassius asked. 'If it's just to be the two of us for a while, I should probably lend a hand.'

'Just your armour, sir. I've not found a spot for that yet.'

Simo pointed at Cassius' mail shirt, folded neatly on top of a pile of bricks. Like all soldiers, Cassius had purchased it with his own money. In fact, he had opted for the priciest and most highly recommended example he could find. The thousands of rings were made of copper alloy, which produced a distinctive silvery tinge. The trader had assured him that it was both stronger and lighter than conventional iron or bronze mail. Cassius did not expect ever to make a more important investment.

Dusting it down first, he lifted the shirt by the shoulders and walked back to his horse. He could see no space on the side Simo was working, so instead examined the other flank. Every available saddlebag was filled: one with food, one with a wood axe, another with his cloak. Cassius could see no obvious solution. Simo intervened.

'Allow me, sir,' he said, taking the shirt. He hurried round the horse's rear and removed the axe from the largest bag. Wrapping it in some sackcloth, he swiftly found a way to fit the axe neatly inside the mail shirt.

'Most resourceful,' said Cassius, running a finger across his chin and resolving to leave servants' work to servants in future.

'I believe we're about ready, sir,' said Simo, surveying his handiwork.

'Let's be away then,' replied Cassius, noting that virtually the entire column was now past them.

'None of the legionaries are to accompany us, sir?' Simo asked.

'No,' Cassius answered flatly as he hauled himself up into the saddle. The horse spent a few moments protesting, perhaps noticing the added bulk, but then calmed down. Simo, now also in the saddle, moved up to take his position behind Cassius, but his master waved him forward to join him.

'It would be better if two pairs of eyes monitor our path in this haze. We'll start by heading for that tree. See there, with the crooked trunk?'

Simo followed the line of his outstretched arm.

'I see it, sir. And did I hear that we're to make for a pass between the first two hills?'

'That's it, yes. I see you are as anxious to establish our route as I.'

'As you say, sir, two pairs of eyes are better than one. I've become rather used to finding the way. Working for my last master it was a daily occupation. I lost count of the times I had to show him the way to buildings within his own estate.'

'Is that so?' asked Cassius as they rode away from the farm-house. 'Still, I'll wager you'd rather be on your way to Rome than stuck out here with me.'

Simo took a while to reply.

'It's not my place to decide how best I can serve, sir. You can be sure I'll perform my duties as well as I can.'

Cassius frowned, feeling slightly guilty that he'd provoked such a statement.

'Oh, I know that, man. I've seen enough of you to know that.'

The two of them fell into an uneasy silence. The only sounds to be heard were the increasingly distant rumble of the column and the annoying thumps and thuds of equipment shifting around on the saddles. As their riders eased their grip on the reins, the horses settled into a slow, steady pace and stared blankly at the ground in front of them, oblivious to the distances ahead.

By the time they finally lost sight of the column, the sun was already beginning its descent. Cassius had been turning round every so often and had just seen the last moving speck disappear behind the pale yellow hills north of Nessara. A few minutes earlier they had reached the crooked tree, stopping to water the horses. Cassius hadn't felt like eating anything and they soon got under way again.

He now realised he had made his first serious mistake. Cotta's words rolled around his head and he found himself struggling to remember precisely what the scout had said about bandits. Given the present situation, he knew his garb would do nothing to deter any would-be attackers. Simo carried a dagger, but he hardly seemed the warrior type, and with his own fighting ability still so limited, he had been stupid not to bring along a couple of the legionaries.

Squinting into the haze, Cassius looked for horses on the plain, or moving along the base of the hills ahead. As they had at least two or three more hours until they reached those hills, he decided to occupy the time with conversation, knowing at least that if they were attacked, it would not be difficult to see their foes coming.

'So Simo. Remind me how it is that a Gaul comes to be so far from home.'

Simo also seemed eager to distract himself and eased his horse a little nearer.

'Well, sir, I have worked for my master all my life, as my father did for his. My antecedents were captured in battle and taken to Rome. My grandfather's grandfather came here in the service of

24

a leather merchant. It was during the time of the Emperor Hadrian – 'the days of glory' as my father would call them. He used to tell stories passed down to him: the building of Antioch's great temples and aqueducts and theatres; the garrison parading the walls, five thousand strong; and the rise of the Christians, of course.'

Cassius rolled his eyes.

'The Christians. I heard almost as much about them in Antioch as the Palmyrans. It seems they are with us to stay.'

'I should say so, sir. My uncle's dwelling in the city is not far from house used by Paul of Tarsus no less. Do you find nothing of merit in their teachings?'

Cassius shrugged. Ever since his earliest days, he had lacked a natural interest in things religious. Here in the East, he had found that every tenet of traditional Roman belief seemed to be a subject for debate, and his interest had declined even further.

'Not particularly. It seems to me that life is short, difficult and dangerous, and one is better off looking to oneself if one wishes to progress. Although I must accept I am in a minority as far as such thinking goes. Of course, if the Emperor and his general Aurelian do well, it may be that one day they find themselves worshipped as divine beings.'

'The Emperor does seem the type to bring the provinces to heel, sir.'

'Indeed, though I must confess I never expected to be involved in such efforts myself. If only that rampaging bitch Zenobia would be content to stay in her lair, I would be spared such a trial. Only a mob of witless barbarians would allow a woman to rule them.'

'Barbarians they are, sir. I have heard tales of their treatment of prisoners that turn the stomach.'

Cassius was relieved that Simo didn't go into any detail.

'There's one issue I might agree with the Christians about. War is one thing but an interest in needless torture and suffering is the mark of a feeble mind. Anyone who's seen the parade of inbreds and freaks emerging wide-eyed from a gladiator contest can attest to that.'

'May I ask something, sir?'

Cassius had just finished another sweep of the horizon.

'You may.'

'Why exactly are we journeying to Alauran? Forgive my question, I wish only for an idea of what awaits us.'

Cassius took a deep breath. When he replied, he found himself listening to his own words with an unsettling sense of detachment, as if they were being spoken by someone else.

'An attack by the Palmyrans is expected. If there is no senior officer present, I will have to do what I can to ensure that the fort and its well do not fall into their hands. As to what precisely awaits us, I advise you take the position I have adopted. I think we're just going to have to wait and see.'

As the sun dipped below the horizon and their shadows stretched away from them, the two riders reached the edge of the plain and turned south at the base of the hills. The pass was still a fair distance away and Cassius decided to make camp at the next suitable location.

It turned out to be a small hollow where a dried-up stream had eaten down into the soil. The site had been used before: several bulky stones lay round a circle of ash and an area at the base of a voluminous boulder had been cleared for sleeping.

'This will do,' said Cassius as he dismounted, 'though a nice little cave would be ideal. The air already feels colder, but we can't risk a fire in the open.'

Shaking the stiffness out of his legs, Cassius drank from his canteen and leaned back against the boulder, watching the last quarter of the sun disappear. Simo removed the saddles and tethered the horses to long ropes, which he tied off round a heavy stone. There was a little grass on the slopes above and both animals soon drifted away to investigate.

'The desert is a cruel land, sir,' observed Simo as he unpacked a saddlebag. 'Not like Italy or Gaul, where the temperature often suits. Here it's too hot by day, too cold by night.'

Cassius was yet to experience such a night, having previously spent the hours of darkness inside either a commandeered building or his spacious officer's tent. Unfortunately, that was now on its way to Antioch.

Simo retrieved six blankets, which he folded over and lay on the ground in the shelter of the boulder. He gave his master four: two to sleep on and two to cover him.

'Leaving just two for you, Simo. Well, you do have more natural insulation.'

'Quite so, sir. Quite so.'

Cassius began to undress. His leather boots had seemed too large at first but now fitted nicely, and it took him a while to lever them off. The merchant who sold them to him had stated that the sturdy hobnailed soles would last for five hundred miles of walking on good road.

Next he removed his sword belt, which hung diagonally from his right shoulder, holding the weapon over his left hip. The arrangement had felt unnatural to begin with but he had soon seen the sense of keeping it free from other encumbrances at his waist, namely the military belt, key identifier of a Roman soldier.

Made of thick, resilient leather, the belts were usually decorated with metal plates, inscriptions or other adornments. Cassius, however, had settled on a simple example with a modest iron buckle. Next off was his dagger, which hung in its own scabbard on the right. These short, wide blades had been in use for centuries and made for formidable sidearms. Cassius lay down both weapons next to his blanket and was about to continue undressing when Simo's broad features emerged out of the darkness in front of him.

'I'd keep your tunic on if I were you, sir. And here's your cloak too.'

Nothing more than a rectangle of heavy wool, the cloak was another piece of standard legionary equipment Cassius was yet to use.

'Surely it won't be that cold?'

'I believe it will, sir,' Simo said firmly.

'Very well.' Cassius took the cloak. He had learned to trust Simo's judgement on such matters.

27

'Dinner won't be a moment, sir. I must just attend to a few other tasks while we still have a little light.'

Cassius sat down on the blankets and pulled the cloak over him, leaning back against the rock. Despite the uneven ground beneath, it felt good to be still and rest his tired limbs. Having never ridden so consistently in his life, he had acquired an unpleasant set of bruises on his thighs and backside. At least the painful blisters on his fingers seemed to be drying out. This was not the only change to them. Since the beginning of training, his hands had been worked so hard that he had actually noticed his fingers increase in size.

Aside from the sounds of Simo going about his work, all was quiet. The darkened plain stretched away in front of him, with only the distant lights of Nessara to remind him where they had come from. He lay down and tried to find a moment's relief from thoughts of Alauran and what turmoil the next few days might bring.

The sky above was cloudless, lighter than the inky black around him, and he passed the time by identifying the few stars he knew. He had long since forgotten the names but one of his childhood tutors had made a point of showing him the most recognisable constellations. They had used the star catalogues within Ptolemy's *Almagest*, of which his father had a good copy. Tracing lines between the stars with his fingers, Cassius succeeded in losing himself for a while, only to be interrupted by Simo, who emerged out of the dark proffering a wooden plate.

'And what delights have you prepared for me?'

'Some spiced pork, sir, some bread, a few dried apricots also.'

'It'll have to do. I'm becoming used to eating like a peasant. I must say though, Simo, you're doing rather well with this outdoor stuff. You've travelled widely in the province?'

'No, sir. My work kept me at my master's house or one of his other premises. This is the furthest I have ever been.' Simo's usual immaculately neutral tone wavered. 'And this is the longest I have spent away from the city.'

'I see.'

'I'll just fetch your wine, sir.'

Cassius found the pork with his fingers. He was about to take a bite when he heard a noise from behind the boulder. It sounded like the scuffing of feet.

Warily lowering the plate to the ground and freeing himself from the coverings, Cassius reached for his sword and slid it gently out of the leather scabbard. Simo was not close enough to hear a whisper so he got to his feet and circled the boulder, crouching low. The slab of rock was easily ten feet across and it wouldn't have been difficult for some unseen foe to hide there, waiting to strike when the two of them were off their guard.

As the angle of the sword changed, the blade caught the moonlight. Cassius stared down at it, eroding what little night vision he had gained. Cursing his stupidity and blinking the glare away, he rounded the boulder and gazed into the darkness. The hillside was as black as the plain and might have masked a hundred men. He could barely see two yards.

'Sir?'

Ignoring Simo, Cassius started up the slope, only to catch his right boot on something. He jumped back and thought he'd perhaps startled a snake. Then he heard a sniff and his fears evaporated. His sight had improved enough to see the eye, then the muzzle, then the head of one of the horses. Cassius kicked the ground and the horse moved away with a grunt, taking the rope with it. He turned away and met Simo as he rounded the boulder.

'Is something wrong, sir?' the Gaul whispered, his hand on his dagger.

'Just one of the horses. I heard something and thought I should investigate.'

'Sir, it may be wise for me to stay awake for the hours of darkness. Please – your wine awaits.'

Cassius followed him back into the little camp and replaced his sword in the scabbard. Simo had decanted the wine into a small jug, which he handed over once Cassius was back under the blankets.

'Apologies, sir. I forgot to pack anything smaller.'

As Simo arranged his own makeshift bed, Cassius drained the jug, savouring every mouthful, despite the low quality of the wine. Determined to keep a clear head, he had been limiting his intake since arriving in Syria, but felt present circumstances justified a little indulgence.

'Sir, I'll go and take a brief look round if I may. You can try to get some sleep.'

'Try is probably all I'll do. You can take first watch but I don't intend for you to keep watch all night, servant or not. Wake me in a few hours and I shall take over. It's been a long day for us both and we'll need our wits about us tomorrow.'

'That's very kind of you, sir,' Simo said as he moved away.

'Not at all.'

Wishing to take advantage of the wine's effects, Cassius lay down again and pulled the blankets up under his chin. Though the air was still cold on his face, his body soon warmed up and he was surprised to find himself appreciating the rediscovered sensation of bedding down under the night sky. It reminded him of his childhood and more innocent times, thoughts of which inevitably led him back to his present predicament.

Even so, the combination of the wine and the strains of the day was a potent one, and he soon drifted off into a deep, welcome slumber.

III

'Ah. I was hoping you would wake of your own accord, sir.'

Cassius yawned and opened his eyes. He expected the black of night, not blinding sunlight.

'It's dawn already?'

'A little past that actually, sir.' Simo handed Cassius his canteen. He looked exactly as he had the previous evening, though his eyes were slightly bloodshot. The canteen was full; the metal chilled Cassius' fingers.

'Why didn't you wake me, man? Don't tell me you've been up all night?'

'Actually I lay down for most of it, sir. I was quite warm enough and I took to walking round the camp every hour or so. There was nothing to cause alarm, just the howl of a dog in the distance. I thought it best to let you sleep, bearing in mind what the rest of the day holds.'

Cassius stood up and let the blankets fall off him.

'I suppose I should be grateful. But next time I give you an instruction, follow it. And don't blame me if you fall off your horse.'

Simo had already done most of the packing and at Cassius' insistence there was no breakfast, just more water, half of which was already gone. Assuming Cotta's estimate was correct, they would reach Alauran mid-morning, so Cassius also allowed Simo to give a little to the horses.

He had just buckled his sword belt when Simo led his mount over. Feeling rather reinvigorated by his night's rest, he launched himself up into the saddle and took the reins. Guiding the animal down on to the edge of the plain, he checked the horizon for any sign of movement.

Threads of smoke could be seen above Nessara and for a moment Cassius thought he could see a rider near the edge of the town but the image shifted, then disappeared. It was too far to be sure. He checked to the north and south but there was nothing of interest, just the familiar haze building again under the newly risen sun.

'All done, sir,' said Simo, tying off the last saddlebag. As he too mounted his horse, Cassius started away along the base of the hills.

The pass turned out to be much closer than expected. After less than half an hour, Cassius spied the dark wall of a narrow ravine. He waved Simo forward.

Though it may have begun life as a natural feature, at some point a significant force of labour had been employed to dig the path through the mixture of sand, soil and rock. The sides of the pass were vertical, topped by hardy bushes, the drought-resistant species Cassius had seen all over Syria.

Simo gestured for him to go first as there was insufficient space for them to enter side by side. Cassius' horse took an instant dislike to the shadows and the damp, earthy odour; it veered to the right and stuck its hooves obstinately into the ground, head flicking up and down.

'What's up with the beast?'

'Perhaps after all the open space it fears an enclosed path,' suggested Simo, keeping well back.

Cassius grunted a reply and gave a hefty kick with the point of his boot. It was enough to change the horse's mind and with only a token shuffle of rebellion, it started forward.

Apart from a few twists and turns to avoid impervious lumps of rock, the path was fairly straight. A few moments after Cassius caught his first glimpse of the far end, a shout boomed towards them. He held up his hand and halted his horse. The path was wider now and Simo was able to draw alongside. Cassius hadn't really made up his mind what to do until he saw the anxious, expectant look on the Gaul's face.

'Stay here,' he whispered before carefully dismounting and handing over the reins.

The path ahead curved left. Cassius advanced slowly, hand on his sword. Thankful his tunic would blend well with the walls, he rounded the bend.

He saw the plain, then a man trotting by on a horse. In a moment the rider was gone, leaving Cassius unsure whether he was a soldier, a trader, a brigand or a peasant, though in truth he doubted his ability to distinguish one from the other in this lawless, alien land.

Wincing at a metallic clank from one of the saddles, he moved forward once more. Darting from shadow to shadow, wall to wall, he was soon just fifty feet from the end of the pass. Half standing, half crouching, he peered over an outcrop of rock as two more riders appeared, then stopped. Their horses stood side by side, one obscuring the other. The man closest to Cassius was clad in some of the richest, most colourful garments he had ever seen: a long, purple tunic embroidered with gold and worn over a pair of matching trousers. The man's head was covered with a wrapping of equally fine scarlet cloth. The outfit seemed as incongruous as it was impractical. From the way he bent over in the saddle. Cassius gathered the man might be rather old. Behind him, a commonly attired young servant held a woven shade over his master.

Another shout came from behind the pair. The old man waved the shade away and the two horses moved off. They were followed in short order by three more men who sped by in close formation. All were bearded, dressed in common robes and armed with long, heavy spears.

Cassius counted to twenty then left his hiding place and edged forward, again sticking close to the wall. As the sides of the pass began to angle downwards on either side of him, he paused, listening intently. Apart from the buzzing of a sandfly around his ear, he could hear nothing. Advancing as far as he could without

33

breaking cover, he first looked left, and saw that there were no stragglers or a rearguard to catch him unawares. Ignoring the vast expanse of desert in front of him, he then peered right between two thorny bushes. There, perhaps eighty yards away, were the horsemen, bobbing up and down in their saddles as they continued south along the edge of the plain. Despite the glare of the sun, he could still make out the lustrous purple of the elderly rider.

Careful to remain hidden, Cassius now allowed himself to look forward. Where previous panoramas had been dominated by mountains and foothills, he knew that he was now seeing the Syrian desert proper. He couldn't help being slightly disappointed by the paucity of golden dunes; even here the sand was more brown than yellow, dotted with plant life and littered by pebbles and stones.

Eyes narrowed and with two hands to shield them, he now looked for any sign of a settlement. Cotta had seemed sure Alauran was easily spotted once through the pass. Cassius was becoming used to the way the hazy horizon seemed to offer a shape only to conceal it immediately, but there was no mistaking the cluster of trees almost dead ahead. He counted nine palms in all. They were in front of a pale, angular structure that seemed to reach half as high. It was, he concluded, one side of a wall.

Five minutes later, Simo offered the opinion he'd been asked for.

'I believe that must be it, sir. I see no other structures at all.'

Cassius, sitting in shade, took a long swig from his canteen before replying.

'How long for the ride would you say? I was thinking three or four hours.'

'I should say more like five, sir, if I'm honest.'

'Well, we shall soon see. I intend to set off when our friends are a little further away. What do you make of them?'

Simo took a last look along the foothills before grabbing the reins of the horses and towing them safely out of sight.

'The colour and quality of the attire you described suggests they may be Emesan, sir. Since the rise of the Palmyrans it has not been uncommon to see them abroad.'

'Would they consider us enemies?'

'It's difficult to say. They are an unpredictable bunch at the best of times and this is hardly that.'

'Unpredictable and a good deal more besides. The boy emperor Elagabalus hailed from Emesa and look at what happened to him.'

'I'm afraid my education didn't extend far into the field of history, sir. My master encouraged me mainly in the ways of trade. Knowledge that would aid me in my work for him.'

Ever busy, Simo took the opportunity to get some more water down the horses before they crossed the plain. As he retrieved an iron pot from a saddlebag, Cassius continued.

'Well, he was yet another Syrian who imagined he would make a wonderful emperor. Power-hungry lot out here it seems. Anyway, his ascent was as convoluted and dull as a hundred others. His reign, however, was, well . . . shall we say colourful. Apart from being devoted to the cult of the sun he was known to prefer the attire of women and to practise indiscriminate copulation. Hardly a rarity in Rome you might say, but his insistence on the senators and their wives participating certainly set him apart.'

Simo looked rather embarrassed at such talk and Cassius decided to move on.

'In any case, it all ended with him and his mother being murdered and cast into a sewer. Mind you, an emperor meeting an ignominious end hardly constitutes a rarity either I suppose.'

Cassius got up and held his horse back so that Simo's could drink.

The Gaul looked up at the sky.

'It seems strange to me, sir, that folk from such a dry, parched place should choose to devote themselves to the sun.'

'Well, not all of them. What about this chap Mani? Wonder what the Christians think of him.'

'I haven't heard his teachings, sir.'

'He's said to consider himself greater even than their precious Christ.'

'I didn't know that, sir.'

'And what about Elagabalus' black stone? You must have heard of that.'

Simo shook his head.

'Quite a tale. He brought to Rome a conical rock said to possess remarkable properties. It was found somewhere not far from here, I believe. Apparently it reflected both the sun and the moon and could speak with a voice from above.' Cassius gave a cynical sneer. 'You have probably gathered that I am hardly a zealot, but a talking stone? Please.'

'As likely as making a blind man see I suppose, sir,' said Simo.

'Yes,' replied Cassius, sensing a rare edge in the Gaul's voice. 'Quite.'

It soon became obvious that both men had been unduly pessimistic with their estimates. Before the third hour of the journey from the pass was up, they had a good view of Alauran.

Having previously resisted the local custom of wrapping cloth around the head, Cassius had given into Simo's urgings and was already grateful for it. He had picked up a good deal of colour in the previous month but could still feel sunburn on his exposed legs and arms. The heat was also beginning to take its toll on both horses; they had slowed to a lethargic amble.

'It might be as well to walk from here,' said Cassius. 'A cautious approach would seem wise.'

Dropping to the ground, he left the horse where it was and gazed at the settlement, now no more than a mile away. Cassius recognised the telltale signs of a spring: the high date palms and clumps of grass surrounding a wide depression in the sand. Though it was high summer and the palms bore more brown fronds than green, the trees somehow clung to life, sustained by the deep subterranean waters that also fed Alauran's well.

Beyond the spring, where the depression ended, was one side of the fort. Constructed of the ever-present cream-coloured brick, the wall was well over a hundred feet long, perhaps ten high. A tall timber structure dominated the south-east corner of the compound. Cassius thought it might be the granary, housing the precious supply of food.

'No smoke, sir,' said Simo thoughtfully.

'And a flagpole with no flag on it,' Cassius added.

Leading the horses by the reins, they walked steadily towards the fort. Cassius stared fixedly at the wall, hoping rather than expecting to see the reassuring sight of a standard or a raised spear.

By the time they neared the closest of the palms, this preoccupation had distracted him from what Simo had already noticed. The Gaul tapped him on the shoulder and pointed towards the tree.

A large, black-feathered buzzard had just hopped out of the palm's shadow. Claws scraping the sand, it shook its head at the strangers. Clasped in its crooked beak was something red with flies buzzing around it. With a single flick of its neck, the bird swallowed the morsel and hopped back towards the palm. Still looking on, Cassius belatedly realised what Simo had been pointing at all along.

Wrapped in faded shrouds, and arranged in an untidy line under the tree, were six bodies.

IV

Covering their noses with cloth unwrapped from their headgear, Cassius and Simo stared down at the corpses. One was no more than a pile of bleached bones, wrapped in a thin sheet that looked like it might blow away at any moment. The shrouds covering the middle four forms were a little newer. A section of cloth covering the face of one had come loose, revealing a portion of sunken, lined skin. This figure was notably smaller than the others.

'A child perhaps,' said Simo quietly. Unwilling to open his mouth, Cassius nodded and turned his attention to the last body. It could not have been there more than a week. Apart from the sweet odour of rot, the skin, visible where the buzzard had pecked a wide hole, had hardly decayed at all. Flies had gathered on the wound.

Cassius felt a wave of nausea, reminding him of the seasickness he had endured during the three-week crossing from Ravenna to Seleucia Pieria, the port that served Antioch. He had eventually resorted to offering daily prayers to Neptune, with no obvious effect.

He clapped his hands, driving the bird away. It hopped towards three more of its brethren, gathered together under another palm.

'Well somebody put them here,' he said.

'Victims of disease perhaps?' replied Simo, following Cassius back towards the horses. Neither of them chose to mention the obvious suspicion. Outbreaks of plague had afflicted the area for years; the disease could arrive at a settlement borne by a single individual and spread to the entire population in weeks. Cassius was fully aware of the risk; his uncle had died during one such outbreak while stationed in Cyprus.

Taking his mount by the reins, he started towards the south-eastern corner of the wall, examining the structure as he walked, knowing he might soon have to depend on it. The clay brick looked solid enough, the edges of each block visible under a thin layer of white paint. The foundations also seemed secure, with little evidence of slippage or subsidence. The top of the wall, however, was rather unconventional: there were no guard towers or battlements.

In the time it took them to traverse the southern side of Alauran, not a single sound was heard from within. It was almost midday; Cassius could not conceive how a garrisoned settlement, even one so remote and undermanned, could remain so deathly quiet.

They reached the corner. Cassius stopped and handed his reins to Simo.

'Your knife is at hand, I see.'

'It is, sir.'

Cassius retrieved his helmet from one of the saddlebags. If there were any troops left, first impressions would count. Having secured the strap under his chin, he took a final drink of water.

'Eyes and ears open then.'

Simo took charge of both horses, looping the reins together as he followed Cassius round the corner.

In the middle of the eastern wall was a small but sturdy-looking gatehouse. The two towers bore the familiar hallmarks of a traditional fortress, though on a far smaller scale. Each was square, perhaps ten feet wide, extending two yards above the wall, with several arrow slits close to the roof.

The gate itself hardly deserved the name: two thick wooden doors mounted on a frame set into the wall. One door was slightly ajar.

Simo's horse snorted. Cassius placed his hand on his sword, concerned that the noise would alert any potential enemy inside. Noting some vulgar graffiti at the bottom of the door, he leaned round it and peered inside.

Directly ahead was a street of sorts, separating two rows of ramshackle housing and leading through to a paved square. Beyond that were a well and a small temple.

Checking that Simo was right behind him, Cassius gripped the edge of the door and pushed it inward. The hinges squeaked, protesting noisily until there was enough space for the horses to pass. He took four steps forward and stopped. Though no people were in view, there were a few signs of life: a line of washing hanging from a roof, a discarded sandal, a large pail in the middle of a doorway.

Fairly sure he could hear voices coming from somewhere, Cassius swept his eyes across the compound. To the left was some kind of encampment where awnings had been strung from the houses to the southern wall. Under the awnings were assorted barrels, amphoras, blankets and several piles of clothes. There was also a well-maintained fireplace, complete with a spit and a stack of cooking pans.

To the right was a U-shaped marketplace with stalls on three sides. Many of the stalls had been cannibalised for wood. Woven baskets of various sizes and shapes littered the ground. They were all empty.

'Keep your eyes on those houses,' Cassius told Simo, turning to look at the inside of the eastern wall. The towers were accessed through a low doorway on each side of the gatehouse. Along the remainder of the wall a number of wooden planks had been affixed five feet from the ground to form a series of rudimentary firing platforms.

Cassius steadied himself, reminded himself of his rank and his orders and set off at a brisk pace towards the square.

'Follow me, Simo.'

Resisting the temptation to examine every potentially treacherous window, he instead pressed on until he could see the rest of the fort. The square was about sixty feet in diameter and paved by alternating grey and white tiles, many of which needed replacing.

The building behind the well was indeed a temple, its narrow doorway framed by two spiral columns. In a larger settlement they would have been marble but these were of some lesser stone. Faded outlines and blotches of orange and red on one side suggested an abandoned attempt at decoration.

Occupying most of the space to the left of the square was the large wooden building they had seen from outside. Its sloped roof was thatched with dried palm fronds, the supporting beams visible underneath. The manner in which the entire structure had been mounted on a series of short thick timbers confirmed it was the granary: by keeping a flow of air through the building, its contents could be better preserved and protected from vermin. At the eastern end was a wide double door. At the other end, separated from the granary by a narrow alley, was a smaller building with three half-doors: undoubtedly the stables.

Equally recognisable was the barracks, situated to the right of the square. Like every other building except the granary, it bore the pale tones of clay brick. There were two doorways at the near end, a number of wide, low windows and a long water trough outside. It looked about the right size to house a century. A few tunics and sheets had been draped over the windows to dry, yet, once again, there was a bemusing lack of activity. At the far end of the barracks were the officers' quarters: a small block fitted with a wooden door and a large, shuttered window. Some throwing javelins had been propped up against the shutters.

Cassius was ready to investigate further when Simo touched his shoulder.

'Sir.'

Coaxing the horses round with him as he turned, the Gaul nodded back towards the gate. Only when Cassius had skirted around the flank of his mount did he see what Simo was so concerned about.

At the opposite end of the street, about a hundred feet away, was a man. He stood absolutely still and wore a long, black, sleeved tunic. Even at that distance they could see a dark complexion and wreaths of hair that hung far below his shoulders.

Cassius was unsure what to do. He was, however, throughly sick of the weighty helmet and thought it best to suggest peaceful intent, not that there was any realistic alternative. Slowly lifting it from his head, he cradled the helmet under his right arm and wiped his brow.

'Might I suggest we retire to one of these dwellings, sir,' Simo said shakily.

As he spoke, the black-clad figure raised an arm.

Cassius squinted into the sunlight, trying to see what the man was doing. He realised after a moment that the stranger's arm was moving in a circle. The arm suddenly accelerated into a blur of motion. Cassius glimpsed something glinting under the sun then heard a loud crack.

'What—'

For a moment, he thought he'd been hit; that he was about to sense an injury somewhere on his body. Then he noticed a small object lying in the sand. It was a leaden ball the width of a thumbnail. Turning the helmet over, he saw a neat hole in the iron close to the crest.

'Slinger,' he said, gulping as he showed the helmet to Simo.

The stranger was now motionless again, arm back by his side.

'If we can get behind the horses,' Cassius said quietly, 'we might have a chance at the closest doorway. Are you ready to move?'

'Yes, sir.'

'On three then.' Cassius could hear what he thought was Simo's breath coming in sharp, shallow gasps. Then he realised it was his own.

'One, two—'

Cassius spied movement to his right. He could not think why Simo would be moving forward but then saw that the figure walking past was certainly not the Gaul.

'I really must apologise, sir, but you know how these locals can be. Back in a moment.'

The interloper must have been sixty-five if he was a day. Despite the inelegant gait produced by his bandy legs, he moved with impressive speed. His hair was snowy white, thinning on top but tied in a long tail. He wore a tatty pair of sandals and a dirty, ragged tunic. He didn't seem to be carrying any weapons. Continuing down the street, the old man held up a hand of greeting to the black-clad warrior.

Cassius exchanged confused glances with Simo, then recalled Cotta's last words.

'Thank you! Barates – is it?'

The veteran stopped, turned and bowed before striding away again.

Simo let out a long breath and patted the nose of his horse.

'Well,' said Cassius. 'Quite a shot. It must be, what—'

'Thirty yards or so I should say, sir.'

'At least.'

Cassius picked up the leaden ball and held it against the hole in his helmet. He knew the iron was vulnerable to arrows but had no idea a slingshot might penetrate at such range.

Barates was now speaking to the mysterious warrior.

Circling back round the horses, Cassius saw that the square was still empty.

'Looks like he has things in hand. Let's see if we can rouse anyone else.'

At the eastern end of the barracks, two stretchers had been left against the wall. Knowing that small aid posts were usually constructed for minor forts such as Alauran, Cassius aimed for the closest doorway, hoping to find a surgeon or attendant inside. He belatedly realised that two men were lying under the stretchers. One was snoring loudly, the other drooling. There were several abandoned wine jugs next to them. Both their mouths were stained red.

'Gods, it's hard to tell if they're even soldiers,' said Cassius. One of the drunkards was wearing a tunic and one sandal. The other was naked except for a sheet he had donned in the style of a toga.

Behind the aid post was a flimsy wooden structure, complete with a poorly thatched roof and a few rough-hewn tables and stools. On the other side of a short bar were several shelves lined with empty wine bottles. It was, in short, an inn.

Shaking his head, Cassius put his hands on his belt and wondered what to do next. He had half a mind to pour water over the two men but there was no telling how they might react, even if they were part of the garrison. He walked past the aid post, then the barracks, glancing inside each gloomy window as he passed. There was little to be seen except the edge of a few bunks and the odd arm or leg sticking out, and there was little to be heard but snoring.

'At least there's a few of them here,' Cassius said quietly to Simo.

Hearing a noisy slurp, he turned to see the horses dipping their noses into the water trough. With more of an angle on the street, he could now see Barates deep in conversation with the warrior. The veteran seemed to be emphasising every other word with some wild gesticulation.

Cassius reflected on what he'd discovered. It now seemed unlikely that any officer remained and that discipline amongst whatever legionaries were left had completely broken down. It was therefore essential to find out as much as he could from Barates about the men and their state of mind.

Deciding it was still quiet enough to take a quick look at the temple, he left Simo with the horses and hurried across the corner of the square. He passed the well, with its four-foot clay surround, and bracket and winch for raising and lowering pails, then ducked under the low doorway of the temple. There was just enough light to see a simple stone altar opposite the door. Two figures had been crudely engraved on its surface. The legend underneath read: TO MARS AND HERCULES. FROM THE MEN OF THE THIRD LEGION. Beneath the altar was an ancient-looking spear, a dagger with an embossed handle and a helmet that had almost rusted away. A pair of candles, standing sentry-like in front of the altar, appeared not to have been lit in a long time. Cassius also noticed that his were the only footprints in the sand that had blown in off the square.

It seemed that the legionaries of the Alauran garrison had forsaken religion along with military discipline.

Exiting the temple, he was surprised to see the horses trudging slowly away from the barracks, their reins trailing in the dust. Behind them, Simo seemed to be drinking from the water trough below one of the windows. Cassius then realised that he was in fact being held down.

As Simo tried to free himself, Cassius sprinted over to him. The owner of the large hands gripping Simo's neck leaned further out of the window. He was a man of about thirty, with curly hair, a blunt nose and a demeanour that suggested he had just woken up.

'Use our trough for your beasts, would you?' he shouted at the back of Simo's head. 'Let's see how you like sharing with 'em.'

'Let go at once!' Cassius ordered.

The man looked up, blinking.

'And what concern is it of yours, boy?' he snarled.

'It is my concern because unless you are some wandering peasant, I will assume from your location that you are a legionary of Rome. With that in mind, I will give you a moment to wipe the sleep from your eyes and a chance to look at me again. Perhaps you might notice the helmet in my hand or the stripe on my tunic?'

Cassius had heard such speeches hundreds of times during training. The words came easily enough but he was less confident of predicting their effect.

After a moment's pause, the legionary released Simo and placed his hands on the window. Grunting, he disappeared into the shadows. Simo, coughing and spitting out water, took a couple of steps backward.

'Sorry, sir. He caught me unawares.'

'Don't worry. Just fetch the horses, would you.'

'Yes, sir.'

As Simo moved away, Cassius waved at Barates and gestured towards the officers' quarters. Barates waved back.

Turning on his heels, Cassius immediately found himself faced by the curly-haired legionary and two of his fellows, all armed with wooden staves. They had clambered out of the low window next to the officers' quarters and now barred his way.

For once Cassius knew exactly what to do. He could not be seen to wait for Barates or show indecision. He strode along the side of the barracks, aiming for a gap between two of the legionaries.

'Good morning,' he said, smiling.

The soldiers frowned as he passed them, struck dumb by the cordial greeting.

Half expecting to feel a stave thump down on his head, Cassius only breathed out when he reached the door of the officers' quarters. It was unlocked. Glancing to his right, he saw that the legionaries had been joined by two more men. All five stood in a row, silently studying him.

He opened the door and stepped inside.

V

Azaf lay flat on the ground, enjoying the momentary shade provided by some rarefied cloud. He closed his eyes and sunk his fingers into the warm sand. The only sound was the distant chatter of his men, gathered together under some hastily arranged awnings. Beyond them lay a wide dusty trail and the outskirts of Seriane.

He couldn't remember the last time he'd enjoyed a moment to himself. The Palmyrans had ridden all night to make the rendezvous and the previous weeks and months had been occupied with cleaning up the remaining pockets of Roman resistance in eastern Syria. So far, it had been ridiculously easy.

The last significant battle had been with three cohorts of the Fourth Legion and the Romans apparently had little else to offer. It was now a matter of rooting them out town by town: usually nothing more than a short one-sided battle; the execution of the uncooperative, the wounded and the weak; and the dispatch of prisoners back to Palmyra. Azaf and his men were bored by their work and he was surprised that the order for the next big advance still hadn't arrived.

It seemed like a long time since he had left the city: Tadmur in his own language, named by the Romans after the palm trees that surrounded it. Azaf was of nomadic stock and he had only visited Palmyra twice. The first time had been as a small boy, travelling with his father to receive payment from a sheikh who recruited local tribesmen to escort his caravans. He had seen his first paved street and stood open-mouthed in front of the city's vast stone columns and arches. Whilst waiting in the courtyard of the sheik's palace, he came across an intricate, multicoloured mosaic that took up one entire wall: a dramatic depiction of a hunting party. He had never seen such craftsmanship and splendour.

On their way out of the city, they encountered a sight that was to make an even deeper impression on the young boy. Not far from the outskirts, amidst dust and eerie quiet, was a collection of narrow, windowless buildings, some standing together, others in isolation. These, his father told him, were the tomb towers. During his fighting years, a soldier of Palmyra would put aside enough money to pay for himself to be interred alongside his brothers-in-arms. The better the record and reputation of the soldier, the higher he would be placed, with the upper levels reserved only for the greatest leaders and bravest warriors. To Azaf, it was a far nobler fate than being buried or burned to ash. He could imagine no greater end.

Years later he had returned to the capital as a man, a soldier and a leader. Along with almost half the entire Palmyran Army, he had lined up on the great colonnaded avenue to hear the Queen speak. Like thousands of his counterparts, he had longed to see her in the flesh since his boyhood years. He had heard some men say that her looks were overstated, others that they couldn't be captured in words. That day in the square, however, he had swiftly formed his own opinion.

Zenobia had inspected every row of soldiers, her aged eunuch attendants struggling to keep up with her. She was tall, statuesque and without doubt the most exquisite woman Azaf had ever seen. She wore an ornate golden diadem that framed a face of almost supernatural beauty. Her eyes seemed huge – brown and deep – and she wore a silver silk tunic that cut a diagonal line across her chest, exposing a single perfect breast.

Azaf was a member of the Komara tribe, raised in a village on the banks of the Euphrates. Barely a month after his father had passed his sword to his thirteen-year-old son, he had been bested by the boy. Azaf's quicksilver hands seemed to defy the limits of physiology, and he was apparently able to see his opponent's next move before they had even decided upon on it.

War was now his vocation. He had been recruited to the army's ranks at fifteen and had killed his first man battling the Persians. Aware of his ability, the more experienced swordsmen had tried to keep him away from the front line, anxious to impart their knowledge and harness this raw, god-given talent.

But Azaf would not be denied. He confounded his fellow warriors, showing that he had been listening and learning: calmly scouring the skirmish line like a veteran, picking on isolated individuals and pairs, dispatching them with clinical ease. He revelled in the first moments of combat, weighing his alternatives in the blink of an eye: the build of the man, the signs of injury and fatigue, the weapon in his hand. Yet he could never recall making any calculation: just acting, generally with lethal results.

He had risen swiftly through the ranks and now commanded a hundred swordsmen, mostly Komara men. He had proven himself to be an adequate tactician but both he and his superior, General Zabbai, knew that his real value lay in the example he gave his men. Azaf's warriors, whether fighting Persians, Egyptians or Romans, had always excelled themselves, each man dedicated to emulating their leader.

Some, he knew, fought for the glory of victory, and the booty and pillage that came with it. Some fought to honour their god Malakbel, and the other deities of the Palmyran pantheon. All would be happy to see the end of Roman rule.

He never spoke of his own motivations. Though he enjoyed command and could not wait to lead his men into battle again, as time passed he became more preoccupied by thoughts of that day in the capital. He could not remember much of what the Queen had said, but he could not forget her. Occasionally Zabbai would let slip some comment and, though he would rather die than betray his true thoughts, Azaf would listen, rapt, eager for any revelatory word.

He had little interest in the vagaries of politics or trade and little understanding of the long, complex relationship between Palmyra and Rome. He knew only that her enemies were his.

Occasionally, though he cursed himself for such idle fantasy, he would imagine himself inside the palace, standing against the Roman onslaught that must eventually come: the last man alive, protecting his queen.

Sometimes, after hours of riding or sleep, he would see her. She never spoke. But she smiled. A smile that told him he was hers and that she loved him for it.

He fought for her. He fought for Zenobia.

'Sir.'

Azaf opened his eyes and rolled over. One of his men was standing over him.

'He's here.'

General Zabbai looked down at the prisoners and scratched his chin. He wore a bright white tunic over a matching pair of trousers embroidered with gold. The brooch that held his light brown cloak together was topped by a spectacular emerald: plunder from a recent victory. Zabbai's broad-featured face was surprisingly youthful considering he was approaching his fiftieth year. His expression remained impassive, despite the scene in front of him.

The Romans had been stripped of their clothes and weapons. They lay naked in the sand, bloodied and battered, ugly welts on their legs and arms. It hadn't taken long for the violence to escalate; eventually spears had been pushed into their stomachs and groins. Both had lost a lot of blood. One man was unconscious. The other stared up at the Palmyrans, left hand covering his groin, right hand over his cheek, where broken bone pushed at the skin.

'How long have you had them?' Zabbai asked.

Azaf emerged from a group behind the general. His skin was much darker than Zabbai's and, uniquely amongst the gathered soldiers, he wore no tunic, only a thin purple cloak with his black, shapeless trousers.

His entire body was knotted with muscle, and his skin seemed to have been stretched tight over his jutting ribs and shoulder blades. He moved with a solid, predatory grace. His jet-black hair reached almost to his waist and, like most of the Palmyrans, he had a heavy beard.

'We picked them up last night, sir.'

'Where?'

'A mile or two east of here. Deserters most likely. They gave us word of the fort at Alauran.'

'And?'

'It's as we thought. The well has been spoiled, the provisions taken. There's little of use there.'

Zabbai smiled.

'They were most cooperative,' Azaf continued. 'Eventually.'

Zabbai's grin disappeared as quickly as it had arrived.

'Their words were false. I've had word that a small garrison still occupies the fort. The granary is half full. And the well runs still, with the clearest water for miles.'

Azaf stood up and drew his sword. He no longer carried his father's blade, though it went everywhere with him, wrapped carefully in oiled cloth.

He had found his current weapon in the hands of a dead Roman. Unusually long and narrow, the sword had viciously sharp edging and a light but solid wooden hilt. He'd been told the design was Mesopotamian but Azaf was not concerned with its origins, he was simply grateful to have acquired a weapon perfectly suited to fast, slashing attacks rather than what he considered to be the clumsy thrusts of a heavier, shorter sword. Such swords were often used with a shield; a piece of equipment he found to be more trouble than it was worth. The only drawback with such a light blade was the risk of losing grip when striking a bulkier weapon. He had solved this by attaching a leather wrist strap to the base of the hilt. Even if the handle was knocked from his grasp, he would not lose the sword. He wiped a speck of dirt from the flat of the blade.

'Azaf,' said Zabbai gruffly, waiting until his commander had turned to face him. 'We need that well. You know how hot it's been this year – the reservoirs and cisterns are running low. And we'll be sending thousands of men and horses through this area.

I'll give you some archers and cavalry. A spy of mine will make himself known to you at Anasartha. He has a man inside the fort. Slay all you find there and secure the well and provisions. I shall return to consult with the Queen. She wants us to strike west, link up with General Zabdas' forces and make for Antioch in overwhelming numbers.'

Azaf nodded. He kicked the conscious prisoner on to his back, then knelt down beside him.

'Do you hear your breaths, Roman? They are your last. You must forget this world. You belong in another now.'

Azaf stood again and lowered the blade into the Roman's mouth, resting the gleaming tip on his tongue. As the young man's eyes widened, the Palmyran gripped the sword handle lightly with his left hand, just enough to hold it in place.

He formed a fist with his right palm, raised it high above the handle, then hammered it down.

VI

Cassius stared out at the square. The men were gathered in small groups, deep in discussion. Some wore their military belt, a few were armed, but most resembled commoners, and not particularly impressive ones at that. Every now and then, someone would point at the officers' quarters. Cassius did a quick headcount.

'Thirty-one. Is that all of them?' he asked, turning away from the window.

Barates had planted himself on a low bench. Despite his wizened limbs and crooked back, the veteran seemed sharp and keen to help, his bright green eyes shining out from his leathery face.

'A few may still be sleeping. Centurion, can I ask exactly why you're here?'

If there had been little reason to correct the assumption of his rank before, Cassius knew it would be insane to do so now.

'We'll get to that,' he said, moving towards a large wooden desk opposite the bench. 'Where is your commanding officer?'

'You approached from the west?'

'Yes.'

'And passed the palms?'

'Ah.' Cassius leaned back against the desk, nodding as he recalled the scene by the spring. 'Who was he?'

'Centurion Petronius. A veteran of the Persian campaigns. Our cohort – the Third – was divided up and sent to man these outpost forts and towns. Our century was assigned to Alauran, though we could barely muster fifty men. Our second in command, Optio Felix, had been given his own century just before we left, so Petronius was our only senior officer. He'd been struggling with an infected wound even before we arrived.

53

He did his best to keep up his duties but eventually slipped into a fevered sleep and never awoke. That was about two months ago. Over time we lost a couple more to disease, along with a local stable lad. And Actius a week ago. Fever again. We'd intended to return the bodies to the capital when the opportunity arose but . . .'

Barates stared forlornly at the floor.

'I take it then that discipline has rather broken down?'

'Some wanted to desert when Petronius died. All I've been able to do is keep them here. Will you take command now, sir?'

Cassius took his time to reply; when he did so he almost whispered it.

'I suppose I shall have to.'

Barates gave a slight smile.

'And what about the locals?' Cassius asked. 'That slinger—'

'He's part of Kabir's group. They are about thirty strong; auxiliaries originally attached to the Second Cohort. Some, as you have seen, are a little hot-headed. I believe Kabir took the rest of them out on a march this morning – he likes to keep them busy. They've made their own encampment in the south-east corner. Probably be back before sundown.'

'They don't use the dwellings?'

Barates shook his head.

'Those haven't been occupied in months. Most of the locals were sent away soon after we arrived. Petronius told them we would leave with the provisions and poison the well – a ruse to deter attack. So far it seems to have worked.'

'And what contact has there been with command?'

'None. We heard some news from a scout but that was—'

'Yes, I know, weeks ago. Cotta. It was he that gave me your name. You have no idea of the wider progress of the war then?'

Barates shook his head.

'In days past we might have picked up word from tradesmen and travellers, but since the spring we've seen little of either. The odd caravan on the horizon. Nothing more.'

Barates clasped his fingers together.

'What is the situation, sir?'

Cassius knew no one within the fort would believe the war was going well, but a full and frank explanation of their circumstances might easily lead to desertion or mutiny. It was unlikely he would survive the latter.

'Reinforcements are on their way. Lead elements of General Valens' cavalry should be here within a few days. I have been ordered to organise the garrison and secure the fort against possible attack. The well and the granary represent a significant prize for our enemies.'

'Indeed,' said Barates, leaning back against the wall, tapping his thumbs together, 'but that has been the case for many months. The last we heard, the Palmyrans had struck south towards Egypt. Are we under immediate threat?'

'I don't profess to know the precise details of the Palmyran itinerary, but if a general gives me instructions, that is evidence enough of their importance for me.'

'And for me, sir,' answered the veteran with a cordial half-smile, 'but it is those outside you will depend on.'

Cassius looked out of the window again and saw that the smaller groups were gravitating towards a larger one. The curly-haired man seemed to be doing a lot of talking.

'Will they follow orders, Barates? Will they follow me?'

'I honestly don't know. A word of advice though: when you address them, speak mainly of the cavalry and relief and the arrival of pay. I must ask, sir – do you have any money? They, we, have received nothing for more than a year.'

'A little. Not enough.'

Ten of the men were now walking towards the officers' quarters. Cassius was not surprised to see who led them. Barates had risen and now stood next to him.

'Who is that fellow? I have already had the displeasure of meeting him.'

'Yes, I saw. That's Flavian. Big drinker and a nasty temper when riled.'

With the others spread out behind him, Flavian stalked towards the door, stave in hand.

Cassius retreated as the men came to a halt outside. They spoke in hushed tones, then there was loud crack on the door. Trying to maintain a semblance of calm, Cassius leaned close to Barates.

'This Flavian. Is he popular?'

'Not particularly. Actually, I should have said – he and three others are not from the Third Legion. They were originally with the Fourth but got separated from their column during a sand-storm. They arrived a month or so after us. Flavian's an idiot but the others want answers too and they'll be happy to let him lead the way.'

There was another crack on the door.

'If he could be persuaded to cooperate, would the others fall into line?'

'Possibly. But if that is to be your tactic, then there is another, a man more suited to the role.'

'Go on.'

Before the veteran could answer there was a third crack on the door, followed by a voice Cassius instantly recognised.

'We want to speak to you, centurion.' The last word was laced with sneering disdain.

'Quickly man,' Cassius whispered.

'His name is Strabo. Something of a rogue but well liked and respected by all. Well, most. He's the guard officer.'

'That makes him next in command now you've no centurion or optio. Why didn't you mention him before?'

Barates grimaced.

'Since Petronius' death he hasn't taken his position very seriously. He's a capable soldier, though, and a man open to persuasion.' Barates got to his feet. 'I didn't see him outside but he likes to gamble most of the day. Usually behind the temple – where it's cool.'

'Fetch him at once.'

The door ring rattled.

'And what should I tell *them*?'

'Tell them I will speak to them in the square within the hour. Nothing more. Just get this Strabo over here.'

'Very well.'

Cassius pointed Simo towards the door. Taking care to remain out of sight, he watched as the Gaul took a firm hold of the metal ring and raised the latch.

'Well? What's going on?' snarled Flavian. 'Does he have any money?'

Cassius could see a portion of his ruddy face between the door hinges.

'Allow me to pass and I might tell you,' said Barates impatiently. Before Flavian could reply, some of the less aggressive soldiers parted to allow the veteran through. Barates spoke as he walked, luring most of the men from the door. Flavian tried to barge his way inside but Simo quickly shut the door in his face.

'I will allow the centurion to explain,' the veteran continued, 'but there is some good news . . .'

Knowing that Flavian would try to look through the window, Cassius slid behind the door. The legionary and several of his acolytes shuffled over to the window and for a moment Cassius feared they might try to climb inside. Then came a bitter curse and the sound of a stave being flung to the ground.

'Come on,' spat Flavian. The men moved away towards the barracks.

Cassius slumped back against the door. Sweat trickled from his armpits.

'Under attack twice already and we haven't even encountered the enemy yet.'

'We may have weathered the early storm, sir,' said Simo. 'Barates seems to be an ally of some worth.'

'Let's hope this Strabo is equally useful. Where's the money?'

'Hidden with your belongings, sir. Shall I bring it all?'

'No. Two hundred denarii should be enough. The rest you can put in there.'

Cassius pointed to the bedroom that took up the back half of

57

the officers' quarters. It was furnished with two beds and a small chest. Though gloomy and poorly ventilated by a single high window, it had one other notable advantage – a thick wooden door equipped with a lock. Simo had already found keys for the door and chest inside the desk. Despite thick layers of rust, both still worked.

The Gaul hurried over to where he had stacked their saddle-bags and gear. Idly looking at the desk, Cassius noticed a pile of papers buried under some dirty wooden plates. Pushing the plates away, he found a collection of faded papyrus sheets, bound together along one side. The pages appeared to be in no particular order. Most of the untidy writing referred to supplies.

Simo handed over a small leather satchel.

'Two hundred as you said, sir.'

Cassius' helmet was still lying on the desk, complete with hole and projectile. He lifted it up and hid the money inside.

'Simo, listen. You do appreciate that we must continue to make no mention at all of my true status? These men must believe me to be a centurion, not just an officer. Common soldiers generally have an extremely low opinion of the Service. Understood?'

'Of course, sir.'

Cassius wandered over to the window. Emerging from the crowd alongside Barates was a character who seemed perfectly to fulfil the veteran's brief description.

The legionary looked about forty. He was tall, a little overweight and unusually broad-shouldered. His hair was thick, black and unfashionably long. As he neared the officers' quarters, Cassius could also make out a large, beak-like nose that had been broken more than once. His beard, however, was well trimmed, as was the current trend, though most of the legionaries at Alauran seemed not to know it. (Cassius was waiting for the wispy hair on his own chin to develop, but progress was frustratingly slow.) Strabo was attired correctly, wearing tunic, belt and dagger, though his sword was missing.

Barates entered first, then held the door open for Strabo. Cassius returned a courteous nod and was struck by the darkness of his eyes; they seemed almost black. Strabo looked him over and Cassius registered a flicker of amused contempt that soon became a thin smile.

'Centurion.'

'Strabo, isn't it?'

The guard officer took a couple of steps inside, then looked down at the saddlebags.

'Barates,' said Cassius, 'might I ask you to check if there are any more men still asleep. I want them all up.'

'I'll do my best,' Barates replied, sighing as he shut the door.

Strabo looked through the bedroom doorway at Simo. Realising he was just a servant, he seemed to relax. He sat down on the bench and casually stretched out his legs.

Cassius leaned against the desk again.

'Forgive my curiosity,' said Strabo, cocking his head to one side. 'but you do not appear to have lived twenty years of life, let alone twenty of service. How is it that one so young carries the stripe?'

Cassius did his best to look annoyed but answered calmly.

'It's common practice to recruit younger officers now. To replace those lost in the East and elsewhere.'

'Really? I see you have an attendant with you. And I hear from your voice that you do not hail from the lower classes. Perhaps that too was a factor in your swift promotion.'

'Perhaps,' said Cassius with a wry smile, determined not to take the bait, 'but my personal circumstances are not important.'

Strabo frowned theatrically.

'Aren't they? Hardly palace duty is it?' he said, waving a hand towards the square.

Cassius couldn't find an answer to that, and he was beginning to doubt this man would help him.

Strabo continued: 'Though I suppose I should admire your loyalty to the cause of Rome in coming here. There are many in these parts who have long since abandoned such commitment.'

'Yourself included?'

Strabo shrugged and folded his arms across his chest. 'A

59

soldier's enthusiasm for war fades when he sees his fellows lost and his purse empty. We are not all Italian nobility out here.'

Cassius noticed the legionary examining his tunic. Though now worn and dirty, it was still identifiable as finest linen, one of three given to Cassius by his mother.

'There are Galicians, Cilicians, Thracians. I myself am from Sicily. Most of us here took an oath to Odenathus of Palmyra, you know, just three years past. Rome may not have called him emperor but it was he that kept the Persians at bay.'

'And yet the garrison remains,' Cassius countered.

'It does while the men await more than a year's worth of back pay. Even the funeral fund is still with the cohort clerk in Antioch.'

Strabo stood up and walked past Cassius towards the window. Catching sight of the hole in the top of the helmet, he chuckled heartily.

'And equally impatient for their money are our local friends. As you may have already noticed.'

Cassius wasn't sure if the Sicilian had seen the satchel but it reminded him of his strategy. He pushed himself off the desk.

'I'm sure Barates told you I have a little money. More importantly, when the reinforcements arrive, you men will receive full recompense. I have an assurance from General Navio.'

Cassius felt far less guilty misleading Strabo than Barates. It was a matter of necessity: with no other officers present, the cooperation of the century's third in command was nothing less than essential.

Strabo stood silhouetted against the bright window, his features almost invisible.

'To be honest,' Cassius continued, 'I don't believe these men will follow me if I act alone. But with your support they might. Barates tells me you're the best soldier here, the closest—'

Strabo chuckled again.

'Barates is an old fool. I know a little of soldiering, yes. But why do you think a man of my age didn't make it past guard officer? I have been in the army for more than half my life and I know one thing above all others. I have no desire to lead.'

'I am not asking you to lead. I'm asking you to help *me* lead.'

Cassius removed the satchel of money from under the helmet and threw it to Strabo.

He caught it one-handed.

'Here. An incentive. Consider it payment in advance.'

The Sicilian investigated the contents.

'A substantial sum.'

'Indeed.'

'You must be desperate.'

'Unusual circumstances call for unusual measures.'

'Of course. But we've heard nothing for months and then you suddenly show up. I'd wager the Palmyrans are heading in our direction. Perhaps they've learned that the food and water remains. No army can fight without that.'

'As I said to Barates, it is possible. Yes.'

Strabo moved closer to Cassius. The glare from the window still shrouded his features and Cassius narrowed his eyes, trying to read the Sicilian's expression as he spoke.

'You do realise that I could run you and your fat friend through right now, take all your money and one of those fine horses you rode in on and disappear. Just like that.' Strabo snapped his fingers.

Cassius was surprised by his words but sensed that they were meant as a test, not a genuine threat.

Simo came in from the bedroom. Strabo ignored him.

'I do,' said Cassius, trying not to swallow nervously, 'but I don't believe you will.'

Strabo moved forward again, his frame blocking out the light.

Cassius met his stare as it slowly softened into a playful grin.

'You're not as young in the head as you are in the face, centurion. I'll give you that.'

Strabo headed for the door, then stopped mid-stride.

'On second thoughts, it might be better if this stays with you and our arrangement remains . . . confidential.'

The bag of coins landed on the desk with a solid thud. Strabo pointed at Cassius.

'I have your word I'll receive it when the garrison is relieved? In addition to my pay?'

'You have my word.' Cassius nodded towards the square. 'As long as you stand by me out there.'

'I'll do as you've asked. For now.'

'Thank you.'

'Thank you,' replied Strabo, grinning as he reached for the door, 'sir.'

VII

The heat in the square was almost unbearable. As he came to a halt beneath the flagpole, Cassius tugged irritably at the straps of his helmet, then wiped his clammy hands against his tunic.

After the meeting with Strabo, Simo had tidied up the officers' quarters and made some useful discoveries: a bronze tuba for sounding orders, a log book and the century roll. Cassius had been through every page of the roll: it listed names, wage levels and dates and places of birth. Petronius had been a conscientious officer; almost up to his death he had made notes in the log about supplies and work details. There was no mention of disciplinary infractions or punishments.

'What do you think, sir? I thought it would be good for the lads to see this again.'

Barates arrived holding a tattered legion flag.

'Excellent idea.'

The veteran, now wearing his belt and sword, unfurled the flag and knelt down in front of the pole.

Squinting through the glare and the sweat running down into his eyes, Cassius turned to face the assembled troops. Most had made some kind of effort and all now wore tunics, belts and swords. A few even sported metal insignia: decorations for honourable action. One group was making a show of ignoring Cassius completely. They included Flavian: the stocky legionary was still wielding his stave and looked rather unsteady on his feet.

Cassius was curious about what Strabo had said to them. The guard officer stood to his right, looking bored, apparently disinterested in taking the lead. Wondering if it was another one of his tests, Cassius decided to get things moving.

'Guard officer.'

'Sir?'

'Get the men into close formation. Three lines.'

Strabo repeated the command, then yawned. The men organised themselves with surprising efficiency. Only Flavian and his cronies dragged their heels, successfully making a mess of the third line.

Cassius felt a tap on his shoulder. Barates pointed up at the flag, now hanging listlessly in the enervating heat. As with all legions raised by Caesar, the symbol of the Third Legion was a bull, in this case rendered in golden thread. Though the red of the standard had faded to a thin pink, the bull itself shone reassuringly bright.

'Well done.'

Barates moved away but Cassius held up a hand. 'Stay here would you, I may need your help.'

'Of course.'

Barates put his hands behind his back and surveyed the men. Strabo was doing nothing to quieten the shuffling feet and whispered comments. Before beginning, Cassius reminded himself to consider his audience and simplify his language. As he had discovered during training, the military was not the place for the embroidered vernacular of the orator.

'I am Centurion Cassius Quintius Corbulo and I am here on the direct orders of General Marcus Galenus Navio. I have been instructed to take charge of Alauran.'

Though the men were listening, Cassius sensed this was due more to curiosity than respect. There were more than a few quizzical looks at the unusually young officer before them.

Flavian was swaying and muttering to himself.

Cassius continued: 'Now, I appreciate the difficulties you have faced over the last few months, but—'

Flavian stumbled forward into the second line. Some of the other legionaries cursed at him.

Cassius turned to Strabo.

'Guard officer,' he said matter-of-factly. 'Deal with that man. He's drunk.'

Flavian pushed his way through the first line.

'Guard officer,' Cassius repeated.

'Sir?' said Strabo flatly.

Flavian stomped forward, bloodshot eyes locked on Cassius. He smacked the stave noisily against his other hand.

'Deal with him!' Cassius shouted, resisting the temptation to turn and run. Flavian was no more than twenty feet away.

'What exactly should I do, sir?' asked Strabo, drawing laughs from some of the men.

'What about your duty!' snapped Barates.

Flavian charged on, a bestial grimace on his face.

'Deal with him now!' Cassius yelled. If it hadn't been for the flash of movement to his right, he would have made his escape.

Strabo covered the distance with surprising speed and his well-timed trip caught Flavian perfectly. The legionary fell forward head first, cracking two tiles with his skull. The stave flew out of his hand and clattered to the ground at Cassius' feet.

Barates squatted down and examined the legionary's head. He was unconscious but still breathing.

'There'll be quite a lump, but he'll be all right.'

'What should we do with him?' asked Strabo.

'Put him in his bed,' Cassius answered, loudly enough for the men to hear. 'I've no use for a drunk.'

Strabo turned Flavian over and waved a couple of men forward to help him. One of Flavian's cronies broke ranks, rounding the first and second lines.

'Hands off, Strabo! We look after our own here.'

'Get back in line, Avso,' said Strabo, dropping Flavian's prone form roughly to the ground. 'This is none of your concern.'

'And since when has taking charge been yours?' countered the legionary angrily.

Avso was not a big man, but he looked wiry and tough. He was probably no more than thirty, but had a gaunt, almost cadaverous face and a head of lank, greasy hair. Cassius also noted his well-maintained weaponry and a livid pink scar that ran diagonally across his right shin.

Two of Avso's supporters stepped up behind him while some of those in the first line exchanged glances with Strabo. There seemed to be a distinct possibility that Cassius' first address was about to deteriorate into a brawl.

However, the guard officer took a breath. He glanced first at Cassius, then back at his would-be adversary.

'Avso, I know you're Thracian but try to keep up. We have a new centurion here and he'd like to finish his speech.' Strabo nodded down at Flavian. 'Take your friend, clean him up and get back here on the double.'

Avso hesitated for a moment, then beckoned the others forward. It took all three of them to carry Flavian off the square and into the barracks.

Cassius let the men settle down, composed himself, then continued.

'As I was saying, I know you've had a difficult time out here – not knowing what's going on beyond these walls and manning such a remote post without pay – and I'm not going to pretend that all is well with the war. The Palmyrans could strike here and we must be ready.'

Reading the apprehension in the eyes of those he addressed, Cassius moved on quickly.

'But there is good news. A cavalry column is on its way: General Valens' men. They should be here in four or five days. When they arrive you will receive all wages due. That's straight from General Navio.' As before, Cassius felt the lie was a risk worth taking. He had to do something to get the men on side and could always plead innocence or ignorance at a later time. 'I have been sent here to ensure that the relieving forces find a well-organised, well-defended fort.'

A man in the second line raised his hand.

'Yes, legionary.'

'What will happen then, sir? Some of us have been out here almost two years. If we could at least get back to Antioch—'

'Yes, of course. I must be honest on that point. I do not know how you will be re-deployed.'

'If I may, sir,' Strabo piped up. 'Seems to me that if there are fresh centuries coming to reinforce the area, they won't want a unit that can barely muster fifty. It might be that we're back in the city before long.'

'And how many times have we heard that before!' came a loud retort. The man was standing in the second line and Cassius took a step left to get a better view. The legionary was of a good age, over forty certainly, with a thinning thatch of spiky grey hair and the battered face of a seasoned campaigner.

'Serenus,' whispered Barates. 'Highly decorated but afflicted by illness for a year or more.'

'Legionary,' said Cassius, 'you and every other man in this square are members of this garrison. Now I am too. We are not brigands or mercenaries or auxiliaries. We are professionals and we will do a professional job.'

For the first time, there was silence.

'Now, once you have been dismissed, I will be deciding on a precise plan of action. Until then, I want each of you to return to your quarters and ensure that your personal kit is up to scratch. If it stinks, wash it. If it's dirty, make it shine. If it's blunt, make it sharp enough to cut the balls off an elephant. Muster parade will be held just before sundown. The roll will be called.'

Strabo dismissed the men line by line. As they broke up, Cassius observed a number of differing reactions. Some of the men trudged off with blank expressions, others walked briskly away, apparently glad to have something to do. A few remained on the square, exchanging comments with their compatriots, weighing up the new officer still standing stiffly below the legion flag.

Though he knew there was precious little of substance to be happy about, Cassius was relieved. Most of the legionaries had at least shown a willingness to follow orders.

He had made a start.

Not long afterwards, the new commander of the Alauran garrison sat at the table inside the officers' quarters. Occupying chairs to his left and right were Strabo and Barates. Simo sat on the low bench opposite him. The Gaul had managed to find some spare papyrus sheets and an old reed pen. Having just made up some ink from a lump of gum and some water, he was now ready to make notes as requested.

Strabo belched loudly.

'Do you happen to know the date?' asked Barates suddenly. 'I have been trying to keep track, but—'

'Late August,' answered Cassius. 'The twenty-fifth, -sixth, perhaps. Simo?'

'Somewhere around there, sir. I could work it out if you like.'

'No matter. Doesn't seem to mean much in these parts in any case.'

Cassius had been bemused to learn that many of the Syrian cities still maintained their own calendars, stubbornly refusing to adopt the Roman system. An officer in Antioch had regaled him with several related tales, the last of which involved leaving one city in March, only to arrive at another in February.

'Well, gentlemen,' he said, keen to get started, 'my mother always says: "If in doubt, make a list." And so we shall.'

Ignoring both sets of raised eyebrows, Cassius continued.

'Our aims are simple and twofold. Firstly, to consolidate the defences of the fort and secondly to turn that rabble next door into something approaching a fighting unit. We need to establish the most urgent tasks and set about them immediately. Barates, you seem to know the place as well as anyone, any thoughts?'

'Several. Number one – the wall.'

'Clay brick, yes?'

'Unfortunately. There are no quarries near here, only clay pits. I believe it's about twenty years old. Originally there was just a village around the spring and at some point the army decided to enclose it.'

'But it's at least in reasonable shape.'

'For the most part yes, apart from the breach.'

Cassius' frown deepened as Barates continued.

'It's behind the barracks. A few months ago a pair of pack horses were startled by something and bolted. They hauled a cart half the length of the fort and it overturned as they rounded a corner. It made quite a hole and over time the area above has collapsed. Perhaps if I show you?'

'Later. How big is this breach?'

'Eight feet across, about the same in height.'

'Why wasn't it dealt with?'

'It happened after all the locals had left. The clay they use here is unusual and, well, I suppose we just never got round to it.'

'You mean to tell me there's no one here who can repair a wall?'

'No one volunteered their help. Needless to say I've had other things to attend to.'

'There'll be someone,' interjected Strabo. 'I'll ask around.'

'Do so. Right then, the walls.'

At a nod from Cassius, Simo made his first note.

'Two – water and food,' continued Barates. 'Although this lot have done their best to get through the contents of the granary, I should say at least three-quarters remains. There's grain, pork, fish, plenty to see us through. Water too – the spring under here must be huge. Even in this season, the well still gives us all we want and what comes up is remarkably pure in taste and colour.'

'Enough for drinking,' said Cassius. 'But we'll need a good deal more if attacked.'

He had received basic instruction on the art of the siege and knew it was likely the Palmyrans would try to fire the buildings before mounting an assault.

'There'll be enough,' answered Barates. 'We have barrels sitting empty in the granary. I'll have a detail fill as many as they can.'

'Right,' said Cassius as Simo made another note. 'What's next?'

'Three – weapons and equipment,' said Barates.

'We'll have a good idea about that after muster, won't we?' Cassius said.

'True, as far as personal arms go. There are also perhaps fifty or sixty of the light javelins. They might prove useful.'

'Perhaps if we had five or six hundred,' replied Strabo. 'I could

69

chuck fifty myself in the time it takes you to cross the square. Anyway, a lot of good they'll do us against oven men.'

'Oven men?' Cassius asked.

'Palmyran cavalry,' said Strabo, leaning forward and thumping his elbows theatrically down on the table.

'They cover themselves and their mounts in a coat of iron. Workmanship you wouldn't believe: joints that move with their limbs, metal hardy enough to deflect any sword, their only vulnerable point a tiny opening for each eye. I spoke with a man who saw them hit the Persian flank at Callinicum. He watched one of their lances go clean through a horse – in one side and out the other.'

Strabo illustrated the blow with a jab of his finger and leaned back, still holding Cassius' gaze.

'Wonderful horsemen. Worth twenty infantry each at least. The only time they lose is when they faint from the heat.'

'But surely cavalry are ill-suited to a siege,' said Cassius optimistically.

'Has happened. To punch a hole at a weak point. And you've seen our gate.'

'Which should be our next area of attention,' said Barates. 'It needs reinforcing.'

'And the gatehouse?' queried Cassius.

'If the enemy bring artillery they'll knock it down in half an hour,' said Strabo.

'Siege warfare is not their speciality as well you know,' replied Barates. 'They prefer to move quickly and there's little suitable material for artillery in these parts. More likely they'll attack in numbers, try to fire the buildings, use ladders for the walls.'

Cassius checked that Simo was keeping up. The ink was a tad watery but the Gaul had written concise notes in a large, clear hand.

'Didn't *we* have some artillery around somewhere?' asked the Sicilian, drawing a look of dismay from Barates.

'As well informed as ever, Strabo,' he answered, taking his own turn at sarcasm. 'There was a light onager and a pair of scorpions but they went east with the legion. Not that we have a trained crew anyway.'

'Do you have any horses?' said Cassius.

Barates shook his head.

'The pair that bolted were our last. Both had broken legs and had to be killed.'

'There are *no* other horses here?' asked Cassius, incredulous.

'No. We have three camels though,' said Barates. 'Difficult beasts, but we have a boy here who takes care of them.'

Strabo laughed. Barates continued.

'With his help I've been able to mount the odd patrol. Evil creatures to be sure and an uncomfortable ride, but they can get us out to the crest and back in a couple of hours.'

Barates answered Cassius' next question before he could ask it.

'A small rise a couple of miles east. It gives a commanding view of the area and several hours warning of any approach.'

'Excellent,' said Cassius, relieved to hear a piece of good news. 'We shall post a permanent guard there. You can show me it after muster.'

'I shall tell Julius to ready the animals.'

'That boy is a cretin,' said Strabo irritably. 'We should have sent him away with the rest of the locals.'

'He has some trouble with his words, I grant you,' answered Barates, 'but there's nothing wrong with his brain. He's been a good deal more use to me than anyone else in recent months.'

'The only reason he is able to deal with the camels is because he has the same level of wit.'

'Strabo, that boy is worth—'

'Gentlemen, please.' Cassius held up his hands between the two of them; it seemed this was a long-running argument. 'We don't have time for this.'

'Sorry, sir,' said Barates, 'but I'm still waiting for our esteemed guard officer to offer a worthwhile point to this discussion.'

'Here's one for you,' said Strabo. 'Probably the most important point of all – the attitude of the men.'

'And whose responsibility is that?' asked Barates.

Strabo held up his hands.

'Fair enough. But remember I never asked Petronius for the job. And the pay is scarcely more—'

'This is not the time for recriminations,' Cassius said. 'Obviously the situation is far from ideal, but if we can't get the men working and fighting together then everything else is for naught. Let's start by grouping them into sections. At least then we know what we have to work with. Simo – the century roll. And the pen to mark it with.'

'What about the Syrians?' said Barates, making way as Simo fetched the papyrus sheets and placed them in the middle of the table. 'They could be a great help to us.'

'You really think they'll stand by us?' said Strabo. 'More likely Kabir will switch sides if he thinks there's gain in it.'

'You seem to get along with the locals,' Cassius told Barates. 'When we're done here, tell this Kabir I will visit him first thing in the morning. There's not time tonight and I think a clear head might be preferable for such a task.'

'That's probably wise,' replied the veteran. 'There are certain niceties to be observed when dealing with them. And as Strabo said, Kabir's no fool. His patience has been sorely tested; they've been awaiting pay even longer than us. If he thinks he's being lied to, there's no telling what he'll do. To be honest, if things turned nasty, I wouldn't fancy our chances.'

Cassius noted Strabo's cynical frown but the Sicilian said nothing, choosing instead to lean forward and examine the roll. Wiping sweat from his top lip, Cassius asked Simo to fetch them some water.

Strabo got to the third page and handed it over to Barates.

'Well it's a little out of date, but everyone seems to be there. Including us three, forty five men in total.'

'Five groups of nine perhaps,' suggested Barates. 'For work parties now, sections if we have to fight.'

'So who is to lead these sections?' asked Strabo tiredly.

'I'll take one,' said Cassius. 'Strabo, you take another, Barates you too.'

'Sir, if I were ten years younger I would gladly—'

'I'm not asking you to carry barrels or wield a sword, merely to organise your section.'

'Don't give us the old man routine, Barates,' said Strabo, 'we know you'd like nothing more.'

The veteran allowed himself a grin.

'You said that Serenus is a good soldier,' Cassius continued. 'And he's obviously not afraid to speak up for himself. What do you think?'

'Could do worse,' said Strabo. 'But we'll need a reserve in mind if he's not up to it.'

'A good choice,' said Barates, marking the names with the pen as Simo poured more water from a pail into three mugs.

'Flavian and Avso's lot for the last section?' suggested Cassius.

'You want to put them together?' asked the Sicilian.

'I believe we should leave fellow with fellow. Men they'll fight with and fight for. Avso for section leader?'

'I don't like the man, never have,' said Barates. 'But he's damned useful in a fight.'

Strabo gave a reluctant nod.

Cassius drank half his water and stood up, adjusting his belt and sliding his sword back over his hip.

'If there's nothing else, gentlemen, please finish up with the roll. Then perhaps you can go and visit this Kabir fellow, Barates. Strabo, you can see how the men are getting on. We shall reconvene in the square.'

VIII

The sun was already sinking below the western wall as the men filed out of the barracks. Standing beneath the flag once more, Cassius was relieved to find the temperature had dropped significantly. Hands tucked into his belt, he watched Strabo and Barates direct each man towards a section. Avso and Serenus were also taking charge, checking weapons and equipment before the formal inspection. Their sections were close together and the men were beginning to intermingle. Cassius walked over and gestured for them to separate. Though the legionaries obeyed, Avso smirked and mouthed something to Serenus.

For the thousandth time in recent months, Cassius forced himself out of his natural passivity and walked over to them.

'Problem?'

'Sorry, sir?' said Avso, eyes narrowing with mock confusion.

'I asked if there was a problem? You seemed to find my actions entertaining.'

'Not at all, sir. I always welcome the assistance of a senior officer.'

This drew a few grunts of amusement from the surrounding legionaries. Cassius felt his new-found confidence ebbing away.

'Then presumably you are familiar with the concept of insubordination. And the punishment that might follow.'

'Oh yes, sir. Very familiar.' Avso ran a finger and thumb down his narrow chin.

'If I were you, legionary, I'd take a little more care with my manner.'

'I'll try to remember that, sir. But I am just a Thracian peasant, not a fine Roman gentleman.'

Some of the men laughed. Cassius stared defiantly back at Avso's sunken eyes for a moment.

'Evidently.'

He turned to Serenus.

'Do you have something to say to me?'

'No, sir.'

Serenus would have once been a striking man but illness had yellowed his skin and clouded his eyes. He had broad shoulders but his belt was pulled tight round a disconcertingly narrow waist. His limbs were lean and veiny; muscled but insubstantial.

He spoke quietly: 'I apologise if we seemed rude. But we know nothing about you. Perhaps if we knew something of your previous experience, we might feel a little more assured.'

Before Cassius could reply, Strabo appeared, barging his way through the crowd. He glanced speculatively at Avso.

'Causing trouble again?'

'Look who it is, lads – the mighty Strabo, our inspirational guard officer!'

Ignoring the ironic cheers and whoops from Avso's cronies, Strabo reached for his dagger.

'That's enough!' Cassius yelled.

Seeing that the Thracian was about to let loose another remark, he pointed towards the temple.

'Avso and Serenus with me. Strabo – get the men lined up in their sections.'

Strabo didn't move; he was too busy eyeballing Avso.

Cassius stepped carefully between them and waited patiently until the guard officer looked at him.

'Now.'

Barates had arrived too. He took hold of Strabo's arm and coaxed him away. The Sicilian shook him off but was soon re-directing his ire towards the legionaries.

'Follow me,' Cassius said, wondering if there would be time to complete the inspection and get out to the crest and back before sundown. When they reached the temple he gestured to a fragile-looking bench.

'Please.'

Avso shook his head. Serenus however seemed keen to rest. After several rasping coughs he sat down.

'So,' said Cassius, 'you wish to know of my background. I have been in the army less than a year. My original assignment was to round up injured in this area and lead them back to Antioch. Yesterday I received orders to take over the garrison. I have never fought in a battle before and this is my first real command. Now you know.'

'Well I have to admire your honesty,' said Serenus with a thin smile.

Predictably, Avso was less generous.

'Whoever decided that first-year recruits can match a man with twenty years under his belt is an idiot.'

Cassius shrugged.

'Possibly. I am not responsible for military policy. But I am responsible for this garrison and I am your centurion.'

Cassius noted that the lie was becoming easier. It had been an exhausting day, not over yet by a long way, and he was in no mood for diplomacy.

'So, unless you plan to walk out of that gate right now, you need to accept that I am in command. You don't have to like it, you don't have to like me, but that's the way it is. Whatever happens, you won't have to put up with me much longer than a week.'

'Assuming we make it that far,' observed Serenus wearily.

Avso said nothing, which to Cassius seemed like progress.

'Strabo and Barates assure me you'll both do a good job with your sections. Serenus, can you manage?'

'I'll do my best. But I should tell you, this is one of my better days.'

Cassius turned to Avso.

'We both know that in another time and place you and your friend Flavian would be up on charges by now. But we're stuck with this time and place and I need every sword hand I can get. You have men to lead and I expect you to lead them well.'

'Is that all? Sir.'

Cassius decided he would have to settle for begrudging cooperation.

'It is. Return to your section. And from now on, address me correctly and show me the respect I deserve in front of the men.'

Avso headed back across the square.

'Not a pleasant man,' said Serenus when he was out of earshot. 'But he's as tough as they come.'

The veteran got slowly to his feet and the two of them started back, watching as Strabo formed up his section.

'Again, apologies for any offence caused.'

Cassius held up an appeasing hand.

Serenus continued: 'You must forgive my wavering temperament. I used to be counted as the most solid man in my century but this affliction leaves one bitter and melancholic. And days such as this, when I can talk and walk and eat – they come with decreasing regularity.'

'What is this ailment?'

'Some imbalance in my airs. That's what a surgeon told me.'

'And nothing eases it?' said Cassius as they stopped next to the flagpole.

'Nothing. I imagine I'll be lucky to see out the year.'

As if to demonstrate the point, Serenus was struck by another coughing fit. He pulled a cloth from his belt and held it to his mouth. Cassius saw several spots of blood as he took it away. Most of the cloth was covered in older stains, faded to brown.

'Perhaps you should retire to the barracks for the moment?'

'No, no. Let's have a look at this rabble first.'

Serenus moved away, straightening as he neared the men and already pointing at a legionary with his sword unsheathed.

Strabo and Barates joined Cassius as Simo brought out the century roll. Avso and Serenus were quick to their work and soon a double line of men traversed the width of the square. Cassius began reading and the legionaries answered their names. There was well-observed silence, even though he had to hesitate now and again while searching for the next name or struggling to read Petronius' writing.

He was about halfway through when his peripheral vision picked up some turning heads. Looking up, he saw that most of the men were staring over at the barracks. Cassius turned too, and found himself gazing at an extraordinary figure.

Walking barefoot with a slow, ambling gait was an individual of such unusual size that he seemed to occupy the space of two normal men. Though he was tall, it was the horizontal dimensions of his body that were unlike any Cassius had ever seen. The huge head was hairless apart from an untidy greying band between the ears and sat atop a neck of equally unnatural breadth. Below, an enormous pair of shoulders and arms stretched the material of a light blue tunic Cassius could comfortably have used as a bed sheet. Patches of thick dark hair covered the upper arms and shoulders. A leather belt was pulled tight at the waist, showing little fat round the man's middle. Beneath the tunic were a bulging pair of legs that somehow matched the vastness of the rest of him.

Without a single glance at the assembled legionaries to his right, the giant rounded the corner of the barracks and disappeared towards the inn.

Barates leaned towards Cassius.

'The Praetorian.'

'A late time to rise, even for him,' said Strabo.

Cassius had been so busy that he had given no thought to the man Cotta had spoken of.

'What does he do here? Will he join us?'

'Probably not,' said Barates.

'Definitely not,' added Strabo.

'If he's in the army, then he must fight.'

'Perhaps you would like to go and tell him that, centurion,' said Strabo. 'Or you could stay here – and ensure that your head remains attached to your neck.'

'I should explain,' said Barates.

'Quickly then.' Cassius held up a hand to the legionaries. 'One moment, men.'

'He was exiled from Rome, serving with the Fourth, but was struck down with some disease of the gut. I've never seen a man in such agony. The pain causes him to cry out; his face contorts as if he's possessed by some evil spirit. All that will ease it is wine. Lots of it. He'll rise in the afternoon, walk the few yards to the inn, down as many jugs as he can, then retire when he's done, ready for the next day.'

'Why was he exiled?'

'The last man who asked that has only just recovered.'

'Broke his arm,' said Strabo. 'Praetorian didn't even get out of his seat.'

Cassius saw that the men were drifting off into conversation.

'Tell me the rest later. Let's get this roll finished.'

They did so quickly. The only absentee was Flavian, now bandaged up and asleep in the barracks. Cassius was happy to leave that particular problem until the morning. With the square now shrouded in the half-light of dusk he, Strabo and Barates began the inspection.

It was reassuring to see that none of the men had allowed their personal arms to fall into serious disrepair. This was, Cassius now understood, one of the advantages of making each man purchase his own.

The legionaries wore a variation of the plain linen tunic worn by soldiers across the Empire. All reached down below the knee, none any further than the calves. About half of the men had cut the sleeves off at the shoulder. Some were decorated with dark lozenges or squares. No one was without his military belt.

Earlier in the day, Cassius had seen legionaries walking around barefoot but all had now managed to locate their boots. Tied together with leather straps, some had uppers, others were open under the laces. Cassius heard Strabo picking on certain individuals whose footwear needed attention. It seemed the guard officer was finally beginning to live up to his title.

Stopping between the second and third sections, Cassius waited for the others to catch up.

'Armour's not so good,' he said as the Sicilian drew near.

There were only a few men with mail shirts. Most were well maintained but none matched the quality of Cassius' own.

'Some of them sold them,' said Strabo.

'What? To whom?'

'Whoever. Fetches quite a price. Even out here.'

Given the wage situation, Cassius decided not to make an issue of it. The trio continued on, passing a couple of legionaries equipped with archaic cuirasses composed of large iron plates held together by leather straps. They afforded good protection to the shoulders and chest but were extremely uncomfortable and difficult to maintain.

'Well at least they all have helmets.'

'They do now,' said Strabo. 'I found a box full of spares in the barracks.'

The helmets looked almost new. They were of an older design than Cassius', one he knew was regarded as superior, and were of bronze construction, topped by a strengthening crosspiece.

Continuing past Strabo's section, he turned his attention to the shields. Other than the personalised designs and graffiti, they were similar to his own: an oval, made of wooden planking reinforced with iron bars and covered with leather.

The next man Cassius passed was young, not much more than twenty. He stood arrow straight, hands clasped together behind him.

'Show me your sword, legionary.'

'Sir.'

The soldier unsheathed his blade and held it up. Every surface was flawless and Cassius could smell the oil he had used to attain such a fine sheen. The wooden handle was engraved with swirling patterns and embossed with some glittering stone.

During a rare spare hour during training, Cassius and some of his fellow officer candidates had visited a smithy where swords were constructed. They had watched, fascinated, as an amalgam of narrow iron bars was twisted into a screw, then hammered and folded repeatedly. This formed the core of the blade, to which the two cutting edges were then welded.

Cassius gave the legionary a nod of approval and moved on to the second line: the fourth and fifth sections. Here, a couple of the older hands were also armed with pila. Based on a wooden or iron shaft up to seven feet long, these heavy javelins varied in design but all were topped by a barbed metal point. Used most effectively at short range, they could wound enemies or puncture shields, weighing them down and rendering them useless. In close-quarter melees, with ranks of men virtually on top of each other, they were ideal for penetrating shield walls or out-reaching shorter weapons.

Given the poor state of some of the soldiers he had encountered in previous weeks, Cassius was relieved to find that every member of the garrison was fairly well armed and equipped. There were a hundred little things he could have pulled individuals up on – a patch of rust here, a loose strap there – but he had at least the makings of a fighting force. Some specialist archers would have been useful, but if the Syrians could be persuaded to fight too, they might form an effective auxiliary missile unit.

He came to a stop at the end of the second line.

'Well?' he said.

'They'll do,' answered Strabo.

'My thoughts entirely.'

Cassius caught Barates' eye.

'You'd best go and ready the camels. And ask Simo to saddle my horse.'

The veteran grimaced.

'I'm afraid camels and horses do not always mix, sir. That's why we're keeping them at opposite ends of the stables. And the three beasts are more biddable when they are kept together. I'd be happy to escort you out there and complete the first sentry shift myself. Julius can bring you back at your leisure.'

'Very well,' answered Cassius. It seemed that the remainder of his first day at Alauran would offer up yet another novel experience.

He and Strabo returned to the flagpole. Turning to face the legionaries, he saw immediately that their goodwill was fading as fast as the light. There were bored, tired expressions all round;

it seemed that the modest exertions of the evening were weighing heavily on those recently unaccustomed to soldiering.

'Well, men, a reasonable showing!' he announced. 'I suggest you all get a good night's sleep because I expect every one of you back here at sunrise. Tardiness will not be tolerated and you should be prepared for a long day's work.'

Strabo coughed loudly.

'Food and drink,' he whispered.

'Ah. Yes.'

This was another point they had discussed before the muster parade. Cassius was not slow to recognise it as a potential point of contention. Having listened to the advice of his deputies, he'd decided to ease the garrison back into a more formal system.

'I intend to reintroduce set meal times from tomorrow. Food will be rationed.'

There was predictable tutting and head-shaking but Cassius sensed a certain half-heartedness. It confirmed his suspicion that many of the men would be glad to get back to normal military routine.

'Report to the granary after you've rid yourself of your gear and the guard officer will ensure that you get your share. I've also asked him to monitor the consumption of wine.'

'And who will monitor his consumption?' asked Serenus good-naturedly.

Cassius just about held back a grin as the men broke into smiles and laughter. Strabo scowled.

'See you at sunrise. Dismissed!'

IX

A hillock of sand fifty feet high, 'the crest' did indeed provide an excellent view of the area surrounding Alauran, particularly the desert to the east. Scattered across its slopes were patches of thorn bush, drained of colour by the summer sun. Aside from a few grasshoppers and sandflies there was no other sign of life. An indistinct track ran west back to the fort and east as far as Anasartha, the closest settlement of any size.

Cassius and Barates were at the top, gazing out across the plain.

'No,' Cassius said, 'I can't see it.'

Barates had assured him that the buildings of Anasartha, less than twenty miles away, would be visible from the crest. The old man sat on his haunches close by, noisily chewing his way through a handful of raisins.

'The sun is low. Perhaps in the morning.'

'At least we'll able to see the Palmyrans coming. One of the few advantages of a desert location, I suppose.'

'One of the few.'

'You're sure Julius is able to find his way back in the dark?'

'Easily. He and I have done this trip a hundred times. The camels could probably do it on their own.'

Cassius glanced down towards the bottom of the crest. He could just about make out the youth and the three camels sitting in a triangle around him. Close by was a ramshackle shelter housing a water barrel and a stash of timber.

Barates had been correct about the boy's ability to control the beasts. There had been a few problems mounting, but once clear of the gates the camels had settled into a purposeful stride, though

83

Cassius had yet to adjust to their lolloping gait. He wasn't particularly looking forward to the return journey. In fact, he was rather enjoying the tranquillity of the crest.

'Then if you'll oblige me, I shall keep you company a few moments more. You were telling me about the big man.'

Barates had embarked upon an intriguing tale. The Praetorian had been attached to a cohort of the Fourth Legion as an adviser, part of a hastily organised counter-attack that had ended in disaster. He had managed to get away and had pitched up at Alauran just after Barates and the rest of the century.

'When he first arrived you could talk to him. He would say nothing about himself, but we would discuss politics, army life and so on.'

'And now?'

Barates expelled a long breath as he eased himself up off his haunches.

'It's been a downward spiral. His rotten gut and drink-addled head have left him in a permanent stupor. On the few occasions he's not drunk, he's in a rage. I don't remember the last time he had a civil word for anyone, even me. He has a room to himself at the end of the barracks and the others just stay out of his way. They'll curse him behind his back – for his snoring, or for emptying every barrel in the inn – but they know better than to say anything to his face.'

Cassius watched the last segment of the sun drop below the horizon, dragging the remaining swathes of orange and red with it.

'Cotta suggested that you valued him as a member of the garrison. Someone who might lead the way.'

'I believe I did say as much to the man, though it's hard to believe now. Back then he would occasionally accompany Petronius and me on patrol or offer a word of advice. His knowledge of tactics and battle is second to none. He knows how to fight these Easterners too. It was his performance fighting the Persians that got him promoted to the Guard.'

'At Edessa?'

Cassius looked out at the desert. The city lay a hundred miles to the north-east and its very name was enough to evoke memories of a momentous Roman defeat. Ten years earlier, before Odenathus and his Palmyran armies had finally driven the Persians back, the Emperor Valerian had met them in battle at Edessa only to be beaten and captured by their leader, Shapur. It was rumoured that Valerian had been flayed alive and his skin displayed on the walls of a temple. Cassius recalled one of his older cousins relating that particular detail with some relish, after his father had announced news of the defeat to the household.

'Yes. He was one of the few to escape alive. He served Valerian's son too, and it was while working for Gallienus that he was exiled from Rome.'

'You don't know the details?'

'A disgrace of some kind,' said Barates disapprovingly. Cassius suspected the veteran had a somewhat parochial view of Roman politics.

'Barates, it's often unwise to assume that those accused and sentenced in the capital are guilty of any real crime, particularly those unlucky enough to serve an emperor. The Guard have suffered as a result of our rulers' intrigues as often as they have benefited. It may be that his unit simply fell out of favour with the wrong prefect or senator.'

'Well, I must admit I would like to think he was innocent. The man was awarded three rampart crowns and they are seldom given to those lacking integrity.'

'Indeed not.'

The crown was given to men who led successful charges against enemy defensive positions, usually city walls. They were not easy to come by. To win three was almost unheard of.

'Well, I suppose I'd better be going. You sure you don't mind being left alone out here?'

'Won't be the first time,' said Barates, putting a hand on Cassius' shoulder. 'And us old ones need less sleep than you youngsters.'

'Very well then. And thank you for all your help today.'

Cassius would have liked to say more than that. He would have liked to express his relief at finding such a willing collaborator in the honest, committed veteran. But these were the sentiments of an anxious youth, not an officer of the Roman Army.

'I will send your relief at first light. Goodnight.'

'Goodnight, sir.'

With that, Cassius trudged down the slope, slowing as he approached the camels so as not to alarm them. Julius walked towards him. Cassius reckoned him to be thirteen or fourteen. He was a skinny specimen, clad in a tatty green tunic, with the dark skin of a local and a mop of unruly black hair.

'Back to Alauran.'

Julius answered with a barely comprehensible 'Yes, sir.' He then got Barates' camel on its feet and led it over to the shelter.

Since meeting Julius at the stables, Cassius had been amazed at how well Barates understood the mixture of noises and garbled words that came out of the boy's mouth. Cassius had met such people before but he soon saw that Julius was not doubly cursed with idiocy as Strabo suggested. He was very skilled in dealing with the animals, and responded quickly and efficiently to instructions. Cassius' mother had always told him to keep an open mind about such people; after all, the first Emperor Claudius had been afflicted with many physical impediments, yet history had cast him as an effective, dynamic leader.

Waiting for Julius to return, Cassius recalled what Barates had earlier told him of the boy's background. He had lived at the fort for as long as he could remember. His mother had died in childbirth and his father had held him responsible, shunning his son and leaving him in the care of his brother, an unmarried metalworker. This man had been pressed into service as an auxiliary with the Third Legion and had left Alauran the year before. Nothing had been heard of him since and Barates had told the boy to assume his uncle was dead. With nowhere else to go, he had stayed on to tend to the camels, even when the last of the Syrian civilians had been ordered to leave by Centurion Petronius.

Julius was not his real name. It had been given to him by the soldiers. If he was to have a Roman name, they said, he may as well have the greatest name of all.

The young man reappeared out of the gloom, then took the reins of Cassius' camel, the largest of the three. He waved Cassius forward to mount. Apparently this camel was the mother of the other two – both males, not yet fully grown. Cassius clambered up on to the saddle. Lurching forward as the camel hauled itself to his feet, he took firm hold of the reins.

The boy moved swiftly over to his own mount and sprang up into position with ease. As the camel rose, he shouted yet more indistinct commands and kicked the animal into action, heading back round the crest towards the track. Without any bidding from its rider, mother obediently followed son.

During the trip out, Cassius had felt on numerous occasions that he was about to be thrown, but had found that by gripping the front of the saddle with one hand and the reins with the other he was able to balance himself. The saddles themselves were of a design unfamiliar to him, with a wooden base that sat upon the hump, topped by a layer of padding and surprisingly fine scarlet cushions.

As the camels plodded on, Cassius felt he should try to talk to the boy, but he knew the task required more enthusiasm and patience than he currently possessed.

He looked about him. With no more light from the sun and the moon obscured by cloud, the plain was a dark, ominous sea. Cassius shuddered, imagining himself submerged within its depths. And as they left the crest behind, he thought of Barates, alone on an island in that sea, and did not envy him his night's work.

Approaching Alauran, they heard laughter and shouting, and despite the fact that Cassius had asked Strabo to man the gate-house for the night, he and Julius were able to dismount and lead the camels inside without a word – let alone a challenge – from the supposed sentry. Cassius thanked the boy for his help and sent him on his way.

Though he wanted nothing more than his bed, letting this pass would inevitably lead to further indiscipline. Gathering himself for another confrontation, he stepped inside the northern tower. There was enough light coming from above for him to negotiate the ladder. He emerged inside the tiny chamber to find Strabo and three others sitting on a thin rug, each in possession of a pile of stones and a small jug of wine, watching as one man prepared to throw a pair of dice. Between two of the legionaries was a clay lamp half full of oil, the floating wick producing more smoke than light.

'Greetings, centurion,' Strabo said cordially as the ivory cubes landed on a wooden board, showing a pair of fours.

'Told you it was my night,' the Sicilian said smugly, raising a toast to his compatriots as each handed over some of their stones.

'Might I have a word?' Cassius asked.

Showing no sign of annoyance, the Sicilian got to his feet.

'Twenty-seven,' he said, pointing at his pile of stones before following Cassius down the ladder and outside.

Reminding himself to be firm, Cassius was surprised to receive a sharp dig in the shoulder as he exited the gatehouse. He turned to find Strabo almost on top of him.

'What do you mean by disturbing my game?' the Sicilian hissed.

'What?'

'You heard me. I've done your bidding all day – kept my end of the bargain. You are trying my patience. I am not some pet of yours.'

Cassius could smell the wine on Strabo's breath. He took two steps backwards.

'Of course not. But you have a job to do. Tonight there's four of you not in the barracks, tomorrow it could be ten – before you know it—'

'Caesar's balls! I'm not that stupid. I spent a good hour making sure each section was in its den. As far as they're concerned, me and my men are on guard duty.'

'And are you? You didn't even ask for a watchword. *Is* there a watchword?'

Strabo shrugged.

'We knew it was you.'

Cassius was glad to see Strabo had calmed down, but he knew the next few days would be intolerable if he allowed the Sicilian to treat him with such disdain.

'Listen, I want you working with me, and that means doing what I ask.'

'And what if I don't?' asked Strabo, eyes wide. Cassius realised he had underestimated how drunk he was. 'What if I walk back in there and continue my game?'

'Guard officer, I will allow you to continue your game, but you must slow down with the wine, and you must keep someone on watch at all times.'

His tone of authority left the Sicilian with little room for manoeuvre.

'Makes no difference to me.'

'Good. I am going to retire. Raise me if you see anything.'

Cassius thought he heard a mumbled curse as Strabo returned to the tower but he paid no heed to it. He was so desperate to get back to the officers' quarters that he ran up the street and across the square.

X

Approaching the peak of a broad dune whipped steep by the desert wind, Azaf coaxed his horse into a turn and raised a hand. The Palmyrans had ridden through the night and he had promised rest when the day's destination was in sight. A tangle of bushes at the base of the dune would provide a little shelter from the early morning sun. Sipping water from a gourd, he watched the men dismount.

Leading the way was Bezda, an experienced cavalry commander, accompanied by twenty-four men. Neither the riders nor their horses were clad in armour; this came behind them in several large carts. Within moments, the cavalrymen were on the ground, tying their mounts together and leaving them in the care of the cart drivers. Other servants were sent ahead to arrange the temporary cover amongst the bushes.

Next to arrive were the horse archers, a hundred strong. No less valuable than the cavalry, these riders could control their mounts using only their legs and voices, leaving their hands free for their formidable bows.

At the rear were the infantry, all clad in maroon tunics. As speed was of the essence, Azaf had chosen only good riders and Zabbai had provided horses for all the infantry too. There were ninety-six of them: Azaf's swordsmen, many of whom had been with him since before his promotion to *strategos* – military commander. The Palmyran people were known for their vivid clothing and red had emerged as the preferred colour of Azaf's swordsmen, related yet subordinate to the rare splendour of his purple cloak. In these times of victory and conquest, such opulence symbolised Palmyran superiority.

To Azaf's bemusement, the benefits of their triumphs had not yet extended to a decent set of armour for every swordsman. He and a few others were well equipped, but despite repeated requests General Zabbai had not seen fit to provide what was needed. Azaf had let his feelings on the matter be known, but Zabbai had brushed off the complaint, blaming supply problems and mocking him for imagining that he might face determined resistance at Alauran.

One of the warriors, a youth named Teyya, broke away from the mass of men. He ran past the archers and the cavalry, sensibly keeping well clear of the horses. He hurried up the slope, then knelt down in front of his leader.

'What is it?' Azaf asked.

'If I may, *strategos*. Something that might interest you. A trick of the gods, a creature like none of us have ever seen.'

'What are you talking about?'

'It's best if I show you, sir. Will you come and see?'

Azaf was already tiring of the young man's exuberance but he couldn't deny he was intrigued.

'Very well.'

Teyya half ran, half leaped back down the slope. He dodged through the cavalrymen and accosted an archer who had just dismounted. After a discussion, the man reached into one of his saddlebags. Out came a small sack, which he held carefully in both hands while following Teyya back towards the dune. By the time they reached it, another ten men had joined them.

Azaf pressed his horse down the slope and met them at the bottom. The archer dropped to his knees and lowered the sack to the ground. The men gathered round.

'Wait,' said one. 'It might startle the horse.'

Teyya and the archer looked up at Azaf, then at each other.

'Here,' said the *strategos*, sliding off his saddle and handing his reins to the man who had spoken up. The warrior led the horse away.

'Hurry up then,' said Azaf, pushing his cloak back over his shoulder. 'I don't have all day.'

The archer delicately untied the twine around the mouth of the sack. A section of cotton bulged as the creature inside moved.

'Don't get too close.'

The crowd, which had now trebled in size, quietened down. The archer gripped the bottom of the sack and flipped it over. For a moment nothing appeared. Then a snake dropped on to the sand.

It was a young, yard-long viper banded by dark and pale brown. A common enough sight to all present, except that halfway along its length, the body divided in two.

Both parts ended in an identical broad head, topped by two black eyes. The tongue of one flicked back and forth, the other remained still. The necks were kept separate by a short stick tied just behind each head. A white dot had been painted on the neck of one, two dots on the other.

'An abomination,' said one man, eyes wide with disgust. 'The familiar of an evil spirit. It should be killed at once.'

He began to unsheathe his sword. Others held him back.

'Observe,' said the archer, relishing the attention. He took two more sticks from his belt. Each ended in a Y-shape. He handed one to Teyya.

'Have no fear,' he said to those facing the snake. 'They are not spitters.'

Simultaneously, he and Teyya clamped the heads down on to the ground. Then the archer removed the stick separating the heads. He put it to one side and took a small leather bag from his belt. Out came the body of a baby rat, which he dropped a couple of feet in front of the snake. The archer then took hold of both clamping sticks and looked round at the fascinated faces.

'Better keep clear for this bit,' he said, slyly whipping the sticks away before anyone could move.

Both heads launched themselves clumsily towards their prey. One sunk its fangs into the rat's body, dragging it away from the other. Recovering from a misplaced lunge, the second head was instantly snapping at the other's neck, causing it to drop the rat and turn on its competitor.

Before they could do any serious damage to each other, the archer trod on the tail and slid the sticks up each neck, bringing them swiftly back under control.

'What do we think of that then?' he said, grinning.

'They are brothers, yet they strike each other,' said Teyya.

'If one injures the other, both will die, yet still they fight,' said the archer.

'What do you think, sir?' asked Teyya.

Azaf looked down at the creature impassively.

'I think it is in the nature of all things to fight.'

He looked up and glanced round the assembled soldiers.

'And I trust each of you is as ready as they are.'

This brought shouts and cheers from the men. Though he was glad to hear it, Azaf was not usually one to engage in such banter.

Bezda had also been watching and now pushed his way to the front.

'It is in the nature of all except the Romans,' stated the cavalryman, 'who would rather build roads and make trade!'

This too brought a cheer and a good deal of laughter. As the noise died down, the archer held up his hands.

'I had been waiting for the right time to let these two at it but now seems as good as any. I'll need twenty coins if you want to see them fight again. The odds—'

As the crowd pressed closer and men suddenly produced handfuls of coins, Azaf drew his sword. The warriors retreated. Before the archer could react, the *strategos* swung his blade towards the ground. He grabbed a handful of the archer's tunic and wiped off the sword edge as the other Palmyrans gazed down at his handiwork. The two heads of the snake had been severed at precisely the same point, just below the neck. Even in death they remained identical.

'There'll be no gambling. Get yourselves and your horses watered and rested,' said Azaf quietly. 'We'll be on the move again soon.'

Anger shone in the archer's eyes but he regained control of himself quickly, lowering his gaze and bowing.

'At once, sir.'

Azaf turned away again and walked back towards the top of the dune, Bezda at his side.

There was no set formal hierarchy within the Palmyran forces. Both men held the rank of *strategos*, but Bezda recognised Azaf's seniority on this occasion because he was acting directly on the orders of General Zabbai. Bezda would retain tactical control of his cavalrymen, but the responsibility for overall planning lay with Azaf.

'There'll be time enough for fun and games when we've taken this fort, I suppose,' said Bezda, shaking sand from his thick, knotted beard. He was a large, bear-like man and rode a horse of commensurate proportions, liberated from a Roman cavalry officer.

'Perhaps. If we find the situation as favourable as the general suggests.'

'You doubt his word?'

Azaf aimed a narrow glare sideways as they neared the top of the dune. He hadn't fought with Bezda before but knew he was greatly respected for his strength and aggression, despite his advancing years. Azaf was glad to have the additional force but found Bezda, like most of the cavalrymen he'd encountered, rather arrogant.

'Hardly. But I prefer to see the situation for myself.'

'Well,' Bezda replied, as they came to a stop, 'that time approaches.'

Whilst travelling by road the column had passed several Roman milestones and they knew they were close. Some of the limestone slabs had been defaced by Palmyran soldiers, who had covered the names of emperors past with that of their queen. Leaving the road the previous evening, they had taken a more direct route across the dunes. It had been hard going, but they had saved several hours.

The two Palmyrans stared out across the plain. Pleasingly short of the horizon lay the angular outline of their last stop before Alauran: the city of Anasartha.

XI

'Ah, what I'd give for a proper bath – half an hour in a hot room then a cold plunge.'

Cassius passed the last of the sodden towels to Simo, who wrung it out above a large bowl.

'Not that I'm ungrateful, you understand. You have acquitted yourself most impressively, given the circumstances.'

'Perhaps when we're back in Antioch, sir.'

'Yes, quite. That's the spirit, Simo.'

They were standing in a corner of the bedroom, Cassius completely naked and glad to be at his cleanest since leaving Nessara.

'You know, it amazes me how you servants manage to awaken before dawn.'

'A lifetime of practice, sir. We are able to sense when it is time to rise.'

Cassius took a fresh towel from Simo and dried himself.

'You'd best attend to this water,' he said, stepping out of the ever-enlarging pool. Before he could start dressing, there was a rap on the half-open door.

'Anybody up?'

There was no mistaking the sarcastic tone.

'Good morning, guard officer,' said Cassius brightly, pulling his tunic on over his head. 'I didn't mark you down as an early riser.'

'Actually I haven't been to bed,' answered Strabo, stepping inside. 'I plan to get the men started and sleep when the heat comes. You'll find the will to work fades sometimes around midday.'

'Not this day, I'm afraid.'

'We'll see.'

Grabbing his belt and dagger, Cassius walked over the top of Simo's bed, leaving damp footprints across his blanket.

'Better than stepping through that water, eh?'

'I suppose so, sir,' replied Simo.

Sheathing the dagger and buckling his belt, Cassius walked out of the bedroom and over to the window. The dark was already receding. No one else seemed to be up.

'Nothing unusual during the night I trust?'

Strabo was perusing the page with Simo's notes from the meeting.

'Only my luck. The dice were kind. My pile of stones grew large.'

'Really? Saving up for a boulder?'

Expecting at least a grin, Cassius found himself subjected to the most withering of gazes. It seemed the Sicilian was not receptive to quips at his expense.

'Each stone represents a tenth,' Strabo explained grimly. 'We'll settle up when the money comes.'

'Ah. I see. About the wall – any progress?'

'I'm not sure we'll be able to put together the local mixture, but a man in my section has a suggestion: if we break the rubble down and mix it with water and camel dung, it should return to something like clay. Then we pack the hole and let it dry.'

'That sounds like a solution. It will show from the outside as a weak point, though.'

'We can find some paint to cover it. In any case, the whole wall is a weak point. If we're lucky they'll only have ladders. Battering rams or engines of any kind will do for us in moments. Flavian with his stave and in one of his rages wouldn't take much longer.'

Simo walked past them, laden with towels. Cassius approached the table and cast an eye across the sheet.

'What about the gate? That'll require some skill.'

'There are a couple of carpenters with Avso's lot. They manned the workshop for a while.'

'Fifth section can attend to the gate then. Third and fourth can take charge of the granary and the well. Remember – we need water in proofed barrels next to all the buildings in case of fire. Tell Serenus to organise the food so that we can get what we need easily. The morning meal will be taken just before midday. I'll set my men on tidying detail. What about the aid post?'

'Hardly deserves the name. A couple of beds, a few surgeon's tools and potions.'

Simo fetched Cassius' boots and placed them carefully on the floor, then pulled out a chair for him.

Strabo smirked.

'You still here?' said Cassius as he sat down. 'We can't do any of those jobs with the men still in bed.'

'At once, Your Highness.' Strabo bowed low and exited with a chuckle.

Flavian still stank of wine. He ran a hand through his curly hair and stared down at the floor. In theory his offence – attacking an officer – could be punished by the harshest sanctions. In normal circumstances he might be whipped, clubbed, even executed.

Behind him were Strabo, Barates and Avso. Behind them, busy soldiers passed the window at regular intervals.

Cassius shook his head disapprovingly.

'Let me make one thing clear to you, legionary. If I didn't need every last man within these walls free to fight, I'd have you clapped in chains and breaking rocks.'

Flavian shrugged, then surprised everyone with his reply.

'No chains here, sir. Or rocks.'

For once, Cassius didn't have to feign anger.

'Perhaps you'd like me to devise a similarly unpleasant task for you?' he shouted. 'I'm sure we can come up with something!'

Strabo and Avso were struggling not to smile. Cassius was beginning to realise that rank alone was not enough to make the sight of a nineteen-year-old berating men twice his age any less amusing to hardened legionaries. He therefore determined to avoid doing so wherever possible in the future. Thankfully, Strabo soon recovered himself.

'Of course we can, sir,' he said. 'Petronius' old cane will be lying around here somewhere.'

Avso's grin disappeared.

'That won't be necessary,' Cassius replied quickly. 'Assuming the legionary can summon an apology, I already have another task in mind.'

'Sorry, sir,' said Flavian. 'It was the drink. Won't happen again.'

Ignoring Strabo's snort of disdain, Cassius nodded stiffly. It struck him that the manner of Flavian's apology seemed almost juvenile. He had previously put his stupid behaviour down to the drink but was beginning to think a limited mental capacity might also be to blame. Avso was certainly the brighter of the two.

'It had better not. And in the meantime, as well as your regular duties, you'll be responsible for manning the gatehouse at night. You will monitor the plain and report anything out of the ordinary immediately. Avso can join you. Any failure in this regard and you can expect serious consequences. Understood?'

'Sir.'

'And if I hear you've had any more wine than your ration, I'll have you driven from this fort. It's a long walk back to Antioch. Dismissed.'

Avso followed his friend out.

'See you around, guard officer,' the Thracian said with a sly grin.

'You will at that,' retorted Strabo, helping the door shut with a kick.

Cassius wandered back towards the bedroom and quietly told Simo to fetch another two hundred denarii.

'That was a mistake,' said Strabo. Cassius turned to face him.

'Really?'

'Will you be able to rest easy knowing those two idiots are on watch?'

'If we can't trust them with a simple guard duty, what can we trust them with?'

'Very little. I thought I made that clear.'

Cassius didn't want to waste time explaining himself. He had assigned guard duty because it meant Flavian was responsible for, and answerable to, the entire garrison. It was not uncommon for legionaries to lynch sentries who fell asleep. Cassius was sure even the men of Alauran would treat such a failure seriously.

Strabo's attention switched to the jangling bag of coins in Simo's hand.

Cassius took the bag and tucked it behind his belt.

'I believe you have a wall to rebuild.'

Glowering, the Sicilian left. Cassius grabbed the door as it swung shut and gestured for Barates to lead the way. The veteran looked exhausted.

'Once we've spoken to the Syrians, you must get some sleep.'

'I won't deny I need it.' Barates had just returned from the crest and dispatched a replacement sentry along with Julius and two camels.

Outside, the first section were collecting up the javelins left by the window. Barates had identified an able second in command to lead them in Cassius' absence: Crispus was short, compact, immaculately turned out and he wore a miniature spear on his tunic, a decoration for bravery.

'Should we take these over to the workshop, sir?' Crispus asked, a bundle of the javelins under his arm. His beady, close-set eyes conveyed the impression that no detail escaped his notice. 'They need cleaning and sharpening.'

'Certainly. Then get started on the barracks. Leave beds, chests and the like for each man, but I want the corridors, washroom and latrine spotless.'

'Yes, sir.'

Cassius had taken a quick look inside the barracks before the muster parade and had not been impressed. The latrine in particular needed attention; the three deep pits at the end of the barracks were giving off a terrible stench.

Barates turned towards Cassius as they set off for the Syrian encampment.

99

'Centurion, I thought you wanted to know a little of their background before meeting Kabir.'

'Yes, you can tell me as we walk.'

'It may take a little longer than that. I wouldn't want to you to go in there unprepared. We can't afford to lose them.'

Cassius stopped.

'Very well. Let's shelter here a while. I can keep an eye on the men.'

The place he had in mind was a shady spot in front of the dwellings. They each sat down on a barrel and Barates began.

'From what I've been able to gather, they are nomads, originally from the mountains of the north. Many of their people traded along the spice roads, travelling with caravans to the Orient and back. But since the rise of Palmyra, Zenobia has banned all but her own from profiting from such trade. They had to seek other means to pay their way – as you've seen, they can be effective auxiliaries.'

'And Kabir?'

'Their tribal leader. He speaks good Latin and knows something of the ways of the world. The others always look to him. Win him over and you've won them all.'

'How do you suggest I do that?'

'The money should help. How much do you have there?'

'Two hundred denarii.'

'A good start. But it is the promise of what they are owed that will keep them here.'

'What is their custom? Shall I give it to him openly?'

'Under no circumstances – he would consider it an insult. He'll probably speak to you privately. Perhaps then.'

'His character?'

'Don't be deceived by his fair face and cordial manner. He'll be observing you, testing you, seeing if you have what it takes to organise the defence.'

Cassius was not looking forward to the meeting, but had been too occupied to give it much thought. Now he felt utterly out of his depth again, as if the encouraging events of the previous hours had never happened.

'Just remember that they are devout,' Barates continued. 'Not like some of ours – visiting the temple just before a battle or offering a prayer when fever strikes. To them, the sun is sacred and all nature's parts are a gift. You should make no complaint about the heat or how much you hate the desert. This is their home.'

'I shall not mention religion or nature at all.'

'You should know also that they do not approve of gambling, debauchery or drinking for the purposes of inebriation.'

Cassius shook his head.

'I can tell this is going to be fun.'

The encampment started halfway along the row of houses and was enclosed by the southern and eastern walls. The Syrians had erected a series of awnings that cast angular shadows across the ground. There were in fact two separate cooking areas, and closer to the houses lay neat rows of blankets divided by small piles of possessions. Washing hung from windows and several pieces of furniture had been moved outside.

Cassius was about to ask where the inhabitants of this silent, orderly camp were, when he caught sight of two figures standing in the corner. Then the rest of the Syrians came into view.

They were all wearing black tunics and were kneeling on the ground, backs straight, arms folded, facing the standing figures. Of these two, one was completely bald. Over his tunic he wore a long, flowing cape tied together at his neck. It too was black but decorated with a vivid collage of orange and red streaks.

'The grand-looking one is Yarak. A kind of priest. That's Kabir next to him.'

Yarak brought his hands together in a position of prayer. Kabir was about to follow when his gaze fell upon the two observers. He whispered something to the priest, who nodded, then started his prayers. Kabir rounded his men and gestured for one of them to follow.

'How do they greet each other?' asked Cassius.

'A bow would be courteous.'

As the Syrian came closer, Cassius understood what Barates had meant about his appearance. To Roman eyes, long hair would always seem somewhat less than masculine, but it was Kabir's green, almost feline eyes that most struck Cassius as effeminate. He was barefoot and wore the same simple tunic as his men. In his right ear was a heavy metal ring that stretched the lobe unnaturally.

The three of them bowed simultaneously. Kabir examined Cassius for a moment. If he was surprised by his youth, he didn't show it.

'Greetings, Roman. I am Kabir Abka Mabeer.'

'Good morning. Cassius Quintius Corbulo.'

'Please.'

Kabir gestured towards the dwellings and gave a series of instructions to his subordinate. Barates seemed to have an idea where they were going and led Cassius through a doorway.

Ducking inside, Cassius found himself in a cool, murky room. Close to the window, several straw mattresses had been covered in cushions and expensive cloth. Next to the far wall was a table topped with all manner of objects, including several oil lamps, a religious figurine and some ornate jewellery. Despite the gloom, Cassius could see that the room had been kept immaculately clean.

'I expect you'd like to sit,' said Kabir, lowering himself on to the cushions and pointing at two stools. As Cassius and Barates did so, the other Syrian arrived with a small bowl. He was tall and almost freakishly lean, though this was not his most unusual feature. That was the curious white scar that began above his left eyebrow and ended just to the right of his upper lip. Whatever blade had inflicted the blow had made a complete mess of his nose. Only a tangled mass of bone, scar tissue and exposed flesh remained. Even with the minimal effort he was expending, the Syrian's breath came in disconcerting rasps.

Inside the bowl were dried olives. As his tribesman exited, Kabir leaned forward and took several.

'I should apologise for the . . . incident yesterday. No harm was meant.'

'Luckily none was caused,' countered Cassius.

'I assure you luck had nothing to do with it. If he had wanted to strike your head, he would have.'

Cassius did his best to look unperturbed. The man returned with a jug and three cups. He knelt down and carefully filled each one.

'It was a simple case of over-exuberance and a certain resentment towards Rome. Isn't that right, Idan?'

The man looked up at the mention of his name but obviously didn't understand Latin. He passed each of them a cup and left with a bow.

'Serving you is part of his punishment,' Kabir explained.

'That helmet was new. The shot went straight through.'

'As I said, apologies. Most would probably have bounced off, but Idan is our best. I have never seen him beaten for power or accuracy.'

'I can well believe it.'

Kabir popped one of the olives into his mouth.

'Barates tells me Alauran is to be relieved.'

'Hopefully in four or five days. General Valens' men.'

'I do not know the name.'

'A commander of considerable repute.'

'And there is some information regarding the Palmyrans?'

'We believe they may be advancing into this area.'

'It is only the favour of the Glorious Fire that has kept them at distance this long. I have often wondered over the last few weeks what it is that delays them so. Had they built on their earlier successes, they might have been at the gates of Antioch already.'

Cassius thought it impolitic to mention the Persian campaigns in Arabia, Palestine and Egypt.

'I must say, your Latin is excellent.'

'Thank you. My father believed a good understanding of language was essential for trade. I have found it to be similarly useful in times of war. How is your Greek?'

'Not bad. I made use of it in Antioch.'

'You have no reinforcements with you,' Kabir continued.

'No. I was in the area on another assignment when my orders came through.'

'You are the youngest officer I have ever seen.' Kabir downed another olive. 'You must be an exceptional soldier.'

'I would make no such claim. I've been ordered here to do what I can before General Valens' forces arrive.'

The Syrian nodded towards the square.

'If the Palmyrans have learnt that the well still runs, our days of peace and quiet will end very swiftly.'

Cassius sipped from his cup. The water held a trace of lime.

'We have posted guards at the crest to warn us of any approach,' he said. 'The garrison is preparing the defence.'

'And you believe these men capable of holding Alauran?'

'Yes,' Cassius said firmly.

Kabir laughed out loud, startling both Romans.

'Forgive me. But such confidence! Before we ever set eyes on the legions, we were told that it was the discipline of the Roman soldier that set him apart. Perhaps it was true when they arrived in these parts but the East seems to have made them lazy. The Persians and the Palmyrans have made a mockery of Roman superiority in recent years. And I have seen nothing to match the discipline of my own people.'

Kabir paused for a moment, then leaned forward.

'We start our boys with the sling when they reach ten years of age. They must fire at bundles of sticks twenty yards away. The bundles move a yard further every week until twenty becomes a hundred. Only when they can hit the target three times in a row are they allowed to eat.'

'It's no secret that I hardly have a crack century here. Nor do I deny that I could use your assistance.'

'And now you will offer me the coins you carry at your belt.'

'Will that affect your decision?'

'Actually, now that you have confirmed we will in all likelihood be attacked, I am inclined to take my men and head north while there's still time.'

'Of course that's your choice. But I know you have waited long for your just rewards. It seems strange to leave when that moment is so near.'

'And what use is a reward if one is not around to spend it?'

'You seem to think we cannot hold the fort. I believe we can.'

Kabir finished his drink and stared back at Cassius. As those emerald eyes bore into him, Cassius thought about whether he actually believed what he'd said, aware also that Kabir was trying to deduce precisely the same thing. The Syrian looked out through the window, then spoke again.

'When one of your armies met them earlier this year, the Palmyrans held significant advantages in neither position nor number, yet they triumphed.'

'I have no doubt that they are a formidable foe. But we have a position to defend. And a unit of slingers who can all hit a bundle of sticks – or a man's head – at a hundred yards. If their leader chooses to fight with us.'

Kabir smiled. Now Cassius leaned forward.

'I can assure you that you will be paid what you are owed. General Valens will want all the help he can get.'

'You say that now. But when the time comes, you will enjoy the protection of your own. What guarantee do I have that we will receive our due?'

'My word.'

'I mean no offence, centurion, but in my experience the word of a Roman is worth little.'

Cassius tried not to think about the myriad of lies and half-truths he had already spouted during the meeting.

Kabir continued: 'Under the terms of our duty with the Third Legion, we are owed six thousand two hundred denarii. I have the agreement with me, signed by their camp prefect. Can you really ensure we will receive every coin?'

'I give you my word that I will do everything in my power to get you your money. Here, we can start with this.'

Kabir held up a hand as Cassius reached for his belt.

'That is not necessary.'

The Syrian looked outside again. The men were chanting: a sorrowful refrain that gradually died away.

'I will talk to them. See how they feel.'

'They will follow you, won't they?' asked Barates, speaking up for the first time.

Kabir gave a wry grin.

'They will, Barates. But we have been away a long time. The signs tell us that we have missed many a birth and death; that our loved ones long for our return. Each man deserves a chance to offer his view. Then we shall see what the Glorious Fire wishes for us. I shall tell you my decision.'

With that, Kabir rose from the cushions.

'Thank you for your hospitality,' Cassius said.

They exchanged bows once more and Barates led the way out. As they left, the rest of the Syrians arrived, their prayers finished. Barates nodded to a few individuals. Cassius ignored the curious stares cast in his direction.

As they neared the square, he looked back, watching the tribesmen gather round their leader.

'Well. What do you think?'

'If you yourself are a believer,' said Barates, 'I suggest offering a prayer or two. With them on our side, I think we may have a chance. Without them, I fear there's none at all.'

XII

Simo had spent the entire morning setting up a miniature kitchen on one side of the officers' quarters. After sweeping the floor clean and laying some dried grass for matting, he now had a small fire going. Though a little smoke hung in the air, most escaped through the window and a yard-wide hole he had cut in the roof with the wood-axe.

The Gaul had also gathered some essential equipment and food from the granary. Pots, bottles, bowls and jugs were now lined up in the corner, along with a water barrel and several jars of fruit. He'd found some smoked pork and combined it with a few vegetables to make a thin broth.

Cassius, sitting at the table, picked up a wooden spoon and took a mouthful from the bowl in front of him. Though the heat sapped his appetite, he knew it was important to keep up his strength. As usual, Simo had done well with the means at his disposal.

'Most agreeable.'

'Unfortunately everything here is preserved,' replied Simo, squatting in front of the fire and stirring the pot of soup.

'I must admit I could do with some nice fresh bread.'

Since leaving home, Cassius had found it difficult not to torment himself with thoughts of the common pleasures now denied him.

Simo placed a small glass bottle on the table.

'Fish sauce, sir. You might add it for flavour.'

Cassius turned up his nose at the suggestion but picked up the bottle and examined it as he ate. He held it up to the light, admiring the curve of the neck and the religious symbols etched on the side.

'Quite beautiful.'

'Glass-blowing originated here in Syria, sir. I've seen the technique myself in Antioch. It's truly an art.'

Directly opposite where Cassius sat, the men of the fourth section were gathered round the well, filling barrels.

'Well, I've got them working, Simo. That's something, isn't it?'

'More than something I should say, sir.'

Cassius looked on as Serenus leaned against the well surround and wiped his sweat-soaked face. The legionaries were working in the full glare of the midday sun.

Cassius stood, skirted around the table to the door and called him over. Serenus gave a few instructions and wearily walked towards the barracks.

'A bowl for Serenus too, please, Simo.'

'Yes, sir.'

By the time Serenus sat down next to Cassius, the soup was waiting for him.

'Please. You look like you need some sustenance.'

'Thank you.'

Chewing on a thick lump of pork, Cassius nodded at the well.

'How are you doing?'

'Twelve barrels so far. Eight are up in the gatehouse, four more by the granary. We'll continue until all the spare vessels are full.'

'Excellent.'

As Serenus took his first mouthful of soup, a large figure blocked the doorway. Strabo's hands were covered in a sticky dark mixture. He ushered in a legionary from the first section, who was holding his left elbow tenderly with his right hand.

Cassius stood again.

'What happened?'

'We were cleaning up the barracks,' answered the legionary shakily, 'and one of the lads forgot about the Praetorian – got too close to his room and woke him up.'

'Ah.'

'Chucked a couple of pots at them,' explained Strabo. 'Luckily they missed, but this lad fell awkwardly.'

'Is it broken?' said Cassius.

'Just a twist,' said Strabo. 'But we have a bigger problem. He's at the inn, drinking already. Normally he's not up for another four or five hours. With this much of a run at it, he could end up in a right state. Perhaps we should wake Barates. He's the only one who might get through to him.'

'No, leave him. He deserves a break.' Cassius casually picked up his bowl of soup and finished it off. This was no show of arrogance; he had simply accepted that it was time to face another difficult challenge. He handed the empty bowl to Simo.

'Soup for these two.'

'What are you going to do?' asked Strabo impatiently.

Cassius tightened his belt and straightened his tunic.

'Something I should have done already. Introduce myself.'

The Praetorian was at the back of the inn, sitting on a bench that looked like it was about to give way. On the table in front of him was a jug and on the floor nearby was a small barrel. With one hand he was tapping against the handle of the jug, with the other he scratched at his neck. His eyes were barely open and his mouth was turned down in an expression of contemptuous distaste.

Cassius wasn't sure if he'd noticed him or not. Only when he moved past the first row of tables did the man react.

'Do you mean to clean me out of here too?'

The voice was far more refined than Cassius had expected; deep and authoritative certainly, but more distinguished than many of the officers he'd encountered. Cassius risked a few more steps forward.

'No. I wish only to introduce myself. I am Cassius Quintius Corbulo. The new centurion. I am here on the orders of General Marcus Navio.'

The Praetorian took a swig of wine then looked Cassius up and down.

'The war must be going badly.'

'It's certainly not going well.'

The Praetorian drank again. He grimaced as he swallowed, then his eyelids snapped shut and his teeth ground together. The man was clearly in a great deal of pain. After a time, he managed to open his eyes.

'Still here?' he growled. 'Make yourself useful at least. Pour me some more.'

As there was no one else around, Cassius decided to play along for the moment, despite the unnerving feeling that he was being toyed with.

'Why not?'

Pushing a couple of chairs aside, he bent down and gripped the sides of the barrel. Though small, it was almost full and difficult to lift. He dumped it awkwardly on the table.

The Praetorian moved his jug closer.

Cassius pulled out the stopper and lifted the barrel once more. As he lowered the lip, wine spilled out of the hole and seemed to go everywhere except the jug; by the time it was full, two-thirds had ended up on the table and floor.

The Praetorian shook his head.

'I'd never make an innkeeper,' Cassius said brightly.

Wiping a hand across his chin, the Praetorian stared once again into the middle distance.

'I'd like to talk to you for a moment if I may,' Cassius said. As he was about to sit down, the giant was struck by another paroxysm of pain. His eyes clamped shut again and his mouth contorted into a snarl as he pressed his hands against his stomach. Only after he had downed more wine did the tension in his body seem to ease.

Cassius' hand was still stuck to the chair.

'Before you take that seat, you should be aware of something.'

'What's that?'

The Praetorian held up the jug.

'This makes me feel better. Talking to idiotic, cack-handed runts who paint stripes on their tunics does not.'

He belched and eyed Cassius malevolently.

Thinking it inadvisable to further antagonise the man, Cassius retreated through the tables and chairs. He was almost to the street when he heard the dull crack of boot on wood.

The Praetorian's kick sent a chair careering into a table with sufficient momentum to knock two more chairs flying. One struck Cassius. He stumbled, then fell, landing awkwardly on his sword handle.

The giant was still guffawing when Cassius hauled himself to his feet. Dusting himself down, he carefully replaced the chairs, not daring to catch the man's eye again but determined to maintain some semblance of composure.

'Run along now, boy!' yelled the Praetorian.

Cassius walked towards the northern wall, just to get away. He turned left and saw Strabo's men up ahead, working on the breach. His hands were shaking and he knew he'd find a nasty bruise on his side later.

Less easy to quantify was how much damage the encounter had done to his confidence. It was a humiliating reverse, but he was thankful no one else had witnessed it. He would simply have to hope that the monstrous man stayed in his stupor and out of the way. Even so, as he neared Strabo's men, Cassius was struck by the inescapable feeling that he might have to face the Praetorian again sooner rather than later.

'Afternoon, sir,' said one of the legionaries, largely to alert his colleagues, most of whom were doing very little. They were gathered round a large wicker basket lined with cloth, full to the brim with the mixture Cassius had seen on Strabo's hands. Next to the basket was a barrel of water and a malodorous heap of camel dung.

'How are you getting on?'

'Well, it's a big hole, sir,' said one legionary.

'It certainly is.'

Barates had been conservative in his description of the damage. To the left of the collapsed section, marks could be seen where the cart's axles had swept along the wall before the impact brought part of it down. The uneven edges of the gap looked about ten feet apart. It was difficult not to visualise a band of marauding warriors simply stepping over it and into the compound.

'I think we need more water,' said another man, stabbing a finger into the mixture. 'This damn sun dries it out so quick.'

'Well get to it then!' snapped Cassius.

'Sir!' came the simultaneous response and the five of them set about the task with renewed urgency. Two worked on the mixture, another set about levelling off the base while the others continued to break up the rubble.

'That's more like it.'

Cassius made his way along the rear of the barracks, stopping at every window to look inside. He could see that his section had done a good job of cleaning the floors and clearing the worst of the mess. When he reached the side window of the officers' quarters, he saw that while Serenus had returned to work, Strabo was still shovelling soup into his mouth from a suspiciously full bowl.

'Enjoying yourself, guard officer?'

Strabo continued eating, undeterred.

'Good cook, this Gaul of yours.'

'I see you've already had seconds. When you're done I want you back out here. That wall's not going to rebuild itself.'

Not waiting for a reply, Cassius hurried on. He passed Serenus' men at the well, then the stables, then took his first look at the workshop. At the front of the open area were two hefty wooden tables. There was also an anvil, a vice and hanging from the walls a host of iron tools, most of which Cassius struggled to identify. He did not tarry long because ahead was a sight of more interest.

In the dark of the previous night he hadn't noticed the four heavy carts lined up behind the granary. He estimated them to be eighteen feet long and seven wide. There was just enough space between them and the granary to squeeze through and he checked each one as he passed. The wheels looked in good condition; it would be easy to move them.

Stepping over the last of the protruding axles, Cassius noticed that someone had nailed six pieces of wood to the granary wall to form a makeshift ladder. With no plan more specific than getting a good view of the compound, he started upward. An avid climber since boyhood, he negotiated the wall with ease.

In more temperate climes, the granary would have been topped by tiles, but the lack of rainfall in the area meant that a timber frame covered by dried palm fronds sufficed. The layers of branches were, however, in desperate need of replacement and there were many gaping holes. Leaning on his side across two roof beams, Cassius looked towards the gate.

Avso and another man were there, pointing things out to each other and taking measurements. Others, including Flavian, walked to and from the marketplace, breaking up the abandoned stalls and returning to the gate with suitable pieces of wood.

Over in the south-east corner, the priest Yarak stood alone. Still wearing his opulent cloak, the Syrian was behaving rather strangely. Having already planted several spindly tree branches in the ground, he was now examining them from various angles. He would occasionally look to the sky and Cassius realised after a while that it was not the branches themselves he was interested in, but the shadows they cast. Tracing the shapes into the dirt with the fingers of one hand, Yarak clenched the other into a fist and hammered the air.

Wondering if this was the method Kabir would use to consult the opinion of his sacred spirits, Cassius offered a brief bow towards the sun.

'Every little helps.'

Removing an annoying palm twig from beneath his backside, he climbed a little higher up the beams until he could see over the apex of the roof. Scanning back across the compound, he couldn't help enjoying the few moments of peace as he observed the activity of others, content to be on his own.

He thought of the tall apricot tree at his father's house in Ravenna. As a child, he would often escape there to avoid a lecture, a beating or one of his mother's endless parties. Clambering up to the high boughs, he would spend hours watching the servants, the family and their guests, often until darkness gathered round him. More than once he had fallen asleep up there.

At some point, someone would come looking for him.

Occasionally it would be one of the servants or one of his sisters but usually it would be his mother. She would stand at the base of the tree, hands on hips, calling up to him.

The precise words would vary but her speech would always centre on the same theme: life wasn't about sitting in trees. Life was about coming down and getting involved; showing one's face; getting things done. As with most of her advice, it had served him well. With a reluctant sigh, he clambered back down towards the ladder.

XIII

'Any word from Kabir?' asked Serenus, slumping down against the wall next to Barates.

'Not yet.'

Cassius, standing opposite them in shade next to the temple, said nothing. He was determined at least to give the impression that the garrison could do without the Syrian auxiliaries.

'By Mars, it's stickier than a camel's crotch today.'

Strabo rounded the corner of the temple, wiping his face with a cloth. In his other hand was a large wooden cup, which he filled with water from the barrel next to Barates. Avso was the last to arrive. Predictably, he stood as far away from the Sicilian as possible.

After several requests for a break, Cassius had eventually relented. The men had been given an hour off and most were either dozing in the barracks or eating outside the granary. The section leaders had been summoned to a brief meeting.

'What about the gate?' Cassius asked.

Avso's lean features twisted into a grimace.

'We've repaired what wear and tear there was and doubled up the main beams, but we can't really reinforce it yet. Not while we still need to keep it open for the camels.'

'What do you suggest then?'

'As long as we get a couple of hours' warning, we can strengthen it outside and in: cover the hinges, mount timber on the wall and across the main planks. It won't stand up to a decent ram but it will be a lot tougher than it is now.'

'Make sure you know how to do it and ready the materials. We'll make sure you get plenty of time to prepare. Strabo, what about the wall?'

'We've got the mixture right and the first layer is drying now.'

'Will it be back up by nightfall?'

The Sicilian shook his head.

'Not a chance. It must be taken a layer at a time or it won't hold its own weight. Late tomorrow at the earliest.'

Serenus was next to report.

'Twenty-one barrels filled. Another thirty or so still empty. Should be done sometime tomorrow.'

He raised the cup in his hand.

'And there's still plenty for drinking.'

'Good,' said Cassius. 'I'm going to have my lot drag those carts out later. We can use them as barricades if the Palmyrans get inside.'

Barates nodded but none of the section leaders said anything. Despite the preparations, it seemed to Cassius that their months of safety within Alauran's walls had led to a misplaced complacency they were still struggling to shake free of.

There was a wider issue. All four were capable in their own way, but they were soldiers of the line; more used to receiving orders than giving them. They could organise the men and offer advice, but ultimately it was with Cassius that decisions would rest. More than ever, he felt ill-prepared to make them.

Worse still, there was a man not thirty yards away, currently drinking himself insensible, who knew the enemy inside and out. A man who could tell him what to expect and how best to prepare for it. If he could just get him to cooperate.

Whilst waiting for others, Cassius had come up with an idea that might work but which was likely to be unpopular. The plan was audacious, dangerous in fact, but nothing like as perilous as facing the Palmyrans unprepared.

'Listen, I want to make sure the men are ready for anything. That's going to mean moving quickly. Simo found a tuba in the officers' quarters. Anyone know how to play it?'

'I believe Minicius from my section used to be a signaller,' said Serenus. 'It's not that hard.'

'You just need a big mouth and plenty of hot air,' added Strabo. He leaned forward to catch Avso's eye. 'Fancy a go?'

'Why don't you take it, guard officer,' replied Avso without looking at him, 'and stick it up your—'

'None of that, thank you, gentlemen,' said Cassius. 'From tomorrow, whenever that tuba sounds, everyone is to assemble round me, fully armed and in sections. Tell your men. We'll work out a proper set of signals later.'

The Sicilian took a swig of water.

'That it?'

'Half an hour more, then get back to it. Strabo, obviously you and yours keep at the wall. The rest of you: when jobs are done, I want the men drilling. Fighting skills, close-quarters stuff.'

Cassius was glad that this rather vague instruction passed without reaction. 'That's all.'

He was halfway back to the officers' quarters when the legionaries in the square suddenly became quiet. He looked up to see Kabir and Yarak walking towards him, again barefoot and clad only in their black tunics. News of the impending decision had evidently spread to the men; Cassius could feel numerous eyes upon him as the Syrians approached.

'Good afternoon. Shall we speak inside?' he said, pointing towards the officers' quarters.

'No, no, this won't take long,' said Kabir.

Cassius felt his spirits sink. There was, however, little to be deduced from the Syrian's expression.

Barates hurried over to them.

'My men and I will stay,' said Kabir.

'I am very glad to hear that,' said Barates, barely able to smother a smile.

'As am I,' Cassius added.

Kabir seemed uninterested in their sentiments.

'You should know this. Though some are keen to avenge those

lost to the Palmyrans and wait for what we are owed, many wished to leave. And some believe we may not receive our due, myself included.'

Kabir glanced sideways at Yarak. The priest watched the Romans impassively, hands clasped together in front of him.

'However, the signs tell us that we should remain. That a great victory will be won. And that some of us will return home rich men.'

Despite his optimistic words, Kabir's tone was neutral, almost cynical.

'I hope the signs are correct,' replied Cassius. 'But forgive me if I say you don't sound convinced.'

'Sir,' warned Barates.

Yarak and Kabir exchanged comments in their own language. The priest seemed less than impressed by what he heard.

'We follow the will of the Glorious Fire, yes,' said Kabir, 'but we are not stupid enough to believe that what is meant for us is always the same as what we wish for.'

'I meant no offence,' Cassius said.

Kabir's expression softened slightly.

'How do you intend to deploy us?'

Cassius had given the issue only the vaguest consideration. He hoped Barates might intervene but the veteran looked blankly back at him.

'Well, how do you think you would best be used?'

Despite the fact that the two were so utterly unalike, the flicker of amusement that crossed Kabir's face reminded Cassius of Strabo.

'We were used as skirmishers. As you have seen, we have no armour but can do considerable damage with the sling. I suggest keeping us in large groups so as to concentrate fire. Preferably from a protected position.'

'Well, that sounds fine.'

'And how exactly will you organise the defence?'

Cassius decided honesty was the best policy: 'We're still planning that. In fact, I'm interested in any advice you can give. You're sure to know more about the Palmyrans than most of us do.'

'Possibly. Though in truth my people have spent more time fighting the Persians over the years. We did not expect to face an enemy so close to home.'

'I'm calling a meeting of my senior men tomorrow. I'd like you to be there.'

'Certainly. Until then we shall set about rearranging the encampment and readying ourselves for attack. I'll need to send a party out to the foothills.'

'Very well. Might I ask why?'

'To look for stones. We have some lead shot but that won't last long.'

'Ah.'

'Tomorrow then.'

'Tomorrow.'

Kabir and Yarak left. Cassius looked at the men, who had all been listening. Most seemed happy.

'All praise the Glorious Fire,' he said with a grin, opening his palms towards the sky.

'Indeed,' answered Barates.

'So, what of our large friend? I assume he's still at it?'

'At the time we need him most, he's drinking more than ever.'

Cassius decided it was time to implement the second part of his plan for the Praetorian.

'Keep an eye out for when he turns in.'

'I'd be happy to, but I was planning to take the night duty out at the crest.'

'Who's out there now?'

'Antonius. Uncouth sort but he has the eyes of a hawk.'

'Pick a couple of reliable men from your section and tell them to follow these instructions. Once the Praetorian's asleep, they should take every last barrel of wine out of the inn and put it in the granary. If you know of any in the barracks or elsewhere, confiscate that too.'

Barates frowned.

'But when he gets up and can find none? The man will go mad.'

'As soon as he's up tomorrow, come and find me immediately.'

'But he needs that wine. He'll do anything to get his hands on it.'

'That's what I'm depending on.'

Cassius found Simo piling up the last of Petronius' papers.

'Some good news. The locals are with us.'

'That is good, sir.'

'You could sound a bit more enthusiastic, Simo. After the fright that scarred fellow gave us yesterday, I'd say recruiting them to our ranks counts as considerable progress.'

'How many of them are there, sir?' said Simo hurrying to fetch Cassius a drink.

'At least thirty I should say. Which gives me almost eighty men.'

Cassius sat down and stared blankly at Simo, his thoughts elsewhere.

'A century of my own after all.'

He took a cup of water from Simo and noted that the Gaul was no longer wearing his dagger.

'I should prefer it if you continue to arm yourself. Especially with that money still lying around.'

'To be honest, sir, I don't like to carry a weapon.'

'You've worn that dagger ever since I met you.'

'Master Trimalchio told me to, sir. So that I might protect you while we were travelling. I've never done so before.'

'Simo, if the Palmyrans turn up outside those gates, you'll be another sword hand for me, like it or not. The men here are from the Third, you know – a legion originally raised in your homeland.'

'I'd really prefer not to get involved, sir. Violence is not in my nature.'

'Neither is it in mine, but aggression and skill with a blade can be instilled in the most peaceful of men. Trust me, I've experienced it first-hand. I shall place you with one of the sections for drilling this evening.'

'Sir, I'd really rather not.'

Cassius was surprised by the Gaul's persistence. He was now moving from insolence towards downright disobedience.

'The decision has been made,' he said firmly.

'But sir, you'll need someone to care for the injured.'

Cassius was about to snap back at him but saw instantly that Simo had a good point. At present there was no one to man the aid post and deal with serious injuries.

'You're pushing your luck, Simo, just be aware of that.'

Simo gave a conciliatory bow.

'But I can't deny you might be on to something there. What do you know of medicine?'

'I'm no expert, sir, but I can dress and tend wounds. And I've had a look at the aid post. We would need to move some more beds inside, but everything else I'd need is there.'

Cassius made a show of considering, but he'd already made up his mind.

'Very well then. Once you've finished here, make a start. You should be prepared for some bloody work though. A battlefield hospital is no place for the faint-hearted.'

'I do not fear blood, sir. I should just prefer to try to preserve life rather than take it.'

Again Cassius was surprised. Though it was clear Simo had acquired a degree of education whilst in the service of Trimalchio, he occasionally made comments that seemed at odds with his station. It was not customary for servants to freely proffer their beliefs to their superiors.

'Well,' said Cassius, 'quite the philosopher, aren't we?'

Simo looked down at the ground. Cassius wished he hadn't said anything.

'You must still wear that dagger.'

'Yes, sir.'

XIV

Serenus took charge of the evening drill, starting the men off with a jog round the flagpole. It was a common exercise, designed to concentrate minds and tire limbs before the first round of swordplay. The weary legionaries struggled not to run into each other or be tripped from behind, but, thanks to Crispus and a few other vocal types, they gradually got a rhythm going, even when Serenus ordered a sprint.

After the warm-up, he told them to draw swords and practise parries and thrusts. Shields, other weapons and manoeuvres could wait. Though unenthusiastic at first, most soon warmed to their task: hitting harder, moving quicker, criticising and complimenting their partners. Serenus offered guidance, altering grips and stances where he saw deficiencies.

Suddenly a high-pitched cry cut through the clanging swords. Cassius and Barates, looking on from in front of the temple, saw a man drop his blade and fall to the ground. The others all stopped as the legionary examined his wounded hand then unleashed a stream of curses at his partner. Cassius didn't understand a word of it. The second man turned to face the crowd.

'What did he say? Anyone speak that Galician filth?'

'Something about your mother, Linus!'

'Your sister too!'

'And what was that about your niece?'

'Not very helpful,' observed Barates.

Enraged, Linus swung a boot at the Galician. Despite his injury, the legionary rolled out of the way and got quickly to his feet. He swapped his sword to his good hand as Linus positioned himself for a lunge. Their blades never met.

Avso swept the Galician's legs from under him in the same moment as Serenus smashed an elbow into the back of Linus' neck. The Galician had barely hit the ground before Avso, ably assisted by Flavian, launched a flurry of kicks at his stomach. Linus, meanwhile, was down on his knees, retching and coughing. Serenus stood over him.

Cassius sprinted over.

'That's enough!'

'No, *that's* enough,' said Avso, with one last kick.

The Galician rolled on to his back, hands pressed against his gut.

'You rat-faced—'

Avso made to kick him again.

'Want some more?'

'I said that's enough!'

Cassius stood between them.

Serenus offered Linus his canteen. The legionary swatted it away and rubbed at his neck.

'What happened?' Cassius asked.

'Almost took my hand off!' yelled the Galician, holding up his wrist. The gash was at the base of his hand.

'It'll be your face next time!' spat Linus.

Somebody laughed. Then the rest of the legionaries laughed too. Cassius was reflecting on the pitifully childish nature of army humour when he turned towards the gate and saw the real cause of the hilarity: Julius, trying to haul one of the camels down the street.

The animal was not cooperating. It had planted its feet and was now jerking its neck from side to side. The boy slapped it across the nose then heaved on the reins with both hands. The camel took a sudden step forward, then stopped again. Julius lost hold of the reins and pitched backward into the sand. The beast shook its head once more, showering him with spittle. By the time Julius was back on his feet, almost the entire garrison was roaring. Even Linus and the Galician managed a smile.

Cassius turned to Serenus and nodded towards the two legionaries.

'This under control?'

'I think so.'

'They're tired. Perhaps you should finish up quickly – avoid any more accidents.'

'I agree.'

Cassius walked over to the Galician, who was now also up on his feet.

'My attendant will see to that wound. Simo!'

The Gaul was already outside the officers' quarters and he now escorted the injured man to the aid post.

'Right, back to it!' Cassius announced. As the crowd broke up, he hurried after Barates, who was off to help Julius.

'Seems a caring sort, your attendant,' observed the veteran.

'Indeed. He was singularly reluctant to join in with training.'

'Forgive me, centurion, but you might consider doing so yourself. The men would like to see you leading the way.'

Cassius had considered taking the session. He could execute the basic routines – stabbing, parrying, sweeping, blocking – his months of training had seen to that. But he couldn't help imagining making some dreadful error and losing the minimal amount of respect he had built up. His silence, he knew, spoke volumes.

'Sorry,' said Barates. 'When one reaches a certain age, one forgets one's station. I am in no position to make such judgements.'

'Forget it. Come, let's help the lad.'

With the two Romans on the reins and Julius pushing at the rear, it didn't take too long to manoeuvre the camel over to the stables. Leaving the other two to get it inside the stall, Cassius took the opportunity to look inside the granary.

Attracting a few stares from the Syrians, he lifted up the plank securing the double doors and pulled one side open. Ideally he would have posted a guard, but Strabo had made it clear to the men that no one was to enter without permission. According to Barates, the Syrians never attempted to take anything as long as they were supplied with provisions when required.

Cassius stepped up on to the raised floor. A five-yard gap had been cleared and the remaining stores piled neatly into stacks, some of which reached almost to the roof.

He was surprised to see just how many barrels there were. Only in the last few years had they begun to compete with amphoras as the main container for transporting food and drink across the Empire, being considerably stronger, larger and easier to move. When lined with pitch they were also virtually water-proof. Though now common in Italy and the western provinces, they were far less prevalent in the East.

A narrow path had been made between the stacks. Cassius passed through shafts of light, disturbing suspended motes of dust that swirled away. Every single container was labelled with white paint, identifying it as the property of the Third Legion. Assailed by a variety of odours, he spied barrels of dates, dried apricots and pears, various types of nuts, olives, cured meat, salted fish, grain, beans and lentils; there were also glass bottles and amphoras containing vinegar, olive oil and wine.

After a few yards, the path followed a zigzagging pattern around vast piles of grain sacks and endless trays of hard biscuit – an army staple that could be softened with water for eating or ground into flour and reconstituted for baking.

The far wall was adjacent to the stables. He could hear Barates talking to Julius and one of the camels grunting away. Here, the concoction of smells was reminiscent of a latrine. Wondering if the foul stench was produced by rats, Cassius looked for any sign of nests or droppings before recalling that this was precisely what the raised floor guarded against. Deciding that the odour must be coming from the camels, he retraced his steps to the door.

As he was replacing the locking plank outside, he heard a few shouts from the encampment. Jamming the plank firmly down, he turned to see a number of the Syrians arriving with large baskets on their backs.

The men lowered the baskets to the ground and the others, including Kabir and Yarak, inspected the contents. Kabir took out a handful of stones and tossed a couple in the air. He seemed to approve.

Twilight was near as Barates left to relieve Antonius at the crest. Cassius saw him off and headed back up the street.

With the drill over, the legionaries were gathered by the granary again. None of them could be bothered to cook, preferring to pick from plates piled high with dried meat, fish and fruit while drinking water and wine from their canteens. Most lay on the ground in small groups, tired from the day's exertions. A few played at dice as they ate.

Strabo's men were finished for the day. Half the breach had been filled and the mixture was holding well. The Sicilian was standing behind a table where he and his section had laid out the provisions. He was drinking wine and talking to Serenus.

'Centurion.'

Cassius was intercepted by two legionaries.

'The Bear,' said one, 'sorry, the Praetorian – he's in the barracks, asleep already. Should we collect up the wine now?'

'Ah, you two are doing that. Yes, after you've eaten. I'll make sure the guard officer knows about it.'

The two legionaries sat down and returned to their meal. Cassius walked over to Strabo and Serenus and swiftly outlined his plan for the wine.

'Are you insane?'

'Keep your voice down, Strabo. It's best if the men don't hear about it beforehand.'

Serenus grimaced.

'At present his behaviour is no more than an inconvenience. If we antagonise him he could become a real problem.'

'A real problem?' said Strabo. 'Caesar's cock! He'll go berserk!'

Cassius rounded the table and coaxed them away from the other legionaries.

'I understand your objections but allow me to explain. This man has been out here for years. He knows these Palmyrans.

How they think. How they fight. If he can help us at all, we must try and talk to him.'

'I thought you already had,' said Strabo with a knowing look.

'You won't change my mind.'

'Then I shan't waste my breath.' The Sicilian took a swig of wine, wiped a hand across his mouth, then wandered off to investigate a nearby game of dice.

'What do you have planned for this evening?' asked Serenus.

'We'll let them eat and rest. After muster they can turn in. Tomorrow we continue the preparations. I want everything that can be done finished by sundown.'

Serenus seemed distracted for a moment; he was staring over Cassius' shoulder.

'What is it?'

'Kabir and his people. Every day they perform this ritual. As the sun rises and sets.'

The two Romans moved closer to the granary, allowing a clear view through the encampment to the Syrians, gathered once again in the south-east corner. In contrast to the earlier ceremony, all were on their feet, facing Yarak and Kabir with arms aloft.

'They certainly put us to shame,' continued Serenus. 'I don't remember the last occasion I saw anyone inside the temple.'

'Give it time,' said Cassius. 'If we spy a horde of Palmyrans charging towards us, you won't be able to get in the door.'

Even from such a distance, they could see the strain in the hands and fingers of the Syrians as they stretched skyward. And they could hear a low but insistent chant that gradually rose in pitch and volume. When it eventually reached a peak, some of the tribesmen leaped and shouted. Others beckoned to the sun as it hovered above the western wall. With a final cry, all except Yarak became quiet and still. Waiting as one for the priest to lower his hands, they finally turned and walked away in pious silence.

XV

Standing between two of the poles that supported the high awning above him, Azaf looked out at the encampment.

Buildings had been commandeered in Anasartha by the local Palmyran commander, but he wanted to keep the men well away from the city. Though the inhabitants had long since been dissuaded from mounting any organised resistance, it was common for fights to break out between local men and the occupying troops, and there was the additional complication of available women.

Azaf had no interest in such distractions. During his last trip home, a neighbouring tribal leader had offered his daughter in marriage. Azaf's father approved of the match and the ceremony would take place when he next returned. He had not seen the girl but had been told she was fine in form and face. Now that he had pledged himself, he could not touch another woman; even his thoughts of the Queen sparked feelings of guilt.

In between the tents spread out in front of him fires crackled and the smell of roasting meat hung heavily in the air. He had ordered double rations and was happy to see the infantry, archers and cavalrymen relax for a few hours. Earlier, five garlanded goats had been sacrificed to Malakbel. Pleasingly, their entrails had been clear of unusual marks or defects: a good omen. He could hear urgent, excited conversations. The warriors knew they were close now; they would reach their objective soon.

Just before sunset, a party led by Bezda had returned from Anasartha with food and timber. Despite the drought, nearby springs and efficient Roman water management had allowed the fields around the city to yield earlier in the year; supplies of grain and fruit were plentiful. The timber had already been used to construct eight solid ladders and a rudimentary ram. These had been loaded on to the carts and were Azaf's only concession to the notion of a traditional siege. What he knew of such techniques had been gleaned from others more familiar with Roman and Persian tactics. General Zabbai wanted a victory in hours, not days, and Azaf was determined he would get it.

It had been a frustrating few months for the general. After leading the Queen's forces against the Fourth Legion, he had been ordered to consolidate gains in the south, ensuring that Palestine and Arabia were secure before pressing north-east towards Antioch: the great prize. What Azaf had seen of Roman resistance so far suggested a complete lack of coordination and appalling morale. On only two occasions had he met serious attempts to defend the walls of a fort or town. The tally for his swordsmen since leaving Palmyra was two hundred and fifty enemy killed, four hundred captured. He had lost thirty-four.

Yet he was wary of assuming it would be as easy this time. Any Roman soldier still at his post between Palmyra and Antioch couldn't be entirely without courage, and the men of Alauran defended a valuable prize. Even so, he felt sure that the archers and cavalry would give him the edge over whatever force he met. If it meant sacrificing a few of them before his swordsmen carried out the main assault, so be it.

Hearing the shuffling of feet, he looked up to see a familiar face pass through the lambent glow of a torch. Razir was an ageing infantryman from Azaf's tribe who'd been with him since the beginning. A seasoned, wily warrior, he also served as his commander's armourer. He was holding Azaf's sword in cloth-wrapped hands, one on the hilt, one on the blade.

'I spent an hour on it,' Razir said proudly, the light from the torch catching the white in his beard.

Azaf put a finger against the cold steel. As usual, Razir had done an immaculate job of sharpening the blade.

'Excellent. And all by firelight.'

Azaf's tent had been pitched at the edge of a copse of palms. A branch snapped.

Both men looked up. A hooded figure had materialised behind one of the trees.

'Who's there?' demanded Razir, raising the sword.

Though he had posted sentries, Azaf knew it wouldn't be difficult for a determined foe to slip into the darkened encampment.

'*Strategos* Azaf?'

The Aramaic was clear but the voice seemed hesitant, as if it were not the speaker's first language.

'Didn't the general tell you I'd make contact?'

Feeling the chill of the night, Azaf pulled his cloak round him.

'Ah. Yes. Come closer. Here by the torch.'

'I think not. And you'll need to dismiss the old one if you wish me to tell all I know.'

Azaf could sense Razir bristling beside him. He placed a hand on his shoulder.

'Leave us.'

Razir reluctantly withdrew.

'I shall be close by.'

Azaf nodded and turned back to face the stranger.

'Well? What have you to say to me?'

The spy moved round the tree and squatted down. He reached up and adjusted his hood so that it covered most of his face. Azaf could see only a thin mouth and clean-shaven jaw.

'You're headed for Alauran, yes?'

'We aim to be there in two days.'

'I've not heard from my man in a while but the last time I did there were fewer than fifty legionaries there. He has three standing orders. The first is to gain all possible knowledge about Roman troop numbers and deployment. The second is to remain there until I personally recall him. The third is likely to be of most interest to you.'

'Go on.'

'Before you begin the assault he will send you a message

130

detailing everything inside the walls: armaments, weak points, anything of use.'

'And how will he get this message to me?'

'One moment.'

The spy retreated into the gloom and picked up something. Turning sideways so as to obscure his face, he placed the object on the ground. Only when he had returned to the shadows did Azaf take it and examine it by torchlight.

It was a small wooden cage and inside was a dark-feathered bird. Azaf didn't recognise the breed. The bird pecked at one of the bars and walked round in tight circles – as much movement as the cage would allow.

'Keep it alive and it shall serve you well. We use them to deliver messages. The strings in their throats are cut so they cannot sing and betray their masters. This one is the mate of another. They will fly hundreds of miles to be joined again. I'm sure you can guess where the other is.'

'Ingenious,' said Azaf begrudgingly.

'The message will be attached to its leg. Tether this bird and release it into the air. My man will send the other. You may have to wait a while but it will come.'

'Who is he?'

'You don't need to know. He has worked for me for many years, sometimes with our enemies, sometimes within our own ranks.'

The spy pointed down at the cage with a single bony finger.

'Water and grain every day. And keep it out of the sun.'

Azaf shrugged and looked down at the bird, still completing its circuitous route.

When he glanced back at the palm, the spy had vanished.

Cassius, barefoot and wearing only his tunic, stood in the middle of the square and looked up at the moon.

He thought again of the *Almagest* and Ptolemy's theories about the motion of astral bodies. He could never quite make sense of those particular concepts and, whether it was full or halved or quartered, the moon had always seemed to him no more than a distant sentinel: ever present, ever watching.

He wondered what it saw to the east, where the enemies of Rome gathered and plotted. Somewhere beyond the weak walls of Alauran were the faceless men who might launch the assault, intent on acquiring the fort for their queen, battling any who tried to stop them. Not for the first time, he felt utterly bemused by the destructive forces that caused men to fight to the death for something as mundane as a clean supply of water.

The compound was eerily still. The animals were quiet in their stables, and with only Flavian and Avso on duty at the gatehouse, the barracks were silent.

It seemed impossible that within hours or days the walls could be overrun; that Cassius and those under his command might meet their deaths out here at the edge of the Empire, so far from Rome that it seemed as distant as the moon.

Despite another exhausting day, he had struggled to sleep and had finally given up. Thinking a walk outside might alter his state of mind, he found there was no escape from the thoughts and questions that occupied him. He wondered what his family would think, if they could see him here. Was this what his father had secretly intended for him? To face danger and emerge in triumph or meet a heroic death? And what of his mother? She had never wanted him to leave, though she could never defy the will of her husband. Cursing himself for his childish weakness, Cassius could not deny that he wanted more than anything to be with her, to embrace her, to feel safe again.

As he turned back towards the officers' quarters, resolving to rest his body even if he could not rest his mind, he caught sight of the temple and stopped.

It had been a long time since he had prayed with conviction. As he left childhood behind, he saw it as something for others, whether they worshipped one god or many, their emperors or their ancestors. To him it seemed futile. His fate would be decided by the turn of battle; by his own actions; by others; and by luck.

On this night, though, Cassius offered a simple prayer, to any force that might listen, and he whispered it, though there was no one there to hear him.

'Please let me see my mother again.'

XVI

Legionary Minicius had done a good job of cleaning the tuba and the early-morning sun flashed off the four-foot bronze cone as he held it aloft. Steadying the weight with both hands, he put his lips to the cone and blew. The note was uneven but powerful, and it seemed to rebound off the compound walls, echoing into every corner. Cassius, Barates and the signaller waited for the garrison to arm themselves and gather outside the granary.

Barates had returned from the crest just after dawn, leaving Antonius to take up sentry duty. He'd been surprised to see the Praetorian up early again and already lumbering towards the inn. As soon as Cassius heard this he sought out Minicius and the three of them hurried across to the granary. It surely wouldn't take long for the Praetorian to realise he'd have to look further afield for his precious wine.

Predictably, the fourth section were first to arrive. Serenus swiftly organised them into a line to Cassius' left.

'Excellent work,' said Cassius, before turning to Barates.

'Avso and Flavian reported nothing of interest during the night. Same for you, I presume?'

'Pleasantly uneventful. Julius was upset about something though. He sleeps in the stables more often than not but ended up in the barracks last night.'

'Why?' Cassius asked irritably, having managed only an hour of sleep himself. He got no answer; Barates had already hurried away to organise his own section.

Strabo, Avso, Crispus and a big group of legionaries arrived. Cassius stayed quiet, relying on his deputies to chivvy their charges along. It was satisfying to see the legionaries respond to the tuba's summons so efficiently.

'There he is,' someone said.

The Praetorian was leaning against the corner of the aid post, a jug in his hand. He watched the last few soldiers exiting the barracks, some attaching their scabbards to their belts as they ran.

'Straighten them out, guard officer,' ordered Cassius. With a few words from the Sicilian, the men formed a solid double line, with Cassius' first section and Serenus' fourth at the rear. Strabo's second, Barates' third and Avso's fifth formed a wider rank at the front.

'Everyone quiet!' ordered Cassius as he took up position next to Strabo.

The Praetorian was still observing the peculiar sight in front of the granary with a bemused frown.

Careful not to make any gesture that could be construed as aggressive, Cassius rested his hands on his belt and waited. Gradually, the heavy breaths of the harried troops died down and the only noise to be heard was from the Syrians: the low hum of conversation and odd clink of a pan or plate. The dust kicked up by the men settled back to the ground.

The Praetorian just kept on staring. Cassius felt sure the giant's eyes were fixed on him.

'This is bad,' Strabo whispered.

The Praetorian dropped the jug. As it rolled away, he pushed off the wall and quickly covered the few steps to the barracks doorway.

'That's worse,' added the Sicilian.

Several hushed conversations began amongst the legionaries.

'I said quiet!' Cassius shouted, spinning round. 'Next man to speak will find himself on permanent latrine duty.'

Turning back, he caught Barates' eye.

'Well?' he breathed.

'He may be looking for wine.'

'Or?'

'Or . . . he may be getting his sword.'

Cassius felt his stomach tighten. He already knew the plan was risky but now saw just how badly he might have misjudged things. Heads turned right, and Cassius saw some of the Syrians by the dwellings, watching events unfold. Nobody said a word as they listened to the Praetorian make his way back through the barracks. His vast frame filled the entrance and he came to a halt, blinking as the sun hit him.

He was carrying a wooden stave, not unlike Flavian's, except that one end had been carved into a neat ball, ideal for cracking heads. The implication was not lost on any of the men standing twenty yards away: he wasn't aiming to kill anyone but those who stood in his way could expect to get hurt.

The Praetorian spun the stave neatly through the air, caught it with his other hand, then started across the square. The broad face was expressionless. His arms hung almost diagonally, forced outward by their own musculature and his immense chest. He was heading directly for the granary door, straight through the middle of Strabo's section.

'Draw swords,' Cassius ordered. His own weapon got caught half way out. Looking down as he freed it, he realised that some, including Strabo and Avso, had not complied.

The feeling of the weighty blade in his hand was familiar but far from reassuring. Cassius associated it with failure and weakness. His instructors had told him that he must learn to love his sword, that it would look after him if he looked after it, but somehow it still felt unnatural. Leaving the weapon hanging loosely by his side, he leaned closer to Strabo.

'Draw your sword, damn you.' The venom in his voice surprised them both.

Strabo stared resolutely at the advancing Praetorian, now just ten paces away.

'I told you. This is a mistake.'

'Not if we stand together.'

The Sicilian ignored him and nodded a greeting to the huge figure approaching them.

'Praetorian, listen—'

Without really thinking, Cassius stepped in front of Strabo.

'Good morning,' he said brightly. 'I expect you want some wine. We'll be happy to fetch you some.'

There was a flicker of surprise in the wide, pale eyes. The Praetorian halted and waved at a fly that had landed in the thick hair covering his shoulders. Cassius could smell a pungent mix of old sweat and wine; he struggled not to show his distaste.

'Then I suggest you hurry.'

Cassius was once again surprised by the refined intonation.

'Of course. I just have one small request. Then I promise you can have all the wine you want, whenever you want.'

The Praetorian looked down at the ground for a moment, then sniffed noisily.

'Bad answer.'

He transferred the stave to the other hand and glanced down at Cassius' sword.

'No good to you down there.'

Cassius had never felt such abject fear. His mouth was horribly dry. Even if he could have found some words he couldn't have got them out.

'Sir.'

Cassius realised instantly that Barates was not addressing him.

'Sir, there's no need for that,' the veteran said quietly, walking forward and holding out an appeasing hand. 'The centurion wishes only to call on your expertise. We face attack and need your help.'

Blinking once more, the Praetorian examined the kindly old face in front of him.

'Barates,' he said quietly, as if they hadn't seen each other in months.

'That's right, sir. How are you?'

'Been better,' the Praetorian said bitterly. 'Need a drink.'

'Would you give us a little of your time later? We need some advice. Midday perhaps. If you take a seat at the inn I can bring a barrel across.'

Though grateful for the intervention, Cassius thought Barates had made a mistake. By giving in, they had thrown away their only element of leverage. On the other hand, if the man stayed relatively amenable, they could at least open some kind of dialogue.

Barates was nodding his head rapidly, as if somehow to speed up the Praetorian's assent. The giant cast his eyes across the assembled troops. It seemed that he was at last registering the fact that some semblance of order had been restored to the garrison.

'I can spare a few minutes, I suppose.' He looked at Cassius. 'Just be quick with that wine, boy.'

The Praetorian turned and walked away.

Before he could stop himself, Cassius replied. He regretted it instantly, and knew he had made a catastrophic mistake.

'Centurion.'

There were sharp intakes of breath from a dozen legionaries. Barates and Strabo turned to face Cassius, similarly incredulous.

The Praetorian stopped. His right shoulder tensed, and for a moment it seemed he might be about to hurl the stave. Some of the legionaries moved out of the way.

Invisible choking hands tightened their grip on Cassius' throat.

The Praetorian looked back over his shoulder, the thick rolls of his neck resisting the turn of his head.

'Be quick with that wine, centurion.' He gave a lopsided grin, then continued on his way, tapping the stave on the ground.

Shoulders sagging, Cassius let out a breath and turned to face the men. Some stared at him open-mouthed, others shook their heads. Serenus dismissed his section, reminding Cassius that the entire garrison was listening.

'Same for the rest of you!' he added. 'Remove your swords, then report to section leaders.' He turned towards Strabo. 'Thanks for the support. I'm starting to understand why you were never promoted before.'

Strabo shrugged and said nothing.

'What kind of example does it set to the men when you ignore a direct order from me?'

'Some orders are best ignored.'

'Is that right?'

'It is.' Strabo pointed a finger at Cassius' face. 'And don't imagine that what just happened proves your point. If not for Barates he would have caved your head in without a second thought. How you got away with that last little effort I'll never know!'

Cassius could see no reason to continue the argument.

'I shall see you at the inn. Midday. Just keep at it with the wall until then.'

Strabo left with a disgruntled sigh.

'I do owe you my thanks,' said Cassius, clapping Barates on the shoulder. 'He's at least right about that.'

'Frankly, I'm just glad the man listened. It's unusual to find him this reasonable. We must see what we can get out of him before he gets himself in a state again.'

'Absolutely. Just give him one small barrel and make sure it's well watered down.'

Looking over at the stables, Cassius was reminded of the conversation they had started earlier. Suddenly it seemed like hours ago.

'What were you saying about Julius?'

'Ah, yes – he heard some queer noises last night.'

'Noises? Like what?'

'I couldn't really understand what he meant. Seemed to think there was a spirit or something around. They're a superstitious lot out here. He's always seeing things when we're at the crest. Never amounts to anything.'

Midday couldn't come quickly enough for Cassius. He wandered around, checking on the men, trying to look purposeful, and eventually found himself up on a firing step close to the gate, staring out at the plain.

He thought of how it might begin. At first the enemy would be little more than indistinct dots on the horizon, the merest suggestion of humanity on the move. Eventually they would clear the haze, pass the crest and descend on the fort. In the past, he had visualised the enemies of Rome as primitive barbarians; a fearsome, undisciplined mass. Despite his time in Syria, he still knew little about the Palmyrans. He wondered what the warriors would look like.

'Don't you trust your sentry?'

Dropping neatly to the ground, Cassius found Kabir's intelligent eyes upon him once more.

'Of course. Just checking.'

'An interesting morning I hear.'

'Nothing special.'

'It takes a brave man to face up to that one. The legionaries call him the Bear, don't they?'

Cassius shrugged.

'It was a minor dispute about provisions, that's all. He's agreed to meet with us at noon. He's fought out here for many years – knows the enemy well.'

'Then perhaps I should stay away.'

'Why?'

'I believe he considers us to be little better than the Palmyrans.'

'That's ridiculous. There are Syrians in half the legions of Rome. Vespasian himself was—'

'I am simply informing you of his attitude. He's not one to be trifled with, as I'm sure you are aware.'

'I want you to be there. There's much to discuss.'

'Very well, but don't blame me if things turn unpleasant.' Kabir looked up at the sky. 'Not long to go now.'

Though the sun was yet to reach its zenith, Cassius' impatience was growing with every moment. This latest revelation made it even more important to engage with the Praetorian before the wine took its toll.

'That's close enough for me,' he said, nodding skyward. 'I think we'll make a start.'

XVII

Cassius led his assorted deputies and allies towards the inn with a haste that belied his trepidation. Barates was at his side, and he knew he would have to rely heavily on the veteran once more. A few steps behind, Avso and Strabo exchanged barbed comments about the progress of their respective sections. Serenus was trying to reassure Kabir that he was welcome at the meeting.

They found the Praetorian in his usual position: back to the wall, a jug of wine on the table in front of him. The barrel Barates had fetched for him was on the floor. Dragging his eyes from the contents of the jug, the Praetorian examined the new arrivals.

Cassius and Barates approached warily and arranged chairs around the table. Avso shouldered his way past Strabo and took a seat directly to the Praetorian's right. Kabir calmly sat down next to the Thracian. Then came Strabo, Cassius and Serenus, with Barates last in line. Only the veteran was granted any form of recognition – a slight nod.

The Praetorian downed a quarter of the jug. Heads began to turn in Cassius' direction. As he was about to speak, the Praetorian aimed a thumb at Kabir.

'Who's he?'

'That's Kabir, sir,' replied Barates. 'He leads the Syrian auxiliaries. There are thirty-two of them.'

The Praetorian gave a cynical grin.

'You trust him?'

Kabir glanced across at Cassius.

'I—' The Praetorian hesitated for a moment, then put a hand to his stomach. The pang of pain he seemed to be expecting never came but he blinked several times before replying.

'I thought you wanted the benefit of *my* wisdom, not some provincial's,' he said sourly, looking around the group.

'Absolutely,' said Cassius, leaning forward. 'But Kabir and his men are essential to the defence. He deserves his place here.'

'This is my table. You are here at my invitation.'

'Of course and I am grateful for it. But let's not forget that several emperors hailed from this province.'

'Quite so, and it's been disaster after disaster ever since.'

'Well,' Cassius said, 'we could debate such matters all afternoon but I don't wish to keep you any longer than necessary. Perhaps if I outline the measures we've taken so far you can give us your thoughts.'

The Praetorian shrugged.

'What of their numbers?' he asked Barates.

'Unknown.'

'We have seventy-seven men in total,' stated Cassius.

'They probably know that,' countered the Praetorian. 'Which means they'll send three times as many at least.'

'How can we stop them?' Cassius asked.

'I doubt you can with so few.'

'Why are you still here then?' asked Avso. 'If you believe we face defeat.'

The Thracian initially seemed unperturbed by the silence that greeted his question but the anxious reaction of the others soon spread his way. Folding his arms across his chest, he leaned back in his seat, away from the vast form in front of him.

The Praetorian wiped sweat from his forehead and flicked it on to the floor inches from Avso's leg. Grinning, he turned towards him and lifted the jug of wine like a trophy.

'Fair enough,' said Avso.

The Praetorian took another swig and let the wine run down his throat before lowering the jug.

'I suppose there are a few things you might try,' he said.

Cassius spotted Simo, peering around the inn wall. Cassius gestured towards the jug, then towards the well. Simo got the message and hurried away.

'You've reinforced the gate I expect.'

Answered by several nods, the Praetorian continued.

'Maybe just leave it as normal – encourage them to strike there. They'll get through in no time but at least that way you can have a couple of surprises waiting for them.'

'Such as?' Cassius asked, planting his elbows on the table.

The Praetorian was warming to his task and seemed almost to be enjoying the attention.

'There are some carts around here somewhere, aren't there? You can use them as barricades behind the gate. Create a killing area. Give them enough space to get in but make your secondary line as strong as possible. The barriers must be arranged so that your men can strike but remain protected. With so few, you must ensure you hold the position as long as possible. If that fails, fall back to the barracks.'

'What if they have cavalry?' Cassius asked.

The Praetorian held up a hand and nodded at the barrel of wine. Avso swiftly filled the jug. As he did so, the Praetorian clasped his stomach once more. Cassius and the others tried not to stare but there was something morbidly fascinating about the routine of teeth-grinding and eye-rolling.

Thankfully, Simo then arrived with the water and the others drank it down in unison while the Praetorian recovered himself.

'What were we—'

'Cavalry,' said Barates softly.

'Unlikely. I suppose they might use them to smash a hole. Of more concern will be the horse archers. There are none better. They'll keep your heads down while the infantry ram the gate.'

The Praetorian looked from face to face.

'There's not much you can do about that.'

'And if we do face cavalry?' asked Cassius.

'Best drop your sword. You'll need both hands to pray.'

Do we have any caltrops?' Avso asked.

'No,' said Barates.

'We can make some,' suggested Serenus.

'It'll take time to get the forge going,' Barates replied.

'Not necessary,' said Serenus. 'Use a heavy hammer and knock three pairs of nails together. They'll do the job.'

'Might unseat a few,' agreed the Praetorian. 'But even then, whatever armour you have will be no match for theirs.'

Strabo was listening keenly. The Praetorian's presence was enough to intimidate even him into compliant subordination.

'Swords will make a dent but not much more. There is—'

The Praetorian stopped again and stared down into his wine. After a while, Cassius and the others began to wonder if he would speak again. Then he looked up.

'There is . . . I heard, once, of a tactic that might be of use. If the cavalry do get inside and you can get them off their horses – that's the time to release some of your men. Armour is all very well while you're on horseback, but in the hand-to-hand stuff it leaves you blind.'

The Praetorian tapped the stave he had left propped up against the wall.

'Men armed with these could do some damage.'

Cassius nodded gratefully. At last they had the semblance of a strategy.

The Praetorian slurped noisily at the wine, then sat back against the wall.

'Having said all that, they'll probably come in over the back wall now. Unpredictable bunch out here,' he added with a provocative glance at Kabir. 'Had to wait for us to come along to understand organised warfare.'

The Syrian ignored him.

'Perhaps we should leave you to it,' said Cassius. Simo collected their mugs as they stood.

'How many men do you have?'

The Praetorian had obviously forgotten Cassius' earlier remark.

'With the auxiliaries, almost a century's worth.'

'*Almost* a century, eh? Then I think you have wasted my time. You'll be better off jumping on the nearest camel and not sparing it until the walls of Antioch are in sight.'

'And yet you choose to remain?' asked Avso. He was the only one of them still sitting.

'As long as the red stuff lasts,' answered the Praetorian.

'And you'll just give up? Allow yourself to be killed or taken prisoner?'

Serenus and Strabo readied themselves to drag Avso away if it became necessary. The Praetorian finally looked sideways at his questioner.

'They won't mess with me. I'll just stay in here. The bastards don't even drink!'

Chuckling, the Praetorian looked on as Avso finally got to his feet and followed the others.

'Cheers!' he said, holding the jug aloft. 'And don't go stealing my wine again, boy!'

Strabo looked warily at Cassius, obviously fearing another reaction.

'Relax, guard officer,' Cassius said as they walked away. 'I have what I wanted.'

'Glad to hear it,' Strabo replied gruffly before turning his attention to Avso. 'You too have a death wish, I see.'

'Relax, guard officer,' said Avso in a poor imitation of Cassius. 'He is but a man. A large one admittedly, but a man nonetheless.'

'And you would take him on, I suppose?' replied Strabo with a sneer. 'You were quick enough to play barkeeper!'

'That'll do,' said Cassius sharply, coming to a halt at the corner of the square. 'Gentlemen, I hope our visit to the inn has given you time to regain some energy. There is yet more work to do.'

Drilling would have to wait. Cassius and his deputies worked out a new plan of action and each section was deployed accordingly.

Serenus and his men were in the workshop, where there was a plentiful supply of large nails. Hammered together in the right manner, the makeshift caltrops would, however they were dropped, offer up a sharp point ready to impale itself in a passing hoof.

Strabo's men had finished repairing the breach and would now assist Barates' section with the barricades. The four carts had been hauled over to the open area behind the gate. When turned on their sides, the vehicles plus the gate would form a five-sided enclosure: the Praetorian's killing area.

Strabo suggested removing one in every three planks from the base of the carts, allowing the defenders to strike out at the enemy. The wood removed (along with that recovered from the marketplace) would be used to reinforce any vulnerable points.

Avso had instructed his carpenters to undo their work on the gate. His section was now outside the fort, filling barrels with sand using entrenching tools. The sand would then be moved inside and used to steady the cart wall. As they toiled away under the burning sun, the men sang bawdy songs about the sexual exploits of their beloved Caesar. Some chose to work completely naked but sweat was soon dripping off them all, so Avso tasked Julius with supplying water. Happy that all were settled to the task, the Thracian too was now busy digging, alongside Crispus and Flavian.

It seemed that his recent efforts were finally telling on Barates. The veteran sat on a barrel in the shade of the dwellings as the others laboured, occasionally passing comment or making a suggestion. He was not the only one observing.

Standing on the roof directly above him were Cassius and Kabir. Though he was grateful for the Praetorian's contributions, Cassius refused to believe that the Syrian and his men would not be of crucial importance. He had taken Serenus aside at the officers' quarters, seeking his advice on how to deploy the auxiliaries.

'Ask their leader,' had been the straightforward reply and Cassius had done just that. Now, having followed Kabir up to the dwelling roof, he watched the Syrian prowl back and forth, surveying the scene below.

'Well?'

Kabir pointed across at the dwelling opposite, on the other side of the street.

'I can divide my men: half on this side, half over there. It's a good position. Assuming the Palmyrans come through the gate.'

'You think they will?'

'I may be Syrian but I know little more of their tactics than you. My people have no experience of knocking down walls and taking buildings. In times of peace it is rare for us even to stay in the same place for more than a few months. We do not see the value of wood and stone as you do.'

'You see the value of water, though, I presume?' said Cassius, pointing towards the well.

'Indeed.' Kabir wandered to the edge of the roof and tapped the low surround.

'It is a shame this isn't higher. Archers will have no trouble dropping a few arrows on our heads once they know we're here.'

'Maybe we can give you a bit more protection. Some timber perhaps.'

'No. Then they will know we are here straight away. I suggest we start on the ground; remain mobile. If we avoid using the slings, any Palmyran that sees us will assume we are common auxiliaries. If they do come through the gate we can move up here. A hail of well-aimed lead might help this "killing area" become a reality.'

'Quite.'

'Yarak can take one half, I'll take the other. Sixteen on each side. I hope this roof will take our weight.'

Kabir stamped down on the brick, taking out a section with his heel. Below was a frame of alarmingly thin planks on which the clay had been set. The Syrian shrugged.

The heat up on the roof was stifling and intense. Cassius could feel the skin on his forearms burning.

'Shall we head back down?' he said, moving towards the ladder. 'I must get out of this damned sun.'

He was on the third rung before he realised what he'd said.

'I apologise.'

Kabir looked down at him gravely.

'It's fortunate that we're alone. Some of my men have a fair

147

grasp of Latin and they are all less forgiving of foreign attitudes than I.'

Kabir pointed at Cassius' mouth.

'Yarak would have your tongue for that.'

Cassius was unsure how to respond. He thought he saw a smile coming.

'Surely you exaggerate,' he said.

The smile never arrived but the green eyes shone as Kabir nodded an acknowledgement.

'Perhaps I do. His Latin is poor at best.'

Cassius could not help laughing.

Kabir waved him downward, finally breaking into a grin.

'Come on, you're right. It is hot.'

They went their separate ways. With not a single legionary anywhere near the barracks, Cassius was satisfied that all were constructively engaged. He wandered over to the aid post.

It was a small room: fifteen feet wide, ten deep. On the right side were three beds, no more than holey straw mattresses supported by rickety frames. On the left were three rectangular impressions left on the sandy floor where other beds had been removed. Lined up against the far wall were four large wooden chests. The first three had been opened. Inside were bandages and splints; probes, hooks and blades; even vials containing medicinal liquids.

The fourth chest was shut and Simo sat on top of it, for once not busying himself with some practical labour, but reading intently from a thick collection of papyrus pages bound by twine. The Gaul was so engrossed that he didn't notice Cassius standing in the doorway.

'Wish I had time for some light reading.'

Simo looked up with a start and dropped the book.

'Sir, my apologies,' he mumbled, recovering the tome and dusting it down.

'Are not necessary,' Cassius said as he entered, turning his nose up at the close, musty air.

'What do you have there?'

'A medical manual, sir. A surgeon must have been stationed here at some point.'

Cassius took the book from Simo and examined the first page. The Greek text was fluid and clear, the work of an expert scribe.

'Nice copy. Ah yes, Dioscorides. One of my teachers was always going on about him. Greek fellow that travelled with Nero. Made a great list of plants and minerals, their medical properties and how to make use of them.'

Simo looked across at the other chests.

'There are a host of treatments, sir. Though I fear some might be past their best.'

'Well, you might be able to make some use of it, but a good supply of water and bandages should be your priority.'

'Yes, sir.' Simo took the book back from Cassius and laid it on top of the chest.

'Best see what you can do about getting more beds in here. We might need them all at some point. Is there anything else you can think of?'

'Nothing I can't attend to myself, sir.'

'Very well. I'll leave you to it then.'

Just as Cassius turned to leave, he saw a small wooden model of a chariot on another of the chests. He picked it up.

'Where did this come from?'

'A keepsake of mine, sir. My nephew made it for me. He loves the races.'

'You have relations back in Antioch?'

'I do, sir.'

'I thought Trimalchio chose you to accompany me because you had no family.'

'I believe my master meant that I had no wife or children of my own.'

'Ah. I see.'

Cassius couldn't think of anything else to say to that. He handed back the chariot.

'But my father lives still,' Simo continued. 'And I have a brother. He and his wife have four children.'

Simo turned the chariot over in his hand.

'You must miss them,' Cassius said.

'I do, sir. Might I ask – do you come from a large family?'

'Three sisters, all older than me.'

Simo smiled.

'They looked after you I expect.'

'They did. Still would given the chance. If we could get the three of them over here, it might be enough to frighten off the Palmyrans.'

Simo smiled again and Cassius thought of the day he left Ravenna. Though two of his sisters were now married, the whole family had gathered to spend some time with him before he left for training. Privately he knew none of them agreed with his father's decision, but there was never any question of anyone trying to change his mind.

In the event, Cassius had left a day early, just before dawn, leaving a note to explain why. It would have been too much for him. Their tears would have become his, and he would have felt even more lost; even more unable to face the challenges ahead.

Helena, Claudia and Domitia had understood. He knew that from the letters sent before he departed for Syria. When he was alone, he would let himself think of them, though he was careful not to get lost in those thoughts. And when he was not alone, he forced himself to push such reflections away; to concentrate on the present and keep himself busy. He was getting quite good at it.

'Well, I better be off.'

As Cassius turned to leave, a last sight of the medical manual sparked an idea.

'One more thing, Simo. When you have a moment, take another look at that book, would you? See what old Dioscorides has to say about long-lasting and painful afflictions of the gut.'

XVIII

The javelin arced elegantly through the air and was just beginning to drop when the tip thudded into a wooden target on the
side of the granary. Three other javelins, Strabo's errant previous
efforts, made a neat triangle around the fourth.

'Ha!' exclaimed the Sicilian, standing in the middle of the
square with the rest of his section. 'The old skills are still there!
Pull them out, someone. Then you can all have a go.'

Still admiring his handiwork, Strabo didn't notice Cassius come
up behind him.

'Very impressive, guard officer.'

'Perhaps you'll take your turn in a moment,' Strabo said over
his shoulder. 'Show us lowly ranks how it's done.'

'Perhaps.'

In truth, Cassius would have been far happier wielding the
javelin than the sword. He had been rated as average during
training and resolved to have a go if time allowed.

A more pressing concern were the fourth and fifth sections;
they had worked all through the afternoon shifting sand and were
in dire need of refreshment.

'Get some food and water out, would you,' he told Strabo, who
nodded and indicated for the next of his men to have a throw.

Cassius made his way down the street to where Serenus and
Barates stood by one of the overturned carts. Two of the vehicles now lay on their side with one end almost touching the wall,
just outside the gatehouse towers. The other two lay next to them,
arranged at an angle so as to meet in the middle of the street.

'Looks solid enough,' Cassius said.

'They will not pass easily, that much is certain,' said Barates, smacking the side of the cart. It was now part of a seven-foot wooden wall. The wheels and axles had all been removed and now formed props at the base of the barricades. Piles of sand a foot high stabilised the whole arrangement. Where the carts met each other, criss-crossing planks barred the way. Only the space between the two central carts had been left open – a four-foot access gap. A nearby stack of wood ensured that it could be plugged swiftly.

'Here come Avso's lot,' added Barates, scratching at his head.

With the Thracian and Flavian in the lead, the diggers filed in through the gate with the drooping heads and shuffling gait of the truly exhausted. Though the sun was low in the sky, most still shone with sweat, brushing sand off their arms as they walked. Only Crispus remained outside; he had volunteered to keep watch while the rest of the garrison ate.

'Well done. Good day's work. Excellent effort.'

Cassius repeated similar phrases as each of the men passed. Only when they were all on their way did he, Barates and Serenus follow. The weary veteran and the afflicted legionary walked slowly and by the time the three of them neared the end of the street, the others had all reached the granary.

There was a sudden flash of movement in the square. A figure stumbled from right to left, propelled by some unseen force, then crashed heavily to the ground. Cassius recognised the man from the second section. He lay sideways on the ground, clutching his shoulder.

The Praetorian staggered into view. He was wearing one boot and could barely maintain a straight line. He was carrying a javelin.

Cassius, Barates and Serenus looked on as the rest of the garrison prepared to take evasive action. The Praetorian stabbed the javelin down, cracking a tile, and shifted his grip back to a throwing position. Some of the men had already found cover. Others didn't dare turn their backs whilst the deadly projectile remained in his grip.

'Teach you to come in my inn!' he bellowed at the legionary, who was being helped away. Then his gaze came to rest on Strabo, who was standing behind the table he had been loading with food. ''Joying your dinner?'

Cassius, Barates and Serenus moved towards the dwellings to their left.

'This could get out of hand,' said Cassius.

'I fear it already has,' replied Barates.

Avso had not hurried away like the others. He was coolly backing towards the granary, one hand on his sword, eyes trained on the Praetorian.

'There's plenty to go round,' announced Strabo with a valiant attempt at warmth. 'Just tell me what you'd like and I'll get it for you.'

With a grunt, the Praetorian retracted his arm, then thrust it forward with startling speed, launching the javelin across the square.

Strabo flung himself to one side. The javelin shattered an amphora, narrowly missed his feet, then slid harmlessly to a halt between two retreating legionaries.

The Praetorian, still hunched over from the effort, tried to stand up straight. Holding his arms out to steady himself, he stared up at the darkening sky for a moment, mouth hanging open. Then he put a hand to his head and turned round. Pointing at the barracks doorway, he lurched back across the square with surprising haste. Tripping as he stepped inside, he bounced off a wall and disappeared from view.

'Thank the gods he missed,' said Barates as he, Cassius and Serenus emerged from the shadows.

The Praetorian's progress through the barracks was punctuated by oaths and impacts until he was finally heard to thump down on to his bed.

Strabo stood and dusted himself down, as did the legionary who had been thrown to the ground. His friends crowded round to investigate what turned out to be no more than a few scratches and scrapes. By the time Cassius and the others reached the Sicilian, he was already talking to Avso.

'You all right?' Cassius asked.

'I'll live,' said Strabo, pouring himself a generous measure of wine. He placed the bottle next to the broken amphora with a look of distaste. It had contained fish sauce and the pungent aroma was already spreading.

Avso cleared his throat, then spoke.

'Though I see he's reluctant to talk of it, the guard officer and I agree on something for once.' Despite the sharp glance he received from Strabo, the Thracian continued. 'We should wait until the Bear is asleep – then cut his throat.'

'You can't mean that!' said Barates.

'And what if that javelin had come your way, old man?' countered the Sicilian. 'You'd have been stuck like a pig!'

'The man is drunk. Haven't you ever thrown your weight around after a few too many?'

Strabo scowled.

'Unfortunately for us, my weight is not the same as his. It'll take half the garrison to hold him down, and though you don't seem to have noticed, we have other matters to concern us.'

Avso spoke up again: 'Mars knows we'd all love to have him on our side but right now he's more likely to kill one of us than the enemy. How can we man the walls with him rampaging around behind us?'

Barates shook his head in disbelief.

'I understand your concern,' said Cassius, ushering the section leaders away from the men. 'Really. But I cannot sanction such an act.'

'It's not something any of us would wish for,' Strabo said. 'But he is a danger to each and every man here.'

'I'll talk to him when he wakes,' said Barates. 'Make him see reason.'

'Oh well, problem solved then! What are we worrying for?'

Strabo finished off his wine.

Cassius decided to bring the discussion to an end.

'Unfortunately, gentlemen, this is not the Senate. I hold the senior rank here and I say no. The Praetorian may have a part to play yet.'

'Oh I'm sure of it,' said Strabo. He slammed his cup down, flattened his palms out on the table and took a deep breath.

'Right,' he said loudly, looking up at the legionaries. 'Show's over. Come and get it.'

Avso leaned in close to Cassius' face.

'You'd best deal with him, centurion,' he said quietly, tapping his dagger. 'Or I'll do it my way.'

'Have you no honour?' asked Barates.

'A little,' replied the Thracian, turning towards the veteran, 'but I've a good deal more sense. And what entitles you to question me, Grandpa? You're a great respecter of rank for one who has spent so long in the army without attaining any.'

Avso walked away.

'Ignore him,' Cassius told Barates. 'Serenus, what do you think?'

Serenus ran a hand through his spiky hair, then rubbed his neck.

'It would be nothing short of murder. But it may be necessary for the greater good. The morale of the men is fragile enough; they don't need an additional burden.'

Cassius winced at his words, not least because they made sense.

'That man is a hero of Rome,' said Barates solemnly.

'Was,' corrected Serenus.

'If we could just get him to fight with us,' said Cassius, gritting his teeth in frustration.

'With respect,' said Serenus, 'I think your efforts might be better employed in other directions. What Strabo and Avso suggest may seem extreme but they have the interests of the garrison at heart.'

'Their only interest is in saving their own skin,' observed Barates.

'That is the one interest we all share,' replied Serenus.

As he too left, Cassius and Barates shook their heads.

'I should be going,' Barates said. 'Antonius will be back later but he is to relieve me again around midnight. Make sure he remembers, would you, he's a little unreliable at times.'

'Of course.'

'Julius can stay here tonight. I can handle one of the beasts.'

Barates was carrying a leather satchel, which he now filled with two canteens of water and enough food to see him through his shift. He grimaced as the weight tugged at his shoulder.

'You've barely stopped these last few days,' said Cassius. 'You look worn out.'

'Just keep an eye on this lot. That will help me rest easy.'

Barates placed a firm hand on Cassius' arm and looked up at him.

'Especially Avso and Strabo. Don't let them do anything stupid.'

'I won't.'

'Tomorrow then.'

'Tomorrow.'

Two hours later, Cassius exited the officers' quarters to find the square dark and empty. A rectangle of light from the barracks cut into the gloom, just as the harsh voices of the off-duty soldiers split the silent desert night. Despite the day's endeavours, Cassius knew it would be a while before they sought rest. Strabo had asked to distribute an extra wine ration – a bottle between three men – and Cassius had readily acceded. The legionaries had worked hard to a man; they deserved a few hours off.

There had been no further trouble with the Praetorian. Crispus had called in with the news that he was snoring away and that they had placed a full water jug in front of his door to warn them if he stirred.

Simo had just returned from the aid post. He had found a recipe in the book to deal with ailments of the gut. Though he couldn't lay his hands on all the ingredients, he was working on the preparation and hoped it would at least approximate the effects of Dioscorides' concoction.

Arriving at the gatehouse, Cassius could see no sign of Avso or Flavian.

'Avso?'

His voice was seemingly magnified by the quiet.

'Up here.'

Wishing he'd brought a lamp along, Cassius entered the right-hand tower. Feeling his way with outstretched hands, he located the ladder and hoisted himself upward. He was soon at the top, gazing at the moon and myriad stars. In the middle of the walkway was the unmistakable bulk of Flavian. He was kneeling down, staring out at the desert. Avso was almost hidden behind him.

'Over here.'

Cassius crawled past Flavian and took up position next to Avso, wiping dust from his hands. He looked to the east. Directly in front of the fort, about a hundred yards away, was a dot of light bobbing up and down, seemingly suspended in mid-air.

'Ah, Antonius. I was hoping to see him.'

'Look towards the horizon,' Avso said impatiently. 'Just to the south.'

Close to where the black plain met the grey sky was a smudge of orange. At that distance it was too large to be a single light.

'What do you make of it?' Cassius asked.

'What do *you* make of it?' retorted Avso coldly.

'A caravan perhaps. Or a column.'

'Obviously. The question is: are they headed our way?'

'Can't see yet,' added Flavian.

'Perhaps Antonius can tell us,' said Cassius, now able to make out the lolloping movements of the camel. He stood up.

'Are we not following military routine then?' asked Avso.

'What's that?'

'The watchword. What if that's the Palmyrans out there? They're known for trying a trick or two.'

'Ah. Of course. Go ahead.'

With an exaggerated sigh, Avso sat up higher on his knees. The three of them looked down, listening to the scuffing steps of the camel as it neared the gate.

'Who's there?' Avso shouted.

'Antonius,' came the tired reply. 'Tide of the Tiber.'

'Approach.'

Berating himself for his stupidity, Cassius realised that not only did he not know or recognise Antonius' voice, he had no idea what the man looked like.

Avso and Flavian got to their feet and hurried towards the right-hand tower. Cassius took the left and descended the ladder as swiftly as he dared. By the time he reached the gate, one side of the door was already ajar and the others were outside. As he passed under the gatehouse, Flavian pulled the other door open.

Avso had disappeared into the darkness but soon re-emerged, holding the camel by its reins. He stopped and took Antonius' lamp as he dismounted. In a moment, four faces were illuminated by its pale, yellow glow.

Now that he saw him, Cassius realised he did know Antonius. He was about thirty years old, with a chubby face that didn't seem to match his muscular physique.

'Well, what did you see?'

'Nothing good. I first saw the lights about three hours ago. Barates agrees that it's a column of some size. If it's the Palmyrans pushing on from Anasartha, that's the direction they'll come from.'

'Are they still moving?'

'We don't think so. Probably made camp for the night. If Barates thinks they're approaching, he'll light the signal fire.'

'Anything else?'

'No.'

'No, sir,' said Cassius.

'Sorry. Sir.'

'Stable the camel, fetch yourself some food, then get your head down. I need you out there again at midnight.'

'Why me again, sir?'

'I hear you have excellent eyes. Count yourself lucky you haven't been digging all day.'

'Don't forget this stinking thing,' said Avso, throwing Antonius the reins. As the sentry led the camel towards the gate, Cassius looked east. Down at ground level, the lights were obscured by the crest. A light breeze pushed his tunic against his skin and sent a chill down his back.

'Well?' said Avso. 'What now?'

Though he couldn't see it, Cassius could picture the long, sneering face and he purposefully took his time replying.

'You two can return to the gatehouse. Wake me if the signal fire is lit.'

'That's all?'

'For the moment,' said Cassius, turning round. 'Yes.'

'You mean to place our fate in the hands of a single man? A decrepit old fool who should have retired before you were born?'

'You're forgetting our able sentries,' said Cassius calmly, walking between the two of them towards the gate. 'Who will remain on duty until dawn.'

Flavian grunted and kicked the ground. Avso spoke up just as Cassius reached the gate.

'Centurion. Shouldn't we man the walls? They might attack under cover of dark.'

Cassius stopped; Avso's use of his title suggested genuine concern.

'There's no point in causing alarm without good reason. Nor do I wish to deny the men a night's sleep when there's no guarantee of any more. We can be ready quickly should the need arise. Still, perhaps some additional eyes wouldn't go amiss. Give it a couple of hours then raise two of your section to man the gatehouse. You two can patrol the perimeter. Don't stray too far. And don't forget Antonius – wake him if he forgets his shift.'

Avso and Flavian, the latter still grumbling, made their way back towards the gate.

Cassius found Strabo and Serenus in the first room of the barrack block, along with most of the men. The legionaries had crowded into every corner to observe a game of dice. There was still a little wine left, plenty of laughter and banter, but no suggestion of excess.

Serenus followed him outside as soon as his face appeared at the doorway. Strabo arrived a few moments later. There was no mistaking the apprehension in their faces as he related the news.

'Keep it to yourselves for now. We'll see how things look in the morning. And try to keep the evening's entertainment to a minimum, would you? We need them well rested.'

Strabo nodded vacantly, his earlier anger and habitual sarcasm replaced by a reflective calm. He returned to the barracks without a word.

'How are you feeling now?' Cassius asked Serenus.

'Better. Well, I was until I heard that.'

'It may turn out to be nothing.'

'Perhaps. Caravans have been sighted before.'

'Quite.'

'Try to get some sleep yourself,' said Serenus.

'I will. By the way, I have a question for you. Tell me about Barates. How is it that one so committed never made it to optio or centurion?'

'Joined up late. I believe he was almost forty. His wife and children were killed – a fire in Rome as I recall. Like a good many others, he sought refuge in army life. Never set foot in the capital again. Goodnight, centurion.'

'Goodnight.'

With that, Serenus returned inside. Cassius cast a last gaze around the compound then hurried back to the officers' quarters. Shutting the door behind him, he found Simo in the bedroom, for once attending to his own belongings. He had located another small chest and was neatly folding his few items of clothing and placing them inside.

'Another long day, sir,' said Simo as Cassius headed for his bed.

'Aren't they all.' Cassius removed his sword belt and his main belt, then lowered both to the floor.

'There are lights on the horizon, Simo.'

The Gaul stopped what he was doing and turned round.

'The enemy?'

'We're not sure.'

Simo returned to his work while he absorbed this news. Cassius lumped down on the bed, then shifted back so he could lean against the wall. He spied a few sheets of papyrus on top of Simo's bed.

'What's that you have there?'

'Just some poetry, sir.'

'Really? Who?'

'Vergilius, sir.'

'Ah,' said Cassius after a long yawn. 'The pastorals?'

'That's right, sir.'

'Read me something. I should like to hear of flowers and green things amidst all this heat and dust.'

'I could not, sir,' Simo said, reddening and again busying himself with his clothes. 'Not with an orator such as yourself for an audience.'

'Hah, I'm fit only for barking orders these days, Simo. I doubt I could manage a verse without stumbling over my words.'

Simo was still looking down, intent on his folding.

'Well, I shan't force you. Another time perhaps.'

Simo nodded gratefully.

'Do you think it is the Palmyrans out there, sir?'

Cassius shrugged.

'It's impossible to say.'

'Then we may be spared yet.'

'We may, Simo. We may.'

XIX

That night, Cassius was assailed by a series of vivid, disquieting dreams.

Endless waves of spectral figures descending on the fort. Glittering blades. Torn flesh. The chaos and carnage of battle.

Disorientated and struck by a sudden thirst, he awoke lying on his side, staring at the wall. Grimacing at the bitter taste in his mouth, he rolled over to find he could see across the bedroom. The dark of night had gone. Just as he was about to fall back into sleep, he spied a familiar figure in the doorway.

'Sir, you better come quickly,' said Simo.

'What is it?'

'Something terrible has happened.'

Cassius got up and pulled his tunic on over his head. He was still buckling his belt as he walked past Simo to the main door.

In the half-light of dawn, a small knot of men had gathered next to the granary. Strabo stood in the middle of the square, his hand pressed against his forehead.

'Well?' demanded Cassius as he neared him.

Strabo simply pointed towards the men. Some of the legionaries saw Cassius coming and moved out of his way. He caught sight of something on the ground; it looked like a pile of sheets or empty sacks. It was the glassy-eyed shock on the faces of the legionaries that he registered next, but when he looked down at the shape again, all was suddenly clear.

Someone had placed a blanket over a body. A small, curled-up body with a patch of wet red sand next to it. Cassius peered over the blanket and saw the face.

It was Barates. His throat had been cut.

Fighting a surge of nausea, Cassius swallowed, trying not to gag as he turned away. He belatedly realised that Strabo had just told him something.

'Say that again.'

'Crispus found him. Just now. His throat's been slashed, probably—'

'Yes. Yes, I see that.'

Cassius looked at the others, all still staring at the body. He bent down and pulled the blanket over Barates' head.

'Crispus, stay here. You others, back to the barracks.'

Not realising that he had spoken so softly that no one had heard him, Cassius was surprised to find no one had moved.

'Go on then!' he barked.

'Go! Move!' added Strabo, shoving several legionaries back across the square. Reluctantly, they edged away.

Cassius gazed down at the mass of footprints in the strip of sand between the tiled square and the granary wall.

'There's nothing to be found there,' observed Strabo. 'Not now anyway.' He circled the body and knelt down beside the head. Lifting the blanket, he examined the wound.

'It was just a few moments ago you say?' asked Cassius.

'Yes,' answered Crispus. 'I had just woken and been to the latrine. I took a look out of the door and saw . . . this.'

'There was no one else in sight?'

'Not a man, sir. I fetched the guard officer at once.'

'The blood has dried,' said Strabo. 'He's been dead several hours.'

Cassius looked over at the gatehouse.

'He intended to return from the crest around midnight. Avso or one of the sentries must have seen him. Fetch them, Crispus. Quickly.'

163

The legionary hurried away.

As Strabo checked the rest of the body, Cassius got down on his knees and peered under the granary. There was no sign of an abandoned weapon or any other clue.

'He's not injured anywhere else,' said Strabo as they both stood. 'It was certainly a knife. A precise cut.'

'Who though?' It seemed inconceivable that the kindly veteran had even a single enemy within the camp.

'I cannot imagine. The man deserved better,' Strabo said bitterly. 'This is an ignoble death.'

Cassius now found that shock was turning to confusion, aware already that there would be little time for grief. This inexplicable act of violence was the last thing he'd expected. As if the threat hanging over the garrison and the added complication of the Praetorian were not enough, this new horror seemed almost unreal.

The Syrians had realised something was going on; Yarak and another man now stood at the corner of the granary, watching. Strabo was all set to move them off when they abruptly left of their own accord.

Attention then switched to the four figures walking up the street, Crispus and Avso in the lead. Behind them were the legionaries Avso had selected to man the gatehouse.

'What are their names?' Cassius asked Strabo.

'Statius and Gemellus. Originally from the Fourth Legion like Avso and Flavian. Decent enough lads though.'

The grim expression fixed on Avso's lean face barely changed as he and the others stopped and gazed down at the body.

'What do you make of that?' asked Strabo levelly.

Avso said nothing. Crispus spoke up.

'Gemellus and Statius talked to Barates two or three hours after midnight.'

'Is that so?' asked Cassius, looking at Statius, the older of the two.

'Yes, sir. Antonius had gone out on time and Barates returned in the early hours. He said there was no change in the position of the lights and went on his way to the stables.'

'He got that far,' added Crispus. 'His camel's in there.'

'Nothing else?' asked Strabo.

Statius and Gemellus looked at each other, then shook their heads. Attention turned to Avso.

'Did *you* observe his return?' asked Cassius.

'No. I was patrolling the perimeter, walking squares about a hundred yards out. I called in at the gatehouse a few times. These two told me Barates was back.'

'You saw nothing else. Nothing unusual?'

'No,' answered Avso quickly, growing ever more defensive. 'I would have told you.'

'And where's Flavian?' enquired Strabo.

'The barracks I expect,' said Avso with a scowl. 'He was of little use to me. Kept falling over his feet and complaining, so I sent him inside.'

'When?' asked Cassius.

'Three or four hours before dawn I think.'

'Before or after Barates' return?' asked Strabo.

Avso hesitated, clearly angry that he had to endure such questioning.

'Around the same time,' he said, his words quiet and deliberate.

'Go and get him,' ordered Strabo.

'I'm not your lackey,' retorted Avso. 'Fetch him yourself.'

The Thracian turned to Cassius.

'And why I am being interrogated so? Hasn't it occurred to you that this may be the work of some scout or spy who managed to get over the wall?'

'Assuming you were doing your job,' Strabo said, 'that seems unlikely.'

'Less likely than Flavian or me being responsible?' demanded Avso.

Strabo shrugged. It seemed to Cassius that he was more interested in annoying his rival than extracting useful information from him.

'Of course not,' Cassius said. 'But we must establish the order of events.'

'Then again,' said Strabo, 'you were the one talking about slitting throats yesterday.'

This was enough for Avso, who barged Gemellus to one side and would have gone for Strabo had Cassius and Crispus not blocked his way. Cassius held a hand up to Avso's chest.

'Ignore him. Just fetch Flavian, would you? Then we can clear this up.'

'He goes too far,' said Avso through gritted teeth.

'I agree. Please.'

With one last malevolent stare, Avso started towards the barracks. Cassius spun round to face the Sicilian, unable to contain his frustration any longer.

'Have you no sense? A man lies dead and you would rather look for a fight than for answers. Where is your honour, man?'

'All right,' Strabo said after a while. 'I wish only to see this murderer caught.'

Cassius ordered Statius and Gemellus back to the gatehouse. Crispus was tasked with keeping the rest of the legionaries in the barracks.

'You cannot make such baseless intimations,' Cassius told Strabo when they were alone. 'Such a matter must be investigated in the proper manner.'

The Sicilian shook his head.

'For it to happen now, of all times.'

'We must not let this distract us from the defence. Think about what still needs doing and hand out details to every section. If they finish, drill them. Keep them busy.'

Strabo gestured towards the body.

'What about—'

'I'll deal with that. Just do as I ask.'

As Strabo departed, Kabir arrived with one of his men a few yards behind. The Syrian stopped a respectful distance from the body, recited a short prayer, then raised a hand towards the rising sun.

'My condolences, centurion. I do not understand how such a

thing could happen. Amongst all here, my men and yours, he was perhaps the most liked.'

'Perhaps, but somebody did this. I'll need to question you and your men. Your camp is—'

'I have already done that.' Kabir gestured to the other Syrian. 'Nidar here is the only one with anything to report.'

'And?'

'I always post a sentry for our camp and he took his turn last night. He saw a man behaving oddly in the darkest hours – creeping round the side of the granary. He assumed he was after food or wine, though he wasn't carrying anything. After a few moments he disappeared.'

'Who was it? Did he recognise him.'

'Yes. There was a little moonlight and he is quite distinctive. A big man, with curls in his hair.'

'Flavian. You mean Flavian.'

'Yes. That's him.'

Simo and Gemellus had wrapped the corpse in a sheet then carried it over to the aid post. Cassius had watched as the small, limp form – borne easily by the two men – had disappeared from view. He found it hard to reconcile such a sight with the energy and ready warmth that had defined Barates in life. It seemed to him that this broken, lifeless body had simply materialised somehow and that the man himself had disappeared; not that they were one and the same.

Now, leaning against the desk and staring expectantly at the door of the officers' quarters, Cassius waited for Flavian and Avso. He was relieved Strabo hadn't heard what Kabir had told him, but was apprehensive about facing the legionaries alone. With an assurance from the Syrian that the information would go no further, he could at least keep his enquiries contained. The last thing he needed was the Sicilian charging around making accusations, and there was no telling how the murder might affect the rest of the men.

Avso was first in. With a wary glance at Cassius, he ushered a dishevelled Flavian inside and shut the door behind him. Flavian waited until Avso moved forward to approach the desk.

Wondering what words had passed between them, Cassius began.

'You've heard about Barates, I presume?'

Flavian nodded.

'Avso tells me you were sent inside sometime during the night. Did you see him?'

'No.'

'I've been thinking,' added Avso. 'It was sometime after that the others told me of Barates' return. Flavian wasn't—'

'The legionary can answer for himself,' Cassius said. 'You returned to the barracks immediately?'

'Yes. I was tired. No use to anyone.'

'And you didn't leave there at all?'

'No. I awoke to all the fuss. Then Avso came and fetched me.'

Cassius hesitated. Flavian was lying, that much was certain, but he was convinced Avso was also somehow involved. There was more chance of gleaning something useful without the sly Thracian in the room.

'I'd like a word with Legionary Flavian in private. There's plenty for you to be getting along with, Avso.'

If he was concerned, the Thracian did a good job of hiding it. He left silently with no more than a blank glance at his friend. Though Flavian was unarmed and there were others close by outside, Cassius was glad to have the desk between him and the burly legionary.

'I'll ask you this once more, and you must consider your answer very carefully. You are saying that you returned from patrol, saw no sign of Barates and proceeded directly to the barrack block, where you remained until you were woken. Is that correct?'

Flavian's eyes dropped to the floor for a moment. When he looked up, his expression had changed. Before he could answer, there was a sharp rap on the door.

Cassius ignored it.

'Answer me, man.'

Flavian swallowed hard and Cassius could now see something close to fear in his eyes.

'Sir!'

It was the voice of Crispus. He hammered on the door again. Cassius hurried over to the window and stuck his head out. 'What is it?'

Circumspect as ever, Crispus looked carefully round before moving in close and answering in a whisper.

'The signal fire is alight, sir. The Palmyrans are coming.'

XX

Without breaking stride, Cassius leaped up on to a firing step and threw his arms over the dusty wall. Despite Crispus' efforts, word had spread quickly and half the garrison were already there. Some were in the gatehouse, some were on the other steps; all were facing east. What they saw was a bloom of fire atop the crest and wisps of smoke drifting high into the windless sky. There was as yet no sign of the Palmyrans. The only figure in view was Antonius, riding hard back to the fort. He had covered about a third of the distance already.

The men were cursing and shouting. Cassius looked for his deputies, anxious to restore order. He had been forced to interrupt his questioning of Flavian and now saw him deep in conversation with Avso.

'Centurion!'

Serenus arrived at the wall.

'Shall we gather the men?'

'Certainly.'

Cassius jumped down and saw that the rest of the legionaries were now up and running through the gap in the carts, eager to join the others at the wall.

'But they'll all want a good look, I'm sure. We'll let them have it, then call muster.'

Strabo, who had just exited the gatehouse, spotted Cassius at once. Dodging through the throng, he hurried over, casting a suspicious glance at Avso and Flavian.

'What are your orders?' he said, almost having to shout above the noise.

Cassius looked round. The last of the men were now up on the wall and had seen what little there was to see.

'That'll do. Get them lined up in the square.'

'In kit?' queried Serenus.

'No. That can wait.'

Strabo began yelling orders. Only the most cooperative complied at once and it took a good deal of persuasion from him and Serenus to drag them all away from the wall. Cassius looked on, trying to put all thoughts of the Palmyrans out of his mind for just a little longer. Avso and Flavian drifted away with the rest of their section. Cassius knew he had missed a vital opportunity, one he might not get again.

The auxiliaries had also seen the signal fire: Kabir and several others were already up on the dwelling roof. Cassius felt his eyes upon him but he hurried after the men. The Syrian would have to wait.

He had to find out more about the night's events. Questioning the men together was hardly ideal but there was no time for anything more subtle.

Under direction from Strabo, the sections were quickly organised into five well-ordered lines facing the flagpole. Serenus and Avso stood on the barracks side, with Strabo in his favoured position close to the granary. Even this scene felt so different without Barates. Cassius looked up at the flag the veteran had raised. As usual, and as now seemed fitting, the flag hung limply in the clinging heat, the golden bull obscured by its folds.

Cassius stood a little closer to the men than normal, keen not to miss any reaction to his words.

'This is a dark day. And not only because of what we see to the east. Barates has been murdered, his throat cut.'

Cassius gestured towards the aid post.

'He lies there now. Somebody within these four walls is responsible. I intend to find out who.'

A few of the legionaries muttered curses or shook their heads.

'Think carefully about these two questions. First, did you see

171

Barates after his return from the crest? Second, did you see or hear anything else unusual during the hours of night?'

Scanning along each line in turn, Cassius noted that Flavian had positioned himself about as far away from Avso as he could.

No hands were raised. Nothing was said.

'Think,' added Strabo. 'Every one of you. Somebody knows something.'

Silence.

'Then let me ask this,' Cassius continued. 'Did any of you, for any reason, leave the barracks during the hours of night?'

More silence. One man coughed. Others looked up at a buzzard lazily circling high above the fort.

Cassius suddenly felt foolish. It bordered on the idiotic to believe that posing such questions to the entire garrison would reveal anything of use.

'Well, so be it. But mark these words: whatever our situation, the perpetrator of this crime will face the full force of Roman justice, as will any accomplice.'

'That applies to our Syrian friends too, I presume,' said a familiar voice.

Cassius immediately locked eyes with Avso, who gazed calmly back at him.

'Of course. I will spare no effort to uncover the truth.'

The Thracian's words had obviously been for the benefit of the other legionaries, designed to divert suspicion from his friend while the chance presented itself. Cassius continued.

'That issue lies in the hands of myself and my deputies. It seems that we now face attack. We are well prepared and organised. We have allies: those fighting alongside us, those coming to our aid.'

As he spoke, Cassius was struck by the change in the men before him. Fear was not absent, it was palpable – the signal fire had seen to that – but it was partnered with a fresh sense of ordered resolve.

'Equip yourselves, arm yourselves, then gather outside the barracks. Dismissed!'

The men hurried away, several bypassing the doorway and vaulting straight through the windows into the barracks.

'Crispus! Statius!'

The two legionaries reversed course.

'Statius, get yourself over to the gatehouse. You're on watch. Crispus, the third section is yours now. I don't like to lose you, but it makes sense.'

'Sir.'

Serenus and Strabo arrived.

'Well?' said the Sicilian.

'Well what?' said Cassius.

'What are we doing? What's the plan?'

'We arm ourselves, man the walls and wait.'

'And then?'

'That rather depends on our enemies, doesn't it?'

'It does,' agreed Serenus. 'Once we see our foe's numbers and how they arrange themselves, we will have to adapt and improvise. But we can establish our basic options, including the Praetorian's plan, and relate them to the men. Otherwise doubt and uncertainty will spread. I've seen it before.'

'You're right. And we must do it now,' said Cassius. 'Crispus, you find Avso. Strabo, you get Kabir. We shall meet, then address the men in front of the gate.'

As they left, Cassius headed for the stables to try to find Julius; he hadn't seen him all morning. Both horses were resting their noses on the doors, sniffing the morning air, and they shuffled noisily as he approached. With a quick pat for both animals, he continued past the empty stalls and found the remaining camels at the other end. The boy was not there.

'Julius!'

The only noise in the compound came from either the barracks or the encampment.

'Julius!'

Met again with no reply, Cassius walked briskly round the end of the granary, past the workshop and along the southern wall. He met Strabo and Kabir leaving the Syrian camp.

'Have you seen the lad?'

'No,' answered Strabo.

Cassius turned towards the granary.

'He's not in there,' added the Sicilian.

'Kabir?'

'Not since yesterday.'

'Strange.'

'Strange indeed,' replied Strabo speculatively. The man made so many underhand comments that Cassius was now hearing some second meaning in everything he said. 'Did you get anywhere with Flavian?' the Sicilian asked.

Before Cassius could reply, there was a shout from the other side of the square. Serenus, Avso and Crispus were already outside the officers' quarters. Thankful for the interruption, Cassius led the way.

Once inside, they sat round the table and Cassius reiterated the basics of the Praetorian's plan. There were interjections here and there, mainly from Serenus and Strabo, but he took care to keep things moving. When it came to the role of the Syrians, Kabir too had his say, once again impressing all with his faultless Latin and calm, logical thinking.

As soon as they turned to other eventualities, and how they might be dealt with, Serenus took the lead. He was as robust as Cassius had seen him, guiding the discussion expertly. Avso was unusually quiet, though even he made the odd contribution, as did the ever-keen Crispus. Struggling at times to grasp certain tactical intricacies, Cassius was content to give way to the others.

Later, when the noise outside suggested that most of the legionaries were kitted up and ready, Serenus clarified a few key points and brought the meeting to a close.

'My thanks,' said Cassius. 'You seem to have a natural grasp of these matters. I shall speak first to the men, but I think it would be preferable if you deliver the bulk of the briefing. Agreed?'

'By all means,' said Serenus.

Leaning back on his stool to peer round Strabo's broad back, Cassius saw sunlight sparkling on newly polished armour.

'Time to move I think.'

They filed out. Kabir left for the encampment while the section leaders began gathering their men.

Simo, sweating heavily, stalked out of the aid post.

'Apologies, sir,' he said, wiping his brow. 'I was wrapping the body. It took longer than I thought.'

'No matter,' said Cassius. 'But I will need my armour and helmet in a few minutes. See to it, would you.'

As he stood there amongst the men, his hand at rest on the hilt of his sword, Cassius' thoughts turned to the prospect of battle.

The enemy were close now; so close that they might be at the wall in a matter of hours. If so, the garrison might be overrun before nightfall. It was possible, probable even, that he might not live to see another day. The thought occupied him so wholly that he barely noticed when those around him fell silent and began to turn in one direction.

Only when a nearby legionary breathed a curse did Cassius look up. Along with every other man in the square, his gaze was drawn to the small figure that had just emerged from the temple.

Julius stared down as he walked round the well, arms hanging by his side. He was barefoot, and his unkempt hair covered most of his face. In the middle of his tunic were several large blotches of dried blood.

XXI

'We cannot stay here long,' said Bezda, surveying the bleak plain that surrounded the column. 'Not without a supply chain back to Anasartha.'

Azaf looked at the men putting the finishing touches to a wide network of awnings – essential protection for the warriors and horses. They had made good progress the previous day, and were now within striking distance of their objective. A short distance away, twenty of his swordsmen were already mounted, ready to join their leader for a scouting mission.

'Your point?' he said.

'My point,' answered Bezda gruffly, 'is that we must strike quickly.'

Azaf glanced at the crest, where the signal fire was now producing only a thin trail of smoke.

'I think it's safe to say we've lost the element of surprise.'

'Clearly. But why give them time to prepare their defences?'

Azaf didn't reply. Though he was prepared to tolerate Bezda's comments out of respect for the cavalryman's station, he would not engage in a debate about strategy until he was ready. Instead, he called out to Razir. The aged warrior was with the scouting party, holding Azaf's horse for him.

'Fetch Teyya.'

Razir passed the reins to another man and jogged away.

'What should I tell my men?' asked Bezda impatiently. Sweat shone above his mouth and on his forehead; he obviously wanted to get out of the early afternoon sun.

'Tell them they should ready themselves for an attack. Is that acceptable to you?'

Humility didn't come easily to Azaf but he needed the cavalry-man's cooperation.

'General Zabbai obviously puts great trust in your judgement,' said Bezda after a moment. 'That's good enough for me.'

Azaf nodded cordially as Bezda wiped his face and strode away.

There was no denying the truth of the cavalryman's words. With the limited supplies of water on the carts, they couldn't expect to stay longer than a day or two. The Palmyran troops could survive on remarkably little, but this was a battle and even a short engagement in the summer heat would tire them quickly. Without adequate refreshment, neither horses nor men would last long.

Zabbai wanted a swift resolution. The men too would prefer a quick assault, and with nothing else to occupy them they would soon become restless. Azaf didn't plan to keep them waiting long, but he was determined to guard against overconfidence. He would not be rushed.

Beyond the scouting party, the other warriors readied themselves.

The infantrymen had unsaddled their horses and left them in the care of the cart drivers. Each man now organised his personal equipment and weaponry. Apart from the distinctive loose trousers and red tunics, their basics differed little from the legionaries'. Most used swords of Roman manufacture, weapons either recently liberated or left over from the days when the Empire supplied the Palmyran armies.

Unlike their leader, most could still find a use for a good shield and, again, many were constructed along Roman lines, reinforced with crossbars and a central bronze boss. Others were of a type favoured in the East: thick, dried reeds, bound by leather, with a V-shaped bottom. Surprisingly tough, they resisted sword thrusts well, absorbing rather than deflecting blows. Then there were the traditional circular Palmyran shields: small, light, easy to wield.

The horse archers were removing all unnecessary clutter from their saddles. Like the cavalrymen, they used the four-horned variety, and would often secure their reins to the forward pair of short wooden poles when firing.

It was Palmyran custom to attach both bow-holder and quiver to the saddle, and before battle each man would adjust the intricate system of leather straps that kept both items in place. Reins and weaponry could easily become entangled and most archers knew from bitter experience the value of such preparation. The sheer physical difficulty of riding and firing simultaneously ensured that no detail was overlooked.

Once satisfied that their saddles were in order, they turned to their weapons. Azaf could see several men working on arrows: adjusting flights, smoothing shafts, sharpening points. Another man was restringing his bow. He needed a fellow archer to assist him; only with their combined weight could they compress the bow into the required shape.

Though Azaf had never made any attempt to master the weapon, he was well aware of its formidable capabilities. The Palmyran bows were three feet long and designed to release arrows with prodigious power. A stiffening section of horn was fixed along the archer's side and a length of ox sinew to the firing side. Stretching as the bow was drawn, the sinew would snap back to its normal size upon release, propelling a well-crafted arrow up to three hundred yards.

None of the archers wore armour, so rare was it for them to fight hand to hand. In fact, many of them wore nothing above the waist, thereby avoiding any additional encumbrances.

Whilst the archers had to ready themselves, each cavalryman was helped by an attendant. The carts containing the coats of mail had been unloaded and the attendants now laid them out on the ground, checking them over thoroughly. A missing section of mail or a tear in the leather undercoat could render the whole arrangement vulnerable.

Lying close by were some of the saddles, removed to give the horses a rest. The four-horned design was also useful for the cavalry. Leather straps attached to the end of a lance could be slipped over a rear horn, providing greater purchase and striking power. The saddles also aided the stability of the heavily armoured riders, especially the front horns, which stopped them sliding forward along the animal's neck.

Azaf knew that Bezda's men would require a good hour's notice if needed; it would take them that long to dress themselves and their horses. Bezda had also stated that they could not be expected to fight for more than half an hour or so under a bright sun.

Clad only in their tunics, the cavalrymen rode bareback, practising charges, turns and stops. They shouted and screamed and struck their mounts with canes, preparing them for the chaos and noise of combat.

Azaf watched his scouting party disperse to let Teyya and Razir through. The youth brought his horse up close.

'You have it?'

Teyya pulled aside the blanket on his lap. Beneath was the caged bird.

XXII

Cassius got to Julius just in time.

The legionaries had swiftly surrounded him. They were examining his tunic and now the lad himself was staring vacantly down at the dark bloodstains. Cassius gripped his shoulder and pointed at the officers' quarters.

'Julius, you must come with me.'

They could hardly move; the crush of faces and bodies had already closed in round them. Strabo and the other deputies seemed suddenly to have disappeared.

'You men, get back!'

'Look there – blood on his hand!' someone shouted.

'Sir, it was him. It must have been,' cried Minicius. Like the others he was now fully armed and equipped, sweating and red-faced under his helmet.

'Just wait. We must—'

A legionary took hold of the boy's other arm.

'You there!' Cassius ordered. 'Let go at once!'

There was a loud crack as the flat of a sword blade smashed into the side of the man's head. His helmet absorbed most of the blow but he staggered sideways.

'Settle down!' Strabo roared. 'That means all of you!'

He barged the man aside and stood in front of Julius, towering over him. Expecting the Sicilian to help him establish order and get the lad out of there, Cassius was dismayed to find he had no such intention. Sheathing his sword, Strabo stared at Julius as the men quietened down.

'Well. What have you to say?'

Cassius looked round once more. Avso was watching intently

from the back of the crowd. There was no sign of Serenus or Crispus.

'Well?' Strabo shouted, slapping Julius full in the face.

Cassius instinctively let go, watching in stunned silence as the boy raised a hand to his cheek.

'I know you can understand me,' said the Sicilian, grabbing his tunic at the collar. 'Say something, boy!'

As Strabo lifted his hand once again, Cassius finally galvanised himself into action.

'Guard officer!'

Strabo hesitated.

'Guard officer, get control of yourself! I will take the boy to the officers' quarters and question him there.'

The Sicilian's dark eyes seemed to have glazed over.

'I will get answers, I assure you,' said Cassius. 'I assure all of you,' he added, looking around.

A little humanity seemed to return to Strabo's face. He loosened his grip.

Julius' head remained bowed.

Cassius spun round as he felt a hand on his arm.

'Easy there,' Serenus said quietly. Crispus had appeared too and was already moving his section away.

'We are needed elsewhere,' Serenus told Strabo, his voice even and firm. 'We must address the men now, while there's time.'

Strabo didn't respond.

'Do you wish to give the order or shall I?'

Clearing his throat, the Sicilian looked at Cassius, then Julius, then back at Serenus. He scratched ostentatiously at his chin before shouting instructions:

'Assemble in sections at the gate. Move!'

The men dispersed. Cassius took hold of Julius' arm once again. The boy was shaking and a small puddle had appeared between his feet.

Cassius led him away, looking over his shoulder as Strabo and Serenus silently regarded each other for a moment. It was an incongruous sight: Serenus' slight, wasted frame dwarfed by the

Sicilian's intimidating bulk. Strabo spat nonchalantly into the dust, then strode off towards the gate. With Barates gone, Cassius now realised just how reliant he was on the cool-headed Serenus to keep Strabo's excesses in check. He would have to hope that the ailing veteran's health didn't deteriorate further.

He peered down at the boy as they walked.

'What happened, Julius? You must try to tell us something. Do you understand?'

Cassius ushered him inside the officers' quarters and sat him down on a stool.

'Fetch him some water,' he told Simo.

Cassius ran a hand over Julius' tunic, to check he wasn't concealing a weapon. When Simo gave him a cup, the boy couldn't close his fingers round it. Cassius put it on the ground.

'Julius. Look at me.'

Julius did no more than wipe a hand across his wet eyes.

'Look at me.'

This time he did, and the mixture of panic and terror Cassius saw in his face startled him.

'You must try to talk to me. Understand?'

Cassius spoke slowly.

'Understand? Nod if you do. Nod your head.'

Julius did so.

'There's something I must do. When I come back you must try to tell me what happened. The truth.'

Cassius backed up to the door and waved Simo over.

'Draw your dagger,' he said quietly.

Simo took out the small, wooden-handled blade and held it by his side.

'You have the key with you?'

'Yes, sir.'

'Keep the door locked and don't open it until I return. I don't think he'll try anything but if he does don't be afraid to use your blade.'

Simo's eyes widened at this but he soon recovered himself, whispering quizzically: 'He is the murderer, sir?'

'I don't know. That mob out there certainly think so. I'll be back soon. Don't take your eyes off him.'

Cassius found the men in good order, arranged once more in their five sections, facing the gatehouse. Lined up in front of it were Strabo, Serenus, Avso and Crispus. Kabir looked on from the dwelling rooftop.

'Quiet there!' snapped Serenus, pointing at men from his own section. Coughing hard, he turned away and pulled the cloth from his tunic.

Cassius stopped next to Strabo. It was important to convey the impression that the argument over Julius was now settled.

All the legionaries had their helmets strapped on and most were now protected by either cuirass or mail shirt. Some had even found time to add graffiti to their shield covers. Painted in white or yellow, the slogans boasted of the strength of the Third Legion, invoked the spirit of Caesar or cast insults at the Palmyrans and their queen. The narrow metal necks of a few pila could be seen, their barbed peaks a foot above the tallest man.

Strabo turned towards Cassius.

'I'm assuming we'll be allowed to prepare ourselves at some point.'

The section leaders were, like Cassius, still in their tunics and armed only with their daggers and swords.

'Of course,' he replied, glad that Strabo had calmed down. He was becoming used to the Sicilian's outbursts and ever-changing moods.

Crispus spoke up: 'Sir, Statius reports that Antonius will be here soon.'

'Good,' answered Cassius. He was about to begin his address but Crispus continued.

'He may arrive during the briefing, sir.'

'Yes?'

Then Cassius realised what he was getting at. Antonius would be in an excitable, perhaps even panicked state. Better to intercept him outside than allow him to rush in and tell the entire garrison what he'd seen.

'Stay at the gate. Fetch me when he's near.'

'Sir.'

Cassius took a moment to compose himself. His gaze fell upon a face in the second line: the man who had taken hold of Julius and been struck by Strabo.

'Your name, legionary?'

'Macrinus, sir.'

Portly and cursed with rather porcine features, Macrinus now stood stiffly, obviously expecting a reprimand.

'Report to me after briefing.'

'Yes, sir.'

'Eyes front!' shouted Strabo as other legionaries turned to look at Macrinus.

Wishing he'd brought his canteen, Cassius cleared his throat and began.

'Legionaries, I spoke in the square of the preparations we have made, the measures we have taken to defend this fort. The principles of discipline and unity have served our army well for a thousand years, and if we hold true to them, they will serve us well again.' Cassius forced himself to look squarely into the eyes of those he addressed. The words came a little easier now. 'The Emperor expects your best. As does General Navio. As do I. Time is short. Listen carefully to what you are told. Your lives, our lives, depend on it.'

He gestured to his left.

'Serenus.'

'We are few. But the centurion is quite right when he speaks of organisation and discipline. Each of you is part of a section and each section has its job. Behind me is the gate – you can see that we have removed the reinforcements. Our intention is to invite the enemy to strike here; our primary scheme centres on a frontal assault.'

Serenus was speaking quietly, taking care not to strain his voice. Cassius looked round to see if anyone had water. A legionary in the front row had a small canteen hanging from his belt.

'Their archers will be able to keep our heads down and we don't have bows or enough javelins to compete at range. We will only man the rest of the walls in the event of a ladder assault. Otherwise, only lookouts will be posted. It is crucial that they know as little of our numbers and readiness as possible. Our Syrian friends have their orders, leave them to carry them out.'

Cassius looked up at the rooftop: Kabir was listening carefully, arms crossed.

Serenus swept a hand back and forth.

'We will concentrate our numbers here, in a defensive cordon behind the carts. Second and third sections to my left, fourth and fifth to my right. First section is our reserve. Whatever comes through the gate we stop. This barrier must hold. We have to assume they will number in the hundreds. A breakthrough here will allow the rest of them to pile in, then they can bring their advantage to bear. If there is a big breach, every man should fall back to the square. We will defend the standard but our final redoubt will be the barracks.'

Serenus stopped.

'A moment,' he said after a while, his voice hoarse.

Cassius clicked a finger at the legionary with the water, who duly offered his canteen to Serenus.

'On that subject,' Strabo interjected swiftly, 'if it comes to it, we will block the barracks door and man the windows – should make for quite a little fort. Injured should report firstly to the aid post, then the barracks if they can walk.'

Serenus drank heartily, then spat several times into the dirt.

'By the way,' Strabo continued, 'when I say injury, I expect to see either a big red hole in you or something hanging off. A stubbed toe doesn't count, right Macrinus?'

The legionary did his best to ignore the laughter.

Serenus continued: 'There are three other methods the Palmyrans may use. First, ladders. Sections two to five will cover a wall each.'

A legionary in the third line raised his hand.

'Questions can wait until I've finished.'

The hand disappeared.

'Second section has the east wall, third has the south, fourth has the west, fifth has the north. We'll use the firing steps, cut them down as they come over. Again, if we're overrun, retreat will be sounded and all must return to the square. Next, these walls might look thick, but they're weak. With the archers' cover they might try to mine us out – dig under them, cause a collapse, or simply knock through. There's little we can do about that, except be ready for them.'

Serenus paused for a moment. They could hear the thud of hooves. Antonius was close.

'Last of all – fire. We have a good store of water and plenty of full barrels. But don't allow yourselves to get distracted by a few flames. There's little wind at the moment and the buildings are well spaced; if they do catch alight we may just have to let a few burn. Now, questions. You first.'

Cassius didn't hear it. He and Crispus had already slipped out of the gate to meet Antonius.

Tugging back on the reins, the sentry brought his ungainly steed to a stop. The wild-eyed camel was breathing hard, its thick pink tongue hanging out at an unlikely angle. Overbalancing as he dismounted, Antonius was helped to his feet by Crispus.

Cassius looked east, half expecting to be faced by a line of warriors charging towards Alauran, but there was nothing.

'Well? What have you seen, man?'

'Palmyrans for sure. I waited as long as I could. They stopped two or three miles east of the crest.' Antonius rubbed at a blood-shot eye with his thumb. 'Damned sand.'

'How many would you say?' asked Cassius impatiently. So much depended on Antonius' answer.

'Three, four hundred.'

Cassius winced.

Antonius nodded at the gate.

'Can I?'

Cassius moved aside and Antonius trudged off, towing the camel. Cassius turned back towards the plain. If the higher figure proved accurate, they faced odds of five to one.

'Not all warriors perhaps,' offered Crispus.

'Ever the optimist, eh?'

Crispus shrugged. As the two of them walked back towards the gate, Cassius realised he'd been stupid to allow Antonius past. He ran after him, warily rounded the camel and gripped the legionary by the shoulder.

'There's a briefing going on in there – wait here a moment. The men are sure to ask what you've seen. You tell them the enemy were too distant to count. Do not repeat the number you gave me. Is that clear?'

Antonius had been frowning as Cassius spoke and he replied with only a taciturn nod.

'I can't say I care much for your manners, legionary. You are not to repeat the number you gave to me. Is that clear?'

'Yes, sir.'

'Good. That goes for you too, Crispus. Antonius, stay here until we're done.'

Attracting considerable attention as he squeezed back through the gate, Cassius ignored the interrogative looks cast his way by Strabo, Avso and numerous others. Serenus was still speaking.

'Two or three days. That's from General Navio. We can hold out.'

'Very inspirational,' muttered Strabo.

Serenus looked back at Cassius.

'Signals?'

Cassius straightened his tunic and stepped forward.

'Most of the time, orders will come directly from your section leaders but we will use the tuba.'

Minicius was just a few paces away, having swapped with another man in order to join the first section. Cassius pointed at him.

'Our signaller. We'll dispense with notes and such like and employ a simple code. There's no need to signal incursions; you'll see those for yourselves. A series of long tones means a general retreat – to the square and barracks. A series of short tones is for the first section – that'll be me calling the reserve to my position.'

Cassius looked at his deputies. 'I think that's everything.'

'May I?' asked Strabo, gesturing at the men.

'Of course,' said Cassius hesitantly, wondering what the Sicilian had in mind.

Strabo swaggered forward until he was standing just a yard or so from the first line.

'I'm not normally one for speeches,' he began, his crude intonation a contrast to Cassius and Serenus. 'But we're still Fifth Century, Third Cohort, Third Legion, and whatever your name is, wherever you're from, you're here now. And you're stuck.'

Thumbs tucked into his belt, Strabo flicked his head to the west.

'Behind us is nothing but miles of desert. You run, they'll chase you down. All we can do now is stand firm and stick it to them. And let's not overrate them. Remember: these half-witted desert-dwellers follow the orders of a *woman*!'

Strabo enunciated the last word with all the considerable derision he could muster.

'My money says we stop them here, wait for our boys to arrive, then chase these dogs all the way back to Palmyra!'

Strabo ran a hand through his hair and gave a lascivious smirk.

'I hear she's quite a beauty, this queen. Well, while you boys are filling your pockets from the palace coffers, I'll be first into her bedchamber – take the saucy bitch myself!'

The men laughed and cheered. Only Avso and Flavian remained po-faced. Strabo waited for quiet to return, then unsheathed his sword and held the blade aloft.

'Caesar fights forever beside us!' he thundered. 'Dyrrhachium! Philippi! Artaxata! These the greatest victories of the Third. For Mars! For the Emperor! For Rome!'

'For Rome!' answered the men, their cry echoing around the compound.

Strabo sheathed his sword and turned round.

Cassius tilted his head.

'Dismissed!'

XXIII

A short queue had formed outside the temple. The section leaders had received several requests from legionaries eager to make a prayer or offering before the battle. Cassius looked on from the officers' quarters. To refuse would have been unthinkable. Few of the men would share his lack of enthusiasm for things religious, and freedom for personal worship was a long-standing feature of army life.

Moments earlier, as he returned from the gate, Cassius had heard chanting coming from the barracks. Not recognising the language, he asked Serenus what was going on. It turned out that a few of the older hands had fought with another legion in Germania many years earlier. After seeing a local auxiliary cohort enjoy considerable fortune as followers of the goddess Viradecthis, they had eventually converted. It was their belief that she had watched over them ever since and would deliver them from the impending battle.

Cassius glanced across at Julius, still sitting by the desk. Simo had been relieved to see his master return; he had swiftly sheathed his dagger and left for the aid post. Cassius tried to clear his head to decide on the best way of approaching the boy, but it was a struggle to focus on anything other than what the next few hours might hold. He walked back across the room and stood over him.

'You must talk to me. You must!'

Julius' eyes betrayed only a vague, blank desperation.

Cassius felt a sudden burst of anger at his dumb silence. Darting forward, he gripped one of the boy's wrists and held it up, examining the dried blood on the tips of his fingers.

'Was it you?' He tightened his grip. 'Was it?'

Julius squirmed in the seat.

'I can't help you if you stay silent. I won't be able to stop them. Who knows what they'll do to you?'

Realising his words were making no impact, Cassius dragged Julius to his feet. He hauled him outside and past the barracks, retaining a solid grip on his spindly upper arm. Half throwing the boy through the aid post door, he found Simo dressing beds. The Gaul looked up, surprised.

'Get Kabir over here. If I can get the lad to speak, I want to know what he says. Be quick.'

Simo stepped carefully past them before hurrying across the square.

Julius was gazing at the white-clad figure lying on the furthest bed to the right. The sheet had been pulled tight round Barates' body and face.

'Did you do that?'

Julius, now kneeling on the floor, stared back at him plaintively. Cassius jabbed a finger at the corpse, then back at Julius.

'Did you?'

Julius winced as if he'd been struck, then looked away.

'Say something! Anything!'

Cassius grabbed him by the collar and dragged him across the floor towards the bed.

'Perhaps I should show you the wound at his neck? Perhaps that might help you remember?'

This time Julius fought back, as if fearful of being close to the body. He clawed at Cassius' arms. His nails dug in and Cassius let go. The boy took his chance and bolted for the door. Cassius sprang after him, then swung out a leg. He caught Julius' back foot and the boy crashed heavily to the floor.

Cassius didn't enjoy meting out such treatment but the time for gentility was long past. He couldn't think of any possible reason for Julius to be the murderer, but the evidence was against him. If he couldn't be persuaded to communicate, perhaps he could be shocked into telling the truth.

Julius recovered quickly and scrambled to his feet. He was set to make for the door again when a large figure all but filled the doorway. Julius froze, then retreated past Cassius and hid behind him.

'Leave this to me,' said Cassius.

'Any progress?'

Strabo was now clad in his heavy mail shirt. His helmet was under his arm, his shield and pila across his back.

'Not yet. Nor am I likely to make any with you around. Shouldn't you be at the gatehouse?'

'That's why I'm here. The enemy have been sighted. A small party on horseback. Scouts.'

Cassius fought his first instinct: to leave Julius where he was and head straight for the eastern wall.

'We must resolve this now,' he said, trying to ignore the boy's desperate moans.

'You should know the men are talking. Some of them want to string him up right now. They are saying it was meant, intended by the gods. There are no animals to sacrifice before the battle, they think—'

'You're not serious, man! He may not be a Roman and he may not be the equal of you or me, but do you really believe I will allow that? An execution can't be sanctioned without evidence of guilt.'

'What do you call that?' said Strabo, pointing down at Julius' tunic.

'That proves nothing. He sleeps over in the stables. He may have found the body. He'd probably tell us exactly what happened if he could. In any case, if he's guilty, why didn't he run away?'

'You are trying to find sense where there is none. Who knows what goes on in that head of his?'

'These men – those who would have him killed. I'll venture Avso and Flavian were amongst them.'

'I didn't hear their view.'

'And what of *your* view?' Cassius snapped. 'You were convinced *they* were responsible two hours ago!'

'You said this needs resolving. You're right. And we must do it quickly.'

Cassius nodded slowly as he replied. Strabo's motivations were becoming clear.

'I see. Regardless of the truth, you'd let him hang – guilty or not – purely to satisfy the men's bloodlust.'

'I didn't say I agreed with it, but we can't just ignore them.'

'As I said before, this is not the Senate. I give the orders.'

'Based on your experience and wisdom?'

'Based on the concept of law. And justice. And what is right.'

Strabo looked over his shoulder for a moment, then turned back.

'Perhaps we could tell them he's confessed? Tie him up, lock him in somewhere. At least it'll be settled.'

'Even though the murderer might still be in our midst? And we would know nothing of what truly happened. Or why. Or what the man might do next.'

'You seem very certain the boy is innocent. And you never answered about Flavian. You are keeping something from me.'

Julius had quietened down now and he looked up at the two Romans, following the conversation intently.

Cassius watched Kabir crossing the square, and decided to tell Strabo the truth, if only to dent his belief in Julius' guilt.

'Flavian was seen at the granary by one of the Syrians.'

Strabo looked down at the floor. Then he punched the doorway, knocking out a section of clay. 'That lying piece of shit.'

He took a deep breath and examined his knuckles.

'Did he admit he was there?'

'No. I think he was about to say something but—'

'Then we'll ask him again.'

'He won't say anything now, I'm sure of it. Avso will have told him to keep quiet.'

'Then I'll beat it out of him,' said Strabo before turning and walking away.

'Wait!' Cassius cried, stepping out into the sun.

Simo and Kabir had just arrived. They looked on as Cassius ran around Strabo and barred his way.

'Don't,' the Sicilian said quietly.

'Just listen.' There was no doubt in Cassius' mind that a confrontation with Strabo on one side and Avso and Flavian on the other stood a good chance of swiftly developing into a riot. 'I'm going to have Kabir talk to Julius in his own tongue. He may be able to tell us something.'

'So might Flavian. And that rat friend of his.'

'They're not going anywhere. Let's just see if we can get anything out of the boy.'

Strabo hesitated.

Kabir stepped forward. He too had readied himself for battle and now wore a thick, sleeveless leather jerkin over his black tunic. Tucked into his belt next to his sword was a sling and a pouch bulging with lead shot.

'You wish me to speak to him?'

'Please.'

'It won't be easy. Barates somehow understood his Latin more than any of us understood his Aramaic, but I will do my best.'

Strabo shook his head, then shrugged.

'Quickly then,' he said, removing his shield and pila from his shoulder. With a grateful nod to Kabir, Cassius hurried past the Sicilian to the doorway. Without getting too close, he gestured for Julius to join them outside. The boy was still kneeling by the bed but he slowly got to his feet. Cassius gave him plenty of space, and Kabir offered a few quiet words of encouragement as he stepped outside. Simo grabbed a stool from the aid post and placed it against the wall. Cassius held Julius gently by the shoulders and sat him down. Strabo sensibly kept his distance, watching with arms crossed as Kabir dropped to his haunches and began.

Hearing pounding footsteps, Cassius turned to see Crispus approach.

'Twenty-two horsemen! They're almost here,' announced the legionary as his sprint became a walk.

'I'll go and take a look at them,' Cassius said.

There was no need to go as far as the gatehouse; the dwellings on the north side of the street were close by.

'I'll join you,' said Strabo. He put down his helmet and pulled his mail shirt off over his head.

Cassius was about to protest but realised there might be some value in leaving Kabir and Julius alone for a while.

'Simo, back to work. Crispus, back to the wall.'

'Make sure the men keep out of sight,' added Strabo, placing his equipment on a window ledge.

As they set off for the dwelling, Cassius noted that the inn was still empty.

'The Praetorian's still sleeping?'

'Noisy swine's been snoring since dusk yesterday,' answered Strabo.

'He doesn't know about Barates then?' Cassius asked as they ducked inside the darkened doorway.

'Do you think he'd even care?'

Despite the gloom, there was enough light coming from the doorway and windows for Cassius to see the ladder in the far corner. Seven rungs later, he popped up in the middle of another empty room already cleared by the men of the first section. Strabo was already on his way up as Cassius crossed to the opposite corner and up the next ladder. Despite a missing rung, it too held and he was soon clambering on to the roof, fingers coated with dust. Taking care to keep his head below the surround, he crawled over to the south-east corner and peered out at the plain.

What first caught his eye was the sun glinting off the armour and helmets of the legionaries gathered behind the eastern wall. He saw Crispus dodge through them and head straight into the gatehouse. As Serenus was nowhere to be seen, Cassius assumed he was already in there, observing the Palmyrans through the arrow slits.

Two hundred yards beyond the wall, eerily still and arranged in remarkably uniform fashion, were the Palmyran horsemen. Their dark steeds barely moved as the men sat high in their saddles, observing the fort. Despite their vivid red tunics, the brown, bearded faces reminded Cassius of Kabir's men.

Breathing heavily, Strabo hauled himself across the roof and close to Cassius.

A horseman close to the centre of the line broke ranks. He headed south, riding parallel to the eastern wall.

'A messenger?' said Cassius.

'More likely an officer, their leader even.'

The rider continued on his way, his gaze fixed on the fort as he turned, now following the southern wall, still staying well beyond effective arrow range.

'Checking the walls,' Strabo continued. 'Making his plans. Might even be a general judging by that fancy purple cloak of his.'

Shifting their position and keeping low, they tracked the warrior over the western wall, losing him for a moment behind the palms. When he appeared again the horse was galloping, his cloak fluttering high.

Cassius imagined what he would see. Above the walls, only the precious granary and legion flag would be visible. He would know now that he faced a fight.

Slowing his mount to a trot, the Palmyran approached the other warriors and gestured to one. The horseman coaxed his mount out of the line and set off back towards the crest at speed.

'What do you think?' said Cassius, turning to Strabo.

'He'll bring up his main force now. Get started while there's still plenty of light.'

'Then we have a little time at least.'

'A little.'

Kabir, who was kneeling close to Julius, stood up as the Romans approached.

'What have you learned?' Cassius asked.

'He heard something in the middle of the night. Voices I think. He got up to investigate and found Barates' body. He says he tried to wake him – I assume that's how he got the blood on his hands and clothes. After that, the story becomes rather confused. I think he hid in the temple because he thought he would be safe there.'

Cassius cast a knowing glance at Strabo, who studiously ignored him.

'There's something else,' added Kabir. 'It's hard to explain, the word does not translate well, but it means something like "ghost". He thinks a ghost killed Barates.'

Strabo snorted and looked across at Julius, who was once again following their conversation keenly.

'A spirit,' said Cassius.

'Yes,' replied Kabir thoughtfully. 'That's closer.'

Cassius turned round and looked across at the granary.

'And still we are no nearer to an answer,' stated Strabo.

'I have dealt with killings amongst my own people,' said Kabir. 'Where men are concerned, women or money are usually the issue. We know one cannot be the cause; I'm assuming the same is true of the other.'

Strabo shook his head.

'Had nothing. Owed nothing.'

'As I said this morning,' continued the Syrian, 'it makes no sense for anyone here to have done this.'

'Except your man saw Flavian,' said Strabo.

'Yes. But even if he was after wine or there was cause for some other dispute, surely it couldn't have led to murder?'

'There's one way to find out.'

'Wait,' said Cassius. 'All we have done so far has been based on the assumption that Barates was killed by one of our men, or by one of yours, Kabir. But as you say, we've known from the start that that's extremely unlikely. Avso thought he may have been killed by some Palmyran scout or spy.'

'Instead of guessing, let's look at the facts,' countered Strabo. 'We know Flavian was there and we know he lied about it. We should be making him talk, not chasing some phantom spy. In any case, how would he have got inside?'

'It would be difficult,' said Kabir, 'but hardly impossible.'

'There is another alternative,' said Cassius. 'What if he was already here?'

XXIV

Outside the granary, four legionaries were piling jars into two large sacks – food for the men. Cassius leaped up the steps past them and through the open door without a word. Not far behind were Strabo and Kabir. They exchanged bemused looks, then followed him inside. He came to a halt in front of the biggest stack of barrels in the granary.

Running his thumb across his chin, Cassius stared at the barrels. They were arranged in neat rows, five high.

'Well?' said Strabo.

'Help me.'

Cassius placed both hands against the second barrel up at one corner of the stack. Pushing back and forth, he created a wobbling motion that quickly spread upward.

'Careful!' said Strabo, joining Kabir behind Cassius so as to avoid any falling barrels.

'I said help me!'

'To do what exactly?' Strabo fired back.

Gritting his teeth in frustration, Cassius gave the barrel a powerful shove.

All three of them leaped back as the third barrel slipped sideways off the second and the two above smashed to the floor. Many of the curved planks that made up the barrels splintered, releasing thick, dark rivers of dates.

'Happy now?' said Strabo, surveying the mess.

Cassius held up a hand.

'Did you hear that?'

'Hear what?' said Strabo dismissively.

'Yes, I heard something,' said Kabir.

With the Syrian's help, Cassius moved the remaining barrels out of the way. Beyond was an identical stack, labelled as olives and meat. Cassius again reached for the second barrel up. Kabir gripped the other side and they began rocking the container. On the fourth push they successfully dislodged it and again narrowly avoided being struck from above.

The three of them were now standing in a heap of broken wood and dried food. Cassius moved closer to the next stack. He pushed his face between two barrels and shut one eye. There was space there – quite a large space. He could see a section of flooring.

Strabo looked on cynically, arms crossed.

'You don't seriously think—'

A flash of movement. Cassius jerked his neck back just quickly enough to avoid the thin blade that shot between the barrels. His speedy retreat caused him to lose his balance on the slippery fruit. Strabo caught him.

With a sharp scrape of metal on wood, the knife disappeared. From beyond the barrels came the sound of scrabbling hands and hurried breaths.

Strabo, staring incredulously at the spot where the blade had been, forgot to let go of Cassius. Pushing the Sicilian's hands away, Cassius got to his feet. Kabir, who had already drawn his sword, moved right, trying to see between the barrels.

'Who—' said Strabo, his face pale.

'I'll cover outside,' said Kabir. 'He may have a way out.'

As the Syrian hurried away, Cassius and Strabo stood still, listening intently. Whoever was in there was moving.

Strabo waved a hand in front of Cassius, then nodded at the barrels. Cassius nodded back and the two of them planted their hands on the nearest stack. This time they simply pushed, aiming to bring the tower down on their hidden foe. Cassius had barely applied any force before Strabo's shove toppled the barrels into the space beyond. Wood splintered, glass smashed and dust kicked up into their faces. They drew their swords and closed in.

The den was about four yards across. There were clothes, blankets, jars of food, even a half-empty barrel of water. Of the occupant himself there was no sign.

'By Mars,' breathed Strabo.

'Look!' cried Cassius, pointing at the granary floor in the far corner of the den. A section of floorboard had been removed; they could see sandy ground beneath.

'He's here! He's outside!' shouted Kabir.

Cassius and Strabo sprinted to the door and cut left.

Standing in their way were the four legionaries. Beyond them, Cassius saw Kabir slip as he darted into the narrow alley between the granary and stables.

'Move it!' yelled Strabo. The soldiers flung themselves out of his way, one straight into Cassius' path. They collided. The legionary was knocked to the ground. Cassius fell on one knee, regained his balance and charged after Strabo.

The Sicilian followed Kabir down the alley. Cassius caught a glimpse of him helping the Syrian up as he himself continued on past the stables. Ignoring the nervous whinnying of the horses, Cassius slowed as he neared the corner. Edging round it, sword held high, he saw a small figure hunched over at the corner of the workshop, twenty feet away.

The man was clad in dark robes, his head covered with brown, matted hair that reached almost to his waist. He carried a satchel over his left shoulder. Suddenly he grabbed a handful of sand and threw it up.

Kabir stumbled into view, clutching at his eyes. The man made no attempt to press his attack, instead scuttling away towards the western wall, robes dragging in the dust.

Cassius dashed after him, wondering where Strabo was. He couldn't understand where the man thought he could escape to. A stray barrel had been left against the rear wall but didn't reach high enough for him to clamber over.

The man flicked his hand forward as he ran. The next thing Cassius saw was the wooden handle of a knife sticking out of the wall a yard above the barrel: a perfectly placed step.

Cassius' long stride had cut the distance between them but the man was still five yards away when he leaped for the barrel. With the agility of an acrobat, he pushed off with his right foot, jammed his left on to the knife, then reached for the top of the wall. With both hands over but his impetus gone, he needed one final effort to haul himself clear.

Cassius had drawn his sword and was all set to swing it at the man's feet when a javelin thudded into the wall just above his head. It had torn straight through the man's robes and now pinned him.

'Don't move!' shouted Strabo in Greek. 'I have another.'

Cassius turned round. The Sicilian was advancing slowly, his arm already back in the throwing position. Cassius realised he must have grabbed the javelins from the workshop.

The man looked back despairingly, eyes full and bright. Legs scrabbling for purchase, he pulled himself upward.

Strabo got him dead centre, between the shoulder blades. The man's grip went instantly. His arms slipped back over the wall and he dropped like a stone, bouncing off the barrel and landing on his side, the javelin still stuck in place.

Cassius moved warily round him and looked down at his face, barely visible through the thick beard and matted hair. His breathing was just audible. One hand pawed at his back, then was still. A thick, foul smell surrounded him.

Wrinkling his nose with distaste, Strabo knelt down and pushed some of the hair away. The man's eyes were flickering open and shut in time with his gasping breaths.

'I know this man. He worked here. One of the locals. Left months ago.'

'So you thought.'

'What have you to say then?' said Strabo, tugging ruthlessly on some of the hair.

The man coughed and his breathing slowed.

By this time Kabir and several others had arrived.

'He's alive?' asked the Syrian.

'Not for long,' said Strabo, straightening up.

'That's Sadir!' said Minicius. 'He was employed in the work-shop for a time.'

The spy was now encircled and as Cassius backed away, excited chatter broke out.

Kabir approached, one eye still red.

'How did you know?'

Watching as Strabo turned his attention to the man's robes, Cassius took a couple of deep breaths before replying.

'Julius had spoken of this "spirit" before. Obviously he'd heard some noises from the granary at night. And there was no sign of rats, yet there was a foul odour there – this fellow. I suppose he must have buried his waste but the stench remained. Then what you said about there being no reason for one of us to have done it – there had to be another explanation.'

'What do you think happened?'

'I imagine he was checking the defences under cover of night.'

'And Barates was unfortunate enough to cross his path.'

'Something like that, yes.'

'I think he's had it,' said Minicius.

Strabo had found something.

'Catch.'

Cassius did so and turned the thin silver disc over in his hand. It was a fairly standard denarius, apart from the youthful, un-familiar face etched on one side. The name that circled the face, however, he had heard before.

'Vaballathus.'

'Zenobia's son,' added Kabir, looking over Cassius' shoulder.

'This announces him as emperor,' Cassius said, examining both sides. Closer inspection showed the coin to be rather inferior in weight and quality.

'I heard there were some of these around,' said Strabo. 'Never seen one though.'

'The nerve of that woman,' said Cassius indignantly.

Jangling a purse full of the coins, Strabo sauntered over.

'Bribe money perhaps. Yours now.'

Cassius took the tatty purse.

'Gone has he?' asked Strabo.

Minicius, kneeling down and listening for any sound of breathing, nodded. The Sicilian planted a boot on the spy's flank, gripped the end of the javelin and yanked it out.

Word still hadn't spread to the men at the gate. Those present either looked on in silence or exchanged quiet comments, apparently still struggling to make sense of the sight before them. Kabir meanwhile had leaped up on to the barrel. He pulled the knife out of the clay and jumped nimbly back down.

'Look here,' he said, holding up the blade as Cassius walked over. 'He didn't even clean it properly.'

Along the edge were several blotches of blood. Cassius felt a surge of relief; they had at last found the murderer.

The Syrian's grim smile suddenly vanished.

'Don't move!' he barked, pointing at the ground.

Behind Cassius, a pair of legionaries had emptied the contents of the spy's satchel on to the ground. Apart from a gourd and a thin blanket, the only other object was a small wooden cage. Inside, a dark-feathered bird pecked at the bars. The door that made up one side of the cage had come loose, and with a flap of its wings, the bird pushed the door open and stepped neatly on to the sand.

'Don't startle it,' said Kabir. 'Look – on its leg. A message meant for the enemy.'

As the legionaries slowly backed away, Cassius saw that there was indeed a tiny roll of papyrus attached just above the right claw. The bird scratched at the ground and stretched its wings.

Despite Kabir's warnings, some of the other legionaries let their curiosity get the better of them.

'You men,' Cassius hissed. 'Stay where you are.'

The legionaries did so but Cassius' words had little effect on Strabo, who was already inching his way towards the bird.

'I wouldn't get any closer,' advised Kabir.

Strabo, hunched over, with the javelin still in his hand, took another small step.

'It'll have been in that cage for months. Probably can't fly.'

'Strabo,' said Cassius.

'Relax, centurion.'

Without taking his eyes off the bird, Kabir called out to one of his men, who hurried away.

'Strabo,' repeated Cassius, louder this time.

The Sicilian shifted his grip to the middle of the javelin and eased it back behind his head, ready to strike.

The bird was five yards away from him, pecking at the ground, oblivious to the impending attack. It was hopping around in circles; Strabo had to constantly readjust his aim.

'Stay still, little birdy,' he whispered. 'Nice and still.'

'Leave this to me,' said Kabir firmly, carefully removing his sling from his belt. Cassius got a good look at the weapon for the first time.

The sling resembled a thick piece of rope but on closer inspection was in fact made of braided hemp. It was half an inch wide and about two feet long. In the middle was a small leather cradle to house the projectile itself. At one end was a small loop of cord that Kabir now slipped over his little finger.

'Who put you in charge, auxiliary?' answered Strabo. Kabir took a piece of lead shot and placed it in the cradle, then took hold of the other end of the sling and held it delicately between thumb and forefinger.

Strabo scowled as the bird moved again.

'Bloody thing.'

Cassius retreated as Kabir raised the sling to shoulder height.

From behind the western wall came the loud squawk of a buzzard. It was a familiar sound to the men but enough to startle the skittish bird. With a few short hops it launched itself into the air and took off towards Strabo. He had no time to adjust his aim and missed with a clumsy swing of his arm. He watching helplessly with the rest of the Romans as the bird flapped higher.

Kabir leaned back and whipped his wrist round. Firing high into the sun, the Syrian had little chance of success and he cursed as his prey flew on unharmed. Every pair of eyes in the west of the compound followed the bird as it circled above, then swooped down towards the wall. It made a rather unconvincing landing on the roof of the stables then paraded back and forth, surveying the crowd below.

'Nobody move,' ordered Kabir loudly, provoking a few glares from the legionaries. He, Strabo and Cassius walked gingerly towards the stables. As Kabir loaded another shot into his sling, Strabo again prepared to throw. Cassius put a hand on the javelin.

'Just leave him to it, would you?'

Strabo reluctantly lowered the weapon. Before Kabir could even raise his hand, the buzzard squawked again and the bird hopped off the roof. It flapped skyward, then wheeled aimlessly about a hundred feet above the fort.

'There!' cried Teyya.

Azaf, Razir and the other Palmyrans covered their eyes and hunched forward in their saddles.

'I see it,' said Razir.

'It looks the right size,' added Teyya, his hands already on the cage.

Azaf looked down at the bird. There was no way to be certain but the timing seemed right. He had limited faith in the spy's scheme, but it had to be worth a try.

'Let it go.'

Teyya opened the door and tilted the cage. The bird slid out and dropped on to the saddle between his legs. The young warrior had already attached a short piece of light twine to one leg and he now tied this to a longer piece looped round his arm. Passing the cage to Razir and freeing the twine, he cupped the bird in both hands then launched it into the sky.

The bird zigzagged away then tried to fly higher. Pulled short by the twine, it struggled for a moment, then landed awkwardly in front of them.

Azaf let out a tired breath. He leaned forward and ran a hand along his horse's neck.

★　★　★

Kabir had summoned ten of his men. They all had their slings loaded and ready.

'It's going higher,' said Strabo dourly.

Cassius could barely make out the minuscule shape in the sun's glow.

'Won't hit it now,' said Minicius. 'Must be forty yards up.'

Cassius made his way through the legionaries to where Kabir was standing, turning this way and that, determined not to lose sight of the bird.

'Shouldn't you try now? Before it gets any further away.'

The bird swooped down again then sped away to the east.

Before Kabir yelled the command, the slingers were already firing. Cassius didn't see a single stone in motion, only the bird climbing higher as it passed over the dwellings.

Everyone chased after it. Two legionaries, eyes fixed on the sky, collided and fell. Cassius vaulted over them, then looked up just as the bird approached the eastern wall. It suddenly lurched to one side, then dropped out of the sky. A cry went up but there was no way to tell if it had landed inside or outside the wall.

'Somebody knows what they're doing!' said Strabo, running alongside Cassius as they followed Kabir into the encampment. The awnings had now been taken down and all possessions and equipment moved inside the dwellings. A crowd had formed next to a section of wall near the gatehouse. The rest of the Syrians were there, and the main mass of legionaries. As their leader approached, the Syrians murmured to each other and moved dutifully out of the way.

'Who else?' said Kabir, glancing over his shoulder with a broad grin.

Emerging from the crowd, both hands proffered before him, was Idan. There was no trace of triumph upon his disfigured face, only a cold calm. In his left hand was the lifeless yet unblemished body of the bird. In his right hand was an unfolded square of papyrus.

*   *   *

Teyya, Razir and the other warriors watched the other bird in stunned silence. The twine had broken and it now circled high above them, perplexed by the demise of its mate.

Azaf coaxed his horse forward and guided it along the line of waiting men. Picking out three riders, he dispatched them to keep watch on the southern, western and northern walls. As they departed, he brought his mount to a halt and addressed the rest of the warriors.

'Dismount and mark a clear line in the sand just ahead of our position. The others will be here soon.'

XXV

After a while, calm returned to Alauran. Then, as the afternoon wore on, it was succeeded by an oppressive air of tension that hung heavily over the compound, suffused with the sapping heat.

Serenus had warned Cassius that some of the men might vent their wrath on the spy's body and the veteran came up with a simple solution: he and three other men disposed of it over the western wall. The legionaries were now gathered in small groups in the shade, fiddling with their equipment and finishing off the food. With the exception of Kabir, who had joined Strabo and Serenus in the gatehouse, the Syrians were back at the dwellings.

Cassius had taken a brief look at the papyrus note before entrusting it to Strabo. His conscience then led him swiftly to Julius, whom he found still sitting on the stool, drawing shapes in the sand with his finger. Cassius had no idea how much he had seen or understood. The boy looked up as he approached. Cassius knelt down on one knee so that their faces were at the same height.

'We know now. We know you did nothing wrong.'

Julius looked wistfully across the square.

'I'm sorry for doubting you. Do you see? I'm sorry.'

Julius stood and walked inside the aid post, head bowed.

Simo met Cassius at the doorway.

'It's true, sir? That man had hidden himself in there for weeks?'

'Apparently. If anyone had taken the time to listen to the boy, he might have been discovered sooner.'

Behind Simo, Cassius could see Julius standing solemnly over Barates' body once again.

'He has been ill-used.'

'He may have faired a good deal worse without your inter-vention, sir.'

'Perhaps.'

Cassius thought of how he had earlier treated the boy, in that very same spot. The least he could do now was try to protect him from the impending battle.

'I'm placing him in your care, Simo. He will act as your assist-ant. Keep him occupied. And put this in the chest, would you?'

Cassius handed over the coin-filled purse.

'Of course, sir.'

Not for the first time, Cassius was struck by, and grateful for, Simo's even temper and composure. Just weeks earlier he had been the respected attendant of a wealthy merchant in Antioch. Now he was stuck at this forsaken fort, facing imminent attack.

'I'm afraid you may be in for a busy afternoon, Simo.'

'I'll be ready, sir. Perhaps you should put your armour on.'

'Yes. Come on.'

Once inside the officers' quarters, Cassius removed both his belts. He lowered the whole arrangement on to the desk, then ran his sword blade back and forth into the scabbard a few times. He didn't want it to get stuck again.

Simo returned from the bedroom, laden down with not only the mail, but also the padded sleeveless shirt worn underneath. It too was an expensive but essential acquisition. The double layer of metal at the shoulders felt like a pair of anvils when in place, but the undershirt also prevented the mail being driven into the flesh if struck. Though grateful for the protection, Cassius had no idea how long he would be able to move in such heat.

He quickly pulled the undershirt on and watched Simo tie the leather straps that would keep it in place. He then raised his arms, allowing the Gaul to lower the mail shirt on to his shoulders. Simo strained to lift the armour high, so Cassius hunched down to help him. The weight never ceased to surprise him.

'It's lucky I don't have to march very far.'

Simo pulled at the shirt until it hung correctly.

'How's that, sir?'

'Fine.'

As Simo took hold of his belt, Cassius looked down at his exposed forearms, wincing as he imagined a sword carving its way through the unprotected flesh. He had seen arm guards on other legionaries but doubted he would be able even to raise his sword, let alone swing it, with yet more weight to bear.

Simo pulled the belt tight. When correctly tied, it took a surprising proportion of the mail's weight off the shoulders.

'And that?'

'Fine.'

Simo secured the buckle and took one last look at his handiwork.

'Thank you, Simo.'

The Gaul looked confused, unused to statements of gratitude. Cassius' father had told him never to thank slaves for doing their work. Generally Cassius followed the advice, and believed it to be wise, but he felt the situation was exceptional.

'Not just for this,' he added, tapping the armour. 'For what you've done, these last weeks. A good many men in your position might have taken the earliest opportunity to stick a knife in my back. You've certainly little to thank me for.'

'Well at least I've seen a little more of the province, sir,' Simo said with an awkward half-smile.

'There is that.' Cassius put his hand through his sword belt as Simo hung it on his shoulder. 'I am frightened, Simo. Truly.'

'I too, sir,' Simo said as he adjusted the belt, 'and every man out there I'm sure.'

'If they are, they don't show it.'

'Then I suppose we mustn't either, sir.'

Cassius took a moment to absorb this, then nodded briskly.

'Quite right.'

Cassius checked the belt, then picked up his helmet. Simo quickly locked the bedroom door and they left.

'Good luck, sir,' said the Gaul as they parted outside the barracks.

'And to you, Simo. And to you.'

Stepping up into the southern tower, Cassius found Strabo slumped in a corner, clad once again in his mail shirt, sharpening his pilum blade with a flint. Serenus was kneeling in front of the arrow slit, keeping watch.

'Anything?'

'Dust trails to the south,' said Serenus without turning round. 'Main assault force I should imagine.'

The Sicilian pointed the flint at Cassius' helmet.

'Might be best to rid yourself of that crest.'

Cassius looked down at the thick red bristles. Though they had been faded slightly by the sun, the colour remained bright. As he had been told many times, the crest was not only a mark of status but the key identifier of an officer during battle. To remove it seemed unthinkable.

'Why would I do that?'

'No sense making a target of yourself – especially if you're up here.'

'Rather goes with the job, doesn't it?' Cassius said, ill at ease with how comfortably he now handled the pretence.

'Were you a veteran I would agree,' said Strabo, 'but it makes no sense for a youngster like yourself to draw attention. You'll have enough to deal with.'

Cassius didn't know how to respond. Strabo's suggestion seemed patronising in the extreme, yet he felt strangely touched by the concern. For a brief moment he toyed with the idea of telling them the truth. Luckily, Serenus spoke up, dispelling the thought.

'Strabo's right. Don't take offence. You've hardly been wearing it anyway – I doubt the men will even notice.'

'Well,' said Cassius, 'it is rather impractical. Gets caught on door frames and such like.'

He examined the helmet. The crest was mounted on an iron

panel that slid between two raised sections. Gripping the bristles, he yanked the crest down, hoping to loosen the panel. It refused to budge.

'Here.'

Strabo took the helmet, perused the arrangement for a moment, then chopped his hand down at an angle, dislodging the panel.

'Another reason I've never sought promotion,' said the Sicilian, 'strutting round like a peacock in barracks, then inviting special attention during battle. No thanks.'

Cassius picked up the square of papyrus lying on the floor next to Serenus. Written on one side in miniature Aramaic lettering was a brief list and several numerals. Kabir had already identified this as an accurate summary of the numbers within Alauran. On the other side was a labelled map of the compound, including the newly erected barriers.

'We've a good deal to thank old scarface for,' said Strabo, now sharpening the pilum again.

'That would have given them quite an advantage.'

'Certainly,' answered Serenus. 'But I can't help thinking they know we are few. Sadir had been here over a year. It's inconceivable that he made no other communication to his masters. They must know four hundred men will be sufficient.'

'Four hundred?' snapped Strabo. 'Caesar's length! Who said anything about four hundred?'

'Keep your voice down!' warned Cassius.

'Antonius and I go back a long way,' Serenus explained.

'I see,' replied Cassius grimly. 'Well, let's just keep it to ourselves, shall we?'

Strabo gave up his sharpening and jabbed the pilum into the clay wall.

'Four hundred? We should have run while we had the chance.'

'What happened to "standing firm" and "sticking it to them"?' said Serenus, with a sideways glance at Strabo.

The Sicilian wrenched the pilum out of the wall and pointed down at the ground where the unseen legionaries were gathered.

'That was for their benefit.'

'Quite a performance,' said Serenus.

Strabo's expression hardened.

'Someone had to offer a bit of inspiration. Left to you two, anyone would have thought we were planning a surprise party, not a defensive action.' Strabo pulled his dice from his pocket. With a casual flick of the wrist he cast them on to the floor close to Cassius' feet. A one and a two. 'We'll be lucky to see the sun set,' he said. Pocketing the dice and grabbing his helmet, he dropped his pilum through the opening and climbed down the ladder.

'Back in a moment,' Cassius told Serenus.

He found Kabir squatting on the walkway, peering out at the Palmyrans, even though they had agreed to use only the arrow slits for observation.

'Don't worry,' said the Syrian. 'It's safe, and there's a much better view.'

Cassius crawled over to him, then got to his knees and looked out over the wall. The horsemen remained as still as ever, though a few had dismounted and were dragging their swords across the sand.

'Some kind of rally line, I presume,' said Kabir. 'They will gather there before the attack.'

'Are those carts?'

Squinting through the haze to the south of the crest, Cassius could see the approaching column. Behind a long line of horsemen three or four abreast were some low, bulky shapes.

'Carrying siege equipment, I expect. And food and water. They know it will not be over quickly, whatever our numbers.'

The sound of raised voices from below drew Cassius to the rear of the walkway. He looked over the edge to find a predictable scene unfolding. Strabo was standing over Avso and Flavian.

'Apologise? What for?' demanded the Sicilian.

'Don't give us that!' snarled Avso, as he and Flavian scrambled to their feet.

'Will it ever end?' said Cassius tiredly.

Kabir motioned for him to go.

'I'll stay here.'

Cassius crawled past him and made his way down the ladder. Stepping over the legs of several legionaries as he exited the tower, he was relieved to find the trio had not yet come to blows.

Avso and Flavian also had their armour on now. The Thracian wore a well-maintained mail shirt that hung loosely from his narrow, sloping shoulders. Flavian, meanwhile, had attired himself in a poorly fitting cuirass. Several plates were missing, others had almost rusted away. His stomach stuck out below the base.

Cassius noticed how Avso held his hands high, close together at the level of his belt, as if always poised for action. The Thracian spat into the dust at Strabo's feet.

Surprisingly, the Sicilian didn't react. He simply glanced down at the newly moistened sand and smiled. Cassius wondered if he wished to preserve his energies for the fight that mattered. He stepped between them.

'Gentlemen. I'd like a word. In there.' He pointed at the northern tower.

Strabo shrugged and ducked inside. Avso and Flavian reluctantly followed. Cassius was last in; the four of them just about filled the area round the ladder.

He began: 'All of us have made mistakes today. We either didn't tell the truth or we didn't recognise it when we heard it. Flavian, you were at the granary last night hunting out wine, correct?'

Flavian looked to his usual source of guidance and received an affirmative nod.

'Yes.'

'Did you get any?'

Flavian shook his head.

'Thought better of it when that darkie saw me.'

Cassius turned to Avso.

'And you told him to lie about it, fearing you might both be implicated in Barates' death.'

'Very good,' answered Avso smugly, without the vaguest hint of shame or regret.

'I remind both of you that at no time were you directly accused of anything by Strabo or myself, though I admit we had our suspicions. You should also remember that the Syrian lad has suffered a good deal worse. And he did *nothing* wrong. Recriminations benefit no one. Our enemies are here. This feud must be forgotten. Now.'

Strabo had already made up his mind. No sooner had Cassius finished than he offered his hand to Avso. Cassius looked down at Strabo's broad, calloused fingers, hoping desperately that Avso would reciprocate. He knew the Sicilian would not make the offer twice.

The Thracian's drawn features were so hard to read that Cassius had no idea what he was about to do until he finally extended his hand. As usual, Flavian followed his example.

The first rank of infantry were now approaching Alauran on horseback, the rest of the force behind them in a snaking line. The leading riders coaxed their horses behind the scouts and arranged themselves into a neat line of twenty. Those behind repeated the procedure until four new lines had been formed. Shuffling hooves kicked up clouds of dust that shifted lazily south with the wind, obscuring the rest of the column.

'About a hundred,' observed Kabir as Cassius sat down beside him. 'These look like swordsmen.'

They turned their attention north. More Palmyrans were fanning out beyond the limits of the initial rally line. They differed from the others in one notable respect.

'Archers,' said Kabir.

Arranging themselves in a double line, staggered to provide each man with a wide field of fire, around fifty of the horse archers eventually appeared on the northern flank. As their mounts settled down, the dust began to clear, revealing an identical deployment to the south. Behind this group, at least ten carts could be seen bringing up the rear.

From the middle of the rally line a hand and a cry went up, directing the archers to spread themselves more thinly.

'Purple Cloak is definitely the leader,' said Kabir.

215

Strabo arrived. Kneeling like Cassius and Kabir, he looked out at the Palmyrans and whistled. Avso and Flavian appeared next. Flavian was carrying a bundle of throwing javelins.

'Three hundred at least,' said Strabo.

'Two hundred and twenty fighting men. The rest are drivers and porters,' announced Kabir. 'Is that what you make it?' he asked Cassius.

Cassius didn't answer; he was too busy staring at the carts.

'What do you think that is?' he asked, pointing towards a group of men tying ropes to something inside one of the vehicles. Others climbed up to manhandle the mysterious object. Following instructions from a gesticulating driver, those on the ground heaved on their ropes. Suddenly several thick, pointed stakes appeared. The men eased them down to the ground. Next out were two large wheels and more timber.

'Ram,' observed Cassius needlessly.

'Hardly deserves the name,' said Strabo.

'Enough to account for our gate,' countered Avso. 'A big one would get stuck in the sand anyhow. They know what they're doing.'

The five pair of eyes were then drawn to a colourful figure walking rapidly in front of the rally line. He carried no sword or shield. Trailing in the wind behind him was a wide cloak of deep red.

Karzai wasn't actually Palmyran; he hailed originally from the coast close to the city of Laodicea. Azaf knew little of his history other than his previous occupation as some kind of merchant. Having presented himself to the Palmyran victors after a skirmish with Roman troops at a river crossing, he had proven singularly useful.

As well as speaking passable Hebrew and Phoenician, he was fluent in Latin and Greek and all the numerous dialects of Aramaic used in both Syrian provinces. He also seemed to have a contact in every settlement they passed through and was always able to lay his hands on food and water for a reasonable price. By way of reward, he took his pick of whatever the Palmyrans plundered along the way.

Azaf had little time for the man, finding his manner pompous, his creed vulgar. But, as he continued to provide solutions for problems Azaf would otherwise have to solve himself, he saw little reason to get rid of him.

'*Strategos.*' Karzai enunciated the word carefully as he bowed. His long hair was greying in places but he maintained the vigour and good looks of a younger man. The ostentatious collection of rings on both of his fingers always amused Azaf. They would make it impossible for him to hold a blade properly. As usual, the man was surrounded by a haze of perfume.

'I want you to speak with them.'

Karzai's thin smile disappeared as he cast an eye at the walls of Alauran.

Although most of the Palmyrans could speak some Greek, Azaf himself knew little and discouraged the men from using anything other than Aramaic. By employing Karzai, it was not necessary for him or any of his men to demean themselves by speaking either Greek or the hated Latin.

'What would you like me to say?'

'The usual.'

Karzai turned hesitantly towards the gate.

Azaf continued: 'Advance until you are halfway between here and the wall. They should be able to hear you.'

'Sir, I'm happy to please as always, but what if—'

'We'll cover you.'

Azaf gave orders to the archers on either side of him, then settled back into his saddle and gestured calmly towards the gatehouse.

Karzai took a moment to compose himself, then set off.

'Well, well. Look at this pretty flower.'

Flavian gave a grunt of amusement at Avso's mocking words.

Cassius was no longer looking at the man walking slowly towards the fort; he was watching the horse archers. Every last one of them had retrieved an arrow from their quivers and now held them in place against the string. Another shout. As one, the archers coaxed their horses forward using only their legs.

'Ah, you never know,' said Strabo. 'Perhaps they're just after a cup of water.'

Nobody laughed. Kabir tapped Cassius on the shoulder.

'They might offer terms. But you should not consider them, whatever they say.'

'I don't intend to.'

'As auxiliaries my men and I might be spared, but you Romans can expect little mercy. If allowed to live, you might be forced to fight in their ranks or spend your remaining years in chains.'

'You needn't concern yourself. Roman garrisons are not in the habit of handing forts over to upstart rebels.'

Kabir looked back at him cynically.

'Forgive me, centurion, but that is a rather naive view. You must be aware that some within your legions have chosen to fight alongside the Palmyrans.'

'Those are rumours, spread by our enemies.'

Cassius felt his face reddening. He was simply repeating what he had heard from other officers in Antioch. For all he knew, Kabir was right.

'Ah,' said the Syrian, amused by his reply.

Cassius decided to end the conversation.

'My orders are clear. We will defend Alauran to the last man.'

Kabir offered a conciliatory nod.

Crispus' head and shoulders appeared from the northern tower.

'Excuse me, sir, but the men are asking what's going on. Should we form up?'

'Tell the men to stand to. They'll get their orders.'

'Yes, sir.'

Cassius looked around.

'Where's Serenus?'

'Down there,' said Avso, aiming a thumb at the southern tower. 'Coughing his guts up again.'

The enemy messenger stopped seventy yards out, flanked on

either side by the archers. The odd horse edged forward or sideways but for the most part the line remained impressively intact.
Another order and each archer raised his bow above his mount's
head.

'Keep low,' warned Kabir. 'This is short range for them.'

A clear, authoritative voice rolled towards the fort in faultless
Greek.

'Whoever lies behind those walls, be he Syrian or Roman,
should listen now and listen well. We, the forces of General Zabbai
of Palmyra, claim this territory and settlement in the name of
our unconquered Lord Imperator Vaballathus and Her Regal
Highness Queen Septimia Zenobia. Your choice is simple:
surrender or die.'

XXVI

'May I?'

Strabo, pressed close to the wall with his head bowed, stared expectantly across the walkway. Cassius realised he would do little for his own authority by letting the Sicilian speak for the garrison, but he feared he might make a mess of it. For all his supposed oratorical skill, he couldn't even conjure a suitably belligerent reply.

'Please.'

Strabo sat back against the rear wall and cupped his hands round his mouth.

'We make our own choice!' he bellowed. 'We choose to fight! Then it is you who shall decide whether to surrender or die!'

The men roared, adding their own insults and beating their sword pommels against their shields.

Cassius heard a shout close by. He looked up and saw Flavian on his feet, a javelin in his hand, jeering at the Palmyrans. Before Cassius could act, something slammed into his helmet and a fiery pain exploded against his left ear.

'Down!' yelled Kabir, dragging him backward.

Still dazed, Cassius put a hand to his helmet, feeling at first only smooth metal, then a small, thumb-sized indentation. The arrow lay next to him, its point blunted. It had hit the surround before striking him, carving an inch-deep furrow in the clay.

Kabir shouted into his ear: 'Stay low!'

Cassius looked up. Flavian was slumped forward, arms over the wall. The two arrows sticking out of his chest had gone clean through the plate armour. The javelin was still in his hand, an agonised snarl fixed on his face.

Avso went to help him.

'Avso, no!' yelled Strabo.

Arrows flashed through the air. The flat trajectory and power of the bows made them impossible to avoid, even if seen in flight. Cassius stared at Strabo's back, unable to drag himself out of a numbing paralysis. Kabir appeared suddenly to his right, shouting at Avso.

'Down! Down!'

But Avso was up on his feet, struggling to shift Flavian. An arrow pinged harmlessly off the Thracian's chest with a metallic whine. Strabo scrambled over, grabbed at his belt and hauled him down. With the two of them finally back below the wall, the hail of arrows ceased.

Flavian managed to raise himself up off the wall but then his body jolted once more: a third arrow had hit him in the stomach. Arms flailing, his weight shifted forward and he toppled over the edge. There was a sickening thump as he hit the ground.

The silence that followed was broken by a distant shout from the Palmyran lines.

'Stay below the wall! Stay out of sight!' cried Strabo, checking his helmet was still intact.

Cassius could also make out Crispus' voice, ordering legionaries away from the walls.

'The tower,' said Kabir, heading left on his hands and knees. Cassius saw Avso spring up and get a quick glimpse over the wall before scrambling away towards the other ladder. Cursing bitterly, Strabo went after him. Staying as low as he could, Cassius followed Kabir to the ladder and down into the tower.

'You'll keep watch?'

The Syrian nodded and planted himself in front of the arrow slit. Cassius continued downward, pushing his sword out to stop it catching on the rungs. Once outside, he saw Avso coming the other way.

The Thracian pushed his way through the legionaries to the gate and grabbed one of the reinforcing planks. Though most of the wood had been removed, the gate could not be unlatched without detaching the three hefty timbers left in place. Before he could draw his dagger and get to work on the nails, Strabo was on him.

'No, you don't. You'll just get yourself killed.'

'Stay out of this!' spat Avso. 'I can get to him! Someone lend me a shield.'

Flavian was screaming now.

Cassius looked on uncertainly. He felt the eyes of some of the younger men upon him. They were waiting for his instructions.

The more experienced legionaries, however, were of one mind and those close by came quickly to Strabo's aid. Eyes bulging, muscles straining, Avso continued to struggle, landing several kicks as he shrieked curses at his compatriots. Strabo eventually managed to get an arm round his neck and wedge himself back against the gate. Other men locked Avso's arms at his side.

Serenus appeared. His eyes were watering and there were droplets of blood on his chin. He held up his hands as he approached Avso.

'You know we can't open the gate! You know that.'

For a moment, it seemed the Thracian was about to give in. Then he kicked Strabo in the shin and managed to get a hand free. Before anyone could stop him, he had wrenched his dagger out and jabbed it back over his shoulder. Strabo grabbed his wrist, halting the blade an inch from his face.

'Let me go, Sicilian,' Avso hissed, 'or I'll put out an eye.'

Serenus and the others took a step backward.

'I have *two* eyes, friend,' answered Strabo evenly, tightening his hold as he spoke. 'You've only the one neck.'

'Centurion!'

It was Kabir, calling from the tower.

'Strabo, you can let him go,' said Serenus quietly. 'As long as he pledges to leave the gate as it is.'

Avso weighed up his options remarkably quickly.

'All right,' he said after two breaths. 'All right. Just let me go.'

Keeping his grip on Avso's wrist, Strabo released his neck. He waited for the Thracian to step forward before letting go. Avso shot him a poisonous glare then made for the southern tower. The legionaries parted to let him through. He grabbed Statius by his tunic.

'You get a rope! Gemellus, with me.'

Statius sprinted away towards the access gap. Avso and Gemellus disappeared into the tower.

'Flavian's as good as dead,' said Strabo. 'And with no one to blame but himself.'

'Centurion!' shouted Kabir again.

Strabo and Serenus started towards the northern tower but Cassius held up a hand, conscious of the disordered state of the men.

'Wait. Get the four sections in position behind the carts. If we need to redeploy then so be it. Let's just get them organised.'

Strabo took a quick look round. It was impossible not to notice the confused, frightened expressions on many of the faces.

'You're right.'

He and Serenus began separating out the men from sections two, three, four and five.

Cassius re-entered the northern tower. Feeling the heat of pain in his ear, he removed the helmet, releasing the chinstrap and squeezing it up over his head. He put a hand to his ear. It was swollen and tender but there was no blood. He climbed up to the first level.

'They're coming for Flavian,' said Kabir, still kneeling in front of the arrow slit.

Cassius dropped down and shut one eye as he peered through the narrow opening. Thirty yards out, a group of eight Palmyrans carrying shields were advancing at a measured pace. The first row of four held their interlocked shields vertically, while the rear four were horizontal, a Roman-style arrangement that left them well protected from missile attack. They were not the only ones moving; both groups of horse archers were now just a hundred feet from the gate. Cassius could see the concentrated calm on their faces as they waited patiently for targets to reveal themselves.

Flavian cried out again. Avso shouted down encouragement.

'What can we do?' Cassius asked, retreating from the arrow slit.

'Nothing,' said Kabir. 'They want him for what he can tell them. Better to kill him now while we have the chance.'

Cassius stared back at the Syrian.

'Better for him too,' Kabir added, standing up. 'Also, I saw them moving the ram up. It won't be long now. I'll divide the men as we agreed and await your signal.'

Cassius nodded vacantly as Kabir clambered down the ladder. He pulled his helmet back on and headed up to the walkway once more. Statius had just arrived with a thick length of rope. Avso tied a double knot in one end and lowered it over the edge.

'Flavian! Take hold of this. We'll pull you up.'

Cassius risked the briefest glance over the wall. The eight Palmyrans had speeded up, though they were careful to keep their shield wall intact.

'Flavian!' Avso shouted. 'Can you take hold?'

'I'll try,' came the weak reply.

Avso was already on his knees and he now straightened up to get his own look over the wall. In trying to see where his friend was he tarried too long. Cassius heard the loud twang of bowstrings. Some of the archers kept up with their flat, low shots; others sacrificed power for accuracy and fired in a shallow arc, trying to drop their bolts over the walkway wall.

Avso's luck held. One arrow stuck itself into the clay inches from his nose, another bounced off the top of his helmet. Statius was quick to react, pressing his body against the forward wall.

Gemellus, however, was stuck behind the others. Before he could get to safety, arrows thudded into the rear wall either side of him. Suddenly his head snapped backwards; a yard-long shaft had embedded itself in his throat. The legionary's chin sank forward and came to rest on the arrow. A ribbon of crimson blood seeped from the wound and down over his tunic. His eyelids fluttered and then were still. Cassius turned away, swallowing the bitterness in his throat.

Statius reached for Gemellus, but withdrew instantly as more arrows hit the rear wall. Avso stayed where he was, facing forward, hands still gripping the rope.

The volley ended as swiftly as it had begun. The advancing Palmyrans could be heard now, their boots shuffling through the sand just yards away.

Flavian cried out again.

'Avso, please!'

'Take the rope! Take hold of it!'

Avso tried to pull the rope in but there was no weight on the other end.

'I can't. I'm all broken up. I can't move!'

Cassius risked another quick look. The raiding party was now so close that they had disappeared from view. Statius grabbed Gemellus under the arms and laid his body down. Now Avso saw what had happened behind him. Spitting curses, he slammed his fist against the wall. Then he leaned back, staring first at Gemellus, then forlornly down at the rope still in his hands.

'Flavian. We – I can't get down there. Just – don't let them take you.'

The Thracian closed his eyes as he spoke again.

'Can you reach your dagger?'

'I can't move.'

Flavian said nothing more. All they heard were his moans as the Palmyrans finally reached him. It was both surreal and maddening to hear their enemies talking to each other just yards away, yet be unable to stop them.

But Avso was not quite ready to give up on his friend yet. He reached for the bunch of javelins and pulled one out from under the binding. He was up on his feet in a flash, arm already back as he looked for a target. He hesitated.

Cassius took another momentary glimpse and saw why. Even as they retreated, the Palmyrans remained in tight formation. Two men were dragging Flavian away while the other six tracked slowly backwards in two lines of three, shields still raised.

The hands of at least half the archers flew up. A bank of dark flecks flashed towards the gatehouse.

Cassius ducked.

A third of the missiles were directly on target, and would surely have done for Avso had he not flung himself to his left, landing on his side, arms outstretched. As the volley ended, he kicked out with a guttural growl, leaving a substantial hole in the wall.

Cassius looked down at him. Avso rubbed a hand across his forehead, breathing heavily.

'There's no more you can do.'

The Thracian left the javelin on the floor and crawled away. He and Statius dragged Gemellus' body towards the ladder.

'Enough!' said Azaf.

Razir shouted the order.

As the archers lowered their bows, the raiding party passed through their lines. The two men with Flavian each had hold of a wrist, hauling him face down across the sand. Part of the arrow in his stomach had snapped off but the remainder caught on the ground, firing further agony with every step. Dropping him close to the rally line, the warriors moved away as Azaf dismounted. He looked down at the Roman, at the two remaining arrow shafts moving up and down with each breath.

Flavian's eyes were open. He squinted up at Azaf, whimpering as he fought the pain.

'If this one's anything to go by, we should have little trouble,' observed Razir. 'Look at the state of his armour.'

Azaf glanced at Karzai, who approached warily, perturbed by the gruesome sight before him.

'Do you wish me to speak with him, *strategos*?'

Azaf nodded.

Karzai knelt down close to Flavian. Preferring not to look directly at him, he spoke softly in Latin.

'Roman. How many men are behind those walls? How well equipped are they? I advise you to tell all you know. These people are not known for their acts of mercy.'

A gurgling sound came from Flavian's throat. He gulped twice, then spat at Karzai. The bloody spittle landed in the sand just a few inches from his mouth.

Karzai shook his head and stood.

Azaf came closer, tapping his fingers against his chest.

'Shall I finish him, sir?' Razir asked.

Azaf stopped, his feet close to Flavian's flank. He reached out a hand and ran a finger up the flight of the nearest arrow. Both lines of feathers were still perfectly straight and soft to the touch. Gripping the end of the shaft, he wrenched it to the side, eliciting a gasping breath from Flavian. The Roman tried to reach for the arrow but was unable to move his arms properly. They shuddered with the effort, then became still. His eyes stayed open: wet, bright and defiant.

'No,' said Azaf. 'I think we can find another use for him.'

He pointed at Karzai.

'You. Tell them to surrender or I'll show them what fate each of them can expect.'

Karzai walked back towards the gatehouse, then stopped between two ranks of archers.

'Give yourselves up now and this man can live. All of you can live. Put down your weapons and you can leave this place as free men! This is your final chance. I say it again: surrender or die!'

Cassius reckoned most of the legionaries heard the second ultimatum but there was barely a whisper. They had already given their answer and the capture of Flavian changed nothing. There was no possibility of bargaining or surrender; the fate of one man was nothing when weighed against the fate of the garrison and the fort. Belief in the primacy of the fighting unit over all other considerations had been drilled into every last soldier present. Though they numbered barely half a century, Cassius knew then that the legionaries of Alauran had not forgotten who they were.

Karzai retreated, followed swiftly by the archers. Those to the north raised their bows as the horsemen in the southern ranks turned their mounts away, walking them slowly back towards the rally line. Once they got there, they turned and raised their weapons, covering their compatriots to the north as they withdrew.

'Sir.'

Crispus poked his head up above the ladder. 'Sections two to five are in place, sir. Section one in reserve. Sentries posted at the other three walls. Guard officer would like to know what's going on, sir.'

Cassius realised he was the only person with a good view of the Palmyrans. He wasn't entirely sure he wanted to be. Still, nothing crucial had changed yet.

'Stay there. You can tell the others when the advance begins.'

Cassius was sweating; his undershirt was already soaked through. The temperature was far lower inside the gatehouse and now the moisture was cooling against his skin. He looked back through the slit. There was a moment of panic when he saw only a cloud of dust and the ghostly, indistinct shapes of retreating horses. Thankfully, what little breeze there was cleared the dust and he saw that the bowmen once again flanked the main force.

'Archers have withdrawn. All now gathered at original rally line.'

Crispus repeated this to someone outside the gatehouse and told them to pass on the message.

Unsure why he hadn't noticed sooner, Cassius spied a group of five men standing ahead of the rally line, less than fifty yards away. One was identifiable by his cloak, the other three were Palmyran infantrymen. The fifth was being held up by the soldiers. Flavian.

'Crispus,' said Cassius without turning round. 'Where's Avso?'

'At the aid post, I think. Serenus is with him. Gemellus is dead, sir.'

Two of the men pulled on Flavian's hands until his arms were parallel to the ground. There was a sudden gust of wind. Azaf's black hair streamed out behind him as he circled the others and drew his sword. He raised the blade high, its oiled surface catching the sun.

Then he swept it down, hacking off Flavian's left arm above the elbow. Even at such distance, Cassius could see blood spurting from the wound. The Palmyran left holding the limb cast it casually to the ground.

'What is it, sir?' asked Crispus, moving swiftly up the ladder.

'Nothing. Stay there.'

Azaf took two steps to his left, then swung the sword down once more, taking off the other arm with symmetrical precision.

To his horror, Cassius saw that Flavian's head was still moving atop his butchered body. His frame jerked horribly, like a manic puppet. Two of the Palmyrans pushed him down on to his knees, then squatted behind him, propping him up with their hands.

Azaf placed the tip of his sword at Flavian's neck, then retracted the blade in a high diagonal arc. He swung the sword once more.

Cassius shut his eyes and turned away. When he opened them again, he found the alert gaze of Crispus upon him.

'What is it, sir? What have they done to him?'

When Cassius failed to answer, Crispus climbed up the ladder. Before he could get close to the arrow slit, Cassius was up off his knees and barring the way. He put both hands flat against Crispus' chest.

'There's nothing to see. Find Avso. Tell him his friend is gone. He was dead before he reached their lines.'

'What did they do to him?'

Cassius' head was already bent over because of the low roof. He leaned in close to Crispus.

'I told you. He was dead before they got him back to their lines. He'll suffer no more. Now find Avso and tell him.'

Crispus took one last look at the arrow slit before stepping back. Then he left without a word.

Cassius took his helmet off and ran his hands across his face and head, wiping the sweat on his tunic sleeves. He closed his eyes for a moment and saw the sword swing once more. Forcing himself forward, he knelt down again.

The Palmyrans were moving quickly. All traces of Flavian had been removed. The leader and his messenger had disappeared. The entire middle section of the first line separated to allow a small group forward. There were ten of them, all fully armoured, all pushing the ram.

XXVII

'How long would you say it's been?'

'An hour and a half,' said Serenus, 'perhaps two.'

Cassius thought it seemed longer. Afternoon had become evening and, to the surprise of everyone within the fort, the Palmyrans had not advanced. The swordsmen had dismounted, their horses sent to the rear, and though the ram had been pushed to the front, the line of infantry remained static. Occasionally a man would hand out water but for the most part the enemy had barely moved at all.

Cassius, Serenus, Strabo and Kabir stood together by the access gap. With Crispus on duty at the gatehouse and the other three sentries still in place, Strabo had instructed the men to seek shade where they could. He had also permitted the removal of helmets, though armour was to stay on and weapons remain within reach.

'So what are they doing?' asked Cassius, aware of the multitude observing their meeting: the legionaries behind the gatehouse; the dark faces gathered at the dwelling windows.

'Maybe Purple Cloak wants it nice and cool for the cavalry,' offered Strabo.

'That's possible,' replied Kabir, 'though he's confident indeed if he expects victory before nightfall. And it would surprise me if he struck first with horsemen.'

'What are the other possibilities?' asked Cassius, looking hopefully at the others.

'Perhaps they await reinforcements,' suggested Serenus, who seemed to have recovered a little strength.

'We can't see any,' Cassius replied, having just returned from checking the other three walls.

'Let's see what Antonius has to say,' said Strabo as the legionary appeared from the southern tower. 'I sent him up there to take a look at those carts. Often sees things others don't. Hurry up then!'

Antonius sprinted over to the group. He was carrying a pilum and, as he skidded to a stop, the long spear almost stuck Serenus in the shoulder. The veteran swatted the weapon away.

'Point up, you idiot!'

'Sorry.'

'Well?' said the Sicilian tiredly.

'There are twelve carts,' said Antonius.

'I know that,' growled Strabo. 'What's in them?'

'It's hard to be sure. But there were bits poking out here and there. Could be ladders.'

'Or firewood?' asked Kabir. 'Torches even?'

'Could be,' answered Antonius with a shrug.

'Anything else?' asked Strabo.

Antonius shook his head.

'Back to your section then.'

'Torches,' said Cassius. 'Do we have any?'

'*We* do,' said Kabir.

'There's a stack in the barracks,' said Strabo. 'We've plenty of oil to keep them alight. And there's a load of dry branches still in the stables too – they just need tying together.'

'Then we should make up some more,' Cassius said. 'I'll get my section on to it.'

He then noticed Simo standing behind Kabir. The Gaul looked anxious about disturbing the conversation.

'Excuse me.'

Cassius ushered Simo towards the middle of the street before speaking.

'What is it?'

'I've finished the preparation, sir. Not with everything, of course, but the key ingredients are there. Ideally it should be drunk soon.'

Though all thoughts of the Praetorian had disappeared since

the arrival of the Palmyrans, Cassius knew it would be foolish to waste an opportunity to get the man on his side.

'Good, good. Any sign of him?'

'Well he's not at the inn, sir. Still sleeping perhaps.'

'And how's the boy doing?'

'Slow to start but working well now.'

'I'll be along soon.'

'Very well, sir.'

Cassius returned to the others.

'I must attend to something – shouldn't take long. Can you three get back to the gatehouse? See if you can work out what's going on?'

'Not much else we can do,' shrugged the Sicilian. The trio marched away through the gap.

The first section were conveniently close, just outside one of the dwellings. Three of them were tightening a leather shield cover, two were decanting water from a barrel whilst two more checked each other's armour. The oldest of them was Vestinus, a man who'd seemed capable and keen every time Cassius had encountered him.

'First section, get finished as soon as you can. There are some branches in the stables that need tying up for torches. Leave enough for the camels then take the rest to the workshop. I want all of them oiled and ready. Vestinus, you're in charge. Quick as you can.'

Back in the square, Cassius saw Avso by the well, splashing water on to his face from a barrel. Cassius stalked towards the aid post with the aim of avoiding him.

'Centurion!'

Wiping wet hair away from his eyes, Avso loped across the square.

Cassius stopped and waited for him. The Thracian's hollow cheeks and sunken eyes made his face a difficult one to warm to, yet there was a trace of vulnerability there now.

'He's dead?' asked Avso quietly. 'You're sure of it?'

Cassius nodded, then glanced around, unsure what to say.

'Never could control himself,' continued Avso. 'Poor excuse for a soldier. I should curse the fool.'

'A friend is a friend. And loyalty is an admirable trait.'

Avso coughed harshly and looked up, his face darkening.

'Save your sympathy for those beyond the gate. They shall need it more than I.'

Simo was wrapping up Gemellus' body. The legionary's boots, tunic, weapons and equipment had been piled at the end of the bed. The smell inside the aid post reminded Cassius of a butcher's just down the street from his home in Ravenna. Freshly killed piglets and chickens would be hung outside on hooks, blood dripping from the carcasses into pails below.

Simo looked up from his work.

'Please, continue.'

The Gaul folded the edge of the sheet twice round Gemellus' head.

'It is not wise to keep bodies here, sir,' said Simo as he finished up. 'Where can we put them?'

'By one of the walls perhaps. I can't think of anywhere else. I'm afraid there'll be more before long.'

Simo nodded solemnly.

'I shall put their belongings back in the barracks.'

'Where's this preparation then?'

Simo moved to the back of the aid post and bent over one of the chests, picking up a small jar of milky liquid.

Cassius took the jar.

'What's in it?'

'Mint, honey, charcoal, some spices. Luckily I still had a little milk left over from Nessara. Oh, and bronze.'

'Bronze?'

'The recipe actually called for copper, sir. It was the best I could do.'

'Where did you get bronze?'

'I shaved some grains from a shield boss with my dagger.'

'Ingenious. And this should work?'

'I have no idea, sir. There are several spices missing, the milk has soured and I've had to estimate the proportions. But the book claims this is a treatment for recurring, painful ailments of the gut, especially lumps and stones.'

'Well, it's worth a try.'

Julius arrived with a small barrel of water, which he placed next to two others by the door.

'Are you sure it's a good idea, sir?' asked Simo, a pained expression on his face.

'Well if it doesn't cure him, it might poison him. Either way you'll have helped.'

Leaving his helmet in the aid post, Cassius made his way into the barracks, holding the jar carefully in his hand. He heard the man before he saw him; the volcanic rumbles emanating from the last room suggested a deep sleep. Cassius peered round the doorway.

The Praetorian was lying face down across two beds, his head atop a rolled-up tunic. His vast from eased slowly up and down with each snore. Below the bed, straw had pushed through holes in the mattress on to the floor. Under the window were no less than five jugs, an amphora, and a half-eaten hunk of dried pork only partially visible through a buzzing cloud of flies. The odour inside the room was a concoction of decaying foodstuffs and human emissions Cassius had little wish to identify.

Opposite the doorway was a large wooden chest. On top was a helmet and an enormous piece of armour. The helmet was almost identical in design to Cassius' but the armour was very different, composed of hundreds of rounded brass scales, sewn by yards of hardy thread to a cloth undergarment. Often favoured by Praetorian Guardsmen, the archaic shirts resembled golden feathers from a distance. Cassius wondered how much it weighed.

Next to the chest was a freakishly large sword, again similar to Cassius' own yet a third wider and longer. There was also a huge rectangular shield decorated with three immaculately rendered scorpions. These, Cassius knew, symbolised the role of the Emperor Tiberius in the formation of the Guard. Despite his

235

current condition, it was evident that the Praetorian had not yet given up every association with his past life.

There was a grunt as Cassius neared the bed. He was unsure how to go about waking the man. It seemed unwise to actually touch him so he decided to use the bed frame. He put a hand on the closest horizontal beam and shook it. There was no reaction. As the giant had slept through all the events of the day, something more forceful was obviously required. Cassius took firmer hold of the beam and jolted it left and right.

The Praetorian's body trembled. The snoring stopped. He sniffed, then pawed at his face.

Cassius straightened up.

'Good evening,' he said loudly.

The Praetorian belched, twisted his neck and looked up at Cassius. He mumbled something then turned over. Lifting each jug in turn, he cast them aside once he realised they were empty.

Cassius held up the jar.

'My attendant has prepared this for you. It will ease your ailment. A recipe by Dioscorides of Greece no less.'

Ignoring him, the Praetorian swung his feet round and sat up with surprising speed. He groaned and ran a hand across his head.

'Here,' said Cassius, proffering the drink. 'I'm sure it will help you feel better.'

The Praetorian rose. As his frame unfolded itself to its full breadth, Cassius instinctively retreated. The large, grey eyes, now lined with red, settled on him.

'You again.'

'Won't you try it?'

The Praetorian was already on his way when Cassius offered the drink once more. With a casual shove, he caught Cassius high on the arm, propelling him towards the corner. Desperate not to spill too much of the preparation, Cassius managed to keep the jar upright but stumbled into the chest, then the wall. Making no attempt to follow, he looked on as the Praetorian shuffled away.

'Well I'll just leave it here then. You can try it later!'

Looking down with distaste at the meat by the bed, Cassius

drew his dagger. He speared the pork and flicked it out of the window. The flies followed their meal.

'Bloody man.'

With a final despairing look at the jar, he placed it carefully on the ground next to the corner of the bed.

Calling in at the aid post to pick up his helmet, Cassius was unsurprised to learn that the Praetorian was now reinstalled at the inn. He was about to leave when Simo produced a piece of papyrus from his tunic.

'Apologies, sir. I meant to show you this earlier.'

Simo unfolded the sheet.

'I copied out a list from the century roll. This carries the name of every man in the garrison. I consulted some of the legionaries. It is accurate.'

'Ah. Well done. I meant to do that myself. We must keep track of the injured and the dead.'

'Yes, sir.'

'Barates, of course. Flavian. And that man there is Gemellus.'

'Yes, sir. I know.'

'You should identify them on here somehow. Those badly wounded, those lost.'

Gazing down at the list, Cassius wondered how it might change over the next few hours; how many of the names would remain untouched, how many more would be marked.

'Cavalry,' Serenus said as Cassius stepped up into the northern tower.

'Where?'

'Forming up behind the infantry in the centre,' answered Strabo, not turning from the arrow slit. 'They came up from behind the crest already armoured. Must have made camp there. I think this is it.'

Kabir, standing next to Serenus, was wiping dust from the front of his jerkin.

'You agree?' Cassius asked him.

'I do.'

'How much light do we have left?'

'Good light? Perhaps an hour. It will have to be soon.'

'May I see?'

Strabo moved aside. Apart from the red tinge in the sky behind the Palmyrans, there was at first sight little change. Then Cassius saw the mounted figures moving around beyond the main mass of infantry. The cavalry were just as Strabo had described.

Each rider was covered from head to foot. Basic protection was provided by a mail shirt connected to the helmet at the neck and reaching far below their knees. The shirts were reinforced by solid chest plates and segmental armour that ran down each limb, even covering the feet. The horses were similarly attired, with only their lower legs unprotected. Some of the men carried swords, some long lances. Every movement of man and beast signified power and grace.

'Rather magnificent, aren't they?' observed Cassius.

'Rather deadly,' added Kabir.

The first two lines of warriors behind the ram fell out of formation then marched south, crossing in front of the horse archers.

'Something's up,' said Cassius.

'Are the bows raised?' asked Serenus.

Cassius checked carefully.

'No.'

'Then we should perhaps observe from above.'

'Agreed.'

Cassius kept watch as the others clambered up the ladder in turn. A group of about twenty archers had broken ranks with the swordsmen and now continued south, walking parallel to the rally line.

Last up to the walkway, Cassius positioned himself between Kabir and Serenus. A second mixed group of infantry and archers was moving north. Each detachment was being trailed by a single cart. The southerly group had now turned ninety degrees, maintaining the two-hundred-yard gap as they neared the mounted sentry opposite the south wall.

238

'Encirclement,' said Serenus quietly. 'They mean to attack the north and south walls too. Probably ladders in those carts.'

'So much for the killing area,' added Strabo.

'I'll fetch Minicius,' said Serenus. He let Avso up before climbing down the ladder.

'Syrian,' said Strabo, 'you should put some of your men at the walls now. If one side falls we've had it.'

'Not yet,' said Avso as he sat down. 'We should still concentrate our main force at the gate. They are.'

'And leave thirty men holed up in houses for no good reason?' countered Strabo.

The three Romans were huddled together, heads below the wall. Only Kabir was still looking out at the Palmyrans.

'We discussed this,' Cassius said firmly. 'The Syrians will be best used behind us, against the enemy in the killing area. If the walls are threatened—'

Strabo cut him off. 'What do you mean "if"? They—'

Before he could continue, Kabir interrupted.

'You may want to see this.'

Azaf was now the only swordsman still on his horse. Just ahead of him was the ram and the ten armoured men stationed by its wheels. Gathered behind him were the ranks of infantry, blades drawn and shields up, ready to move. Azaf had insisted that Razir repeat the orders to his lieutenants now at the northern and southern flanks. What he had planned was unconventional and not without risk. It would require considerable patience and discipline.

'Give the order.'

'Yes, *strategos*.'

Razir unleashed a deep, penetrating cry.

'Forward!'

The Palmyran forces on three sides of Alauran – swordsmen, cavalry and archers alike – advanced as one.

★ ★ ★

Realising his helmet was loose, Cassius reached for the chinstrap. The floor below him was pocked with marks created by boots, spear ends and sword points, revealing the pale grey clay under the white paint. He stared at it, eyes glazing over. Now it was the turn of the Palmyran infantry to beat their sword handles against their shields; a rhythmic, insistent clamour that dulled the senses. It took Cassius a while to realise he couldn't adjust the strap because his fingers were shaking so much. Clenching them tightly, he saw that the others were ready to leave.

'At least the waiting's over,' said Strabo, shouting over the noise of the enemy.

'Good,' added Avso.

'We should be with our sections,' continued the Sicilian.

'Where's Minicius?' Cassius asked.

'Here, sir,' said a shaky voice.

Minicius was already up on the walkway and sheltering behind Avso, the tuba between his feet.

Kabir crawled away and was followed swiftly down into the tower by Avso.

Cassius felt a sudden surge of panic. Things were happening quickly now. Too quickly.

'Come on,' Strabo said, his tone almost paternal as he gestured for Cassius to follow him.

A shout from Minicius halted them.

'Sir!'

'What is it?'

'They've stopped.'

Whatever Minicius was talking about, Cassius knew it wasn't the clattering of the shields: the rumbling cacophony suggested the Palmyrans were just yards from the gate.

'So they have,' said Strabo.

'How far out?' asked Cassius.

'Eighty feet. Bows still down. Even the rammers have stopped.'

Strabo then checked the flanks.

'The others too. Strange.'

It soon became clear that this was more than a momentary

interruption to the assault. The noise continued – archers and cavalry adding to the clamour – but still the advance did not come. With Strabo keeping watch, Cassius and Minicius crouched down, eyes locked on the Sicilian, awaiting any clue as to what might happen next.

'What game is this, Purple Cloak?' said Strabo.

Abruptly the noise stopped and the end of a shouted order was audible.

Strabo checked the flanks once more.

'Just standing there.'

'What do you make of it?' asked Cassius.

'Perhaps they wish to confuse us. Wear us down.'

As they sat there, awaiting the single shout that might finally signal the start of the battle, Cassius realised how much the temperature had dropped. Twilight was near. He looked across at Strabo.

'You seemed sure they wouldn't attack at night.'

'I was.'

Azaf sensed unease all round him. The men didn't understand why they had been ordered so close to the walls only to stand to. Neither did they understand why he had delayed the attack throughout the afternoon and evening. Still, it was not their place to question his methods. Even Razir had not voiced his concern, simply passing on the orders without comment.

Bezda, however, was another matter. When the messenger finally arrived from the rear, Azaf was surprised it had taken so long. The nervous-looking cart driver was escorted forward by Razir. He at least had the sense to bow. Azaf told him to speak.

'Sir, a message from Master Bezda. His horses and men are tiring. With respect, he asks when the attack will commence. Or whether it will commence at all.'

Azaf looked up at the darkening sky. Around him, men listened intently.

'Tell him he will have a decision soon.'

'Yes, *strategos*.'

The driver bowed again and began his trip back through the lines.

Razir paced in front of Azaf's horse, twisting tufts of his beard between finger and thumb. After years spent living and fighting together, Azaf could tell when his most trusted warrior had something to say.

'Spit it out then.'

Razir put a hand upon the horse's neck, looked up at Azaf, and spoke to him in hushed tones.

'The light fades, sir. If I knew what you had in mind—'

Azaf gave a thin smile.

'Patience, Razir. Patience.'

As the red sun dropped below the horizon, the silhouettes of individual horsemen and soldiers merged, then were lost to the darkness. Blinking and rubbing their eyes, Strabo and Cassius peered out, trying to discern any suggestion of movement. Occasionally Strabo would turn north or south, concerned that the forces on either flank had already begun some covert advance. Cassius would turn too, convinced the Sicilian had seen something. After one such occasion, they turned back east just as the Palmyrans lit the first fire.

What began as an orange dot was soon a blaze several feet high, joined by another, then another. Sparks drifted into the sky. Sometimes a shape would pass close by, illuminated by the flames. The first three fires marked the rally line but before long more were alight to the north and south.

To Cassius, the message seemed obvious: the Palmyrans didn't want the darkness to offer the Romans even the slightest relief. Alauran was still surrounded; the garrison was still trapped. The attack would still come.

XXVIII

There were only two fires burning inside the walls of Alauran when darkness fell. One had been started by the Syrians to light their torches, the other was at the officers' quarters, where Simo had a large pot of water boiling to clean sheets for use as bandages.

The men of the first section waited patiently at the door while Serenus used a stick to light each torch in turn. The tops of the tightly bound bunches of palm branches were covered by oil-soaked goatskin. Serenus was dispatching the torch-bearers to each corner of the compound and the centre of each wall. All were issued with a spare for later on and he repeated the same orders to every legionary.

'Don't climb upon the wall. You are there to guard against incursions, not show the enemy where you are.'

With typical foresight, Simo had lit nine small oil lamps. Two of them were on stands inside the officers' quarters, two in the aid post. Four more had been swiftly claimed by passing legionaries. The last one he had kept in reserve.

'For you, sir.'

'Well done,' said Cassius, taking the lamp as he passed the aid post and slowing down to avoid spilling the oil. Minicius was with him, tuba in hand. Cassius had just sent the men of the third, fourth and fifth sections to the remaining three sides of the compound, with orders to space themselves out evenly, listen for any signs of movement and report any sign of attack. Strabo and his section were manning the gatehouse.

He found Serenus inside, returning the lighting stick to the fire.

'Any change?' asked the veteran.

'Some movement. Nothing definite.'

'It is odd. But if they do plan to attack under cover of night, I see no reason for them to delay. We should check the perimeter at once. Shall we start with the rear wall?'

The first legionary they came across was Vestinus, who had just arrived at the north-west corner. He was facing the wall with the torch held well away from him, listening carefully. Above them, the branches of the closest palm rustled in the dark.

'Anything?' asked Serenus.

'Not so far.'

'Let me borrow that.'

Serenus took the torch and held it high as he walked along the rear wall, examining the edge. He turned round after a few yards and returned it to Vestinus.

'Check now and again as I did. If you see or hear anything, cry out at once.'

They continued along the western wall, passing Crispus and the third section. Serenus kept up a quick pace and stopped regularly to check the view from the firing steps. There were still no fires visible to the west but they had agreed that the rear wall must remain as well guarded as the others.

The camels snorted and shifted in their stables as the trio started along the southern wall. Then the horses began to whinny and pace.

'They share our disquiet,' said Cassius.

'Perhaps,' answered Serenus. 'Legionary, if I hear that tuba scrape on the ground one more time, I'm going to make you carry it above your head one-handed.'

'Yes, sir,' replied Minicius.

Halfway along the southern wall they encountered another torch-bearer.

'Anything?'

Before the sentry could answer, a cry went up.

'Over here!'

'The north wall!' yelled Serenus.

They ran round the front of the granary and across the square.

Wishing he could get rid of the lamp, Cassius heard the pounding of feet to his right. Half a dozen Syrians appeared, torches held high, wavering light glinting off their blades.

'Look out!' someone shouted. One of the Syrians pointed into the air.

Three flaming arrows had just reached the apex of their flight and were dropping towards them.

Luckily, they had been fired so high that the defenders had time to get out of the way. Two landed harmlessly in the dust, another embedded itself in the wall of the closest house. One of Kabir's men plucked it out of the clay then snuffed out the flame with his boot.

Cassius caught up with Serenus just as he climbed up on to the nearest firing step. Wheezing, the veteran raised his head above the northern wall.

Three more legionaries arrived.

'Started just now, sir,' said one.

More orange flashes streamed into the sky. Serenus half fell off the step, landing heavily next to Cassius.

'Many torches. Moving,' he announced as Cassius helped him to his feet. 'They may be closing in.'

At least ten flaming arrows had landed inside the compound. The legionaries set about extinguishing all those they could reach. Several had hit the barracks. Serenus requisitioned a torch from one legionary and sent him there at once.

'Quickly! There are barrels there if you need them.'

Kabir could also be heard shouting orders as his men rushed inside the dwellings. Though grateful for his help, Cassius was confident fire would not quickly take hold there; the rooms had been emptied and the parched clay brick would not burn easily on its own.

Once more holding the torch high, Serenus led Cassius and Minicius east along the northern wall. They walked slowly, listening carefully for any suggestion of advance. Shapes appeared, moved and disappeared to their right as the Syrians made their way through the houses.

Serenus paused as they neared what had once been the market-place. Cassius spied the torch-bearer at the corner and saw a faint glow within the doorway of the northern tower. He wondered what Strabo had seen of the attack.

Serenus turned and retraced his steps. As he swapped the torch from one hand to the other, a burning twig landed on Cassius' arm. Shaking it off, he managed to flick oil out of the lamp on to his wrist, barely stifling a yelp.

The veteran hurried on. They drew level with the barracks. A legionary leaned out of a window and dropped two blackened arrows into the dust. Cassius bent down and examined one. There was no metal or stone at the point. The wooden shaft had been sharpened and the top half wrapped tight with cloth soaked with something flammable.

He caught up with Serenus again. Even in the dim glow of the torch, he could see the variation in colour and texture over the area of wall repaired by Strabo's section. Serenus stopped. Cassius shut his eyes, trying to pick up any noise from beyond the wall. Only when he heard a pained cough from Serenus and opened his eyes did he realise why the veteran had halted. The light from the lamp illuminated Serenus' mail shirt, now stained with saliva and blood. He tried to speak but produced only a rasping sound.

Cassius quickly placed the lamp on the ground and took charge of the torch. Serenus wiped his chin and put his other hand against his chest.

'Here.'

Cassius helped Serenus sit down on a nearby barrel.

'We must—'

'Don't talk. Wait here a moment.'

Cassius jogged round to the side window of the officers' quarters. Simo wasn't there. He reached through the window and down to the floor; to where he knew the Gaul kept his canteen. As his fingers found it, the fire flickered: a large figure had entered the room.

'Ah, Simo—'

It was in fact Strabo, torch in one hand, pilum in the other.

'What's going on?' the Sicilian demanded.

'Fire arrows were shot over the northern wall. Serenus is ailing.'

'I'll come round.'

Taking the canteen with him, Cassius called over to the nearest man at the wall and passed him the torch. It turned out to be a young legionary named Priscus. Cassius had noticed him around because, though tall and well built, Priscus was quite possibly the meekest soldier he had come across. He assumed this was at least partly due to the lurid maroon birth mark that covered half his face. The youngster bit nervously at his lip while he listened.

'Here. I want you to check the entire perimeter. Report back—'

'Leave that to me,' said Strabo as he arrived.

'Very well. Anything to the east?'

'Nothing new.'

'Come on,' Strabo said to Priscus.

The two of them receded into the darkness towards the temple. Cassius blinked as his eyes readjusted. He hurried back round the barracks to Serenus and passed him the canteen. The veteran drank heartily, then let out a long breath.

'Better?'

'Yes.'

Serenus looked down at his armour and wiped away the rest of the bloody spittle.

'That was as bad as I've had it. My chest burns so.'

'Should you talk?'

'Probably not. But the worst has passed.'

Cassius listened for any sign of another attack but all was quiet. He tried not to think of the Palmyran warriors skulking just yards away.

'Rest easy. I'll wait here with you a while. Strabo's checking the walls.'

'The Sicilian has done well,' said Serenus, matching Cassius' hushed tones. 'The men like him. Always have.' He grinned. 'We must have seemed like a bunch of brigands to you on that first day.'

247

'Given the circumstances, I wasn't entirely surprised. You have known Strabo a long time?'

'Before coming here, only by his face. Our cohort was completely reorganised before we left Raphanea – the legion's headquarters. What I'd give to be behind those walls now – solid stone two yards thick.'

Serenus drank some more and leaned back against the uneven clay wall. The compound was quiet again. It seemed the brief attack was over.

'And Centurion Petronius?' asked Cassius, 'you knew him well?'

'Quite well. I had hoped we would have been able to get his body back to Antioch by now. His wife deserves that much.'

'He was married?'

'Yes. Many of the men here have wives. Syrian girls mostly. I too.'

Cassius was surprised. Though he knew many of the legionaries had been stationed in the East for years, decades even, he somehow imagined that if they had wives, they would be back home.

'It's been so long since I've seen her I can hardly recall her face,' continued Serenus. 'It's a pretty one. I know that.'

'She lives in Antioch?'

'No. A village on the river about ten miles upstream. We were married three years ago, though it's more than two since we parted. I bought a small farmhouse close to her family's lands. There are a few goats, some figs, endless olive trees. Her father runs a small press and the oil fetches a good price in the city. She has her brothers to help her and makes enough to get by. At least she did. I hope all is well with her.'

'Her name?'

'Eskari. Has a nice ring to it, does it not?'

Serenus looked down at the ground, clearly preoccupied by thoughts of his past life.

'I'll go and find Strabo,' Cassius said. 'You wait here until you feel ready to move.'

'Very well.'

Lamp in hand, Cassius marched quickly past the barracks and turned right past the inn.

'Which idiot's trying to start a fire?'

The Praetorian was sitting in complete darkness. Once again, the slurred pronunciation and combative delivery couldn't entirely disguise his urbane intonation.

Cassius stopped. It was impossible to see anything inside the inn, so he simply stared at where he knew the Praetorian's usual seat to be.

'Our enemies fired them. They have surrounded us.'

There was a grunt, then the sound of wine being slurped down. The Praetorian fumbled with his words but managed to finish the sentence.

'—what all the noise was about.'

For a moment, Cassius thought about talking to him. He could have told him about Barates, perhaps shown him the body; appealed to him again, persuaded him to fight. Then he recalled what Serenus had told him about not wasting time on the man and he resolved to waste no more. Grateful that he was at least happy to continue his drinking and cause no further disruption, Cassius went on his way.

The hours of night wore on and still the Palmyrans didn't attack. Finding Strabo back at the gatehouse with nothing new to report, Cassius completed another tour of the perimeter with identical results. Serenus was up on his feet and checking his own section, as was Avso. Kabir had placed men on the roof of every dwelling.

Cassius had completely lost track of time, so decided to fetch his hourglass. It was another seldom used item but he was fairly sure Simo would have packed it. On the way to the officers' quarters, he asked four legionaries how many hours they thought had passed since sundown. The answers varied greatly but averaged out at three.

He found Simo building up the fire.

'My hourglass is in the chest, isn't it? Do you have the key?'

Simo took the key from the purse on his belt and passed it to Cassius.

'Sir, might I ask you for something. A small favour.'

'You may.'

Simo pointed over at the desk. In one corner was a folded sheet of papyrus.

'I've written a letter, sir. For my family. In case . . . well, in case.'

'I see.'

'I wondered where I should put it – so that it might be found. I've included my father's address.'

Cassius didn't have the heart to tell Simo just how incredibly unlikely it was that such a letter might find its way back to Antioch.

'Perhaps with the century roll and Petronius' papers. That might be the best place.'

Simo nodded gratefully.

'Have you thought of doing the same, sir?'

'No, not at all,' Cassius replied honestly. 'I haven't the time.'

'Then perhaps you would like to leave a few thoughts with me, sir. I could pass them on if—'

'If I were to die.'

Simo bowed his head.

'I prefer to try not to think of such things, Simo. I don't believe it helps.'

'I understand, sir, of course.'

The chest was under Simo's bed. Cassius put his oil lamp to one side, hauled the chest out, unlocked it and flung the lid open. To his annoyance, the hourglass had tipped on to its side and had sand in both ends. He had just locked the chest shut again when Simo cried out.

'What is it?'

The Gaul was at the door, pointing outside.

'Arrows! There!'

'Take this,' Cassius said, throwing the hourglass to Simo.

He darted out of the doorway, still balancing the oil lamp in one hand. The sky was lit by a dozen sizzling orange streams. Bolts landed in the compound across the length of the southern wall as Cassius ran across the square.

'Hold your positions!' he yelled, repeating the order over his shoulder. One arrow had hit the northern side of the granary roof, lodging itself in the palm branches; it would surely take only moments for the flames to spread.

Scrambling past the granary steps, Cassius almost collided with two legionaries. One was holding a torch, the other a pail of water. Both were staring dumbly up at the southern side of the roof where two more arrows were alight.

Cassius put his lamp down.

'What are you doing? We must act now!'

Without allowing himself a second thought, Cassius reached for the makeshift ladder he had climbed two days ago. He planted a boot on the bottom rung and started upward.

'Sir, what—'

Cursing the darkness, Cassius climbed steadily, trying to ignore all thoughts of his exposed position and the Palmyran archers. He stopped only when his helmet clanked against the roof edge. Reaching up, he felt his way through the dry palm and found a sloping beam.

Pain pulsed through his fingers. Assuming he had spiked his hand on some sharp twig, he raised his head over the edge only to see flames licking round his wrist. He instinctively let go and would have fallen had his left hand not found purchase lower down the beam.

There were shouts from all around. Cassius couldn't decide if he was hearing Latin or Aramaic. He was trying to remember what he'd intended to do once he got up there.

Suddenly a hand gripped his leg.

'Here, sir! Here!'

Cassius reached down. He expected to feel the strap of the pail but it was a wooden pole being passed up to him.

'Take it, sir.'

His fingers closed round the pole.

'What— What am I supposed to—'

'Tear the branches down, sir! It's a sand rake!'

Cassius dropped his grip to the middle of the rake, wedged his chin over the roof edge and reached as high as he could. He pulled the rake down, dislodging most of the fiery branches. As they slid towards him, he twisted his arm round and swept them off the front of the granary. The first of the fires was out.

The second arrow had landed closer to the top of the roof. The area aflame was no more than a yard across but much harder to reach. Resting the rake along the closest sloping beam, Cassius clambered up until both knees were on the roof edge. His armour made every action doubly taxing, but with one hand braced on the beam he was able to extend the rake high enough to reach the burning branches. Flaming leaves dropped down into the granary.

'Inside! Somebody get inside!'

As he continued to flick the branches off the roof, Cassius checked to his left, surprised but relieved to find no more arrows had landed on the granary.

'Get back down here!'

Not sure if the shout was meant for him, Cassius was reaching for the last of the flaming palm fronds when something hit his right shoulder.

The force of the impact knocked him forward on to the beam. He came down squarely on his chest, somehow maintaining his grip on the rake. Aware of light and voices below, he lay there for a moment. He felt no pain in his shoulder and hoped the mail had done its job. Looking up, he saw that only a couple of palm fronds were still alight. He knocked them down into the granary, hoping someone was there to extinguish them.

'Come back down!'

It was definitely Strabo; he sounded close by.

So much of the palm had now been raked away or incinerated that Cassius could see the other side of the roof. The fire there was out. He slid back down the beam and dropped the rake to the ground.

Fighting the urge to hurry, he took care to get down safely and dropped the final few feet, finding himself amongst a crowd of legionaries and Syrians. Like the Romans, Kabir's men were facing the southern wall, all holding their slings. Cassius looked along the granary roof, then at the dwellings: there was no sign of fire.

'A job well done,' said Strabo, looming out of the dark, torch held high. 'That took some balls.'

'What about inside, there were—'

'Crispus dealt with it. The other side of the roof too.'

Cassius turned round.

'Check my shoulder, would you? I think I was hit.'

Strabo held the torch above the armour. 'You were. Lucky you've such a fine piece of mail. A couple of dented rings but that's all. Made a right target of yourself up there. We chucked a couple of javelins and heard a cry or too. I think they've backed off again.'

'Good.'

Cassius realised now how out of breath he was. He turned his hands over and examined his fingers. In places, the skin bore the purple shine of a slight burn but there was no real damage.

'Next time send one of the men up,' advised Strabo. 'You must learn to – what's the word?'

'Delegate?'

'That's the one.'

A group of Syrians separated and Crispus appeared, a rake still in his hand.

'Sir, Avso reports that the Palmyrans have moved back. No torches closer than their original position.'

'Another feint,' said Strabo thoughtfully.

'Well done, sir,' said Crispus.

'Well done yourself. Why would they try and burn this down? They must know it's the granary.'

'I think those were strays, or there was an error in communication,' answered Crispus, wiping grime from his face. 'After those first few hit, the rest were aimed at the dwellings.'

253

Cassius turned to Strabo.

'Anyone hurt?'

'Not that I know of.'

'We should get the men back to their positions then.'

'I'll do it quietly,' said the Sicilian, 'in case those beyond the wall speak Latin.'

The crowd began to break up, leaving Cassius to catch his breath. He checked his belt: both dagger and sword were still in place. The mail shirt, however, had ridden up. Pulling it down, he noticed a glow behind him.

There on the ground, almost under the granary, was his oil lamp. It was still burning bright.

XXIX

The last few grains of sand dropped on to the golden mound below. Cassius flipped the hourglass over.

'Six hours gone,' he said to no one in particular.

The cold of the desert night had penetrated every corner of the compound. Those at the walls were wrapped in their cloaks and the torch-bearers no longer resented their burdens. Cassius and the section leaders were gathered together in the officers' quarters, sitting on stools in a half-circle before the fire. Only Avso was absent, taking his turn to check the perimeter. Having just served some hot wine, Simo had left for the aid post.

Though his efforts at the granary had tired him, Cassius felt glad to have made a direct contribution to the defence. There was, he sensed, already a subtle difference in the way the legionaries viewed him.

'I've know some long nights over the years,' said Strabo, his hands circling the cup of wine, 'but I fancy this might be the longest yet. Mind you, I recall a few nasty waits around the time old Odenathus started taking charge.'

'You've been in Syria that long?' asked Cassius.

'Twelve years, I think. Might even be thirteen.' Strabo's eyes were fixed on the fire. 'Things were fairly quiet when we first arrived, then Dura fell to the Persians and we found ourselves marching east. Luckily the Palmyrans got the worst of it. We were camped out close to the Euphrates. For three nights they told us we'd see action the next day, but it never happened. Bad information from the Security Service as I recall. Not that anything good ever came from that nest of snakes.'

Cassius observed the nods of agreement from the legionaries.

Based on what he'd heard in Syria, the Service's reputation amongst rank-and-file soldiers was not far short of atrocious. He hadn't enjoyed lying to the men about his identity, but was glad he'd followed General Navio's counsel.

'Odd, is it not?' said Serenus. 'That we now find ourselves at war with our former allies.'

'*Odenathus* was our ally,' said Strabo sharply. 'Some would say he went too far, but we've not known many emperors as strong in a good many years. That whore wife of his is another matter. Fancy knocking off your husband at a birthday party.'

'That's just a rumour, isn't it?' said Cassius.

Strabo gave a cynical look as he downed more of the steaming wine.

'Are you married?' Cassius asked him.

'No,' Strabo answered quickly, almost indignantly. Cassius wished he hadn't asked.

'The guard officer cannot afford to take a wife,' said Avso, appearing suddenly from the gloom outside. Gathering his cloak about him, he took up a stool and glanced speculatively across at Strabo. 'Isn't that right?'

The Sicilian finished off the wine and set the cup down.

'At least I've had offers. And not, like you, solely from pox-ridden streetwalkers.'

'Why don't you remind us how you came to lose your life savings? Quite a tale.'

Strabo's eyes stayed on the flames as he replied.

'Before you came in, we were discussing what can happen when alliances are broken. How swiftly ally can become enemy.'

'Just making conversation,' said the Thracian. 'Didn't mean to cause you embarrassment.'

'The tale doesn't embarrass me in the least. Fortuna simply chose not to smile upon me that night.' Strabo glanced at the door. 'I'm assuming all is quiet out there?'

'Like a temple on pay day,' replied Avso.

'I shall take my turn,' said Serenus, who seemed to have recovered himself.

The Sicilian crossed his arms and begrudgingly began.

'It was a couple of years ago. I was on leave in Tarsus with a few other lads from the century. We'd been playing doubles all week. Anyway, there was this bunch from—'

'Doubles?' queried Cassius.

'By Mars. A soldier that doesn't play dice.'

Cassius shrugged. His family had always taken a dim view of gambling. Dice in particular was seen as a game for the lower ranks of society.

'Two players. For every round both roll three dice. Highest total wins. Simple. Except the loser can "double" – challenge. As long as he has the money. The winner has to accept. So they both double their stake. When the money's in, they roll again, and so on. It's high risk, usually doesn't last long. You need balls – big, hairy balls – to make much out of it.'

Cassius nodded.

'We were staying in the same inn as a bunch from the Fourth Cohort. I'd cleaned out all our boys, one of theirs had done the same. Name of Glaucus, ratty-looking type, not unlike our Thracian friend over there. Someone decided we should play this big game. The place was packed: officers, men, locals. I started well and it just got better. This Glaucus kept losing, then doubling, then losing again. I had thousands piled up. But this fool wouldn't let it go.'

Strabo shook his head ruefully.

'Then I rolled an eight. He got ten.'

'So he had won?' asked Cassius.

'Unless I doubled.'

'You did it?'

'Three thousand two hundred denarii. I had two thousand with me, the rest in Antioch, which the legion clerk stumped up. I rolled a fourteen. Great score. Glaucus made ten or eleven, I think. I'd done it. But then *he* doubled. Nobody could believe it. He'd lost everything, but all his mates chipped in. They said he'd never lost a long game before. So I had to accept, even though it would mean every coin I had in the world if I lost. I made

257

nine. The lucky son of a bitch hit sixteen. I can still see it now – two fives and a six.'

'You lost over six thousand denarii?' said Cassius, eyes wide. It was a huge sum, enough to buy a decent house in Rome.

'Only if I dropped out. I wanted to double again. My mates wanted to help me out – for a share of the winnings, of course. They'd never seen *me* lose. But Petronius and the other centurions put a stop to it. I never forgave him for that.'

'So you had to pay?'

'I'd been in the army ten years. A decade of hard slog all gone in one night.'

Avso leaned forward, closer to the fire.

'That's not quite where the story ends, though, is it, guard officer?'

Strabo didn't react.

'The way I heard it you refused to pay up because the game had been stopped. You head-butted this Glaucus and it turned into a brawl – Third Cohort versus the Fourth. The inn was virtually destroyed and two hundred sober Sarmatian auxiliaries had to be ordered in to break it up. You only got out of it by bribing half the officers in Tarsus with a stash of looted emeralds.'

'Shouldn't believe everything you hear, Thracian,' said Strabo with a grin. 'Though I believe there was a small scrap after the game – probably down to a spilt drink or something.'

Avso nodded knowingly. Cassius smiled.

'Still,' Strabo continued, 'Fortuna has been pretty kind ever since. I paid what was owed and my luck has held.'

He looked around the room, then out of the doorway.

'Well, until now I suppose.'

With that, an uncomfortable silence settled over them.

After a time, Kabir appeared at the door.

'Is something wrong?' Cassius asked him.

'Not at all. May I?'

The Syrian pointed at the fire.

'Please,' said Cassius.

Kabir squatted between two of the chairs and warmed his hands.

'How are your men?' asked Cassius.

'Anxious. It has been a long time since we last fought. I have placed half of them inside the dwellings to take what rest they can. They will exchange places with the others before long.'

'Perhaps we should do the same?' suggested Cassius.

'We have less than forty men out there as it is,' said Strabo. 'Do you really think half that number can cover all those yards of wall?'

'I can move my men out alongside them if you wish,' offered Kabir. 'The Palmyran tactics are clear. Twice they have made attack seem likely, then halted. By harrying us through the hours of darkness, they mean to weaken our bodies and minds.'

'Obviously,' answered Strabo impatiently, 'but what of *their* bodies and minds? They were standing out there for hours in the heat, now the cold; they're worse off than us.'

'You think all those men remain there still? I doubt there's more than a hundred at the wall. The others will be sleeping back at their camp.'

'Even if that's true, we don't have the luxury of men to spare,' countered the Sicilian.

Avso spoke up: 'But if this is a long night, tomorrow is sure to be the longest of days. A few hours' rest could make a big difference.'

Cassius turned back to Kabir.

'You don't think they will attack before morning?'

'I don't.'

'Strabo?'

'We cannot know. This Purple Cloak is a sly one. Do not assume we can read his intentions.'

'Avso?'

'I think they'll attack at first light. Ideal for the cavalry.'

'Then we shall divide the men into two shifts. Take every other man off the wall and send them to the barracks for three hours. Then we'll swap them. Kabir, you will redeploy your men?'

'I'll do it now.'

The Syrian left. Cassius and Avso stood up. Strabo stayed on his stool and shrugged.

'Fine, just ignore me then.'

'You'll benefit too,' said Cassius. 'What's good enough for the men is good enough for us. Serenus and I shall take three hours of sleep first. Then you two can take a turn.'

With half the legionaries in the barracks, Cassius was on his way back to the officers' quarters when he heard raised voices.

'What do you think this is, man – a drill? Look at me, you dozy bastard!'

Cassius ran over to the north-west corner. Avso, his gaunt features lit by torchlight, turned as he approached. Strabo was there too, facing a legionary pressed up against the wall. His knee shot up and the soldier doubled over.

'What's going on here?'

'Asleep at his post,' explained the Sicilian, staring contemptuously at the cloaked figure. Cassius moved his lamp lower. The man twisted his head and narrowed his eyes against the light. Spotting the dark blotch of the birthmark, Cassius realised it was Priscus.

'What have you to say for yourself then?' he asked.

Priscus tried to reply but he was still winded.

Strabo spun his pilum over in his hand and swung the solid wooden handle against Priscus' right knee. There was a sharp crack and the young legionary collapsed to the ground with a cry. His cloak fell from his shoulders and he lay there moaning, reaching for his knee.

'Bloody useless!' said Avso, before landing a light but deft kick to Priscus' mouth. The legionary rolled on to his back. Blood seeped from a gash in his lip.

Had they continued, Cassius would have intervened, perhaps pointing out that they needed every man fit for battle, but he saw that Strabo and Avso were satisfied with the effect of their actions. Priscus looked desperately up at him, expecting help. Cassius knew he couldn't give it.

'Get up then!' he said. 'You've another three hours to go. Then you can sleep.'

Priscus slowly raised himself. At his full height he was actually taller than Strabo, yet he backed away until he was touching the wall again. Still wary of some final blow, he sheepishly reached down for his cloak and hung it over his shoulders.

Strabo again spun the pilum in his hand and leaned closer, the edged point of the spear an inch from Priscus' chin.

'I'll be checking on you every hour. And those eyes better be wide open or you'll be getting this end next time. Do I make myself clear?'

'Yes, sir,' stammered Priscus.

Avso moved away.

'And wrap that cloak round you properly,' added Strabo. 'It's like winter out here tonight.'

Not long afterwards, Cassius lay across his bed with two blankets to cover him. He had kept his tunic and boots on and his belt was close by; he could move quickly if he had to. The oil lamp, now a valued companion, burned bright atop the table next to him. Next door, Serenus rested by the fire.

Cassius stared up at the shadowy recesses of the roof. He tried to recall and order the events of the day but soon found himself back in that moment where the Palmyran blade had swept down upon poor Flavian. Gruesome though it had been, some part of him valued exposure to such brutality. He hoped it might toughen him, and he knew he would face much, much worse.

Barates. Flavian. Gemellus. The first men lost under his command. He tried to summon images of their faces but they were vague and indistinct, composites of others: men from the garrison, those he had trained with, people from home.

Despite such dark thoughts, fatigue finally took its welcome course. Shortly after hearing Serenus turn the glass over, he fell asleep.

The rest of the night passed without major incident.

Cassius was awoken two hours later by Serenus. They passed Avso and Strabo on their way to the gatehouse.

In the second hour of the shift, with dawn not far away, another small volley of arrows were fired over the northern wall. The flames had already been put out by the time Cassius arrived. He waited until the men were settled back at the wall, then returned to the gatehouse.

Later, he and Serenus sat side by side on the walkway, watching the colours of dawn. First came scattered cracks of a deep, ominous red; then mottled swirls of purple and pink; and finally, etched round clusters of cloud, a striking pale yellow.

XXX

Fully armoured and refreshed from a good night's sleep, the cavalrymen pressed their steeds along in a slow trot, the newly risen sun at their backs. With so much movement to and from the camp, a clear track had been etched in the sand. The riders were in pairs behind Bezda, who sat high in his saddle, eyes fixed on the crest.

Azaf had just passed the cart drivers leading the swordsmen's horses back to the camp, and now he moved up past the cavalry, keeping wide of the track until he drew level with their leader. Bezda, cradling his immaculately maintained helmet in one arm, glanced sideways.

'All went well during the night?'

'I believe so. I left Razir in charge and he did what I asked. And your men?'

'One lamed his mount while riding back in the dark, but nothing more serious. I see now the logic of your actions yesterday.'

'Your men would enjoy fighting in this temperature I imagine?'

'I too. Especially against such wearied foes.'

'You may well get your chance.'

'I must tell you: our water is running dangerously short, and our feed for the horses.'

'Do not concern yourself,' answered Azaf. 'I doubt this will last much longer than the morning.'

Alauran was still cloaked in gloom and the clammy cold of night, and the soldiers warmed themselves with activity. Cups were filled from the water barrels and the remaining morsels of food finished off. Torches and lamps were collected up, cloaks and blankets returned to the barracks. Helmets, armour, belts and boots were checked and checked again.

The Syrian auxiliaries were split between the two houses. Four of the five Roman sections were lined up behind the carts. The only real noise came from the first section as they hammered nails into the timbers now in place across the access gap.

Serenus, Avso, Crispus and Kabir were with the men. Cassius and Strabo remained in the gatehouse, surveying the ranks of Palmyrans arranged precisely as they had been the previous day. Despite all the delays and feints, the garrison would face a straight-forward frontal assault after all. Only the sentries at the other three walls were not looking east; they remained focused on their Palmyran counterparts.

Strabo was kneeling in front of the arrow slit. 'Cavalry's coming up.'

'What about Avso and his staves?' asked Cassius, crouching behind Strabo and peering over his shoulder.

'We've handed them out to some of the more experienced lads. Avso found Flavian's in the barracks. He's been carving skulls into it all night.'

'And the caltrops?'

'I moved the boxes up just now. Two on either side.'

Cassius saw movement behind the southern line of archers.

'Here they come now,' Strabo said. 'Purple Cloak too. Must have had a bit of a lie-in.'

Azaf handed his reins to Razir as he dismounted. He took a brief look at Alauran, then at the well-spaced lines of archers along each flank and finally at the main body of his troops. There was now a clear gap between two similarly sized sections.

'You have divided them as I asked?'

'Yes, *strategos*. Our most experienced men are at the rear. The others will go in behind the ram. Every second man has a spear. All have shields. Young Teyya understands his task.'

Azaf watched the cavalry return to their predetermined places.

'Let us waste no more time then.'

When the cry went up, the ten men at the ram bent their backs and the wheels began to turn. As it trundled across the sand, four more moved in front and raised their shields.

'I'll stay here as long as I can,' said Strabo. 'Watch them until the last moment.'

'Very well,' answered Cassius. 'I'll check the barricades.'

Strabo gripped Cassius' forearm.

'Those barriers must hold. Even the smallest breach can turn a scrap like this.' He smoothed down his hair and pulled on his helmet. 'And keep that tuba close by.'

'I will. And you be careful.'

'You forget,' said Strabo, aiming a thumb at his chest as Cassius made his way down the ladder. 'Fortuna's friend. I rolled my dice again at dawn – a five and a six. We might get out of this yet.'

Cassius found Minicius standing where he had left him. The signaller was chewing at his bottom lip.

'Come on.'

The planks closest to the wall on both sides had been temporarily removed. Cassius and Minicius squeezed through on the northern side.

'Block it up at once,' Cassius said to two nearby legionaries.

Close to the ground and adjacent to the edge of the cart, three holes had been carved into the wall. These would accommodate short, rounded timbers to help support the carts. Once all the planks were reattached, the timbers would be slotted in. It was Avso's idea; he had overseen an identical arrangement at the southern barricade.

Manning the positions behind the first cart were Serenus' fourth section. The unoccupied men milled around with swords already drawn. Mounds of sand had been shovelled on to the edge of the cart to improve stability and they had a good supply of replacement timber nearby. Serenus himself was perched on the edge of a wooden box. He had armed himself with a pilum and now leaned against it, head bowed. Cassius saw that the box was full of the makeshift caltrops.

265

The veteran looked up.

'The ram is on its way,' Cassius said, drawing the attention of all the legionaries within earshot. 'You all right?'

'Just saving my strength,' said Serenus with a weary smile.

Minicius took one of the caltrops out of the wooden box and dropped it on to the ground. Two of the three pairs of nails acted as legs, leaving the third facing straight up. With a nod of approval, the signaller returned the sample to the box.

Anxious to move on, Cassius next encountered Avso and the men of the fifth section. The Thracian was close to the second cart, surrounded by legionaries. He was crouching low, one arm holding his shield, the other demonstrating an upward sword thrust.

'Like so – in amongst the groin and guts. Or like this.'

With the shield in a central defensive position, he straightened up and altered his grip. Then he reached high and stabbed downward.

'Below helmet, above chest piece. Tear chunks out of their neck if you're lucky.'

Avso frowned at one of the legionaries.

'No shield?'

'No.'

'Then you get this.'

Avso walked over to Statius and snatched the pilum out of his hand.

'That's my property!' Statius protested.

'You have sword and shield. He'll pay for any damage.'

Avso handed the pilum to the other man.

'You stay behind the rest of us. See something you can hit, have a dig.'

Avso picked up a stave lying on the ground close by, then noticed he was being watched.

'Not long now,' said Cassius.

Avso pointed across the street.

'In that case, you might want to have a word with the locals.'

Before Cassius could find out what the Thracian meant, he was intercepted by Vestinus and the rest of the first section.

'We've boarded up the access gap, sir. Not much is getting through there.'

Vestinus pointed over his shoulder. The criss-crossing collection of planks left only a few small holes and looked as solid as any other part of the cart wall.

'Good. Stay here for now. If you see a breach, do what you can to help but don't get too involved. You're my reserve.'

Cassius glanced through one of the dwelling windows and saw the Syrians inside. He hurried round to the doorway and found them at prayer. Again Kabir and Yarak stood at the front, with the rest of the men kneeling forward, heads bowed so low that they almost touched the floor. Kabir noticed Cassius. He held up a finger, indicating Yarak was almost done. Cassius could barely believe what he was seeing, but thankfully the priest finished almost immediately. The men repeated a single line of prayer and were swiftly up on their feet.

'My apologies,' said Kabir, 'but dawn prayers cannot wait.'

'Clearly not. The ram is coming. Make sure your men stay out of sight unless they're needed.'

'Of course.'

Cassius moved on to the southern barricade where first he found the third section. Crispus was pressed up against a gap, eyes fixed on the gate. Cassius tapped him on the shoulder.

'Ram is coming. Ready your men.'

As Crispus passed on the order to draw weapons, Cassius moved on to the next cart, where the second section were stationed. With both Avso and Serenus on the northern side, he had thought it wise to take up position to the south. Now, however, looking round at the grim, determined expressions on the faces of Strabo's grizzled friends, he realised his presence was hardly crucial. None were particularly large, but they carried themselves with the same presence and composure that characterised the big Sicilian.

'Sorry, sir.'

Minicius arrived, breathing hard. 'Broken bootlace. Shall I sound a tone when they advance, sir?'

'Don't bother. I think we all know what's coming.'

Cassius drew his sword. This time it came out easily; a good omen he hoped. To the right, one of Strabo's friends yawned and rested his shield against the cart. The legionary was left-handed and Cassius noted how the ridges in the bone of his sword handle were dulled and black with dirt. Cassius glanced down and looked between his own fingers: the gleaming surface was shiny and unsullied.

Suddenly, there was a shout. Then a loud crack. Cassius looked up and peered between two planks. Another crack. The gate shuddered, releasing a small cloud of dust that floated slowly to the ground.

The wooden doors that made up the main gate were each mounted on a pair of iron hinges. The hinges were set into a timber frame embedded in the clay wall.

The Palmyrans struck first at where the doors met. Progress seemed minimal until one of the reinforcing planks nailed across the divide abruptly popped out, swiftly followed by the other two. With one more concerted blow the locking plank itself snapped and the doors swung slightly open.

'Come on in then!' shouted someone from the northern barricade.

With a splintering crash, the southern door buckled. The next impact knocked out the top hinge, leaving the door hanging at an angle.

Cassius imagined the enemy troops heaving the ram backwards, then lining it up for the next blow. They aimed low and they aimed well, taking the bottom hinge out cleanly, along with most of the wooden frame. The door flew backwards and toppled into the dust. It had taken them only moments. The Palmyrans cheered.

'What are you waiting for?' came the voice again. Cassius belatedly realised it was Avso.

A wide-eyed mass of infantry clustered close to the gate, shields and swords at the ready. Though the second door could now simply be pushed aside, the ram was slowly retracted once more.

Strabo suddenly materialised at the southern-tower doorway. He darted for the barricade, flung his pilum over the top and disappeared from view. Cassius leaned back and saw two legionaries part to let him through. They already had timber, nails and hammer ready and instantly began covering the gap.

Strabo recovered his pilum and hurried over to Cassius.

'Fifty or so infantry. Some well armoured.'

The second door was struck. Two vertical planks were shattered by the first blow.

'Here, pass me a couple,' ordered Strabo.

A legionary handed him two of the light throwing javelins from a nearby bundle. Leaning his pilum against the cart, Strabo took a javelin in each hand and nodded at two others.

'Gulo, Iucundus, you too. Let's see if we can slow them down a little.'

Gulo was a sturdy, rough-featured man with shoulders as broad as Strabo's. Iucundus was taller and narrower, with unusually fair hair that stuck out in tufts through the joins of his helmet. Though Cassius hadn't previously known their names, he recognised them as Strabo's fellow gamblers.

The ram was thrust forward once more and two of the sharpened stakes were driven between door and frame. The Palmyrans began to lever the hinges out.

With one javelin in his left hand, Strabo weighed the other in his right, then took several steps backward. Gulo and Iucundus stood beside him.

As its hinges were finally torn free, the door keeled over, lying at rest close to its counterpart.

The noise from the Palmyrans rose until it became a single bestial roar. The ram was withdrawn and before long, nothing could be seen except the red-clad swarm of warriors. The first rank stretched out their sword arms, held their shields high, and charged.

XXXI

Strabo, Gulo and Iucundus all got their javelins away as the first of the Palmyrans cleared the gatehouse.

Fighting the urge to retreat as the onrushing bodies surged towards the carts, Cassius saw one of the missiles hit home, piercing the upper arm of a swordsman who had lowered his shield. The warrior stumbled and fell, tripping two more behind him. All three were soon overtaken by the second wave of men.

The sight of what blocked their way did nothing to slow the Palmyran charge and in moments the first of them smashed up against the carts. The scrapes and thuds of metal on wood fused with the cries of attacker and defender alike until neither words nor language could be heard.

The opening in front of Cassius was suddenly covered by a striped shield. It was then wrenched aside and a narrow spear thrust towards his face. Cassius saw it in good time and stepped backwards, swinging his blade left. The sword caught the head of the spear, knocking it aside with a metallic clang.

The unseen warrior retracted his weapon and unwittingly presented Cassius with an exposed section of tunic. Cassius centred his sword and stabbed into the space but he was too slow and hit nothing; his opponent had already moved away.

Now was the time to check the rest of the line. To his right, the second section looked in good order. The legionaries stood at an angle to the gaps, shields protecting them as they sought vulnerable spots to attack. Strabo directed affairs, yelling orders and pushing the men into position.

The third section seemed to be doing equally well. Crispus slammed his shield against a gap and leaned into it. Two men fell in beside him, jabbing their swords through the spaces above and below the shield.

'Sir! Look there!' cried Minicius, pointing left.

Perhaps realising they would struggle to batter their way through the carts, the Palmyrans were now attacking the network of connecting timbers close to where Cassius had just been standing. One length of wood splintered, then cracked in two. A Palmyran boot kicked through it.

Strabo arrived, pilum in hand, as another piece of timber was struck. Scrabbling fingers appeared at the edge of the plank but still the Sicilian held off. Another blow knocked one end of the plank away and now the unprotected belt and tunic of a Palmyran infantryman were visible.

'Ha! Idiot!'

Strabo leaped forward, holding the pilum with both hands, and drove the point into the top of his victim's thigh. An agonized shriek cut through the din. The blade had sunk at least two inches in and the Palmyran's hands clawed desperately at the shaft as Strabo twisted it from side to side. Blood gushed on to the sand below.

'Have some of that!' the Sicilian thundered before wrenching the point free, leaving a ragged, gory mess behind. Hands gripped the Palmyran round the waist and he was dragged away.

'Killing area—' said Strabo, grinning as he shook a bloodied piece of quivering flesh from the pilum's point '—good idea!'

Minicus, who had been watching alongside Cassius, bent over, dropped the tuba and spewed up what looked like the entire contents of his stomach.

'Ha! Good lad!' said Strabo, slapping the legionary on the back. Cassius took a deep breath and turned away, narrowly avoiding the same fate. With the southern side of the barricades holding well, he decided to check the north.

'I'll be back!' he shouted. Crispus, still pressed up against his shield, nodded grimly as Cassius passed by.

Some of the Syrians, including Kabir, were gathered outside the closest dwelling.

'Just give the word if you need us,' he said, leaning nonchalantly against the wall.

The apparent ease with which the carts were holding worried Cassius. It occurred to him that the first wave of Palmyrans might have no intention of really breaking through the barriers; that they were meant only to occupy the Romans while others attacked elsewhere.

He found the first section where he had left them, shouting encouragement to those manning the barricades.

'Vestinus, take another man and check every part of the perimeter the sentries cannot see. I want you up on the steps, looking for any sign of enemy movement. Then report back to me.'

A second legionary volunteered himself. The two of them dropped their shields and jogged away down the street. Minicius had by this point managed to catch up and he joined the others, his face still pale.

'The rest of you follow me,' Cassius said as he continued on towards Avso's men.

'Are those carts?'

Bezda had left the rest of the cavalrymen at the rear to join Azaf, standing just in front of the horse archers. The ram had been withdrawn and the warriors had also removed both doors; firstly to clear the way, secondly to prevent the Romans from making further use of them.

'Possibly,' answered Azaf. He waved Razir over and pointed towards Teyya, who was standing just outside the gate.

'Tell him to pass this on. I want men on the other side of those barricades. Any way they can. Pick of the spoils to any man who gets through!'

Just as Cassius arrived at the northern barricade, one of the fifth section was suddenly pulled forward by a Palmyran hand on his shield. As the legionary tried to wrench himself free, two enemy spears shot towards him. The first blow deflected off his

272

helmet, but the second caught him in the cheek. The soldier did not cry out or fall; he just stood there, blinking, as blood ran down his face.

Other legionaries hauled him away. Palmyrans appeared in the spaces they had guarded, kicking and striking at the cart with their swords and spears, trying to make a hole big enough to fit through. The fifth section closed ranks as the enemy warriors pressed up against the entire length of the creaking cart. A breakthrough seemed imminent.

Cassius pointed his sword forward.

'First section! Help them there!'

As the men rushed forward, Avso appeared. Seeing the danger quickly, he grabbed a pilum and leaped up on to the joining timbers between the two carts. He climbed on to the upturned side of the vehicle, used one hand to steady himself, then jabbed the spear down into the thronging enemy below. His first victim was a Palmyran whose shield and shoulder were almost through a gap when the spear gouged a chunk of flesh out of his neck. He gasped and fell backward.

Avso struck again, at another warrior trying to pull one of the timbers from the side of the cart. The pilum glanced off his helmet but the Thracian's attack had drawn the attention of all the Palmyrans close by. The legionaries drove forward with their shields once again, plugging the holes.

Avso didn't remain atop the cart for long. Several spears had by now been trained on him and one flew past as he dropped adroitly to the ground. He checked that the legionaries were back in control before approaching Cassius.

'No more than fifty infantry. No second rank coming in.'

'What are they doing?'

'Just probing perhaps. They know they'll make a hole sooner or later. Might reinforce then.'

The injured man moved past them, assisted by another member of the fifth section.

'Hold there,' Avso said, examining the legionary's face. The spear had cut across his cheek rather than into it.

'You'll be fine on your own. Get back here as soon as it's dealt with.'

The injured man staggered away. Avso pushed the other legionary back towards the cart. Cassius continued on.

The fourth section were not as close to the cart as the others, preferring to stand back and lash out at any exposed flesh or protruding blade. There were no significant breaches; the tactic seemed to be working. Serenus was directing operations, a canteen in his spare hand.

'That's it, lads,' he rasped. 'Keep at it. Hold them there. We can keep this up all day!' he added as Cassius approached.

'We may have to!'

One of the legionaries turned away from the cart. It was Priscus, who pointed back over his shoulder, shouting something neither Serenus nor Cassius could hear. As they hurried over, the top of a Palmyran helmet appeared close to the wall.

'They're climbing the firing step!'

In an instant, the warrior had leaped up on to the side of the cart. His bearded yet youthful face bore not a trace of fear. His only protection was a sleeveless mail shirt, his weapon a short stabbing sword. The Palmyran hurled himself into the air, leaping clean over Priscus and Cassius. Rolling athletically in the dust, he sprung to his feet and launched himself at the Romans.

He first grabbed Priscus' shield and wrenched it downward, then swung his sword. The blade sang as it struck the mail on Priscus' shoulder then caught the side of his helmet, knocking him into the wall.

The Palmyran was still facing the tall legionary as Cassius closed on him, raising his sword with both hands. But as he drove it down towards the warrior's wrist, the Palmyran turned and yanked his arm away. The blade missed, and Cassius' clumsy swing left him off balance and vulnerable.

The Palmyran saw it and readied himself for an upward slash, straight into Cassius' face.

But Priscus had by now recovered and he charged, shield up.

Knocking the Palmyran's blade to one side, he smashed the shield into his opponent's chest.

Serenus and another legionary rushed past. As a second enterprising Palmyran hauled himself on to the cart, they drove their pila up at him. Neither weapon connected but the warrior lost his footing and fell back.

In forcing the first Palmyran to the ground, Priscus too lost his balance and stumbled forward. The enemy swordsman kicked out as the legionary came down on top of him, hitting the shield and knocking him to one side. As soon as the Roman hit the ground, the Palmyran was on him.

The paralysis that had struck Cassius up on the gatehouse returned. Impulses and actions seemed to require double the effort and his leaden legs moved him towards the battling duo with a ruinous lack of speed. He knew he would be too late.

As Priscus tried to rise, the Palmyran smashed his left elbow down into the Roman's face, then plunged the sword into his gut. Priscus' head jerked to one side and he screamed.

Then Cassius was there. The Palmyran turned to face him but couldn't raise any defence. Cassius swept his sword diagonally downward from right to left. The tip of the blade scraped across the mail at the Palmyran's chest, then across his arm. The warrior's sword fell from his hand.

Leaving his sword in the dust, the Palmyran scrambled away.

'Don't let him up!' someone shouted.

Cassius had taken only three steps after the swordsman when something flashed across his field of vision.

The Palmyran collapsed to the ground as if his legs had been cut away. Lying sideways, he reached downward, fingers outstretched.

Impaled in the middle of his left calf was the barbed iron shaft of a pilum. The seven-foot spear swayed from side to side.

Avso strode towards the fallen warrior and drew his sword. The Palmyran held up his good arm, his only remaining defence. Avso kicked it away, stood over him, then jabbed the sword straight into his throat. The Palmyran's body spasmed twice, then fell back, releasing the slick, red-stained tip of the blade. Avso wiped it clean on his victim's tunic, then looked at the pilum. Seeing that removing it would take time, he walked away.

'Never let them up,' he told Cassius as he passed him.

Serenus and Minicius knelt by Priscus. The legionary looked strangely calm as he drank water from the canteen Minicius held to his mouth. Serenus, meanwhile, was widening the tear in his tunic, trying to examine the injury.

Cassius couldn't bear to look over their shoulders. He had no wish to see the wound that would probably kill the young legionary; an injury that could have been avoided had he moved a little faster, had he defended Priscus as Priscus had defended him.

Instead he sheathed his sword. Even this took two hands, so badly were his fingers shaking. He glanced over at the other legionaries and imagined what they would be thinking. Their new 'centurion', for all his youthful enthusiasm and grand words, had turned out to be no more than a slow-witted liability, incapable even of dispatching an injured man at his feet.

'Here,' said Serenus to Minicius. 'Place your hands across the cut and push down. It will hurt him but it must be done until the flow of blood slows.'

Minicius' face was now as pale as Priscus' but he did as he was told.

Serenus stood up and looked at the barricades. Avso had taken charge of both sections and was now moving along the line at pace, directing the men where necessary. Serenus took his cloth from his belt and wiped his fingers.

'Mars has favoured him. It is a deep wound but more in flank than gut.'

Priscus was gazing up at them, trying to hear what was being said.

'He'll survive?'

'Probably, if the wound stays clean.'

Cassius felt a slight surge of relief.

'I shall fetch Simo.'

Serenus shook his head.

'I shall send someone to do that. Were you struck?'

'No.'

'Call out if you need me,' Serenus said to Minicius before he and Cassius hurried back towards the carts. Two more attackers hurled themselves at one legionary's shield, knocking him off his feet. Another man saw them off with his sword while Serenus and Cassius helped the legionary up. He returned instantly to the line, slamming his shield in place between two planks.

'By my estimation, that gate is at least eight feet high, perhaps ten wide.' Bezda turned towards Azaf. 'Enough for two horses to pass easily. Especially if there is clear space beyond.'

Razir and Teyya ran back from the fort side by side, the older man's steady lope a contrast to the youngster's eager trot. The sun had still not fully risen, and the gloom obscured their faces until they came close.

'Well?' asked Azaf.

'I think one man got over, sir, but no other breakthroughs.'

'How many of them are there?' asked Azaf.

'No more than fifty I should say, sir,' replied Teyya, slightly breathless. 'Well armed and equipped.'

'Any sign of a reserve?'

'No, *strategos*, though I couldn't see much beyond the barriers. They are carts turned on their sides, arranged in a half-circle and reinforced. The Romans guard each hole with shield and lance. We have suffered some casualties but—'

'How many?' asked Azaf.

'Five injured, five dead at the last count, sir. They have prepared well.'

Bezda leaned forward, resting a hand on his mount's neck.

'Any sign of heavier weaponry? Horse lances, mounted cross-bows?'

'No, sir. Not that I saw.'

Azaf gestured for Razir to come closer.

'Your counsel?'

'With a greater number of men directed in one area, we could create a breach, I am sure of it. Perhaps use the archers to soften them up first.'

Azaf looked beyond him, towards the walls of Alauran.

'What about ladders at the corners? Put men in behind these barriers, distract them from the main assault.'

'*Strategos*, please,' interjected Bezda smoothly, 'why risk dividing your men when we have such an advantage in numbers? My cavalry will account for those carts in moments. We shall push them aside or tear them to pieces. Allow us to smash a hole, then pour your infantry in behind us.'

'You would risk your horses in such a confined space?'

'Any battlefield is a confined space once a charge is done. And trust me, it would not remain confined for long. They will have no answer, I am sure of it. If you are willing, you may mass your men at the gate behind us, ready to exploit any advantage.'

'Razir?'

'They have been unable to do us much harm. It's a reasonable position to defend but that's all they have. I don't see what they could do to the cavalry.'

Azaf looked at the gate once again. There was a good deal of logic to what the others had said but he maintained his doubts about deploying the cavalry against static defences, weak though they might be. The thought of the armoured horses mixing with his infantry at close quarters did little to ease his fears. Still, Bezda seemed confident.

'The sun will grow hotter,' said the cavalryman, 'and my men have been in their saddles almost an hour. If you do intend to employ us, it will have to be soon.'

Azaf nodded curtly.

'Teyya, listen carefully.'

'How are we doing?' Cassius asked Strabo as he arrived back at the southern barricade.

'Well, we've killed three of them,' said Strabo, without looking away from the cart. 'How are the others faring?'

'Not bad. Two of ours injured. Avso got at least two of theirs.'

'Only two hundred and fifteen of them to go then,' said Strabo, drawing grins from Gulo and Iucundus. 'I just took a look over the wall. Purple Cloak is out there getting an eyeful. I reckon he's just testing our numbers.'

Cassius moved back behind the legionaries and examined the scene in front of him. The fighting had now settled into a pattern. Men on both sides were keeping their shields between themselves and the enemy at all times. With the additional complication of the carts and the criss-crossing lattice of supporting timbers, accurate thrusts of lance or sword were few and far between. The initial fire of the Palmyran charge had died, while the legionaries were emboldened by the success of their defences. The Romans were now content to stand back and wait for the attackers to take the risks.

To Cassius' left, Crispus was helping a man hobble away from the line with a nasty gash above his knee. Kabir sent over a pair of his warriors to escort the legionary to the aid post, freeing up Crispus, who eagerly recovered his sword and shield.

'Can't say I like it though,' noted Strabo. 'Makes me anxious about what's coming next.'

The watching Syrians separated and Vestinus appeared. Sweat was pouring from his face and neck; the top of his tunic was sodden.

'No sign of the enemy except out front, sir. All three sentries said the same thing.'

Cassius then realised that the noise had lessened. He and Strabo scanned the line and saw that fewer Palmyran shields and weapons were now visible. Sections of dusty earth came into view beyond the barricades. They heard the shuffling of dozens of pairs of boots.

'They're falling back,' said Strabo.

The Romans moved up and saw that the Sicilian was right. There would, however, be no easy shots at the retreating warriors. The Palmyrans withdrew expertly, slowly backing towards the gate with shields up. Not one of the infantrymen rushed or turned. Cassius saw an injured man being dragged away.

Gulo and Iucundus grabbed javelins and readied themselves for a shot.

Strabo held up a hand.

'Save them for a clear strike.'

The legionaries and the auxiliaries pressed up against the carts as the last of the Palmyrans reached the gate. The manoeuvre had been carried out with admirable speed and efficiency.

'Any century would be proud of that,' observed Iucundus.

'Wild tribesmen they are not,' added Strabo.

From the northern side of the barricades a victorious shout went up. Many other voices followed, including some close to Cassius' position. They were soon silenced.

'Quiet!' shouted Strabo. 'Save your breath!'

The Sicilian then spoke in a whisper. 'You're sure to need it.'

XXXII

Though he knew the lull in the fighting wouldn't last long, Cassius was determined to check on Priscus. On the way to the aid post he passed the injured man returning to the northern barricade. The soldier held a wet cloth against his cheek and stared blankly at the ground as he walked.

Cassius found Simo and Julius attending to the legionary from Crispus' section, Julius carefully elevating the leg while Simo wrapped a bandage round the knee. Though there was now enough light to see by, Simo kept several lamps burning. One sat on a wooden chest, casting a golden glow over Priscus, who lay on a bed to the right.

Cassius squeezed past Simo and looked down at him. The legionary had been covered with a cloak and his arms were wrapped round his chest but he was shivering. Cassius couldn't tell if he was conscious or not.

'Can't you do anything else?'

'I've dressed the wound, sir,' answered Simo.

'He's cold.'

'It's not practical to build a fire in here, sir.'

Cassius took a blanket from a nearby bed and laid it on top of the cloak. He tucked the edges under where he could, covered Priscus' shoulders and drew the material up under his chin.

'Do your best for him.'

'Of course, sir.'

The other injured legionary looked up at him brightly.

'Be back out there before you know it, sir.'

'Very good,' Cassius answered stiffly. He hurried out of the aid post and wondered how the legionary's attitude towards him might have differed had he seen precisely how Priscus had been wounded.

Instead of marching back along the street, he crossed to the middle of the square. Though he couldn't see the gate itself, it was obvious from the behaviour of the men that the next attack was not yet imminent. Vestinus' report had partly eased his concerns but he was still desperate to see the Palmyran lines again for himself.

Though it took only moments to climb up to the position he and Strabo had used the previous day, Cassius felt hot and weary as he crawled across the roof. He slumped against the surround and kept his head low.

The deep, vibrant orange of the sun coloured a thin ceiling of cloud and all the lands to the east. Cassius imagined the Palmyrans might think themselves blessed by some portent of victory and he was grateful the more credulous of the legionaries wouldn't see it. He wondered too how Kabir, Yarak and the other Syrians might view this particular manifestation of their Glorious Fire.

The sun was so low and bright that he could hardly make out anything except the returning enemy infantry, slowly realigning themselves between the ranks of archers. The intense glare made him turn to the south. Standing on a firing step just left of the granary was the sentry assigned to the southern wall. His opposite number stood by his horse a hundred yards out. The Palmyran suddenly looked east.

Cassius covered his eyes and saw what had drawn the sentry's attention: a double line of cavalry cantering towards the gatehouse. With the bottom of their mail coats obscured by the dust the horses seemed almost to be floating across the plain.

Though he knew he should already be moving, Cassius was momentarily transfixed. They neared the gate, the riders holding their lances vertically, their mounts taking short, high steps. It reminded him of the cavalry he'd seen during training, when the animals were forced across specially furrowed fields to develop the distinctive gait that enabled them to generate great speed over a short distance. The heads of the horses jerked this way and that as they sensed contact with the enemy.

Only when the first pair had passed out of view behind the gatehouse tower did Cassius finally crawl back across the roof and climb down.

The leading riders were already entering the fort as he sprinted down the street towards the barricades. The second, third, fourth and fifth sections readied themselves as the Palmyrans fanned out from the gate. He could hear the animals snorting heavily under the thick layers of mail.

Though the overturned carts were seven feet high, Cassius now saw to his dismay that, atop the large cavalry horses, some of the Palmyrans could see clean over the sides; they would be able to bring their weapons to bear on the defenders.

Focused wholly on the enemy, Cassius lost his footing and slipped. He slid harmlessly on to his side, unnoticed by the legionaries of the first section standing just yards away. Hauling himself to his feet, he looked up as a large rider loomed, reining his horse in before it reached the barricades. The cavalryman carried no shield, only an iron lance longer and thicker than a pilum. He looked inhuman, like the product of some terrible nightmare, with only two dots of eyes visible beneath the smiling metal face mask.

Bezda yanked on the reins, pulling his horse towards the southern barricade. He took a moment to appraise the defences in front of him: the reinforced carts, the Romans with their weapons and shields blocking every space. He decided they had done well with limited resources. But not well enough to stop his cavalry.

Cassius pressed on to the cart wall and watched the rest of the horses follow their leader towards the southern barricade. There were at least a dozen of the mounted warriors now beyond the gatehouse. They had advanced into the compound as adeptly as the infantry had retreated from it and were yet to make contact with a single Roman blade.

Cassius thought of Strabo's earlier comment.

'Wild tribesmen they are not,' he breathed as he ran past the apex of the carts to find the Sicilian standing well to the rear, watching the advance. In front of him was Iucundus, javelin in hand.

Cassius drew his sword.

Iucundus took two steps forward, expelled a powerful breath and launched the javelin low over the cart wall, striking a cavalryman full in the chest. The javelin simply bounced off the chest plate and dropped to the ground between two horses. The Palmyran paused for a moment, checked his armour, then forced his mount on again.

Bezda held out his lance and swept it across the length of the cart closest to the wall. He waved five men forward and continued the advance, only halting when the horses were two or three feet short of the timbers.

'What about the caltrops?' Cassius asked.

'Not yet,' said Strabo, moving to his right. 'We must draw more of them in first. Gulo, stay back for the moment! And you others!'

Keeping the lance in one hand, its point lowered towards the ground, Bezda now urged his horse forward until its nose was inches from where the cart met the wall. The other riders filed in alongside him, mail coats scraping against one another, until they covered every yard of the cart's length.

'I'd hoped for some hothead,' said Strabo, 'but this one's no fool.'

The Sicilian took a deep breath.

'Let's get stuck in then, second section!' he shouted, dodging past the other legionaries and raising his pilum. He thrust the spear through a gap towards Bezda's horse. There were shaped holes in the armoured coat for its mouth, eyes and ears. Strabo caught the animal halfway down its muzzle.

The horse seemed momentarily stunned but recovered swiftly

284

as Bezda kicked down hard on its flanks. It shuffled forward and its armoured chest knocked the entire right side of the cart backward. One of the poles embedded in the wall snapped.

Bezda dropped his lance on to the side of the cart and jabbed down towards Strabo.

The Sicilian saw it coming and easily ducked out of the way, leaving Gulo to retaliate. The wily legionary knew better than to try to shatter the thick iron shaft so he instead grabbed it, hoping to pull it out of Bezda's hand or, better still, pull him off his horse. He was so intent on doing so that he didn't realise the other Palmyrans were now level with their leader.

A second cavalryman drove his lance towards Gulo. He struck with unerring accuracy, avoiding the Roman's segmental armour and catching him just below the armpit. Cassius heard a horrifying crunch as the sharpened iron head tore into Gulo's ribs. The Palmyran backed up, pulling the lance with him. Gulo fell limply to the ground.

Strabo cast his pilum aside, held the legionary by his armour's shoulder straps and dragged him away from the cart. As soon as he stopped, a thick puddle of blood spread out under Gulo's body. His eyes were shut tight, his face still. Strabo knelt close to him and put an ear to his mouth. After a moment, he shook his head.

All along the cart, the cavalry horses inched their way forward. Every lance was now pointing down at the Romans, daring them to attack. Led by Iucundus, three of the second section sheathed their swords and dodged under the lances. Crouching low, they held their shields against the timbers, trying to hold the cart in place.

Strabo left Gulo where he lay. Stepping casually between two of the lances, he grabbed the bundle of javelins and backed up, not taking his eyes off the enemy. There were five of the projectiles left.

He grabbed the first, aimed it at the Palmyran who had killed Gulo, and let fly. Though the range was no more than five yards, the Sicilian's fury got the better of him and the javelin flashed over the cavalryman's shoulder, disappearing somewhere over the gatehouse.

Cassius moved aside as Strabo reached for a second weapon and brought his arm back again. He took a breath this time and his shot was the better for it, hitting the Palmyran two inches above his eyes. The impact knocked him off balance and he slid sideways off his saddle. The Romans could all see the dent in the metal plate as he grabbed at the mail of the adjacent horse, then righted himself. The cavalryman shook his head, then raised his lance once more.

'Leave that whore-son for me!' snarled Strabo before dropping the rest of the javelins and recovering his pilum.

As the Sicilian charged back into the fray, Cassius forced himself to ignore the body of the dead legionary and called over to Minicius, who was standing with Crispus' men.

'Get ready.'

Minicius raised the tuba.

'Short tones. We need the first section here.'

Minicius wiped some dust from the mouthpiece, then lifted the instrument high with both hands. His cheeks and his eyes widened as he blew. The notes were high-pitched and wavering, but loud enough to cut through the sound of the skirmish.

Just as he finished, the Palmyrans surged forward again. Two of the legionaries leaning up against the barriers were knocked to the ground as the cart jolted backward, splintering several of the joining timbers that connected it to the other vehicle. Strabo cast an anxious look at Cassius before jabbing his pilum back towards Bezda.

'Crispus!' Cassius shouted, moving to his left. 'Men with shields over here!'

Crispus patted the shoulders of three legionaries and pointed them in the direction of the second section. Strabo told them to stand with the others against the cart, shields up.

Bezda turned round in his saddle and beckoned more of his men forward. These riders fell expertly into line alongside the others, facing the carts manned by Crispus' men, until no less than fourteen of the armoured horses covered the entire width of the southern barricade.

A Palmyran lance shattered a plank then embedded itself in one of the third section's shields. Crispus rushed to the man's aid and the two of them heaved the shield backwards, wrenching the lance from the Palmyran's grip. The cavalryman reached forlornly for his weapon as the Romans dragged it through the cart. A weak cheer went up as Crispus prepared to turn the weapon on its former owner.

Before he could make much use of it, Bezda looked down the line and signalled another push. The most eager were those who had just joined the melee. Three of them were close to the point where the carts met. The Palmyrans tied off their reins around the saddle horns and used only their legs to control the animals, leaving both hands free to wield the lances. In a few short moments, they had succeeded in dislodging or smashing half of the reinforcing timbers that stretched across the join.

The few legionaries close by did their best, hacking at the lances whenever they could, but it was an uneven contest. Thankfully, at that moment the men of the first section arrived.

'There,' cried Cassius. 'Aim high!'

The soldiers pressed forward as a group, swinging their swords and driving their pila at the Palmyrans and their horses. Now forced to defend themselves, the attackers withdrew.

'That's it!' Cassius shouted. 'Keep them back!'

Strabo suddenly appeared in front of him, cradling three short timbers, a hammer and a handful of nails. He collared two legionaries and dropped the wood and tools in front of them, then pointed at the join, barely visible through a tangle of legs and tunics.

'Do what you can to shore it up.'

As the men set about their task, Cassius looked over his shoulder at where Kabir stood.

'Should we use some of the Syrians?' he asked Strabo.

Just as he spoke, yet another defender was knocked to the ground as the cart shook with repeated impacts.

The Sicilian grimaced.

'I'd hoped we could keep them out of sight – a surprise for the infantry – but yes, we must. If we can hold on, the cavalry will tire eventually. If they turn or break up we'll use the caltrops.'

Cassius ran over to where Kabir was standing, surrounded by his men.

'We need some help.'

'Our shot will be of no use against *them*,' warned the Syrian.

'Not for that. We need more hands to keep the carts upright and in position.'

Kabir called out a series of names and commands. Eight of his men ran over to the barricades and Strabo directed them towards the base of the carts. Avso had also arrived, three pila under his arm.

Another of the Syrians ran up and reported to Kabir, who then turned to Cassius.

'Yarak is up on the roof. He says the northern barricade is clear for now but the rest of the cavalry are by the gate and all the infantry are massing behind them. A hundred perhaps.'

Cassius nodded, trying to absorb this new development. It was hardly unexpected but it now seemed clear that the short engagement had already reached its critical point; the Palmyrans were poised to force their way through the southern barricade.

Cassius started back towards the carts. He glanced at Minicus, still dutifully following him around. The legionary, his face tight and slick with sweat, looked terrified.

Cassius too felt suddenly hot, almost feverish. His head throbbed and his eyes stung. His stomach felt hollow yet heavy. He saw Gulo's body, already a remnant of the battle. He remembered the revolting sound of the lance impaling itself in the man's chest; the piteous scream of Priscus; Azaf's sword slashing silently towards Flavian's neck. Wracked by a febrile desire to wrench his helmet off, Cassius' hands were halfway to his head when Strabo shouted.

'It's going!'

The Sicilian, along with Iucundus and the Syrian reinforcements, was now solely occupied with propping up the cart, leaving others to fight the Palmyrans. Though they had succeeded in keeping the lances from further damaging the barricades, the steady, relentless pressure of the cavalry advance was finally beginning to tell. Strabo was closest to the wall, shoulder against his shield. He turned his face away just as the second of the embedded poles splintered, then snapped.

'Here! Over here!' he yelled, now almost horizontal, his boots sliding on the sand.

Bezda turned in his saddle and ushered forward the riders held in reserve. They now formed up behind the front rank, the chests of their steeds pushing against the animals ahead, piling yet more force against the barricades. Even the Palmyrans lined up against the third section now looked to their left, so sure were they that a breakthrough was coming.

'Go on!' Cassius told Minicius. Dropping the tuba, the legionary hurried over and filled the only remaining space at the base of the cart. There was now little danger from the lances as most of the horsemen held their weapons in a defensive posture, protecting the horses' heads as they urged them on.

Cassius tried to slow his breathing. The sound of Strabo and Avso yelling at the men receded and he felt strangely detached from the scene unfolding in front of him. Something had to be done quickly but he could not imagine what. There was no point moving men from the northern barricade; they might be required any time soon to protect their own position. The boxes of caltrops were close by but with the cavalry so closely packed, few would even reach the ground. What they needed was something, anything, to stop the Palmyrans and their mounts moving forward.

Iucundus left his position in the middle of the cart. Shield in hand, he hurried past the others, exchanged a few words with Strabo, then stood over the remaining embedded pole. He held the top of the shield, then shoved it downward, wedging it between the pole and the cart. The shield itself was of an old-fashioned design: heavy, rectangular and straight-edged, perfect for what the resourceful legionary intended. With some of the pressure on the pole now redistributed against the shield, he set himself against it. Strabo joined him. Their arms shook with the effort.

Cassius thought suddenly of a small, airless room he had spent hours in whilst training back in Ravenna; a chamber where veterans lectured the new recruits on strategy. One such man, a one-legged ex-centurion named Exuperatus, had easily been the most engaging speaker. He would often drift off the prescribed subject, preferring to regale the young officer candidates with humorous or unlikely military tales from the ancient past. Cassius now recalled one in particular.

He rushed over to where Strabo stood and bent down, close to him.

'We've only moments!' shouted the Sicilian. 'Get ready to sound the retreat!'

Cassius shook his head.

'Not yet.'

'We've no choice! Move sections four and five back towards the barracks at once!'

'Just listen! I have an idea!'

XXXIII

'The Battle of Sardis!'

'What?' cried Strabo, licking away a rivulet of sweat above his mouth.

An impact from above shook the beleaguered planks of the cart, showering them both with dust.

'Cyrus the Great,' added Cassius, stumbling over his words. 'Remember, he—'

'Yes, yes, I know the tale. Doesn't mean it'll work on these!'

'But Barates said that they—'

'Sometimes. Usually they just ignore each other.'

'We have to try something!' Cassius ducked as a lance thudded against the cart next to his head. 'Now, Strabo. That's an order.'

The Sicilian took a breath.

'All right. I'll see what I can do.'

Cassius crouched down and placed his hands against the shield. Strabo waited until he had a good grip on the handle, then slid aside.

'Hold steady, lads!' he shouted. Loping past Kabir, he pointed back at the barricades. 'Every hand to the carts.'

The Syrian ordered his remaining men forward, directing two of his warriors towards a long, thick piece of timber. Three others stood over Cassius and Iucundus, adding their weight.

Though the back of the cart was still wedged in place by the last pole and Iucundus' shield, the top was creaking and bending under the weight of the Palmyran drive.

Kabir drew his dagger and began carving out a small hole just behind Cassius' back foot. Though covered with sand, the ground was well impacted underneath and he had soon created a shallow rut. The two men lowered one end of the timber into the hole, then wedged the other into the corner of the cart. They leaned on the support to keep it in place.

'Good! Good!' shouted Iucundus.

Cassius could tell that the timber had made a difference to the weight against Strabo's shield. He risked a quick look around. Avso had abandoned his pila and was now pressing his own shield against the barricade. Kabir pulled a piece of lead shot from his bag.

Azaf couldn't keep his eyes off the red legion flag. Though he couldn't make out the insignia, the dawn had brought a slight westerly breeze and the banner now fluttered rather more proudly than before. Azaf looked forward to the moment when it would be torn down and burned, and that moment now seemed close.

He stood alone, thirty yards from the gate, with virtually his entire force gathered before him. At the front were the remainder of the cavalry, keenly straining their necks to see how their fellows fared, eager to join the fight. Behind them were the infantry, those from the first engagement now mixed in with the experienced swordsmen. Razir was in there somewhere too, ready to lead the charge. Though they may have been tempted to exchange news of the assault and thoughts about what awaited them, the warriors stayed silent to a man, as they had been instructed. At the rear, close to Azaf, were half the archers, now on foot. They waited patiently, bows at hand, providing Azaf with mobile firepower to deploy within the walls as required. The remaining fifty archers were to the rear, along with some of the drivers and handlers, now in charge of more than a hundred riderless mounts.

Teyya, who had kept up his observations from the gatehouse, ran back towards Azaf once more, barely able to mask his excitement.

'Sir. The cavalry are almost through. Master Bezda has asked for the rest of his horsemen. Should I pass on the order?'

'At once. And inform Razir that my next command will be for him to advance.'

'Yes, *strategos*.'

As Teyya sprang away, the wind dropped. Azaf's cloak settled to the ground; the sand that had been sliding over the tops of his boots disappeared; and, in the distance, the Roman flag crumpled in on itself.

Although Bezda was content to press forward, deterring any adventurous defenders with his lance, some of the less experienced cavalrymen were running out of patience. Two of the horsemen to his right waved back those behind them and managed to retreat several yards, then drove their mounts straight into the cart. The horses turned their necks at the last moment but the impacts were almost simultaneous; powerful enough to knock the supporting timber out of place.

It fell down and to the right, striking Iucundus across the back. His howl of pain was curtailed as the air was driven from his lungs and he slammed into the ground. Two of the Syrians instantly replaced him at the shield, babbling away to each other as they desperately tried to keep the crucial chunk of metal upright. Close to Cassius' feet, Iucundus struggled for breath, unable even to push the timber away. With both hands occupied, Cassius couldn't help him.

Kabir sent one of his men to aid the fallen Roman. Cassius looked over his shoulder to find that the Syrian had loaded his sling but hadn't fired.

'Can't you do anything?'

Though range was obviously not a problem, Kabir could see almost nothing to hit. The eye slits on the Palmyran helmets were narrower than the lead pellet in his hand.

Bezda, the rider closest to him, craftily ensured that his bare hands remained out of sight.

The two riders who had just charged, however, were not so careful. They held their lances high, still trying to smash through the planks. Their hands, sticking out from the sleeves of their mail shirts, were utterly unprotected.

Kabir had kept his sling down by his side. The lead shot was now cradled in place and his finger and thumb were secure on the release strap.

When one of the cavalrymen momentarily rested his lance against the top of the cart, the Syrian took his chance. Almost casually raising the sling to his shoulder, he whipped it round in an instant, releasing the shot before any of the attackers even realised what he was doing.

There was a sharp crack as the shot shattered the top of the Palmyran's hand. Too shocked even to make a sound, he stared down dumbly at the torn flesh and broken bones. The lance slipped out of his hand, no longer held by functioning fingers.

Confusion struck those around him. Even Bezda paused for a moment as they all stared at the hand. One man reached out to prop him up, instantly presenting Kabir with his second target.

Having reloaded the instant the first shot was away, he fired again. This one was slightly high, ricocheting off the Palmyran's mail just above his wrist.

Now Bezda had run out of patience. He spun round in his saddle and saw that the rest of his force were now inside the gate. There were three ranks behind him, all of his twenty-four cavalrymen.

He extended his spare arm, waved it across the width of the assembled riders, then pointed directly at the cart ahead. Those at the front now withdrew their lances and concentrated solely on forcing the cart aside, backward or over. Any gaps still remaining between the ranks of horses disappeared. The heads of the animals next to the carts were forced up as their hooves pummelled the ground.

Cassius looked up for a moment and saw the edge of the cart bending once more. He could smell the familiar oily musk of the horses, hear them puffing and snorting as the Palmyrans forced them mercilessly on.

A stray elbow smacked against his helmet as one of the Syrians lost his footing. The second man couldn't hold the shield alone and the last pole snapped, sending the shield straight into his legs. Cassius turned in time to see him tumble backwards, clutching at his shins. As Kabir dragged the injured man away, Cassius helped the other Syrian to his feet. Just as he got his hands back on the nearest plank, it snapped in two, one half spinning away above his head, the other hitting the ground between his boots.

He glimpsed glittering chain mail to his right as Bezda's horse finally forced its way into the gap, pushing the cart a full two yards away from the wall. Bezda kept his lance horizontal, protecting the head of his steed. The smile etched on his face mask now appeared fittingly triumphant and to Cassius the unblinking eyes above now seemed lit by fire.

There were sixteen defenders trying to hold the cart in place but they were no match for the combined might of the cavalry horses. Bent low, Cassius watched his boots being pushed back in the dust.

The Palmyrans were cheering; a triumphant cry that rose in volume with every inch gained. Like the Romans, they knew that a large breach in the barricades would effectively end the battle.

Cassius glanced again to his right. Bezda switched his lance to his left hand and reached for his sword.

Cassius knew then that he had to move. All other thoughts had been forgotten in the struggle to defend the barricades, but that battle was lost. Strabo was nowhere to be seen. He had to leave before it was too late: round up the others, grab Minicius and sound the retreat.

He let go of the cart, stood up and turned round. What he saw stopped him cold.

Trotting towards the eastern wall, necks bobbing up and down, were the three camels. Close behind were Strabo, Statius and Antonius, all wielding flaming torches and intent on driving the animals towards the barricades. As they passed through what had been the Syrian encampment, Statius sprinted left to cut off the narrow gap between the carts and the corner of the houses.

The big female, perhaps disturbed by the noise of the battle or smelling the many horses ahead, veered to the right. Strabo was there in an instant, waving the torch at the animal's face. With a flash of teeth, she swung her neck away, the others in tow as she cantered towards the eastern wall.

At first it seemed Strabo's efforts had been for nothing. The camels slowed as they reached the wall, turned away from the carts and edged towards the corner.

Bezda hadn't drawn his sword. Cassius saw that the Palmyran too was fixated on the bizarre scene in front of him. Though his horse was now halfway through the gap, his right leg was still stuck on the other side of the cart.

Strabo, Statius and Antonius formed a line and stalked towards the animals, torches held out in front of them.

'Closer!' Strabo shouted. 'Push them left!'

Antonius cut off the path to the south-east corner. Now Strabo and Statius had the camels trapped against the wall.

'Towards the horses!'

The men at the barricade realised what was going on. Heads came up, hands eased. There was a sudden jolt as the cart was prised further away from the wall.

'Keep at it there!' yelled Avso.

Bezda's leg was now past the cart; he was finally free to attack the Romans.

His horse, however, had suddenly become still, nostrils flaring, ears twitching. The riders behind him slackened their reins and looked on.

The camels were now just five yards from the barricades. At the shoulder, the big female was a good foot taller than the cavalry horses. Swinging her head from side to side and scraping her hooves against the ground, the enraged beast bared her teeth and spat; some landed in the sand by Bezda's horse.

'Yah!' shouted the Palmyran, kicking downward again, desperate to force his animal into action.

There was a curious moment of quiet. Then, with a shrill whinny, the horse jerked its head up and lurched suddenly to the left, smashing into the wall and knocking a sizeable dent in the clay. Bezda lowered the grip on his lance and brought it down hard against the horse's side but it had no effect. Straining to turn its neck away, the animal dug its hooves in and began to back up.

Seeing a chance, two daring Syrians closed on the retreating beast, but Kabir called out and halted them mid-stride.

Bezda stifled a grunt of pain as the horse threw itself sideways again, this time to the right, slamming his leg against the cart.

Whether it was the sight and smell of the camels, or the reaction of Bezda's mount, fear spread quickly through the closely packed horses. Suddenly, all the riders in the front rank were fighting for control. Any horse that sensed space behind or beside it retreated or turned. The animal directly behind Bezda's began to buck uncontrollably. Its rider was thrown against the wall. He fell, then screamed as he was trampled by his own steed.

Bezda pulled down hard on his reins, trying to keep his horse facing forward. He lashed out again with the lance, desperate to keep the breach open.

Braving the wrath of the camel, Strabo lunged forward and waved the torch close to the horse's head. The flaming branches passed within inches of the animal's mouth. Rearing wildly and letting loose a high, almost human screech, the horse drove itself backward. Bezda just managed to hang on and somehow threw his lance one-handed at Strabo. He was off balance, however, and the weapon missed completely, landing harmlessly in the dust.

'Now! Push it back!' bellowed Strabo, galvanising the watching defenders. With almost no pressure from the other side, the cart was easily shunted back into place. Iucundus, recovered enough to stand, shoved one of the broken staves back into the wall.

Cassius felt a hand on his shoulder.

'Grab that! We must be quick!'

Avso, his hair hanging down over his eyes, nodded at a box of caltrops. He already had his hands on another box, which he dragged away towards the northern barricade.

Cassius squeezed between two legionaries and grabbed the edge of the second box; he found he needed both hands to shift it. As he hauled it past Crispus' men, Strabo threw his torch aside and took command at the barricades once more.

The female camel took her chance and charged for open space, towards where the Syrian camp had been. As the other two followed, Antonius sensibly sought the safety of the southern wall. Statius, however, got caught in the middle of the onrushing beasts. Despite the torch still in his hand, the female bolted straight at him. He dived to one side but a bony knee caught him on the flank, sending him spinning to the ground. Lucky not to be caught by the hooves of the other animals, the resilient legionary dusted himself down and got to his feet.

Cassius reached Avso's section. He dragged his box a few more yards, then let go.

'Over the top!' shouted Avso.

With little regard for his hands, the Thracian took handfuls of the caltrops and threw them over the cart into the midst of the Palmyrans. Others, Cassius included, were slower, picking out one at a time.

'Quicker, damn you!' yelled Avso. 'Quicker!' He ran towards the cart.

As the legionaries crowded round the box, Cassius crouched down in front of a damaged plank and looked out. At its widest point, the killing area was just forty-five feet across. While the horses were under control, this lack of space hadn't been a problem. But now, with so many animals acting on instinct and completely unbiddable, there was now almost no room to manoeuvre. A few of those who had seen the danger early had been able to drive their horses out of the gate. Those animals close to the only route of escape were now crushed together, desperate to squeeze their way through the narrow space.

Fear created panic. Some of the disorientated cavalrymen found their horses charging for the barriers, believing the few small gaps might offer a way out. Others were thrown to the ground and left somehow to escape the deadly crush.

Seeing a slight gap, one riderless animal launched itself between another and the gatehouse wall. Its shoulder went clean through the clay surround and straight into one of the vertical supporting timbers. Both horses became stuck.

Avso had clambered up on to the cart again.

'Here!' he cried. 'Pass me the boxes!'

The athletic Crispus appeared and was up beside him in a flash, soon helping to haul both boxes on to the side of the cart. Squatting so as to maintain their balance, they flung caltrops with both hands. Over to the left, Serenus had every man of the fourth section hurling the deadly contraptions over the barricade.

They soon took effect. The formidable coats of armour could do nothing to protect the horses from this danger and within moments a number had been lamed. The sharpened nails drove up into the hooves and stuck there, doubling the agony when the animals took another step. A few of the injured animals limped on or simply stopped. Many were approaching exhaustion.

Panic created chaos. The defenders watched the first horse topple over. It had been backing towards the northern barricade when both of its back legs were impaled. The animal's rear collapsed and it dropped heavily to the ground, the coat of mail splayed out around it. The rider dropped his lance and dismounted, spinning round to face any attacker.

The men of the fifth section had done a good job of throwing caltrops into the main mass of cavalrymen close to the gate. When animals began to fall there, any remaining chance of recovery evaporated. Two, three, then four horses were seen to falter, then tumble over. Their flailing legs caught other animals and riders were sent crashing to the ground in all directions.

'Remove the planks there!' shouted Avso to his men. 'Gather staves! And somebody find the Sicilian!'

Another rider came close to the northern barricade. In trying to keep his horse away from the deadly crush of struggling animals and men, he had inadvertently guided it into the worst of the caltrops. Seeing his mistake too late, he jerked back on the reins just as one of the horse's front legs gave out.

The Palmyran was thrown violently forward, somersaulting through the air before landing on his back. As his horse writhed

299

on the ground beside him, the rider sat up. He raised a hand, only to find it heavier than usual: it had been spiked clean through by two thick nails.

Recoiling in disgust and feeling the now familiar bitterness rising in his throat, Cassius backed away from the carts. It seemed incredible that the tide of the battle had turned so quickly, but again he felt anxious that he couldn't see the main body of Palmyran troops. With the gatehouse blocked and the Romans occupied, it seemed likely that they might try to strike elsewhere.

'Crispus! What do you see beyond the gate?'

With both boxes empty, Crispus and Avso now observed the suffering and destruction they had wrought. Another stricken horse tripped and crashed into the cart, almost knocking them from their perch.

The young legionary had heard Cassius though. He stood up and covered his eyes as he looked east, then quickly squatted down again. Avso dropped back down behind the barricade. Crispus quickly followed.

'Infantry and bowmen, sir. All just standing there!'

'At last,' said Avso as Strabo arrived, panting and covered in sweat, though he still had sufficient energy to smack Cassius on the shoulder.

'That was clever thinking. Sorry I delayed.'

Avso chucked one of the heavy staves to Strabo. The Sicilian caught it one-handed.

'The gate is blocked,' said the Thracian. 'We have to take out as many as we can now, while they're on the ground. We won't get another chance.'

Already assembled around them were the six men Avso had previously assigned a stave. They included Vestinus, Statius and Iucundus, who now seemed back to full strength. All had abandoned their shields.

'Let's get to it then!' said the Sicilian, thumping the stave against his free hand.

'Wait a moment.'

Serenus approached the group. Even though he had taken little active part himself, the battle had clearly taken its toll. He was using his pilum to hold himself up and his lips had turned almost white.

'Those men are still armoured. And some are still on their steeds.'

'We won't see cavalry off a second time,' said Avso firmly, already moving towards the cart.

'If we can tear the heart out of that lot it will shatter the spirits of the others,' added Strabo. 'It's worth the risk.'

Serenus accepted this with a weary nod. The legionaries had by now removed several planks, leaving a two-yard gap for Strabo and the others. Avso led the way.

'Let's get them down and finish them off. We stay together. Clear?'

'Clear!'

Strabo was at the rear, waiting for Statius and Iucundus to follow the others into the killing area.

'Watch yourself,' said Cassius.

Strabo grinned.

'Fortuna's friend, remember?'

XXXIV

None of the Palmyrans gathered outside the fort knew what had caused the chaos they now observed. Razir had ordered the front ranks back but all had seen the crush at the gatehouse, the frenzied horses unseating their riders and falling to the ground. Even the five cavalrymen who had managed to escape were either injured or still struggling to control their mounts.

Azaf had no idea why the reverse had been so sudden and dramatic, but the result was precisely what he'd feared. Pacing up and down beside the archers, he forced himself to look away and block out the noise of stricken horses and men. He had to clear his mind; decide how to regain the initiative.

Any common soldier knew that cavalry were most effective when used sparingly against a vulnerable flank or running down scattered infantry. He cursed himself for allowing himself to be persuaded that they might be effective against solid defences with so little room for manoeuvre.

Azaf had long believed that months of uninterrupted success had bred overconfidence within the Palmyran ranks. Despite this awareness, it seemed he too had fallen prey to it, and now he had a costly mess on his hands. General Zabbai would not be interested in excuses. Even so, he might overlook the mistake if Alauran could still be taken swiftly. Azaf had at least lost only a handful of his own men and the day was still young.

Not far away, one of the cavalrymen sat on the ground, his horse circling him, head bowed. Its coat of armour had been pulled clean off and strips of skin torn from its flanks. The rider had removed his helmet and armour and was cradling one arm in his lap. Azaf walked over and saw that the arm had been crushed below the elbow: a pulpy mass of flesh over broken bones.

'*Strategos*,' he said, still gulping for air.

'What happened?'

'The horses at the front, they became crazed. It spread. Then they bolted for the gate. I got out, but the others—'

Azaf looked over at the gatehouse. Two of the vertical timbers had been damaged and half of the southern tower had collapsed, leaving a pile of rubble that made escape even harder. Razir and several others were now desperately trying to free the trapped animals and release those behind.

Azaf knew he couldn't do anything until they had cleared the gate. He ran over to take charge.

Cassius went to check the southern barricade and found Kabir hunched over, watching the killing area through a jagged hole. Every one of his warriors was occupied. Several were carrying injured men to the dwellings, others were helping the legionaries with running repairs or collecting up weapons and equipment.

'I can't fault their courage,' said the Syrian, glancing up at Cassius. 'Though I fear they might regret leaving the defences.'

Cassius got down beside him and looked out. Despite the flurry of horses still charging this way and that, he could see the small group of legionaries. Bunched together as Avso had ordered, they ignored the main mass of cavalry still trying to make their escape and picked out isolated Palmyrans already on the ground.

The group split in two as they rounded a lifeless fallen horse and closed in on their first victim: the man with the caltrop in his hand. He saw the legionaries coming for him and was just scrabbling to his feet when Iucundus swung the stave down on top of his helmet, knocking the Palmyran out.

The Roman raiding party had attracted the attention of two cavalrymen close to the northern barricade. The riders had managed to stay clear of the melee and in control of their mounts. Incensed by the defenders' audacity and the failure of their assault, they exchanged a few words, then charged.

'Look out!' yelled Vestinus.

The Romans spun round as the Palmyrans bore down on them, lances tilted at the legionaries' heads. Without their shields, Strabo, Avso and the others were dependent on their agility to avoid the onrushing cavalry. The group scattered.

Vestinus found his way blocked by the fallen horse. As he tried to scramble over it, one of the Palmyrans caught him with a full-blooded thrust of his lance. The blow propelled the legionary ten feet back into the dust, a fist-sized gouge in his thigh.

The others were luckier. They all got clear of the second Palmyran in good time and Strabo and Iucundus were able to make a grab at the horseman as he passed. The Sicilian couldn't quite get a grip on the saddle but Iucundus made a successful lunge for the Palmyran's belt. He hung on grimly with both hands and was hauled off his feet. Then the additional weight told and the two of them tumbled to the ground in a heap as the horse bucked away. Somehow avoiding serious injury, they instantly dragged themselves up, each ready to attack the other.

Strabo was at his friend's side in a moment, first smashing the stave down on to the Palmyran's wrist as he reached for his sword, then sideways into his head. It was enough to account for the cavalryman, who slumped to the ground unconscious, his legs bent under him.

'Quickly! Before he returns!' shouted Avso.

He and two other legionaries sprinted after the first rider, who was trying to turn his horse. The Romans were on him before he could get the animal moving. Avso grabbed the lance just below the point and wrenched it down, pulling the Palmyran halfway out of his saddle. The horse veered away from the other legionaries, tipping its rider on to the ground. He landed heavily on his side, with no chance of defending himself. Avso swung twice at his head, denting the helmet over each ear, then looked down with satisfaction at his fallen foe.

The Palmyrans had finally freed the trapped horses. Under Azaf's orders, they had cut away at the damaged side of the tower with their swords to create space. They had then dragged the animals out by anything they could lay their hands on – reins, armour, even hair. The stricken beasts managed only a few shaky steps before collapsing.

Bezda had his horse back under control and was now occupied with keeping it on its feet. All around him were injured animals and riders. By staying close to the southern barricade, he had at least kept clear of the caltrops.

He was, however, exhausted. It was a struggle even to lift his arms and manipulate the reins. The movements of his horse were similarly sluggish. He had already resolved to kill the accursed Roman beast, assuming he ever got the opportunity. It seemed an age since he had seen anything through the eyeholes of his mask other than clay walls, wooden barricades and the chain mail of the other riders.

Suddenly the horse in front of him lurched forward. He looked towards the gate and saw that the mass of animals and men was at last breaking up. Most had dropped their lances and many were hunched over their horses' necks, desperately urging them on before they or the animals fainted. Bezda already knew that the best he could now hope for was to escape with the majority of his men and their mounts still alive.

Behind the surging mass, to his left, he saw the cost of his failure to exploit the breach and press home the attack. He had already counted five fallen men and as many animals when he spied the group of Romans.

The eight legionaries had knocked out or killed every unmounted Palmyran they could see, as well as putting several horses out of their misery. Vestinus and another injured man had withdrawn to the barricades and Avso had ordered two more to drag the unconscious Palmyrans back through the gap in the carts. Now he, Strabo, Iucundus and Statius stood in the centre of the killing area.

★　★　★

Mazat was one of Bezda's longest-serving and most reliable riders. As strong, experienced and expert in the saddle as his commander, he too had seen the Romans. Similarly enraged by the sight of his fallen fellows being dragged away, he turned and found Bezda just behind him, sword freshly drawn.

Though there were now only two horses between him and the gate, Mazat wheeled his mount round and brought it alongside Bezda. The cavalry commander nodded at him and aimed his sword at the Romans. Mazat turned round and dropped the loop at the rear of his lance neatly on to a saddle horn.

'Look there!' yelled Iucundus, pointing at Mazat. 'See the dent above his eyes where the javelin hit? That's the bastard that did for Gulo!'

Just as the Romans formed up to face the Palmyrans, the cavalrymen launched their charge.

The legionaries separated: Avso and Statius to the left; Strabo and Iucundus to the right. Strabo would get no immediate opportunity for revenge as he and Iucundus now faced Bezda, who was fractionally ahead of Mazat. The two Romans had already dropped their staves and drawn their swords. They waited until Bezda was just yards away before dividing again, springing to the side, then turning back, hoping to grab hold of something.

Bezda guessed their intentions and yanked his reins to the right. Iucundus was unable to react in time and the horse's chest caught him high, knocking him to the ground. With the animal almost stationary after its dramatic turn, Strabo took his chance.

He lunged at the Palmyran's belt with his free hand, but though he got a good grip, Bezda twisted round and slashed downward. Unable to bring his sword up to parry in time, Strabo had to let go.

Just yards away, Avso and Statius were standing together, swords at the ready. Mazat had missed them with his first charge and now brought his steed round. He kicked on and the weary horse managed enough stuttering steps to get up some speed. This time

Mazat aimed straight for Statius and locked his eyes on the Roman, his lance wedged under his arm.

Retreating as the horse bore down on him, Statius' foot caught one of the caltrops and he stumbled backwards. By the time he had recovered, the Palmyran was on him.

Mazat struck an unerring blow just above the top of the legionary's segmental armour. The weapon ripped clean through his neck and, had it not been for the saddle horn, Mazat would have lost it.

Statius died instantly, blood geysering from the wound as his body crumpled.

Mazat wrenched the lance free and wheeled his horse round to face Avso.

Worried that more of the men might be tempted out into the killing area to help, Cassius hurried back to the northern barricade. He arrived to find that Serenus shared his concern: the veteran was watching the fight unfold with his pilum blocking the way of any overzealous legionaries. Several were shouting encouragement and jabbing their swords in the air. Cassius squeezed through and stood at Serenus' shoulder.

'Sir, can't we help them?' asked one man.

Serunus spun round and glared at him.

'I've already told you twice, soldier. That gate is wide open and there's more than a hundred men outside. We hold the line. No one else leaves this barricade.'

Strabo had already hit Bezda three times, to no obvious effect. He could see that the Palmyran was tired, his defensive parries were lethargic and weak, but while still in the saddle Bezda maintained the upper hand.

The Sicilian stepped back and looked around. Statius' body was close by. He could hear the sounds of blade on blade behind him. There was no sign of Iucundus.

He swung one-handed and Bezda blocked again. This time, however, Strabo pushed his sword up, forcing the Palmyran's

307

blade back while he reached out with his other hand. Gripping a handful of mail, he hauled downward, trying to dislodge his foe. Only the combination of the four-horned saddle and Bezda's horsemanship kept him in place. He tried to turn his horse away but the exhausted animal was no longer capable of moving; it was struggling even to support the weight on its back.

As the two of them fought, Strabo caught a glimpse of movement below him. He looked down. A large, brown hand appeared.

Mazat's horse was also fading fast. As Avso advanced, eyes fixed on the point of the lance, the Palmyran flung the weapon upward. The handle turned over in the air and the blunt end landed on the Roman's arm, knocking the sword from his hand. Mazat swung one leg over the saddle horns and dropped to the ground, drawing his sword just as Avso recovered his own.

The cavalryman knew his own strength was almost gone. Over Avso's left shoulder he could see the last of his fellow riders making their escape through the gate. Seeing the agile-looking Roman raise his sword, he decided on a simple tactic.

Avso was unprepared for the charge. By the time he got his blade up Mazat was already on him. The larger man slammed into the Thracian's chest.

They hit the ground hard. Avso was pinned; he couldn't move his sword arm. Blinking through the sunlight, he saw a gleaming blade closing on his throat. He somehow got his spare arm free and clamped his hand on the Palmyran's wrist.

Strabo continued to spar with Bezda, their blades clanging as they exchanged half-hearted strikes, neither able to mount a telling attack.

Suddenly the horse's armoured coat seemed to slip, then the saddle too. Strabo saw Iucundus crouching under the horse, gripping the main saddle strap. The lanky legionary hauled it towards the ground, catapulting Bezda sideways.

Strabo only just leaped back in time to avoid the falling cavalryman. Bezda landed heavily on the ground at his feet.

Iucundus caught a hoof in the stomach for his troubles. He lay on the ground, winded, as the animal charged away towards the gate.

Strabo readied himself to drive his sword pommel down on to Bezda's head.

'Avso!' cried Iucundus, unable to help the Thracian himself.

Strabo whirled round to see Mazat dwarfing the helpless figure beneath him, forcing his sword down towards Avso's neck.

Just as Strabo turned back, Bezda threw a handful of sand up into his face. Half blinded, Strabo clawed at him but the Palmyran was intent only on escape. He tripped over a horse and stumbled away towards the gate.

Eyes streaming, Strabo ran the few yards to the grappling opponents. He couldn't see well enough to risk a swing of his sword so he dropped it and stood behind the kneeling Palmyran. He ran his hands down over the front of Mazat's helmet, grabbed the bottom rim, then pulled upwards. Hoping to expose the Palmyran's neck and distract him long enough for Avso to use his blade, he pushed his knee into Mazat's back, gripped hard with his fingers, then wrenched the helmet up again.

The sickening crunch that followed was heard by many of those watching from the barricades. Feeling the Palmyran's head go limp in his hands, Strabo realised he had snapped Mazat's neck. He let the lifeless body tip over, then stood aside, still wiping his eyes.

'My thanks,' said Avso.

Strabo helped the Thracian to his feet.

'My pleasure.'

Bezda fell to his knees, undid his chinstrap and tore off his helmet, taking a good deal of hair and skin with it. His face was more red than brown, his cheeks almost purple. Coughing hard, he pushed matted strands of hair from his face.

He glanced up to see Azaf walking past him.

'*Strategos*. I—'

With not even the slightest acknowledgement, Azaf continued

on, past the archers, towards the infantry. Razir hurried over to meet him.

'Withdraw all ranks to the rally line,' Azaf said calmly. 'Allow them to rest and have water brought up. I'll address them soon.'

XXXV

Strabo and Avso stood in silence, helmets under their arms, solemnly staring down at Statius. Someone had wrapped a sack round his throat to cover the terrible wound. Iucundus was there too; he had removed his armour and held both hands against his ribs, grimacing with every breath. Cassius and Serenus were close by, supervising the other legionaries as they worked manically to cover the gap with fresh planks of wood.

'Where was he from?' asked Strabo.

Avso said nothing. The Sicilian turned towards him. 'Avso. Where was he from?'

'Thrace. Some village in the mountains. I don't remember the name.'

The mention of Avso and Statius' homeland reminded Cassius that they were not members of the Third Legion. Avso had now lost all his fellow soldiers from the Fourth: Flavian, Gemellus and now Statius.

Strabo looked over at Cassius.

'How many more injured?'

'I'm not sure. They've all been taken to the aid post. I'll check the roll.'

Avso stepped over Statius' body and stalked towards the open space that had once housed the market. Ahead of him were the Palmyran prisoners. Their weapons and helmets had been removed and they lay on the ground, guarded by three legionaries. There were nine of the cavalrymen in all, though only four were conscious.

Cassius was in little doubt about Avso's intentions and started after him. Strabo put a hand on his arm.

311

'Leave it,' he said quietly.

'Those prisoners are my responsibility.'

'You should not interfere,' said Strabo, his voice steely as he tightened his grip.

'Let go of me,' said Cassius, outraged that the Sicilian should go so far.

The legionaries close by looked on.

'Let go, Strabo.'

The Sicilian bent his head towards him.

'You will not intervene?'

Avso ordered the others to strip the prisoners of armour and equipment. The Thracian drew his sword and held it over the first Palmyran as the legionaries pulled at his belt.

Cassius wrenched his arm away.

'I shall do as I damn well please.'

'Centurion.'

Despite the cordial expression on his face, Serenus now blocked Cassius' way. 'Perhaps you would accompany me to the aid post, to check on the wounded. I've posted a lookout at the eastern wall. It seems matters are in hand here.'

'You too wish to dictate to me? Perhaps I can remind you both of the relevant regulations: prisoners are to be disarmed, then—'

'By Mars,' said Strabo.

Serenus concluded Cassius' sentence: 'Prisoners are to be disarmed, then restrained or guarded unless doing so compromises the completion of a military action.'

'Exactly,' said Cassius.

'The action is the defence of this fort,' Serenus said patiently. 'We cannot spare men to guard prisoners.'

Strabo wasn't interested in arguing any further. He drew his sword, pushed past Cassius and made for the marketplace, with Iucundus not far behind. Cassius watched the first Palmyran wriggling in the dust as the Romans held him down. Avso jammed a boot into the warrior's stomach.

'Come,' said Serenus, tipping his pilum towards the street. 'If you see no transgression, no offence need be reported.'

'That is not the issue,' said Cassius grimly, turning back towards the barricades. He had no wish to see another death.

'Come,' repeated Serenus. 'We have much more work ahead of us. The enemy have not retreated far. They may strike again soon.'

There was no cry from the Palmyran but Cassius could see from Serenus' face that the cavalryman had been killed. Another could be heard pleading quietly for his life. With no real alternative left open to him, Cassius walked away up the street. Serenus followed him past a small group of Syrians attending to minor injuries.

'Would you slow down a little?' asked Serenus, his voice hoarse.

Cassius did so. Nearing the square, they saw wounded legionaries gathered outside the aid post.

'I know you have not seen such things before but I have, many a time,' said Serenus. 'There is seldom much room for clemency once blood is spilt.'

Cassius thought then of Flavian and the manner of his death. He wondered why he had not thought of it sooner. The legionary had been the first casualty of the battle; his death the most cruel.

'So it would seem.'

Over the past few months, Cassius had spent many hours trying to imagine what real combat was like. He knew now that such endeavours had been in vain. He could have spent a lifetime training for battle, heard endless stories of war; nothing could have prepared him for its savage realities.

'You value life,' said Serenus. 'It does you credit.' The veteran stopped by one of the dwellings and leaned against the wall to catch his breath. 'But if your conscience troubles you, consider this; Avso and Strabo have lost brothers here today. They have made up their minds. Neither you nor I can stop them.'

Leaving Serenus to rest, Cassius hurried on towards the aid post. Close to the western wall, Julius and Antonius were struggling

313

to get the big female camel under control. The two smaller animals were tied up to the well.

'There you are!'

Cassius had given no thought to the Praetorian and was therefore surprised to see the giant shuffling towards him. He was barefoot, buckling his belt as he walked, and for once there was no cup of wine in his hand. Cassius still found himself amazed by the physical dimensions of the man, this time noticing the plate-sized hands and enormous fingers, easily double the width of his own.

'That stuff,' said the Praetorian, blinking into the morning light.

'Sorry?'

Though they were just yards from the aid post, the Praetorian seemed not to have noticed the injured men. Cassius wondered if he even understood that Alauran had been attacked.

'That milky stuff you left in my room. I think it did me some good.'

'Oh.'

'My guts feel better. Is there any more?'

Though his eyes were still bloodshot and his delivery stilted, the huge man seemed as sober as Cassius had seen him.

'I'll try to get you some.'

The Praetorian rubbed his hands together.

'Good.'

'It may be difficult. There are injured men.' Cassius gestured towards the aid post but the grey eyes rested on him and him only. 'Others are dead. We must prepare for another attack.'

The Praetorian nodded vacantly and Cassius realised that this new-found lucidity applied only when the man was focused on his own welfare. The wall of intoxication and self-interest he had created around himself would not be easily breached. The Praetorian turned, staggering slightly as he made for the inn.

'Just get me some more of that mixture.'

'I'll try.'

'Good lad,' he mumbled, walking away.

The legionaries outside the aid post had observed the encounter.

One, holding a folded tunic against a wound on his knee, nodded towards the inn as Cassius approached.

'The Bear's up early, sir. Perhaps he will fight with us now.'

'I doubt it,' said Cassius as the men moved aside to let him through. 'He's more interested in his next cup of wine.'

The soldier shook his head. The disappointment amongst the assembled legionaries was palpable. Though Cassius had earlier resolved to abandon all thoughts of winning the Praetorian round, the reaction of the soldiers reminded him of how such a man might embolden them, not to mention the effect his presence might have on the enemy. Everything about his behaviour suggested he would do nothing to assist the defence, but Cassius was not quite ready to give up on him yet.

With a swift about-turn he rounded the corner and found the Praetorian bent over the bar, grunting as he foraged for another barrel. A cup sat on the bar next to him.

'Excuse me.'

Still empty-handed, the Praetorian pushed himself up and turned round. He blinked a couple of times, then picked at his nose.

'Ah. You have it?'

'No, not yet. I just thought I should tell you something. My servant is an expert in these matters. He said that wine will counteract the effects of the preparation.'

'Huh?' The Praetorian's bushy eyebrows formed a V as he frowned, apparently unable to comprehend the notion of abstinence.

'He said it will negate its effects. Your pain will return immediately.'

The Praetorian leaned back against the bar and stared at the floor.

'He has plenty of ingredients,' Cassius continued. 'There's no reason why he can't suppress the pain indefinitely, perhaps even cure you.'

The Praetorian looked up. Cassius examined his face for traces of suspicion but he saw only contemplation, then what might even have been hope. Encouraged, he moved closer, took his canteen from his belt and held it out.

'Here. He said that water would help. As much as you can drink.'

The Praetorian took the canteen, removed the plug and drank. Though the water from Alauran's well was the sweetest Cassius had come across in Syria, the Praetorian winced like a child forced to ingest a particularly unpleasant tonic. He tilted his head back and blew out his cheeks.

'Now it's my head buzzing!' The great hand that slammed down on to the bar split a plank in two and sent his cup flying. 'Mars knows why I've been cursed so!'

Despite his youth, Cassius knew a little about the effects of heavy and repeated drinking.

'You crave the wine to dull the pain – a common enough pattern. But it will pass. Your condition, however—'

Scowling, the Praetorian perused the tender underside of his hand. Cassius began to wonder if he was alive to his machinations. He decided to fill the silence.

'My man has helped many. Some say his powers have been bestowed from above. If you return to your quarters, I'll have him bring you more of the preparation. Perhaps even a meal.'

The Praetorian gave the canteen back, then rubbed his chin.

'Food. Don't remember the last time I ate.'

Cassius gestured to his left.

'Please. I'll send him along presently.'

The Praetorian finally began to move but halted after just two strides, looking longingly back at the bar.

'Surely a cup or two wouldn't—'

'He said not even a mouthful.'

The Praetorian tutted, sniffed loudly, then continued on his way.

The aid post was now reserved for those most in need, and Priscus had been joined by four more badly wounded legionaries. Cassius picked his way between their weapons and armour, then grabbed a mail shirt and passed it back to a man with only minor wounds.

'Remove this gear.'

He stepped carefully over two of the beds and stood over Simo, who was treating Vestinus. The legionary lay on his back with one hand clamped over his eyes. Simo was pouring water from a bowl over the wound in his thigh, cleaning away the sand and dirt. Cassius tried not to look at the section of shiny white bone below the torn flesh.

'Simo. I need more of that preparation.'

Simo did not look up, replying as he reached for a bandage.

'I'm afraid I haven't the time, sir. There are many others to treat.'

Cassius shook his head and wondered how many more times people supposedly under his command were going to disobey him.

'Simo. Over here for a moment if you please.'

Cassius walked to the back of the aid post, in amongst the chests and piles of sheets. Simo lay the bandage over the wound, put a soothing hand upon Vestinus' arm, then joined him.

'I need it as soon as possible,' Cassius said, trying to remain composed. 'The Praetorian seems to think it helped. If he continues to feel better, I may be able to persuade him to fight.'

Simo offered a faint appeasing smile then gestured towards the injured soldiers.

'Sir, these men require attention immediately. That preparation is probably useless.'

Cassius slammed his right fist into his left palm.

'Just do it, Simo!' he shouted. 'Remind yourself of who is servant and who is master. I decide how your time is spent.'

Simo looked down at the floor.

'Yes, sir,' he whispered.

'There's no need to spend hours on it,' Cassius said, lowering his voice. 'As long as there's plenty of it and it looks and tastes roughly the same. Give him some food as well. And do nothing to arouse his anger.'

317

'I understand, sir.'

'Best get back to it then.'

Simo retreated with a bow.

Cassius saw a small clay pot next to one of the oil lamps. Inside were some of the lead identity tablets worn round the neck of every Roman soldier. One had belonged to Gemellus, another to Barates. Cassius still didn't have one because he hadn't been officially assigned to a legion. Next to the pot was the reed pen and Simo's amended copy of the century roll. Cassius took both with him.

He met Strabo coming up the street. The Sicilian was cleaning the tip of his sword with a cloth. He kept his eyes on his work as he approached, his face expressionless.

'Any change?' Cassius asked as they passed each other. They would have to communicate sooner or later and he saw no reason to delay.

Strabo stopped.

'No. Still gathered where they were. I was just going to fetch a little food for the men.'

'I'll give you a hand.'

Strabo shrugged and they set off towards the granary. Away to the right, Antonius had managed to tie the female camel to the well surround, and he and Julius were now towing the other two towards the stables.

Cassius thought it best to try and clear the air while he and Strabo were alone.

'Perhaps I shouldn't have intervened. You have a right to avenge your friends. The Palmyrans have shown little interest in mercy.'

'Is that an apology?'

'No.'

Strabo gave a narrow smile. He sheathed his sword and tucked the cloth into his belt.

'Well, you should know that they at least died quickly. We've put all the bodies against the northern wall. Our men too. Three of them. What's that you have there?'

'Copy of the roll. Simo has been keeping track of the injured and dead. There are six or seven more who cannot fight.'

'About thirty of us left then. We shall have to reorganise the sections. Let's have a look.'

Strabo sat down on the granary steps and took the sheet of papyrus and the pen. Simo had underlined the names of the dead and put a dot against those too injured to fight. Strabo dotted the name of Vestinus and another man, then found the names of Statius and Gulo and underlined them both.

The Sicilian looked up at the sky for a moment.

'Rufus Marius Gulo. As honest as they come that one. Never once saw him cheat or shirk a task.' Strabo spat into the dust. 'Least he wasn't married.'

He stood, hurried up the granary steps and removed the locking plank. Just inside the door were several small barrels of wine and two sacks of food: one full of mixed dried fruit, the other dried pork. Strabo pushed one barrel and both sacks towards the step. Cassius picked up the barrel. The Sicilian paused, his frame in shadow.

'Centurion. I should not have put my hand upon you. That is an apology.'

'We'll say no more about it then.'

Dropping the sheet and pen on top of Cassius' barrel, Strabo took one sack under each arm and jumped down to the ground. As they walked back across the square, he glanced towards the well, where Julius and Antonius were once again struggling with the big camel.

'If we make it through this, you might consider that beast for a commendation.'

Azaf took his time with the instructions, repeating them twice to the gathered swordsmen and archers. He had considered the three-way assault strategy, but Bezda had made a reasonable point when arguing against a division of the force. Men assaulting by ladder would be vulnerable and he still maintained a huge advantage in numbers. This time he would lead the men in himself. There would be no retreat.

Four of the horses lay on the ground not far away. Beyond help, they had been killed and stripped of their valuable armour and saddles. Virtually all the cavalrymen were either injured or exhausted. Some had had to be physically removed from their armour and they were now in the carts, returning to the encampment, to a man shamed by their defeat.

Bezda had made no further attempt to speak to Azaf. He had summoned enough energy to supervise tying the remaining horses to the carts and had been the last to haul himself up into the rear vehicle. He sat there now as the cart trundled away, head bowed.

Azaf finished his orders, then selected twelve of his best men. He directed them to one side then approached one of the older archers.

'You. Pick out four of the worst shots.'

The man hesitated.

'Quickly.'

Reluctantly, the archer walked along the front rank of his fellows. Not daring to tarry, he swiftly identified four men who all glared at him as they exited the ranks and stood close to Azaf. He sent them off to join his twelve swordsmen, then turned to Razir.

'Take the main group up close to the gate. Twenty-five of ours, then twenty-five archers, then the same again. All the others as a reserve on the rally line.'

Razir shouted the command.

Azaf led the twelve swordsmen and four archers to a pile of equipment Razir had assembled earlier. He turned first to his swordsmen. They were all battle-hardened: reliable and strong, ideal for their assigned task.

'Take a lance each.'

Razir had rounded up twelve of the cavalry weapons.

'You know what to do. Now join the first rank.'

Those swordsmen with shields dropped them before taking up the heavy lances and moving off.

'Now, you four. Drop your bows and take a large shield.'

The archers did so uncertainly, unused to wielding such a weight.

'When I pass that gate the four of you stand before me, two in front, one at each side, and you hold those shields high with both hands. And if a missile comes within a yard of me, you can expect to feel my blade at your back.'

XXXVI

Though few of the legionaries had time to get any food down, several cups of wine were still being drunk when the third attack came. Cassius hadn't touched a drop; he wanted to maintain a clear head and was determined to fight his fear through will alone. A faultless job had been done of repairing the carts and three new supporting timbers had been placed where the southern barricade met the wall. The first section had been divided amongst the other four, with Avso in charge of the northern side, Strabo and Cassius still together to the south. Serenus had been struck by another painful bout of coughing. Despite his protests, Cassius had sent him to help out at the aid post. Antonius and the other lookouts were back in position. The only enemy activity was to the east.

Strabo had just taken a quick look over the wall and seen the ranks of infantry and archers. Like Cassius, he was surprised that the Palmyrans had chosen to attack through the gate again.

'Perhaps those weren't ladders in the carts after all,' Cassius said, one hand on the top of his newly reclaimed shield.

Strabo finished off his wine and chucked the cup on to a barrel.

'I'm not sure. Maybe Purple Cloak thinks those bowmen might make the difference.'

He looked around.

'Everybody got their metal on?'

A couple of the legionaries had appropriated Palmyran cavalry helmets. Macrinus would have pulled on an entire set of armour had Avso not stepped in.

Shouts went up from beyond the gate. The Romans moved

forward, keen to see the next advance. Kabir exited the dwelling and ran over to Cassius and Strabo.

'You have seen the archers? They are barely armoured. No helmets. Some of the infantry too.'

'Suitable prey for your boys?' asked Strabo.

'Certainly,' answered Kabir. 'We have good supplies of shot and stone. All my men are in place.'

Cassius looked speculatively at Strabo.

'We're thin on each side. Can we spare them all?'

'Down here they're just another pair of hands, up there they can do some real damage.'

Cassius could hear Avso already taunting the Palmyrans. There was little time for rumination.

'It's decided then. But Kabir, keep them out of sight until the enemy are well inside. One note from the tuba and you open fire.'

Kabir was all set to leave when Strabo held up a hand.

'Syrian. Remind your men that that first volley is essential. After that you will draw the fire of the archers and they outnumber you. And tell every man this: if they catch sight of Purple Cloak—'

'Of course,' said Kabir.

As he departed, Cassius looked up at the dwellings. There was not one sign of the Syrians on either roof; they had done an excellent job of concealing themselves.

'Men, keep your faces away from the carts,' warned Strabo. 'At this range those bolts will go through almost anything.'

The legionaries duly withdrew, though all made sure they could still see the Palmyrans.

The advance through the gate was far slower and more ordered this time, with the warriors facing the added complication of six dead horses in their way. With an instruction from Razir, the first Palmyrans turned to the south. Leading the way were half of Azaf's lance-wielders, well spaced and a pace in front of the next line, a solid rank of red-clad swordsmen. At the shoulder of every one of them was an archer, bow ready but aimed skyward. Razir stayed close to the gate as he sent the second group towards the northern barricade.

At his next command the swordsmen made way for the archers. The bows swung down and in a moment there was a sliver of sharpened iron aiming at every gap or trace of a defender. Those who couldn't see a section of armour or tunic simply trained their bows on a vulnerable piece of planking somewhere between knee and head height. Immense traction was required to draw the bowstrings, so the archers left them only a quarter drawn until the last moment.

'Shields up!' shouted Strabo.

Though it would mean they could see little of the enemy, the Romans readily complied. Cassius had left his sword undrawn. He squatted low and used both hands to steady his shield.

Strabo had earlier placed Minicius at the corner of the dwelling: within earshot but safe from the Palmyran arrows. The Sicilian turned and waved to him.

Minicius lifted the tuba.

The archers shielded Azaf well as he walked through the gate, leaving him free to examine the damaged wall to his left and the detritus of battle still on the ground. Aside from the dead horses, there were sections of armour and leather straps torn away in the crush; lances and swords, some damaged, some as good as new; and patches of blood, still moist enough to shimmer under the low sun.

Azaf had his own armour on now, a light mail shirt that he wore under his cloak against his skin. He only ever put it on at the last moment and detested the way it hung heavily on his shoulders, restricting his arms. It would, however, be foolish to enter the fort without some protection, and he hoped not to be wearing it for long. Razir had chosen to go without, a gesture of solidarity with the other swordsmen.

Azaf counted eight steps, then ordered the archers to halt. The men readjusted themselves, carefully fitting the edges of the heavy rectangular shields together, checking that the *strategos* was well protected. Azaf could see both sides of the barricade and about half of his men. They looked steady and calm. There would be no loss of control this time. No retreat.

Razir arrived.

'All are positioned as you instructed, *strategos*.'

'Begin.'

The echoes of Razir's cry were still reverberating around the compound when the archers set their bows. With thumb and fingers clamped round the string, and sinewy arms trembling with the effort, each made a final adjustment of aim, then let go.

On their own, neither the timbers of the carts nor the leather-covered wooden shields would have been anything like sturdy enough to resist the power of the Palmyran bows. Together, they saved the lives of most of the Roman defenders at the barricades.

Cassius felt no impact against his own shield but saw two men down to his right. One was on his back, shield lying across him, an arrow in his knee. Incredibly, the legionary did not cry out. Another, who had been standing next to Iucundus, was also silent. He too lay on his back, tunic gathered in folds at his waist, an arrow shaft sticking up out of his forehead. Iucundus didn't even bother to check him.

'Now!' yelled Strabo.

Minicius blew and the deep note sounded, clear and even this time. Cassius looked up at the dwelling roof.

The Syrians rose as one above the surround, a huddled black-clad mass, each of them with one arm already in the air. Their wrists spun and the cloud of lead whizzed away.

There were low pops and thuds as the projectiles struck the massed Palmyran troops. The sheer number of screams told the Romans that most of Kabir's men had found unprotected targets. The next sound to reach Cassius' ears was the familiar splintering of wood. Just a yard to his right was Strabo, peering over the top of his shield.

'They've got those big cavalry lances. They'll try to punch holes while the archers cover them!'

The Sicilian moved towards the barricade and drew his sword.

Cassius shuffled left to check on Crispus and his section. Two legionaries had been hit. The five still on their feet were warily approaching the cart, shields up. Crispus went to help one of the fallen legionaries, kneeling down in front of him and propping his shield up to protect them both. The arrow had caught the man high on his left arm and was stuck fast. He was sitting up, eyes tightly shut.

'It'll have to be cut out!' Crispus shouted.

Cassius tapped the soldier on the leg.

'Can you stand? Try and get yourself back to the aid post.'

The legionary opened his eyes. He stared blankly at the arrow shaft as he was helped to his feet. With an order from Cassius, Minicius dropped the tuba and escorted him away.

As Cassius and Crispus turned back to the barricades, two more lances smashed through. They were retracted, then thrust forward again, knocking a plank away. The timber fell at the feet of a legionary who swiftly advanced to defend the breach. As he moved, his shield dropped slightly. Before he had taken his second step, an arrow flashed through the gap and lodged itself in his face, knocking him straight on to his back.

More arrows flew through the gap. Cassius, Crispus and the other legionaries scattered. The injured man thrashed around in the dust, hands flailing. Cassius saw that the arrow had gone straight through his right eye socket. The eye itself had disappeared but the other was open, wide and alert even as the body became still. There was not a single drop of blood.

Strabo charged up and planted his shield across the top of the gap.

'Crispus. Cover there!' he shouted, nodding downward. Crispus was there in an instant, the top of his shield against the bottom of Strabo's, completing the makeshift barrier.

Another arrow sliced through a plank and whistled past Cassius' ear. He dropped down on his backside behind his shield.

'You! Take over here!' ordered Strabo.

Another legionary came forward and placed his shield behind Strabo's, allowing the Sicilian to withdraw.

Cassius, still down on the ground, felt something tugging at the sleeve of his mail shirt. Macrinus was there on his hands and knees.

'Four men down, sir. We need help.'

Strabo knelt down next to them.

'Are the carts holding? Is there a large breach?'

'More than one!' answered Macrinus. 'We can't get close to the lances!'

A caltrop landed in the sand between them, thrown by some enterprising Palmyran. Unperturbed, Strabo looked up at the dwelling roof. Only one Syrian was visible above the surround. Strabo grabbed Cassius by the shoulder.

'See how it looks from up there. Tell them to keep firing. They must take out the archers.'

'Shall I send some of them down?'

'Not yet. Just tell Kabir – the archers!'

Cassius scrambled away, holding his shield to his right as he made for the dwellings. The wounded man had gone but Minicius had returned. Cassius handed him his shield.

'There. With Strabo.'

Minicius reluctantly took it. Before he could move, an arrow thudded into the side of the house. The signaller retreated.

'Get low. Go!'

As Minicius crabbed away, Cassius took a quick count of the defenders. There were only nine legionaries still on their feet behind the southern barricade.

Inside the house he found his way barred by a Syrian descending the ladder. The man was using only his right hand to climb down; a Palmyran arrow was sticking out of his left shoulder. As the Syrian's foot reached the ground, his eyes rolled up and he stumbled backwards. Cassius just managed to catch him. The warrior was still conscious but unable to keep himself upright.

'Here. Let me help.'

327

Serenus appeared at the doorway. Cassius lowered the Syrian to the ground and the veteran took charge. Cassius started up the ladder.

The Palmyran archers were far from craven but they were used to operating hundreds of feet from the front line, safe in the knowledge that their horses could move them swiftly away from danger if need be. Few had ever fought on foot. None had ever experienced such an assault.

Caught completely unawares by the first Syrian volley, almost twenty of their number had been downed by the lead shot. Without the protection of a helmet, any kind of blow above the eyeline could inflict a serious or fatal injury.

Azaf knew the archers lacked the grit of his swordsmen.

He had shouted orders directly at them, instructing them to train their bows on the Syrians. Confident there was little danger from the barricades, he now looked out between two shields.

There were still at least fifteen active archers on both sides. And with only the two roofs to cover, they were able to keep the Syrians pinned down. Despite their speed, it took the slingers several moments to raise themselves, then complete the throwing action before release. The Palmyrans had already taken out several men on each roof before they could get their shots away.

Azaf moved close to the men at the northern barricade. They could now use their lances to tear the barricades apart plank by plank. Behind them, his swordsmen waited patiently for their chance.

Cassius crawled up into blinding sunlight to find the Syrians flattened against the roof. Five or six across, they were almost on top of each other in places, some lying on their chests, others on their backs. To his right, two men lay against the surround. One was dead. His legs had been folded back towards him to make space. The second stared up into the sky, still holding his sling, a Palmyran arrow lodged deep in his thigh.

Cassius stayed on the ladder for a moment, trying to spot Kabir. He caught sight of the scarred face of Idan, who reached across another man and tapped his leader on the shoulder.

Pushing two sets of feet out of the way, Cassius crawled on his belly towards the front of the roof. Twice his belt and sword got caught up with those he passed, but he freed himself swiftly and was soon alongside Kabir.

While down on the ground, he had imagined he would get a good view of the killing area from the roof but he now realised that was impossible. Not one of the Syrians seemed willing to raise themselves above the level of the surround.

'You must keep firing!' he shouted.

'We cannot,' answered Kabir resolutely, his face just inches away from Cassius'. 'Any man that stands will be struck at once.'

Cassius had no doubt that Kabir's fears were well founded, but there was simply no other option.

'You are auxiliaries and part of this garrison. My men are sacrificing themselves. So must yours!'

Kabir looked away. His hair fell across his face.

Cassius heard a rasping voice to his right. He turned towards Idan. The tribesman looked past Cassius at Kabir; he seemed to be asking a question. Kabir stared down at the roof for a moment, then nodded.

'We'll try something.'

Kabir put his sling down, turned to the left and cupped his mouth with both hands. He shouted out a single word. *Yarak.*

Despite the noise of the battle below, they clearly heard the priest's bellowed reply. Kabir gave an order and all those around Cassius readied their slings: loading them, checking each strap, keeping their arms clear of each other as they prepared to rise. Two men scrambled forward on either side of Cassius. Kabir slid backward.

'Come. Unless you wish to join the front rank.'

Kabir, Cassius and Idan took up the space vacated by the two others, their feet just in front of the ladder. Kabir loaded his sling and placed the release strap carefully between his thumb and forefinger. He got to his knees and hunched low. His men all copied him until Cassius was the only one still lying down.

The Syrian shouted a series of short words.

Cassius realised he was counting.

Azaf was still looking up at the southern dwelling when the Syrians rose. Their heads and chests appeared only in the moment before they ducked instantly down without even raising their slings.

All the skittish archers on both sides of the barricades were fooled by the feint and loosed their arrows. Eight found their targets, hitting Syrians on both roofs before they could drop below the surround.

Azaf screamed at the archers to reload. Acting on well-honed instinct, most already had their hands to their quivers as soon as the strings had snapped tight. Some even managed to lower their bows and place the indented base of the next arrow up against the string. Only two had managed to raise their bows by the time the Syrians stood again to take their turn.

Not one Palmyran archer got a shot away before them.

Kabir's men surged forward, ignoring the fallen warriors. The air came alive again as a fresh hail of lead fizzed down towards the archers.

Of the five Syrians who had made up the front rank at the southern dwelling, three were dead, killed instantly by shots to the head. The two still alive were trying to crawl to safety between the legs of their comrades. Cassius scrambled towards one as the others reloaded and sent down the second volley.

The collective composure of Kabir's men had gone. They screamed down at the Palmyrans, whooping when a shot hit home, desperate to avenge their own and destroy their enemy before they could strike back at them.

Holding the injured man by the wrist, Cassius hauled him clear. As the warrior twisted on to his side, his bag of shot emptied itself across the roof. He had been hit in the middle of the chest, two inches below the base of his neck.

Cassius sat up beside him and pushed the man's hands away from the arrow. He looked at his back and saw the iron tip sticking out between the Syrian's shoulders. Stuck to the end of it was a scrap of black cloth.

More than half the archers were now down. Many had been hit in the eyes or nose, others had had their cheeks caved in. Of those still alive, several lay or knelt amongst their fellow warriors, hands against their wounds, praying to Malakbel for salvation.

The Syrian fire was so quick and accurate that the eighteen still standing on the roofs were now able to attack without fear. Any Palmyran who raised his bow was subjected to a withering barrage of shot.

By the time the Syrians unleashed their fifth and sixth volleys, fewer than a quarter of the Palmyrans were still able to fire their weapons. At this point, morale collapsed.

One man, not far from the gate, found himself completely surrounded by dead or mortally wounded fellow archers. Yelling curses, he pushed his way back through the swordsmen.

Azaf saw only a glimpse of him. Before he could take action, three more were past him and through the gate. When he saw that some had even abandoned their bows, he realised that the archers would take no further meaningful part in the battle. Like Bezda's cavalry, they had proven themselves to be powerful yet brittle. When broken, they became a liability.

He made no attempt to stop the last of the stragglers, even ordering Razir to let those from the northern barricade out. With a final look of disgust at the men still running towards the rally line, he ordered his shield-bearers to his right, faintly surprised that they were still following orders.

He called out to Teyya, who, like the others, was now torn between attacking the carts and defending himself against the slingers. The youth scuttled over to him.

'Tell my swordsmen in the reserve that they are to kill any archer who retreats beyond their position. Run!'

★   ★   ★

331

'Leave him,' said Kabir, turning towards Cassius as he reloaded. 'It is a fatal wound.'

The warrior had lost a huge amount of blood, yet somehow he held on. Cassius had been able to do no more than steady him during the most violent spasms; offer feeble assurances in a language the dying man didn't understand. The Syrian's head lolled to one side as Cassius laid him down. Blood frothed between his lips.

Kabir dragged the other wounded man several yards across the roof and dumped him close to the ladder. An arrow had gouged a coin-sized hole in the side of the warrior's neck. He had a hand over it but blood was flowing freely through his fingers.

As Kabir rushed back to the surround, Serenus heaved himself up the ladder with a wheeze.

'What's happening?' he said.

'I'll check,' answered Cassius. 'Help this fellow down, would you?'

Cassius got to his feet and moved warily towards the Syrians. Staying well away from the twisting arms and spinning slings, he looked down at the killing area. The only archers still inside the compound were on the ground, their faces contorted by pain. None of them were firing.

Though the lance-wielders had done a good job of pulling the carts to pieces, they and the swordsmen were now far more concerned with the lead shot raining down upon them. Those with shields raised them high and tried not to trip over the injured archers.

Cassius looked across at Yarak and the other Syrians. They had lost men too, more perhaps; he could see several prone forms lying behind those firing. The priest had placed his sling in his belt and was standing with one leg up on the surround. Screaming exhortations, he pointed down at the Palmyrans then raised a clenched fist towards the sun.

Though he had told himself there could not be another withdrawal, Azaf knew with a sudden certainty that he had no choice.

His men had been close to breaching the barricades on both sides, but with the slingers in such a commanding position, continuing the fight on the defenders' terms would be suicidal. His hatred for the hired Syrians who dared to fight alongside the Romans would be put to one side for the moment. They would pay later for their poor choice of allies.

There would, however, be no chance for revenge if he allowed stubbornness to cloud his judgement. With every passing moment, the losses amongst his own swordsmen mounted. Concerned with defending themselves, they would be unable to inflict serious losses on the Romans.

The attack hadn't been a complete failure. Many of the archers had made kills and he knew now that the legionaries were so few that they could do no more than cower behind the barricades. Including the slingers, he doubted they could muster thirty fighting men. He still had treble that number, assuming he withdrew his warriors swiftly.

Azaf called out to Razir and waited patiently for him to reappear. There would be no panic or signal of defeat. His swordsmen would retreat around him. He would be the last to leave the compound.

He would still have that flag.

Sidestepping more injured Syrians, Cassius hurried back through the dwelling doorway. Having seen the mass of Palmyrans from above, it was doubly shocking to see the handful of legionaries at the southern barricade. Both carts were riven with holes, but Strabo had made sure there was a shield or two up against the biggest gaps.

The Sicilian was standing next to Crispus, bawling at the Syrians. 'Keep firing! Kill as many as you can!'

The character of the noise coming from the Palmyrans changed. 'They're retreating again,' said Iucundus with a half-smile.

Strabo was still yelling at the Syrians, though not one of them showed any sign of stopping. The legionaries lowered their shields to see what was going on.

Still under fire, the swordsmen backed away as speedily as they could. There were many more dead and injured men this time. The Palmyrans aided those who could stand but many were left on the ground. Some of those blinded or struck in the head pawed at their comrades, begging for help.

The Syrians were merciless. They fired again and again at the maimed warriors until they became still.

'There he is!' shouted Strabo.

He grabbed his shield and pilum and sprang away towards the northern barricade, Iucundus not far behind. Cassius was still staring after him when Serenus arrived. The veteran looked out at the retreating Palmyrans.

'Purple Cloak.'

He turned towards Cassius.

'Strabo means to kill him. You mustn't let him leave the line again.'

Cassius wasn't sure if Serenus had judged Strabo's intentions correctly but he knew he had to find out. Leaping over an injured man, he set off after him.

If anything, the situation at the northern barricade was even more desperate. He passed four dead men: all impaled by two or more arrows. Amongst them were Macrinus and Minicius. The signaller had been hit in the cheek and in the forehead.

Somehow forcing himself on, Cassius passed an open section of planking and looked out. Just in front of the gate was a cluster of shields. Below it, in amongst the tangle of legs, he spied a section of purple cloak.

As Cassius neared the cart closest to the wall, Avso disappeared through a freshly created hole, closely followed by Iucundus. Strabo was waving up at Kabir again, shouting at him to stop firing. He waited for the Syrian to give the order, then made for the gap. He was halfway through when Cassius grabbed his arm. The Sicilian turned, surprised.

'Let go.'

'Strabo, you can't risk it again. I need you here.'

'We won't get this close again. We can finish this now. Let go!'

'You will remain here. That's an order.'

334

A strange look of calm resignation appeared on Strabo's face. 'Then I'm sorry, centurion.'

Before Cassius could respond, Strabo had hooked a leg behind his knee. Flicking Cassius' arm off his shoulder he pushed him hard in the chest. Cassius saw a flash of blue sky, then landed flat on his back three yards away. He rolled over and pushed himself up on to his knees.

When he turned back towards the cart, Strabo was gone.

XXXVII

The last group of retreating swordsmen had just passed Azaf and Razir when they heard the Roman battle cry.

The four archers dropped their shields and sprinted out of the fort, leaving Azaf and Razir completely exposed. By the time they saw the charging legionaries, it was too late to run. They separated to give each other space to fight. Azaf pushed his cloak away from his waist and drew his sword.

The Syrians and the rest of the Romans looked on as the entire battle was suddenly distilled into a fight between five men.

Avso was there first, a few yards ahead of Iucundus. Razir stepped forward into his path and the Thracian slowed, skidding in the sand as he struck. Razir blocked his first thrust expertly.

Iucundus rounded Avso on the right. Azaf didn't move out to meet him, instead waiting for the Roman's attack. Iucundus feinted a wide slashing blow from right to left, then jabbed the blade forward, hoping to catch Azaf on his unprotected face.

The Palmyran dropped his shoulder and twisted out of the way. Then, with Iucundus' weight on his front foot, he swung down towards the hilt of the Roman's sword. The honed tip of the blade sliced across the legionary's hand, cutting off his thumb at the knuckle.

Iucundus, eyes still locked on his foe, tried to tighten his grip, then realised why he could not. He looked down, and Azaf struck again, knocking the weapon out of his hands. Before the Roman could retreat, Azaf darted forward again and drove his blade between two plates of segmental armour, inches below Iucundus' heart.

Just yards away, Avso and Razir traded blows. Avso knew already that he had the measure of the ageing warrior. The veteran was composed and skilful but simply by swinging faster and harder, Avso had already forced him on to the defensive.

Strabo had seen it too, and made straight for Azaf. He came to a halt just as Iucundus dropped to his knees. The legionary reached for his chest, let out a final wheezing breath, then keeled over. Azaf looked impassively down at the dead Roman, then at his blade. The top third shone red.

Enraged though he was, Strabo advanced slowly, sword high and straight.

Noting the muscled forearms of his opponent, Azaf swapped his weapon to his left hand, swiftly passing his right hand through the wrist strap. He gripped the hilt again and retreated, waiting once more for his opponent to strike first.

Avso, meanwhile, had engineered an opportunity. Razir was already tiring and a well-timed blow low on the Palmyran's blade loosened his grip. As Razir tried to regain control of the hilt, Avso lashed out with a boot, catching the Palmyran's hand. Eyes frozen in shock, Razir watched his sword fly from his grasp. Even as his scrabbling fingers found the dagger at his belt, Avso was on him. With a jubilant cry, the Thracian jammed the sword straight into Razir's unprotected gut. Grabbing a handful of tunic, he drove higher, up under the ribs. Teeth bared, he twisted the blade, then slid it out. The Palmyran collapsed to the ground, spewing blood from his lips.

Though he knew Razir had fallen, Azaf didn't take his eyes off Strabo, who continued to advance, snarling and whispering to himself.

Avso stepped over Razir and took up a position to Strabo's left.

'You are ours now,' he hissed in Greek.

Azaf's back was six yards from the northern tower.

'Get either side of him,' said Strabo calmly, moving to his right.

Avso stepped left, grinning wolfishly at the Palmyran.

Azaf could no longer watch them both. He had to stare down at the ground, relying on his peripheral vision to tell him where they were.

With every step they took, his chances of escape faded.

He had to attack now.

Cassius had recovered himself and was busy grappling with a legionary intent on charging out to help. Thankfully, some older men pulled him away and Cassius looked on as Strabo and Avso circled Azaf.

Glancing up at the rooftop, he saw that Idan had his sling loaded and was ready to fire. Kabir stood next to him, a restraining hand held up in front of his marksman, also transfixed by the scene below.

As Avso passed out of sight behind his right shoulder. Azaf leaped forward and swung the light sword towards Strabo's chest. The Sicilian twisted his heavier weapon into a parry but the blades never met.

Azaf stopped swinging halfway through the arc and dropped low. As he expected, Avso had closed in on him and slashed at his neck. The Roman's blade cut through the air a yard above Azaf's head as the Palmyran spun round. Avso's hands were stretched high, his body exposed.

Azaf leaped up and hacked towards Avso's head. The point of his sword cleaved through the Roman's helmet above his left ear, slicing across his forehead.

In what appeared to be a single movement, Azaf brought the sword back over his head into a slanting block as Strabo swung down at him. The edge of the Roman's blade hit the flat of the lighter weapon and, though it didn't break, the impact knocked Azaf off his feet.

He allowed himself to be thrown sideways by the blow and rolled nimbly across the sand. He sprang up instantly, knowing he had only moments before some opportunistic slinger took a shot.

Strabo wished he had his shield. He had fought without it before, often in training, occasionally in battle, but he saw that his enemy was far more comfortable with just a blade. Over his

338

opponent's shoulder, he saw Avso stagger backward, blinded by his own blood. Then the Palmyran charged at him.

Azaf darted right then left before launching a series of short, chopping strokes towards Strabo's right shoulder. The Sicilian blocked solidly, narrowing his eyes as sparks flew from the blades.

Azaf's sixth stroke was high. Strabo was still struggling to match it as the Palmyran rotated his wrists and swept downward, inside the Roman's defences. He slashed diagonally under the base of Strabo's mail shirt, cutting across both thighs.

Bloodied and incensed, Strabo thrust straight at his enemy's unprotected throat. Again, Azaf made no attempt to block. He simply ducked under Strabo's arms and pushed off his right foot, swinging his blade upward.

The tip missed the sleeve of Strabo's mail shirt by an inch and sunk deep into the underside of his wrist, almost severing his hand. He somehow still managed to turn and face his enemy. It wasn't until the sword slipped to the ground that he stared down at the blood gushing from the wound. Only a thin flap of skin was keeping his hand attached to his arm.

Azaf was about to strike again when he glimpsed a whirl of motion to his right. He ducked low and heard the lead shot hit the wall behind him. With the wrist strap taking the weight of his sword, he leaped behind Strabo just as the Roman fainted, catching him and locking his hands together round his chest. Thick gouts of blood splattered the sand below as he dragged him towards the gatehouse.

Cassius could watch no more. He was first through the gap, closely followed by the few legionaries at the northern barricade.

Azaf was just two yards from the northern tower. Looking over his right shoulder, he saw that a small group of swordsmen and archers had advanced, ready to cover his retreat. In amongst them was Teyya, carrying a shield. He darted forward and placed it next to the corner of the tower.

Azaf unlocked his fingers, pulled his arms clear and hurled himself towards the shield.

Kabir was shouting even as Strabo's inert frame hit the ground.

Idan was way ahead of him, but he was simply not prepared for the Palmyran's preternatural speed.

As the shot left the sling, he cursed, knowing he had missed.

The lead ball kicked up a puff of dust next to the shield.

Azaf had escaped.

Two legionaries passed Cassius as he neared the fallen trio. They hadn't seen the Palmyrans and seemed intent on pursuing Azaf beyond the gate, only stopping when a volley of arrows flew towards them. Three hit the first man, who was knocked off his feet. The second man threw himself behind one of the dead horses, then scrambled back behind the northern tower.

Cassius heard Kabir cry out again. The slings whirred; shot whizzed overhead.

He looked down at the three legionaries. The fight had lasted only moments; it seemed impossible that Iucundus, Avso and Strabo had been defeated with such ease by the Palmyran leader.

None of the Romans were moving. Crispus knelt down beside Strabo. The Sicilian's eyes were shut tight; the bottom of his tunic soaked through with blood. Crispus reached for the injured arm and lifted it up. As he did so, the flap of skin finally tore and the hand dropped into the sand. Crispus held the arm high, trying to slow the flow of blood.

'Get your servant, sir!' he yelled. 'Now!'

Dragging his eyes away from the mutilated arm, Cassius ran back to the barricades. He passed Serenus, who was helping Avso.

The Thracian was spasming wildly, his boots kicking up dust. With one hand, Serenus held him down by the shoulder, with the other he scooped out the blood pooling in his eye sockets.

XXXVIII

Strabo regained consciousness while he was being carried to the aid post. As all the stretchers were occupied, they used a blanket; Cassius, Crispus and two other legionaries taking a corner each. Simo trotted along beside them, having just bandaged the stump of Strabo's arm.

Avso was dead. The single blow from Azaf's sword had been a fatal one, cutting through his forehead and into his brain. He had lasted only a few moments.

All the legionaries were now back behind the barricades.

Strabo's face was ashen and wet. He gazed up at the sky, mouth hanging open as the blanket swung from side to side.

'Still with us, guard officer?' asked Crispus as they reached the end of the street.

'Still with us,' Strabo replied weakly.

'We must take him to the barracks,' said Simo. 'There's no more space in the aid post.'

'Yes there is,' came a voice from up ahead.

Vestinus hobbled towards them, using his pilum as a crutch. Though there were more men awaiting treatment outside the aid post, Roman and Syrian, none were as badly off as Strabo and they readily made way. Cassius recognised one as the soldier Crispus had helped at the carts. Julius was tending to his wound. The arrow was still lodged in his arm.

Manoeuvring carefully through the narrow doorway, the four men lowered Strabo down on to the free bed. Only one of the other injured men was conscious. He propped himself up on an elbow to see the new arrival. Simo squatted down next to Strabo and took hold of the mutilated arm, straightening it at the elbow.

341

'Hold it up like so,' he said to the nearest legionary. As the man complied, another clasped his hands together and whispered a prayer to Apollo, god of healing. Simo undid the chinstraps and gingerly removed Strabo's helmet. Then he folded the heavy mail shirt back on itself, a job that required both hands. There were two neat tears in the sodden tunic, which Simo also folded back. The cuts were far deeper than any of them had expected: thick rents in the flesh, still seeping blood.

The Sicilian must have seen the shocked reaction of the other legionaries yet he showed no sign of it, instead nodding nonchalantly at his arm.

'Can't believe that long-haired little bitch took my hand. Did anyone grab my silver ring? Some bastard will have it otherwise.'

The legionaries exchanged relieved smiles and some nervous laughter.

'I'll get it,' Cassius murmured, pushing past the others. The brilliant morning light made him feel as if his every expression would be exposed and he set his jaw as he strode away, knowing he was about to lose control of himself.

Luckily there was no one else close by. Serenus was further down the street, looking on as the men dragged the fallen legionaries towards the northern wall. Kabir was there too, watching as his own dead were carried from the buildings.

Cassius was barely through the door of the nearest dwelling when the tears came. He put a hand to his mouth and took refuge in a darkened corner. He leaned back against the wall as he sobbed. Warm tears ran down his cheeks and over his fingers.

He had cried during training, more times than he could remember, especially during the first few weeks, but only ever at night and never loud enough to be heard. Balling his left hand into a fist, he pressed it against his brow, as if he might somehow expel the feelings within.

There was a sound from outside. The tears stopped. Shame, it seemed, could vanquish even this pain.

Cassius waited a while but heard nothing more. His eyes dried and with relief came reflection. Of everything he'd seen, he

342

wondered why it was the sight of the stricken Strabo that had affected him so. He had come to depend on the big Sicilian, he knew that much.

The doorway suddenly darkened. He had heard something after all.

'I thought I saw you come in here,' Serenus said as he stepped inside.

Still sniffing, Cassius wiped his hand across his eyes.

'Please. Go on your way.'

Serenus turned to leave, then hesitated.

'Are you all right, sir?'

Guilt bloomed within Cassius again. He felt inadequate. Weak. Undeserving of the veteran's concern.

'I apologise, Serenus. Once more I have proven my uselessness.'

'There are a few words I might use to describe you. Young. Inexperienced. Frightened. But useless? No.'

'Then you have a poor memory.'

'Actually that is one of the few faculties yet to desert me.'

Serenus coughed and dabbed at his mouth, yet Cassius could feel his eyes still upon him.

'Tell me, who was it that stood up to the Praetorian; got him to speak to us for the first time in weeks? Who discovered that spy in our midst, when none had thought such a thing possible? And who thought of a way to stop those damned cavalrymen smashing us to pieces? Not Strabo. Not Avso. And certainly not I.'

Cassius barely heard these words. He'd been struck by an unforeseen desire to tell Serenus the truth.

'I am not a centurion. Not really. I did complete training but I actually belong with the Security Service.'

'A Service man? What about your tunic? Your crest?'

'In theory, I have a rank equal to centurion.'

Serenus shrugged.

'You're still the senior officer here.'

Cassius looked up.

'What use is a leader who can't lead?'

'I think it is you that suffers from a poor memory. Don't you remember the state of the garrison when you first arrived? Leading is not always the same as fighting. If Strabo had remembered that, Avso and Iucundus might still be alive.'

As ever, Serenus' words carried the weight of logic and experience. Whatever the nature of his past failures, Cassius realised he was now also guilty of self-pity. The wave of emotion had passed; he had to regain his composure.

Serenus' breathing seemed suddenly to accelerate and he put a hand to his chest. He then held out that hand, as if to deflect Cassius' attentions, but could not stop himself staggering forward, spluttering yet again. Cassius helped him over to the nearest seat: the low window ledge.

Serenus took out his cloth. He tried to speak but no words came.

'Rest here,' said Cassius. 'Take your time.'

He stood there, waiting for Serenus to recover himself, drying his eyes a second time.

After a while, the veteran pointed at the door, still unable to speak.

'You're sure?'

Serenus nodded resolutely and with that Cassius left him.

Three-quarters of the way down the street, he found Kabir and Yarak standing under an awning, facing one of the dwellings. Laid out on the ground in front of them were ten dead men. Their arms had been folded across their chests, their weapons and equipment laid out beside them. Yarak moved carefully between them, wafting smoke from a small clay pot over the bodies. Cassius recognised the aroma.

'Frankincense,' he said quietly, stopping next to Kabir.

'To cleanse them,' said the Syrian, staring down at the closest body, that of a youthful-looking warrior perhaps only a year or two older than Julius. 'Yarak thought it best to do it now. While we can.'

344

Cassius glanced across at Kabir, at the blank desolation that now masked even his fair face, and wondered if he had given up hope of victory.

If so, the battle for Alauran was already lost. Cassius guessed there might be about a dozen legionaries still fit to fight, and with three of his five deputies dead, he was now utterly dependent on the auxiliaries. A simple glance down the street told him as much. There was not one legionary at the carts; the few on their feet were busy with the dead. The Syrians, however, still twenty strong, were spread out at the barricades, looking warily towards the gate. He saw one man duck back through a hole in the carts with a handful of lead shot recovered from the killing area.

'My sister's boy,' said Kabir, nodding down at the warrior. 'She asked me to leave him behind but I could not appear to favour my own kin.'

Kabir looked on vacantly as Yarak continued his work, sometimes chanting quietly, sometimes blowing the scented smoke over the wounds of the dead.

Cassius felt great sympathy for the Syrian but there was no time to spare. He had to somehow break this reverie.

'Without their sacrifice we would never have been able to repel the Palmyrans. We must ensure now that they were not lost in vain.'

'You Romans are not known for your subtlety, are you?'

Cassius said nothing.

'You fear perhaps that I have lost the will to fight on.'

'Not at all. But time is of the essence.'

Kabir tilted his head backward.

'Time. Another Roman obsession. The whole world must follow your hours and weeks and months.'

'You believe the Palmyrans will wait?' said Cassius fractiously.

'I believe they will wait long enough to catch their breath. Perhaps even take a moment to honour their dead.'

Cassius stepped away. There was nothing more to be gained by pressing Kabir further. The Syrian held the upper hand now and he seemed to know it.

'I shall be at the barricades,' Cassius said quietly. 'Perhaps you will join me. When you are ready.'

Kabir held out a hand.

'Wait.'

He knelt down and gently plucked some errant hair from his nephew's face, then took a moment to tidy the boy's tunic. His expression softened as he stood.

'You're right. We must act now.'

Kabir spoke a couple of words to Yarak as they walked away down the street, then turned towards Cassius.

'Strabo?'

'Well he's alive.'

'Purple Cloak, as you call him, will not make the same mistake again. They must know how few we are. If they have ladders, they will use them now.'

'We should abandon the barricades?'

'I think we must.'

They came to a stop by the carts.

'Your lookouts are still in place?' asked Kabir.

'Yes. No movement yet.'

Cassius glanced back along the street, recalling the original reserve plan.

'I had thought we might use the barracks as a redoubt but we haven't the men to defend it now.'

The two of them stood there in silence for a while, taking in defences and defenders with a new eye. Before he knew it, Cassius was gazing at the double line of bodies by the northern wall. Though the Romans had been covered with blankets, the Palmyrans had been left exposed. Hundreds of flies hovered around them.

'Do you have it, sir?'

Cassius turned to find Crispus staring expectantly at him.

'The ring, sir. Strabo's still asking for it.'

'Ah. No, no,' Cassius answered meekly, knowing he couldn't face that particular task. In truth, it had been little more than an excuse to get away. 'Perhaps you could—'

'I'll fetch it.'

Kabir pointed up at the dwellings.

'My men should remain on the roofs where we can do most damage. Closer to the square perhaps, a central position. In range of all four walls and able to move if necessary.'

Cassius wondered where he should deploy the remaining legionaries. He could see no obvious answer. Kabir was now the best source of advice left to him.

'What about us?'

The Syrian pointed back up the street.

'I assume you wish to protect your standard?'

'Of course.'

'Unfortunately it's rather exposed. Vulnerable to attack from three sides. Such a small force could not hope to last long.'

Cassius turned back towards the barricades.

'With a bit of protection we might. What about reattaching the wheels and moving two of the carts to the square? Use them to make a triangle with the well at its base, the flagpole at its peak.'

'A sound idea. But wouldn't it offend your gods to fight so close to the temple?'

Cassius shrugged; at that moment he couldn't have cared less. If the gods were watching over the garrison, he'd seen no sign of it. Their survival so far had been won solely through courage and ingenuity, and at considerable cost.

Kabir turned towards the square.

'They have shown little interest in the western wall; the uneven ground and the palms make an assault awkward. Assuming they scale the walls to the north, south and east, they would not be able to see your position. Better to lead them to where we want them.'

'What if we block the gate with a cart and make a token effort of resistance at the walls. Once they appear in numbers we shall retreat to the flag.'

Cassius knew already how to divide the men; he and Crispus would take half each.

Kabir continued: 'With my men on top of the roofs next to

the square, we will be able to attack as they approach. You draw them in and we will strike at their backs.'

Cassius nodded and they stood again in silence, each mulling over the makeshift plan.

Crispus approached, carrying the hand. The fingers remained frozen in a clawed grip, like the legs of a dead spider. Cassius had to look away.

'Couldn't get the ring off,' announced the pragmatic legionary. 'Stuck fast.'

Cassius pointed back at the square.

'Just get it to him, would you? Then gather the men and bring them here at once.'

Though none of them said a word, Azaf could sense the reverence of his swordsmen as he walked along the rally line. It had been a long time since they had seen him fight. Now he stood before them without a mark on him, having dispatched three of the enemy and fought his way out alone.

He knew he had been reckless, arrogant even, in retreating last of all and exposing himself so. Still, the Roman attack had surprised him. It had been brave of those men to take him on. Brave but futile, and in fact he had been more concerned about the Syrian auxiliaries and their slings. He had been lucky to emerge unscathed, but the men seemed oblivious to this element of fortune. As he passed them, some bowed, others held their blades aloft. One swordsman simply clenched his fist over his heart.

'Check your weapons,' Azaf ordered. 'Then divide yourselves into ten groups of equal size.'

Karzai approached, riding alone. He slowed his horse to a trot and guided it round the injured. They were mostly archers, waiting for the carts to return them to camp. Several bore horrific wounds to their heads and looked close to death. Until help arrived, they were on their own.

Ten ladders were now lined up behind the swordsmen. Once everyone was organised, Azaf planned to issue what he hoped would be his last set of instructions.

Karzai pulled back on his reins and Azaf held out a hand to stop his horse.

'A message?'

'Yes, *strategos*. A scout carrying word from General Zabbai. The first of his men will arrive in Anasartha tomorrow, his main force the day after that. He seems to be assuming that the fort will be within our hands by that time.'

'And so it shall,' replied Azaf firmly.

'Of course.'

Karzai looked at the warriors. Those few with any water left were emptying their gourds.

'There are a couple of barrels left. Shall I have them brought up?'

Azaf looked thoughtfully at the swordsmen for a moment.

'No. Their thirst shall drive them on. Soon we shall have all the water we need.'

XXXIX

As the remaining legionaries shuffled into a loose line in front of him, Cassius gazed beyond them, again drawn to the bodies by the northern wall. Below the knee of one Palmyran a patch of flesh had been somehow peeled from the gleaming, blood-streaked bone.

Cassius turned away, struck by a recollection of his old life. Often, after a night of heavy drinking, images of violence and gore would appear amongst his thoughts. The visions had always distressed him and he could think of no logical explanation for them. They were products of his imagination, not based on anything he'd seen or experienced.

Now the images were real. Death, injury, pain and ruin in all their peculiar forms. Men reduced to nothing more than lifeless matter, decaying already under the pitiless glare of the desert sun. Though he felt a certain shame at his disgust, Cassius wished they could simply pile all the bodies on to a pyre and set them alight.

'Fourteen. Sixteen including us,' said Crispus, finishing a headcount.

'That's all?' asked Cassius, doing his best to concentrate.

'All that can fight.'

Aside from Crispus, Cassius knew the names of only two in the line before him: the surly lookout Antonius and the resilient Vestinus, who was leaning against his pilum, grimacing at even the slightest movement of his leg. It seemed incredible that so many of the prominent faces and characters he had got to know over the last few days were gone.

Vestinus' scabbard clinked against his pilum and Cassius

realised that the eyes of the men were upon him. To his right, Crispus stood still, arms crossed. The legionaries looked weary. Their tunics were stained with blood and grime, their dark skin shiny with sweat. Several hadn't even bothered to sheathe their swords.

Cassius cleared his throat and began. The men listened in silence as he briefly outlined the plan. Their faces betrayed only resigned exhaustion and he could not tell if they approved of the scheme or not. It hardly mattered; there was no time to change it now. He could hear Kabir talking to his men not far away. On the roof above them, Yarak and Idan watched the Palmyrans.

There were a few reassuring nods from the legionaries as Cassius described how they would defend the standard with the temple at their backs. As he finished, Vestinus raised a hand.

'Yes?'

'Sir, there are three or four others like me in the barracks – wounded about the legs. We'd be no good on the ground, but if we could get up somewhere high—'

Crispus caught Cassius' eye.

'We recovered some enemy bows and quivers from the other side of the carts.'

'The barracks roof?' Vestinus suggested. 'A good field of fire looking down on the square.'

'Sounds like a good idea,' replied Cassius. 'Go and tell the others and I'll send someone to help you get up there.'

Cassius made way for Vestinus as he hobbled off down the street. Looking back along the line of expectant faces, he recalled Strabo's rousing words of the previous day.

He knew the legionaries would fight on; every man had proved himself. But he needed more than that. He needed them to believe victory was still possible.

'Alauran is still ours. Still Rome's. And those outside the walls still have to come in here and take it from us. Today is the fifth day since I received word from General Navio. Valens' men could be here any time. We *must* hold on. We *can* hold on.'

All the legionaries were looking at him. A couple smiled grimly to themselves, another smacked his hand against his chest and took a deep breath.

Crispus drew his sword. Like Cassius, he spoke quietly but with unwavering resolve. 'Caesar fights forever beside us, sir.'

'Well, I'm not with the Third Legion,' said Cassius with a grin. 'But I hope he's alongside me too. Even if it's just for today.'

'For Rome!' shouted Crispus.

Cassius joined in with the others.

'For Rome!'

'Let's ready ourselves then,' Cassius said when the cries had died down, 'and recall the words of Publius Terentius. *While there's life, there's hope.* I'll see you in the square.'

There were two stops to make before overseeing the arrangement of the carts. A quick word with Kabir confirmed that there was still no sign of advance from the Palmyrans. They agreed also that half the Syrians would now move to the roof as sentries, while the rest would help Crispus and the legionaries move the carts.

Still carrying his helmet, Cassius jogged back up the street to the aid post. He found it surprisingly quiet. Apart from those occupying the beds, the other injured men had all been moved inside the barracks. There was no sign of Simo or Julius.

Strabo, lying closest to the door, was covered with a blanket. He lay still, eyes shut, his head propped up on a cushion against the wall. It seemed he had been holding up his wounded arm with his good hand but it had slipped down. The bandage was soaked through with wet, fresh blood. Cassius wondered if he was already dead.

Suddenly there was movement to his right: Simo stood up from behind one of the large wooden chests.

'What are you doing over there?' demanded Cassius, struggling to keep his voice down.

'I was praying, sir,' Simo replied, almost in a whisper.

'Forget your damn prayers! This man needs your help.'

Simo hurried forward. Strabo stirred as the Gaul held up his arm again.

'Temples are for prayers. This is an aid post.'

Nodding again, Simo began unwrapping the bandage. Cassius noticed his clammy cheeks and realised the Gaul had been crying. He thought for a moment what it must have been like, treating the wounded, watching men die.

Simo placed the sodden bandage to one side, leaving only one layer round the stump, still steadily issuing blood.

'He was asking for you earlier, sir,' Simo said, retrieving a new covering from a sack.

Cassius forced himself to look at the arm.

'Can't you burn it or something? That stops the bleeding, doesn't it?'

'I'm not sure quite how it's done, sir. And I fear the shock of it might kill him. The flow has lessened but he has lost a huge amount of blood.'

'Too much I think.'

Strabo's voice was surprisingly loud. His eyes had opened a fraction and he raised his good hand, beckoning Cassius towards him.

'That you, centurion?'

'It is.'

Cassius knelt down opposite Simo and pushed his scabbard back so as not to catch it on the floor. The Sicilian's eyes opened a little more, the dark pupils accentuated by his pallid skin. Cassius thought of his grandfather. In the days leading up to his death, the old man's skin had acquired a shade so pale it seemed almost translucent. Strabo turned his head a fraction.

'There'll be no burning? Understand?'

'If that's what you wish.'

'You know the boy was in here earlier – looking after me. He has a short memory.'

'Perhaps he has forgiven you,' said Simo as he re-dressed the wound. It looked agonising but Strabo showed no sign of discomfort. His face, usually so animated, was almost serene.

'You are in pain?' Cassius asked.

'Not any more,' replied Strabo with a faint smile. 'I was cold but I feel quite warm now. And light. I dreamed I was at a beach before, just floating back and forth in the shallows.'

'Sounds good to me.'

The Sicilian looked towards the doorway.

'How are the men?'

'Not bad, considering. We'll be ready for them.'

Strabo reached out and took a firm hold of Cassius' wrist.

'You must remember: the wages and the funeral fund. All the men deserve a proper cremation and many have families to take care of. The papers are all in Petronius' desk. In Antioch you will have to find the legion chief clerk. I can't remember his name, but—'

'I will deal will all of that, I give you my word.'

Simo finished tying off the bandage.

'I think the flow is slowing at last,' he said, laying the arm down carefully across the blanket.

Cassius could hear the men moving around outside.

The Sicilian continued: 'One more thing. My back pay will just about cover what I still owe. That two hundred denarii you offered puts me in profit. I'd like to have it now, hold it in my hand. It means something to me.'

Though he hadn't the time, Cassius couldn't bring himself to refuse.

'Very well.' He got to his feet, hurried out of the aid post and ran along the barrack block. Several more of the injured could be heard through the windows: moaning, crying out or praying. Nearing the officers' quarters, he realised he could make his second stop without going inside.

Warily approaching the window of the Praetorian's room, Cassius put his hands on the ledge and leaned inside. The man was either dozing or asleep, his head turned towards the wall. Below the window was a half-eaten plate of food: some strips of dried pork and a few cooked lentils and beans. Surrounding the plate were at least three new jugs, all of them empty.

Shaking his head, Cassius noticed that the huge sword and shield lay next to the bed. The Praetorian had been looking at them perhaps, but whatever his reflections, they hadn't been enough to snap him out of his habitual oblivion. Cassius knew then that he had, once and for all, to put all thoughts of the man aside. It seemed likely he would now meet his end as he had lived these last few months: drunk and dead to the world.

'Not much to show for twenty years' hard graft, is it?' said Strabo when Cassius returned with the bag of coins.

'Enough for a stake. A good run at "doubles" and you'll be on your way again.'

Strabo forced a smile. He weighed the purse in his hand once more, then offered it to Cassius.

'At least now I can say I ended up with more than I started. Here, put it towards the funeral fund.'

'But it's yours.'

'Take it.'

'You might need it. Who's to say you won't be up and about in a few days? That'll pay for your passage home. Maybe you'll find some nice Sicilian girl to wait on you day and night. Might be the best thing that ever happened to you.'

Cassius felt unsure about such levity but he didn't know how else to respond.

Strabo summoned another grin.

'I haven't the energy for an argument. Here, take it.'

Cassius handed the purse on to Simo. Hearing the distinctive rumble of the approaching cart, he looked out and saw Crispus and the other legionaries towing the first vehicle into the square.

'Go on,' said Strabo, pointing at the doorway.

Cassius stood.

'I'll see you later.'

Despite his condition, the Sicilian's eyes had not lost their arresting gaze.

'You will. And remember, lad – don't go quiet on 'em. They need to hear your voice. Chin up. Back straight.'

★   ★   ★

Every spare pair of hands was needed to turn the first of the carts over. All the able legionaries plus six of Kabir's men readied themselves, gripping the edge of the vehicle or one of the hefty wheels. Cassius joined them just as Crispus was counting down from three. He squeezed between two Syrians and flattened his palms against the rough timber siding.

'Two, one, lift!'

Those crouching low at the wheels gave the first boost of power and the others pushed on, shoving hard until the cart passed its tipping point, then holding on to stop it flipping on to its back. Blinking as a cloud of sand rose up to engulf them all, Cassius stepped away. The rear of the vehicle was perhaps a yard from the well, a space large enough to give them access but small enough to defend.

'About right, wouldn't you say, sir?' asked Crispus, waving dust away as he approached. The others were already removing the wheels.

'I should say so.'

Cassius heard voices behind him and turned to see Vestinus and his small group of prospective archers emerging from the barracks. Two were limping along carrying a ladder, two more held bows and quivers. Not all of them had been injured in the leg; one man had his head bandaged and looked decidedly unsteady on his feet.

'All right, you lot,' said Crispus. 'Let's fetch the other cart.' With the legionaries and Syrians in tow, he jogged away.

Cassius' proximity to the temple reminded him to be thankful for small mercies. To still have the irrepressible Crispus by his side at this late hour was a blessing indeed. He wondered if Serenus was still inside the dwelling; there was no sign of him elsewhere.

That matter would have to wait; with no one free to assist Vestinus and his group, Cassius hurried over to them. The man with the head wound looked up at him. He was one of the oldest legionaries, perhaps even older than Serenus. He had sustained a black eye and a broken nose. Dark streaks of blood had dried around his mouth.

356

'You sure you're up to this? Shouldn't you be back in the barracks?'

'I must confess I'm a little dizzy when I'm walking around, sir, but I'll be fine once I'm up there.'

Vestinus steadied the ladder and signalled for the first man to climb up.

Cassius looked at the bow and quiver over his shoulder.

'How's your aim?'

'Not bad, sir, but these things are damned hard to draw.'

'Well anything you can do will be a great help. Even if it serves only to distract the enemy.'

'We intend to do a good deal more than that, sir.'

Before Cassius could reply, Vestinus pointed towards the granary. Antonius was there, waving frantically. Cassius waved back.

'There'll be no signal,' he told Vestinus. 'Just stay low and don't shoot until the last moment.'

'Sir.'

As Cassius ran across the square, he saw that Crispus and his men had set one of the carts flat against the gate as instructed. They were now attaching the wheels to the other one bound for the square. Cassius passed the granary and jumped up on to a firing step next to Antonius.

'What is it?'

'They're on the move, sir.'

Keeping as low as he could, Cassius immediately saw a group of Palmyran warriors walking parallel to the wall about fifty yards away. Three of them were carrying a long, solid-looking ladder. Cassius dropped to the ground.

'Stay here. I'll be back soon.'

After the Palmyran swordsmen had divided themselves, four of the ten groups remained with Azaf in front of the fort. Three more were stationed to the north, three to the south. There were eight or nine men in each section. Teyya led the southern group.

Azaf now realised he had to do precisely what Bezda had

357

advised against. He would attack from three sides. He would force the undermanned Romans to divide themselves. His swordsmen would swarm over the walls as they should have with the very first attack.

The men milled around, sharing out the last of their water or quietly exchanging opinions. Others prayed.

Azaf squatted close to the ground some way ahead of them. He lay his sword across an abandoned shield, examining the blade and hilt for any sign of damage. Heavy blows could knock the blade out of alignment, crack the handle or chip the metal. Though he hadn't drunk all morning, he took just a few gulps from his gourd and dripped the rest along the blade. He then used a length of cloth to clean away what blood and dirt remained. Only when every inch of the blade shone did he stand and replace it in the scabbard. He thought of Razir, how the old warrior had taken such pride in maintaining the blade. He would enjoy avenging him.

The sun was hot now, yet Azaf felt cool and calm. He barely felt the weight of the mail shirt; the harsh metal against his skin.

These were the moments he lived for. Easy victories were no test of a warrior; now he would truly prove his worth. He would give the general his staging post and extend the reach of the Palmyran armies deep into Roman territory.

It was said that of late the Queen had taken to personally honouring her most successful commanders. General Zabbai had told Azaf about another young *strategos* he had escorted to the great palace in Palmyra. While he waited for the Queen, her eunuchs had presented him with several gifts: an embossed dagger studded with jewels, a luxuriant robe of finest silk and a silver ingot engraved with the insignia of Zenobia's own house. Zabbai had described the objects with typical relish, but it was something else he mentioned that seized Azaf's attention.

As Zabbai and the soldier were about to leave, the Queen herself had appeared. Ignoring the general, she ushered the young *strategos* into an anteroom. He returned moments later and would not speak of what had occurred. Later that night, however, with his tongue loosened by wine, he told Zabbai what had happened.

Without a word, Zenobia had led him to a corner and placed her hand on his head. She had then brought his face to hers and kissed him on the lips. Then she had bent his head down, slipped her tunic from her shoulder and offered him her breasts.

There had been more than a suggestion of jealousy in Zabbai's voice when he related the soldier's observation that the Queen had enjoyed the experience as much as he had.

Azaf had tried to consign what he had heard to the recesses of his mind and he did his best not to think of it often. In fact, he wished that the general had never told him; the tale simply fuelled the fantasies he already struggled to contain. He believed that they weakened him. Strength came from discipline and control. An excessive interest in the baser desires could, he thought, be the ruin of any warrior.

Still, he did not chastise himself this time; a man about to face battle deserved a momentary indulgence.

But now came the time to concentrate. He thought back to the fight with the Romans; when his mind had emptied and his instincts had taken over. They had always served him well and when the time came he would give himself up to them again.

Azaf clasped his hands and closed his eyes. He breathed deeply and imagined a white blankness setting over him.

It would, he knew, be a glorious victory.

XL

The first indication that the fourth attack was really under way came just as Cassius and six legionaries rejoined Antonius. It was the sound of quick-running steps, the Palmyrans closing in on the southern wall.

The seven Romans were close to the granary steps. Behind them, Kabir and half his tribesmen were hidden inside the dwelling at the end of the street. Yarak and the rest of the Syrians were similarly concealed in the dwelling opposite the inn.

Vestinus and his archers were now up on the barracks roof, lying low. To the preoccupied attackers they would be almost invisible. Crispus and his six men were gathered between the inn and the dwellings close to the northern wall.

Despite the fact that he had just downed half a jug of water, Cassius' throat felt sore, his mouth dry. And even though he had emptied the rest of the jug over his head, the water had already been usurped by sweat and the damnable helmet felt a size smaller.

He and the other legionaries had already drawn their swords. Pila and shields would have been useful had they intended to put up serious resistance at the walls, but extraneous equipment would slow their retreat. Cassius had ordered that it be left behind the newly erected barricades.

Two of the legionaries suddenly glanced left and he moved forward to gain a better view. He saw the twin poles of a ladder above the wall, not far from the south-east corner. By the time he had scanned the entire length of the wall, five more ladders had appeared, one directly ahead.

A sword materialised, then a helmeted head. Though they never heard or saw the shot, the Romans knew it was a lead pellet that had hit the Palmyran between the eyes.

Teyya's last expression was a combination of surprise and disbelief. He fell back.

Cassius looked left again. Five enemy warriors were now over the wall and striding towards the Romans. Several were wearing small wooden shields strapped to their forearms. More men dropped down and joined their ranks.

Antonius tilted his blade towards the square.

'Now, sir?'

'Wait.'

Cassius turned and saw Crispus retreating from the northern wall, his men behind him. They suddenly broke into a run.

Spinning back round, Cassius looked right and saw that yet more Palmyrans were inside the compound, advancing along the side of the granary.

'Now! Retreat!'

The legionaries turned and ran.

Crispus' group were already well past the inn, making for the carts as the Palmyrans gave chase.

One of Cassius' men stumbled and would have fallen had Cassius not grabbed him under the arm and helped him regain his balance. The moment's delay left them yards behind the others. As they raced away, Cassius could hear the pounding footfalls of the enemy behind him; the Palmyrans had taken the bait.

There was no sign of Kabir or any of the Syrians. Cassius resisted the temptation to glance at the dwellings.

The two groups became one as the Romans ran hard for the barricades, legs and arms pumping. Tiles cracked under the boots of the charging legionaries. Cassius kept his eyes down, determined not to lose his footing.

Crispus was first behind the carts. He darted neatly through the gap, then the men funnelled in behind him.

Cassius had almost reached the well when he heard the welcome whir of the Syrian slings. He was the last man inside, and he hurried forward while the other legionaries picked up their pila and shields.

Percussive thuds echoed across the square as the lethal projectiles found their targets. The closest Palmyrans fell ten yards short
of the carts, all struck in the head or neck. Cassius couldn't believe
they weren't wearing helmets or armour. The legionaries whooped
and cheered as red-clad swordsmen tumbled to the ground across
the width of the square.

It didn't take long for the Palmyrans to realise where the shots
were coming from. Kabir's men were lined up above each roof
surround, all either firing or reloading. More could be seen below,
half concealed by the shadowy windows as they continued to
unleash shot at a prodigious rate.

Their onslaught had halted all those chasing the Romans
and soon every Palmyran in the square still standing was
running back towards the two dwellings. Leaving at least twenty
fallen warriors behind, they flooded towards the doorways or
windows, desperate to get out of the firing line and stop the
deadly barrage. Both ground floors were overrun in moments.
The few Palmyrans left outside pressed close to the walls or
raised their shields to protect themselves from the slingers
above.

Shouts drifted across the square towards the Romans. They
looked on as the Syrians bent over the roof surrounds, looking
for new targets. Others had already gone down the ladders to
meet the Palmyrans.

'How many would you say, sir?' asked Crispus, leaning in close.

Cassius didn't answer. The Syrians had again done a superb
job of depleting the enemy ranks, but by striking so early they
had now drawn the full attention of the attackers.

'Must have been fifty or so,' Crispus continued. 'But where
are the others?'

As Cassius considered this, one of the Palmyrans by the
northern house slid to the ground, an arrow sticking out of his
gut. The warrior standing next to him bent over the wounded
man but was then struck in the side himself.

Another triumphant cry went up from the legionaries. Cassius
peered out at the barracks. There was Vestinus, up on one knee,

training his bow at the Palmyrans, the three others beside him. His bow straightened and another bolt flashed away.

Four Palmyrans disappeared behind the aid post, intent on taking out the Roman archers. Those left behind pushed their way inside the dwelling.

'Look there. The roof!' someone shouted.

There was only one Syrian still clearly visible. He was on top of the southern house, waving the Romans forward. Sunlight glinted off a familiar earring.

'That's Kabir,' Cassius said.

The fact that Idan had left him showed how desperate their situation was.

'Shouldn't we help them, sir?' asked one legionary.

Cassius looked down at the ground and tried to shut out the noise. He knew that if he delayed much longer, the decision would be irrelevant. Next to him was the flagpole. Protected by the barricades and the legionaries, the standard still flew. But with the Syrians wiped out, the Palmyrans could regroup and attack the carts. With their greater numbers, they would surely prevail.

'Let's hit them now, while they're bottled up,' suggested Antonius.

Crispus tapped Cassius on the arm and leaned round the flagpole.

'But sir, what about the other Palmyrans? There are forty more of them out there somewhere.'

Cassius had made up his mind. To sit and wait for the enemy to wipe out their allies before turning on them now seemed folly.

'We will not abandon them.'

He spoke to the rest of the men.

'We go to their aid. Bring your shields and pila.'

Cassius was first out. He looked to the rear and was relieved to see that no Palmyrans had circled round behind them. He warily led the legionaries across the square.

They showed little mercy to those left alive. Every warrior wounded about the head was finished off with a jab to the throat or heart.

Up on the barracks roof, Vestinus and his men were still firing, aiming at the windows whenever they caught clear sight of a red tunic.

Cassius and the others glanced anxiously to their left and right as they approached the houses but there was no sign of any more Palmyrans. Crispus was already heading for the southern dwelling with most of his section behind him.

'My men here!' shouted Cassius, aiming for the northern house and belatedly realising he'd left his shield inside the barricades. He thought he was moving quickly, but he was swiftly overtaken by Antonius.

Two of the Palmyran swordsmen saw the danger and bolted, one man throwing himself from the window. Antonius slammed his shield into the warrior's shoulder as he tried to get up, then stabbed down into the base of his back.

The second Palmyran came from the door. Antonius blocked his way. The legionary's flank was dangerously exposed.

The Palmyran raised his sword.

Cassius forced himself not to think. He threw his blade forward as the swordsman swung down.

There was little strength in Cassius' extended arm but his weapon absorbed most of the blow and the blades tapped harmlessly against a segment of Antonius' armour. The burly legionary turned from his first victim and was about to swing again when another Roman rammed a reversed sword pommel into the Palmyran's face. Three separate blades slid into the warrior before he hit the ground. With a brief nod to Cassius, Antonius joined the others as they swarmed inside.

Cassius looked over at the other dwelling. Crispus and the others had planted themselves in front of the doorway and window. Shields high, they jabbed at the Palmyrans.

Above, Kabir was taking matters into his own hands. He had just clambered over the surround and was now lowering himself over the side. His legs hung just inches from the first-floor window where his tribesmen fought hand to hand with the Palmyrans. It must have been a ten-foot drop but the Syrian rolled athletically to one side as he landed, then sprang to his feet. Yelling in Aramaic, he drew his sword and made for the door.

He was right on Crispus' heels as the Roman drove his shield into a Palmyran and barged his way inside. From within came an agonised screech.

Cassius moved to the doorway of the northern house. Several bodies lay on the floor. The remaining Palmyrans had backed towards the ladder in the far corner, eyes and blades glinting as they lashed out at the legionaries. The Romans were shouting to each other as they hacked their way forward.

Suddenly there was a loud crack. A section of timber fell to the floor.

With neither Yarak nor any of the other Syrians on the roof, Cassius suddenly realised just how packed the second floor must be. Another timber gave way, showering the legionaries with dust.

'Get out!' Cassius yelled. 'It's coming down!'

Not one of the legionaries moved.

Cassius darted inside.

'Out! All of you – out!'

A couple of the legionaries turned round but Antonius and three others were locked in a deadly struggle on the other side of the room.

A third crack and the supporting timber across the door frame gave way. It landed in two halves behind Cassius.

'Out! Out!'

He pushed the two closest legionaries towards the window. Apart from Antonius, the others had also seen the danger. They passed Cassius and made for what remained of the doorway. Only a single Palmyran was left on his feet, shrinking into the corner behind the ladder.

'Antonius, now!'

Cassius grabbed one of Antonius' armour straps and wrenched him round.

'We are leaving! Now!'

Wood, mud and straw fell round the two Romans as they charged for the window.

The cart blocking the gate had finally been pushed clear. Azaf ordered three men inside. Seeing there was no danger, he followed them, stopping in the middle of the killing area as the rest of the swordsmen spread out behind him.

He looked for the standard but it was now obscured by the curious pall of dust rising above the street.

Cassius and Antonius had landed in a heap outside just as the dwelling collapsed. By the time they got to their feet, everything around them had been enveloped by dust; they could barely see three yards. Coughing hard, Cassius waved his arms in wide arcs to clear the air.

He could hear Crispus inside the other house, still yelling orders. More shouts, none of them in Latin, emanated from the second floor.

The dust began to settle; and Cassius saw that virtually the entire building had come down, with no more than five feet of wall remaining at any point. One legionary was already climbing up the pile of rubble. In amongst the tangle of timber and clay, the Roman was searching for Palmyrans still alive and finishing them off with his sword. Two others went to the aid of a pair of Syrians pinned by a large beam. Both were still breathing. One held up his hand, fingers outstretched towards Cassius.

Next to them, just visible beneath a pile of straw, was the top of a distinctive head. A shattering blow had punched a fist-sized hole in the side of Yarak's skull.

A heavy hand landed on Cassius' shoulder and he spun round. It was Antonius.

'Centurion, we can hear them coming up the street!'

'You three!' Cassius shouted. 'With me!'

The two legionaries had managed to pull the Syrian men clear. They joined the third, who had finished his murderous work, and duly followed.

To his surprise, Cassius found nine legionaries already gathered in the middle of the street. Only Crispus and another man were missing. All now looked towards the gate.

The Palmyrans had spread out across the full width of the street. Purple Cloak was in the centre, a pace ahead of the others. He marched on, cloak billowing behind him, sword still undrawn.

Some of the legionaries backed away.

'The barricades?' asked one.

For once, Cassius knew precisely what to do. Much of the rubble from the house had fallen into the street, narrowing its width to four or five yards.

'Men with shields – form a wall!'

The men were all set to sprint back to the barricades. They looked at him doubtfully.

'Hurry there! All of you!'

He grabbed Antonius and placed him at the edge of the rubble. The legionary seemed so surprised that he barely resisted. Cassius took hold of another man but the soldier shrugged him off.

'I know the drill, sir.'

'Come on! You seven with shields – complete the linc. Form the wall!'

The standard command was enough to galvanise the men into action. Without a second order they planted their feet and began interlocking their shields.

'The rest of you with pila – over the shoulders of the front rank.'

The other men got into position and readied their spears.

Crispus lurched out of the southern dwelling. The slight legionary looked utterly exhausted. He could barely hold up his shield and the point of his sword was trailing in the dust, leaving a red line on the ground.

'House cleared, sir,' he said between breaths. When he caught sight of the forty Palmyrans he'd been so concerned about earlier, he gazed despairingly up at the sky.

Next to emerge from the now silent house were Kabir and Idan. If anything, they were in worse condition. Kabir had lost

367

his jerkin and his throat was covered in purple welts. Idan's hands and arms were covered in blood and there was a nasty rent in his earlobe where a ring had been torn away.

Without looking at Cassius, Kabir led Idan to a position at the corner of the collapsed dwelling, guarding against an enemy advance across the rubble. The Syrian didn't seem to notice his tribesmen lying just yards away. His eyes were blank and distant. He and Idan sheathed their swords and took their slings from their belts. Kabir had lost his bag of shot. Idan handed his leader a stone, then took one for himself.

Azaf had expected heavy losses amongst the first wave but he couldn't understand how the Romans were still fighting. It incensed him to see they were still able to organise themselves and that yet more of his men had been sacrificed just to take this accursed fort and its precious well.

The standard was within reach now; he had no intention of letting it slip from his grasp again.

At last he drew his sword. Raising the blade high, he charged straight for the middle of the shield wall.

Cassius was vaguely aware of hearing something behind him but he didn't turn round. Instead, he watched as the Palmyrans struck.

Each defender skidded back a yard or more but the wall held. The front rank made no attempt to strike back at the enemy warriors, so intent were they on keeping their shields together. The second rank moved up, jabbing into the enemy wherever they could.

Feeling something tug on his mail shirt, Cassius turned to find Julius at his side. Cassius pushed him away but the boy persisted, dodging his arm and dropping a bundle of javelins at his feet. Julius pointed towards the Palmyrans.

Cassius switched his sword to his left hand and slid one of the javelins out.

Just as he lifted it, Simo appeared. He was unarmed and unprotected, his tunic covered in blood.

'You will fight?'

Wiping his sweat-sodden hair from his forehead, the big Gaul bent down and picked up a stray Palmyran sword. He mouthed prayers to himself.

Cassius nodded back with a grim smile.

Julius, however, was another matter.

'Back inside,' Cassius said, pointing the way. 'They may spare you. This is not your fight.'

Thankfully the lad did as he was told, following the two injured Syrians as they too sought refuge in the barracks.

Backing away until he was ten yards from the shield wall, Cassius flung the javelin low over the heads of the legionaries into the Palmyrans.

Like all those in the front rank, Azaf was in danger of being crushed by his own men. He waved them forward nonetheless, sure that their weight would soon force the Romans back.

He heard the whir of a sling close by, then the impact and a howl of pain.

Raising his arms above the crush, Azaf held his sword with the blade facing down and slid it across the closest shield, aiming to find purchase between two edges. At the first attempt, the tip of the blade simply bounced off but with the second he managed to force it inside. Driving the blade further, he levered the hilt, prying the two shields apart.

As Simo handed him another javelin, Cassius watched Kabir and Idan. Relentless and implacable, the Syrians stood side by side, plucking stone after stone from Idan's bag, whipping shot into the enemy flank.

Cassius took careful aim and threw the second javelin. This one landed close to the rear of the Palmyrans. He didn't see it hit but heard a scream. Gesturing for Simo to stay back, he took up another javelin.

Suddenly the shield wall broke. Two men in the middle were knocked aside and the Palmyrans flooded through, hacking at

369

everything in their path. So many were through in such a short time that Kabir, Idan, Crispus and the rest of the second rank had no choice but to retreat. Cassius caught a glimpse of Antonius, his face mauled, being crushed into the dust as the Palmyrans trampled over him.

Kabir and Idan put their slings behind their belts and drew their swords. They lined up beside Cassius, closely followed by the remaining legionaries.

Crispus, his reserves of energy finally depleted, had not been able to keep pace with them. The others looked on helplessly as the Palmyran leader swung low at the Roman's legs, slashing across the back of his knees. As Crispus fell, two more swordsmen drove their blades under his helmet and into his neck. His whole body shuddered, then was still.

Four Palmyrans walked casually out from behind the inn and joined the others. With a glance at the rooftop, Cassius concluded that Vestinus and the rest of his archers were dead. One man's head hung over the side of the barracks roof. Blood ran down the pale wall.

There was no one else left. Just Simo, Kabir and Idan to his left, the five legionaries to his right.

The Palmyrans numbered at least thirty and, judging by the fiery intent in the eyes of their leader, they didn't intend to tarry any longer than necessary.

Cassius' head was pounding. He gripped his sword tight.

At least the torment would be over soon. He could do nothing more. Alauran was lost.

A line from Euripides, words he had thought of many times, returned to him then.

Dishonour will not trouble me once I am dead.

XLI

Azaf thought he had killed at least one of the senior legionaries and was therefore surprised to see the young man bearing a centurion's stripe. The Roman was tall and slender, almost boyish, with the pale face and delicate features of a scholar, not a warrior.

Next to him were the treacherous Syrians. Azaf considered whom to kill first. The auxiliaries were both injured but they looked able and strong. He aimed his sword to the right and several of his men broke away to cut them off. With a similar motion to the left, he sent others to occupy the remaining legionaries and isolate their leader.

He reminded himself to relish the moment of victory.

The young officer would die first.

Cassius bent his elbows and held his sword straight as he had been taught, giving him the best chance of getting something in the way when the Palmyran struck. He tried to shut out all thoughts of what he'd seen of the warrior before. Then he said a prayer, though it was not to the gods.

If you ever intend to aid me, great Caesar, please, aid me now.

He was so focused on his opponent's slow, almost tortuous advance that he only noticed something had caught the Palmyran's attention when the man actually stopped, his gaze no longer on his prey.

Cassius sensed a presence behind him. Then he was wrenched five feet backwards and almost off his feet. The same hand that had grabbed a handful of his mail shirt steadied him, then let go.

The Praetorian lumbered past, sniffing contemptuously as he neared the enemy. He wore no helmet and no armour, only the

371

light blue tunic that stuck to his sweat-soaked back. In his right hand was his sword, in the left his shield. Slung over one shoulder was a long pouch with several javelins poking out of the top. He had also put his boots on.

With the eyes of every man present upon him, the Praetorian came to a halt five yards in front of Azaf and the rest of the Palmyran line. Settling into a fighting crouch, he raised the great shield, then swivelled his sword, cutting eights into the air. The Palmyrans stared at the three white scorpions upon the Praetorian's shield. Cassius wondered if the symbol meant anything to them.

He could not imagine what had transpired in the last hours to make the man willing and able to fight, but it seemed that his prayer had been answered.

When Azaf saw the Roman giant, he almost took a step backwards. The man was enormous, yet he wielded his weapon with practised ease. Noting the huge dimensions of his foe's sword, Azaf secured the leather strap round his wrist.

Here at last was an opponent worthy of his skills. Provided he could avoid being hit, Azaf knew he could beat him. It would make the victory all the sweeter.

Quiet settled over the watching warriors. Those close by could have attacked either man but all were transfixed by the sight of the disparate pair circling each other. Cassius knew instantly that a tacit agreement had been made: no one on either side would interfere until the duel reached its conclusion.

A dead glaze covered the eyes of the Palmyran but the Praetorian matched it with a cold, unblinking resolve. Occasionally he would look away, as if suggesting his enemy did not occupy his full attention, daring him to strike first.

In fact, it was the Roman who took the initiative, closing the space between them as Azaf feinted and weaved. The Praetorian kept his sword out wide, pushing his shield towards the Palmyran, forcing him to retreat.

Azaf took only three steps back before launching his first attack. Knowing he could avoid the sweeps of the bulky blade, he simply darted to the right of the shield, grabbed the edge with his spare hand and pulled himself forward.

It was a completely unconventional move, instantly opening up the Praetorian's defences. Azaf was about to swing for the Roman's head, but such was the man's strength that he simply pivoted neatly round, wresting the shield from Azaf's grip.

The Palmyran withdrew and the circling continued. While Azaf stayed on his toes, his movements fluid and swift, the Roman shuffled sideways, letting his shield do the work. Azaf was breathing evenly but the Praetorian was already puffing, every inch of his skin glistening with sweat.

Azaf feinted left then ducked low, disappearing from the Praetorian's view behind his shield. The Palmyran dropped to his knees and aimed a one-handed slash at the Roman's knees. Any other opponent would have been caught but so great was the Praetorian's reach that the blade met only air.

Azaf reappeared to his right, hair and cloak whipping through the air as he swung for the Roman's neck. The Praetorian knocked the blade aside with the edge of his shield. Azaf struck out again, two-handed this time, and again the Roman simply angled his shield, deflecting the blow with ease.

The Palmyran didn't stop. Leaping forward again, he launched a series of scything sweeps, disguising every blow expertly, forcing the Roman on to the defensive. Chips of leather and wood were hewn from the shield's edge as the Praetorian was pushed back by the flurry of blows.

Cassius and the legionaries retreated, still watching.

The giant seemed to be slowing. Azaf attacked again. He chopped downward, trying to catch an elbow; then swept high at the unprotected head; then thrust towards the sword hand.

The Praetorian seemed to stumble backwards.

Reading it as a feint, Azaf hesitated.

There was a curious pause, then the Roman opened his stance, lowering the shield and raising his sword arm.

Azaf saw the opening in a flash. He moved before the Praetorian even had his arm back, hacking two-handed towards his chest.

Still the Praetorian's blade didn't move.

His shield arm, however, shot up: not as a defensive block, but a powerful thrust driven towards the sword. Such was the force of the impact that the blade sliced clean through the cover and lodged itself in the wood.

Before Azaf could free it, the Praetorian dragged the shield down. Azaf's wrist, still circled by the leather strap, went with it and he was hauled helplessly on to his knees. Even as the great arm swung down towards him, Azaf somehow shook his wrist free.

With the first and last swing of his blade, the Praetorian swept the sword down upon the Palmyran's neck, just as Azaf flung himself backwards.

Cassius, along with everyone else in the square, believed he had missed.

Azaf, sitting in the dust and leaning back on his hands, stared dumbly at his sword, still stuck fast in the middle of the Roman's shield.

The defenders watched as the thin horizontal tear across the Palmyran's throat turned red. The blade's tip had sliced an inch out of his neck, enough to release a rivulet of blood that swiftly became a thick stream, cascading down through the rings of his mail shirt.

With his face registering no more than a stunned frown, Azaf's arms buckled and he slid backwards on to his cloak.

Cassius later learned from Simo that, at the moment their leader fell, there were still thirty-one Palmyrans left alive in the square and just ten defenders. It did not matter.

The Praetorian took only a moment to savour his victory.

'Amateur,' he said quietly, throwing his shield aside. He reached over his shoulder and plucked one of the javelins from the bag, then drew his arm back and flung it at the nearest Palmyran, skewering him an inch above his belt.

Before the man hit the ground, the Praetorian was aiming a second javelin at another warrior who had time only to turn and take a step before the projectile punctured his back, emerging between two ribs as he toppled to the ground.

The remaining Palmyrans fled.

One of the legionaries gave a cry and they set off after them, leaping over the bodies that littered the way. The Praetorian followed at a light jog. Two more Syrians appeared from the barracks and gave chase too. Cassius was the last man out of the square.

As he lay there alone, his head resting against the soft cloak, Azaf wondered why he now seemed to have a mouth in his throat and why he was coughing up so much water that it was wetting his neck and chest.

He stared up at the sky, so blue and pure, until a subsuming fog edged across his vision and a perfect silence settled in his ears.

He saw for a moment the desert beneath him, the rolling dunes of his homeland, and there, in the distance, the towers. Where he wanted to rest forever.

And then he thought of her. Always her.

XLII

Cassius caught up with the others just outside the gatehouse. The fleeing Palmyrans had dropped every piece of weaponry and equipment and were now sprinting for the crest.

The Praetorian slowed, then stopped. The legionaries halted too, watching as he reached over his shoulder for another javelin. Cassius couldn't believe he was going to try; even the slowest Palmyrans were at least fifty yards away. The Praetorian weighed the missile in his hand for a moment, took four quick steps, then launched it. The weapon was in the air for so long that Cassius had time to glance round at the legionaries as they followed its flight.

The javelin thudded into the ground a yard behind the trailing warrior. The Praetorian swore and smacked his hand against his thigh. The legionaries cheered the attempt, then bawled insults at the retreating enemy.

Kabir and Idan had stopped a little further out. They reloaded their slings quickly and now threw yet more shot at the enemy. Firing at a low angle, they both hit men in the back. The warriors collided with each other and fell, then scrambled to their feet and went on. Idan left his sling by his side but Kabir kept at it, frantically whipping away shot after shot.

Cassius sheathed his sword and walked over to him.

'Kabir.'

The Syrian leader fired again but hit nothing; he was shooting wildly and the Palmyrans were almost out of range.

'Kabir.'

Cassius put a hand on the Syrian's shoulder. He spun round, wild-eyed, breathing hard.

'It's over,' Cassius said.

'By the gods it's not,' said one of the legionaries. 'Look!'

Cassius turned and followed the line of the soldier's outstretched arm. In the distance was a swirling tower of dust reaching high into the azure sky. At its base was an indistinct mass of riders, heading straight for Alauran.

'It can't be,' cried the legionary, falling to his knees. 'It can't be!'

Cassius felt a flash of heat in his head. He put his hands out to steady himself.

'No, no, no,' he whispered.

'Get up, you idiot,' said the Praetorian, passing the kneeling legionary as he walked back towards the fort. 'They're coming from the north. That's your relief column.'

Cassius knew instantly that he was right. Fear had robbed him of all logic.

The legionaries stared dumbly after the Praetorian for a moment, then at each other, then at the column again. Realisation became relief. They ran until they were parallel with the north-east corner of the fort. Cassius and Idan followed them.

'Caesar be praised!'

'I can see the standards! I can see the scarlet and gold!'

Each man took his own time to be certain, but soon they were all shouting, jumping up and down, embracing each other, and praising Jupiter, Mars, Fortuna and every other god they could think of.

A grin crept across Idan's disfigured face.

Cassius felt curiously numb. One of the legionaries turned towards him.

'It really is them, sir. You might allow yourself a smile.'

Cassius took off his helmet. He felt light-headed, faint. A sickly, sweet smell reached him. He looked round and saw a dead horse just yards away. Its head lay on the ground, its lips pushed up over its teeth to form an obscene grin. Flies walked across its eyes and its wounds and the piles of dung on the ground.

Cassius threw up. What came out was mainly water but he had

to just stand there, bent over, hands on his knees, until there was nothing left in his stomach.

The legionary gave Cassius his half-full canteen. He was a squat, barrel-chested character with a huge purple bruise on his right cheek and a split lip.

'Your name?' Cassius asked when he had finished the water.

'Domitius, sir.'

'Thank you, Domitius.'

Cassius straightened up and looked over at Kabir. The Syrian was now kneeling in the sand, facing east. Cassius walked back towards him. Kabir suddenly clasped his hands tight over his face. Cassius squatted down next to him.

'The signs were right, Kabir. A great victory.'

The Syrian was whispering to himself in his own language. His hands stayed over his eyes.

Cassius left him.

He found Serenus exactly where he'd last seen him before the fourth attack: sitting upon the window ledge with his feet planted on the floor. He was slumped forward, head and arms hanging between his thighs. On the ground by his feet were the old stained cloth and fresh spots of blood.

Cassius knelt down. The veteran's eyes were shut, his mouth frozen in a placid half-smile. Cassius reached out and touched his neck. The skin was cold.

'We wondered where he could be,' said Domitius as he and another legionary walked in.

'It was the illness that killed him,' Cassius said.

'We'll look after him, sir,' said the second man.

Cassius made way for them, now realising they had been members of Serenus' section. He nodded gratefully and went outside. Glancing down, he noted that the only real damage to his helmet was the hole left by Idan's slingshot four days previously. Pulling the mail shirt off over his head, he slung it over his shoulder and started up the street.

Around him, the dead lay at every possible angle, some on

378

their sides, some on their backs, others with their faces pressed into the dirt. A few were still gripping their weapons. Limbs belonging to at least five different warriors stuck up out of the ruins of the collapsed dwelling.

Skirting round the rubble, he saw the Praetorian back at the inn. Standing with one foot up on a stool, the giant was carving into his sword handle with a dagger. Lying on the table next to him were his javelins and a wooden cup. He saw Cassius and waved him over.

'Your fat servant won't make me any more of that milk.'

'I daresay he's more concerned with the wounded.'

The Praetorian shrugged.

'What chance any of them have out here without a surgeon I don't know. Still, I'll admit he knows his potions well enough. And I suppose I should thank you for getting it down my throat.'

The Praetorian stopped carving for a moment.

'I did not think I missed clarity of thought. Until it was returned to me.'

'Forgive my curiosity, but I passed your room not long before the battle and you were sound asleep – with three empty jugs by your bed.'

'Emptied indeed. But of water, not wine.'

The Praetorian smiled at Cassius' reaction.

'Yes, lad. I did listen to you.'

He looked towards the square.

'I should have done so earlier. We might have fared a little better.'

Cassius turned round and his gaze rested instantly on the Palmyran leader.

'I must thank you. You saved my life.'

'Life?' repeated the Praetorian scornfully. 'Lucretius was the only one with something sensible to say about life. *One long struggle in the dark.*'

He put his knife down and picked up his wine, then began idly swinging the sword. He aimed the tip at where Azaf lay.

'He was quicker in hand than he was in head. Only a fool ties himself to such a light blade.'

'Do you know how that colour is made?'

'What?'

'That very bright purple. His cloak. I met a trader with one just like it on the boat up to Antioch. He told me about it. There are these little sea snails that can be found all along the Syrian coast. When wounded, they secrete tiny amounts of a purple liquid. He said it takes tens of thousands of them just to make the dye for one cloak like that.'

The Praetorian slurped his wine.

'So?'

'I told him I thought it seemed wasteful. Cruel even. He said that's the way of the world. Suffering and death are necessary – to achieve something of note.'

Cassius glanced at the Praetorian. There was a look of faint amusement in the grey eyes.

'Is this something of note?' Cassius asked him, opening a hand towards the square.

The Praetorian paused for a moment, still swinging the sword. Then he shrugged.

'It is a victory. And you are alive in a place where most have met their death. Forget your musings. Be thankful you are still on your feet.'

He put the wine down and started carving again. Cassius nodded at the tally etched on the handle.

'Quite a number.'

'Not really,' replied the Praetorian, finishing the final mark. 'This is my fifth sword.'

Cassius found Simo outside the barracks. His expression was blank, his face drained entirely of its usual colour and warmth. His hands were wet; he had tried to wash off the blood, but his hands and forearms were stained pink.

Cassius gripped his shoulder.

'Help is on its way. The relief column.'

'It's true?'

'They'll be here soon.'

Simo clasped his hands and fell back against the doorway, eyes closed.

'And you didn't have to fight.'

Simo opened his eyes and let out a long breath.

'Strabo?' Cassius asked.

Simo shook his head solemnly.

'He gave Julius something for you. He went peacefully, sir.'

Cassius glanced warily at the aid post. He knew he couldn't bring himself to go inside. Ex-legionaries with a missing arm or leg were a common sight and he had held out a little hope that the Sicilian might pull through. But there had been so much blood. Too much. Strabo had known it.

Simo took Cassius' helmet and mail shirt from him.

'Sir, I'm afraid I need to—'

'Yes, yes, of course, get back to your work. Simo, do you have that pot with the identity tablets?'

'Yes, sir, I just collected the last of them.'

'Bring it to me, would you.'

Simo headed inside the barracks, passing Julius on the way. The lad was carrying something carefully in one hand. He indicated that Cassius should open his palm and meticulously placed two small objects there. Cassius knew what they were before Julius removed his hand but when he saw Strabo's dice, he realised why the boy had been so particular. They were upturned just as they had fallen that morning, when the Sicilian had claimed the day would bring triumph.

'A five and a six,' Cassius said. 'Fortuna's friend.'

He looked up to see Domitius and the other man carrying Serenus' body towards the barracks. The other three legionaries hurried past them. They were carrying bunches of reeds gathered from the spring.

'What's all that for?' Cassius asked.

'Tradition, sir,' said one man. 'No one's going to make the relieving troops proper grass crowns out here so we thought we'd do it ourselves. Sign of our gratitude.'

'They're almost here, sir,' said another.

Simo returned with the pot. It was full, almost overflowing. The tablets were covered in grime and blood. Almost as soon as he looked at them, Cassius felt that he would cry again, so he left Simo and the others and walked away towards the officers' quarters.

The men filled cups with wine from a barrel. As they drank and began weaving the crowns together, Domitius started up a song of victory. Even a few weak voices from the barracks joined in.

Cassius placed the pot on the window of the officers' quarters. Then he walked over to the well and picked up a pail of water and a cloth. Returning to the window, he sat down, facing away from the men, and took each tablet from the pot in turn. He cleaned each one thoroughly, wiping every mark or stain from the dull lead, then placed them in neat lines to dry.

As he worked, the noise of the approaching column grew louder.

When his eyes picked up the names inscribed on the lead he would look away. But he could not stop himself thinking: thinking of how each tablet had found its way into his hands, taken from the lifeless necks of those who had fought so hard to win them and had worn them with such pride. He thought of where each tablet had been, carried for years, decades even, by the legionaries as they slept and marched and ate, as they lived and loved and fought.

Then he did read the names, and tears ran freely down his face. By the time he put the last tablet on the ledge, the top of his tunic was wet. He gathered water from the pail and cleaned his face, then closed his eyes for a moment and composed himself. He turned round and walked over to the legionaries.

Domitius saw him and nodded to the others. The five exhausted legionaries dragged themselves to their feet, all holding their cups of wine. Smiling, Domitius gave another full cup to Cassius.

'Here's to you, sir. You did us proud.'

Domitius held his cup high.

'Centurion Corbulo.'

'Centurion Corbulo,' repeated the men.

Cassius raised his cup and took his first sip of wine in almost a week, savouring every bitter drop. The sound of the approaching cavalry was now thunderous. The tip of a standard appeared over the eastern wall. Glancing back at the legionaries, Cassius knew with a sudden, irresistible certainty that he could lie to them no longer.

'There's something I must tell you. I am not a centurion. I haven't even been assigned to a legion. I am an officer of the Imperial Security Service.'

'A grain man?' said one man incredulously.

'Out here?' said another.

'Yes. Syria is my first posting. I thought I would be doing . . . paperwork.' Cassius smiled and shook his head. 'I thought I would be behind a desk.'

The legionaries stayed quiet, staring at each other in disbelief. The ground-shaking impact of hundreds of hooves had reached a crescendo. They turned to see a line of horses being skilfully guided past the collapsed dwelling, through the scattered bodies and abandoned weapons. At the head of the column was the standard-bearer: a muscular veteran with flecks of grey in his heavy beard. Mounted on the pole in his hands was a flag bearing the legend of the Sixteenth Legion.

A smaller, younger and far more noble-looking man urged his horse past the standard-bearer and brought it up close to the barracks. His tunic carried a broad blue stripe and he wore a fine scarlet cloak over his armour. He removed his helmet, smoothed down his hair and looked impassively down at the small band of legionaries.

'I am Tribune Gallio Artorius Andronicus. Who is in charge here?'

The legionaries were standing between Andronicus and Cassius. Not one of them said a word.

'Well?' demanded the tribune. 'Who is in charge?'

After a moment, Domitius turned round and looked at Cassius. With a trace of a smile and a slight nod, he moved aside. Another man turned, nodded to Cassius and moved out of the way. One after another, each of the other legionaries did the same, until there was clear space between the two officers.

Recalling Strabo's last words, Cassius straightened his back and raised his chin.

'I am, sir. I am.'

HISTORICAL NOTE

I have made every effort to be historically accurate where possible. What follows are a few comments about some of the more contentious issues relating to this period and some 'confessions' regarding the few occasions when I have knowingly strayed from the historical consensus.

With the exception of Claudius II, Aurelian, Odenathus, Queen Zenobia, General Zabdas and General Zabbai, all other characters in the story are fictional. Alauran itself is also an invention.

The story takes place in the summer of AD 270. In some general or older historical texts, Claudius' date of death is placed early in the year but in most modern volumes focusing on this era, August or September is suggested. A short period of uncertainty followed until Aurelian came to the fore.

Historians remain largely in the dark about the details of the Palmyran revolt. Recently, there has been a cluster of texts focusing on this event, particularly on Zenobia herself. Several authors now question whether the term 'revolt' is even appropriate. Zenobia has been traditionally (and often romantically) cast as 'the rebel queen', but there is considerable evidence that she tried to reach an accommodation with Rome. (It should also be noted that there is in fact little convincing evidence that she was involved in her husband's death.) Multiple reasons have been offered for the deterioration of relations and her real motives, but the fact remains that sometime around late 269 or 270 her forces occupied Arabia, Palestine and Egypt. It is probable that the invasion of Egypt occurred later than I have suggested in Chapter I.

This story, of course, takes place in Syria and the question of the extent to which Palmyra already 'controlled' the province remains confused. It is possible that after Odenathus' victories over the Persians, the Roman administration operated under the aegis of Palmyra. The Romans certainly honoured Odenathus – grateful that he had filled the 'power vacuum' – but his precise role remains obscure. We do know, however, that after his death different factions expressed a variety of attitudes towards Zenobia's rule. One of her supporters may have been Paul of Samosata, the Bishop of Antioch who caused such controversy with his 'heretical' theology and unconventional behaviour. (I should mention here, however, that many modern texts doubt that any such alliance ever existed.)

Very little is known about the precise nature of the military confrontations that took place. We cannot even be entirely sure which legions were stationed in Syria, certainly not which ones remained loyal to the Roman cause and fought the Palmyran units that had so recently been their allies. We do know that the Third Legion (*Legio III Gallica*) was based in Syria both before and after this period, so it seemed a logical choice.

There is evidence that Palmyran operations in northern Syria were led by General Zabbai and that they had still not achieved a complete military victory by 271. This raises the spectre of a protracted campaign, and provides the backdrop for the events of this novel.

Had the garrison at Alauran or any similar Roman detachment won such a victory, it would in all likelihood have been fairly short-lived. Though it is clear some form of organised opposition held up the advance, by the end of 271 Palmyran forces had reached deep into Asia Minor – as far as Ankara in modern Turkey.

Zenobia, too, had little time to enjoy her triumph. The Emperor Aurelian struck back at her in 272 and by the autumn Palmyra was back in Roman hands. The Queen, according to most accounts, was put on trial, then taken to Rome in chains.

The next story in this series is set during the aftermath of the Roman victory, with Cassius hunting a stolen Persian standard crucial to the signing of a peace treaty.

★   ★   ★

Legionaries would have been used to young officers; after all, serving tribunes were often in their twenties. Centurions, however, would generally have been seasoned veterans in their thirties and forties promoted from the ranks. Young, directly commissioned centurions were rare. It is widely acknowledged, however, that well-connected individuals could attain the rank in this way.

The term 'Imperial Security Service' is my own invention but the details about the organisation in Chapter I are accurate. It has been variously described as a 'secret police force', 'internal security force' or 'secret service'. The reputation of its operatives was as bad – if not worse than – I have suggested here. Most of its agents would have been recruited from the legions but I don't think it's beyond the realms of possibility that a young man such as Cassius (with the right connections, of course) could have been directly appointed to its ranks. The 'grain man' nomenclature is also accurate, the Latin version being *frumentarius*.

Some other issues: regarding the ethnicity of the legionaries at Alauran, it's likely that many of them would have been Syrian. I chose to make most of them from other provinces to heighten the differences between the Romans and Kabir's local tribesmen. We do know that many Thracians – such as Avso and friends – fought in the Syrian legions.

The coins featuring Vaballathus, discovered in the possession of the enemy spy, would probably not have been minted by the summer of 270 but it was a point of interest I really wanted to include.

Cassius' reference to the Battle of Sardis during the cavalry attack concerns a recorded incident from the year 546 BC. Knowing the effect that camels could sometimes have on horses, Cyrus the Great of Persia removed the baggage from his pack animals and ordered his cavalry to chase them towards the advancing Lydian steeds. The enemy horses reacted badly and fled, forcing their riders to dismount. Cyrus' actions turned the tide of the battle; the Persians were victorious.

★   ★   ★

Historical novels are impossible without the work of historians. I am greatly indebted to those academics whose texts aided the completion of this story. I would encourage any readers with an interest in Queen Zenobia to investigate all the recent publications and their differing takes on this fascinating, if somewhat opaque, period.

Of all the many texts I used, there is one that I returned to time and again, and which continues to be a trove of useful information as I work on the second Agent of Rome novel. That book is the vivid and accessible *Roman Syria and the Near East* by Professor Kevin Butcher of the University of Warwick.

Those more learned than I may take issue with certain details and aspects of the story, but that's precisely what it is. Any errors are mine.

ACKNOWLEDGEMENTS

I began this novel in 2005 and the road to publication has been a long one. I must take this opportunity to acknowledge all those who have offered me unstinting support not only during that period but ever since I started writing.

Principal amongst them is my dad Neil. He has read every page of every manuscript I have produced. Always positive, he has been there through thick and thin (mostly thin if I am honest!). Calling to tell him *Agent of Rome* was being published was a fantastic moment.

The next person I called was my aunt, Anne Attwood. She has always been unfailingly enthusiastic and helpful in encouraging my writing.

My cousin Matthew Amiss and his wife Becky have been cheerleaders for the book since day one. Their support provided me with a genuine boost when things were looking grim.

My editor, Oliver Johnson, has been a real ally. His attention to detail and forthright opinions have been hugely beneficial. I must also thank Sophie Missing and all the numerous others at Hodder & Stoughton who have contributed.

This book would not exist without my agent David Grossman. I will always be grateful to him for seeing the potential of the story, securing the deal with Hodder, and the advice he has given me over the last year.

Thanks to my old pal Neil Harrison for the map of Alauran.

Other friends took the time to read various drafts and provide me with some very useful feedback: Adrian Smith (mostly over a pint or five in the bars of Warsaw), Kate March and Lindsay Roffe.

I must also mention all the other people who have shown an interest and provided encouragement over the years: My brother Joff and his wife Emma, Daniel & Emma Amiss, Renata Sledziewska, Sarah Taylor, Justin Highstead, Tony Roffe, Andy Layzell, Dominic Watson, Mark & Diane Taylor, Chris & David Orwin, Bob & Iris Illingworth and Lorry & Sue Vanner.

Finally, I must express my heartfelt gratitude to my beloved late mother Joan. Her contribution dates back to before I even started writing: she gave me the confidence to believe I could do it.

Nick Brown, Warsaw, November 2010.